The
Last Woman
Standing

Tia McCollors

The
Last Woman
Standing

MOODY PUBLISHERS
CHICAGO

All Scripture quotations are taken from the *New King James Version.* Copyright © 1982 by Thomas Nelson, Inc. Used by permission. All rights reserved.

Published in association with the literary agency of MacGregor Literary, 2373 NW 185th Avenue, Suite 165, Hillsboro, OR 97124.

Editor: Suzette Dinwiddie
Interior Design: Ragont Design
Cover Design: 1721 Media, LLC, http://1721media.com
Cover Image: Jupiter Images (jupiterimages.com)
Author Photo: Mic Nash

Library of Congress Cataloging-in-Publication Data

McCollors, Tia.
  The last woman standing / Tia McCollors.
    p. cm.
  ISBN 978-0-8024-9863-2
  1. Triangles (Interpersonal relations)—Fiction. I. Title.
PS3613.C365L37 2009
813'.6—dc22
                                        2009014091

1 3 5 7 9 10 8 6 4 2

Printed in the United States of America

To Reagan Victoria—
May you always stand up and walk in the truth
that you are fearfully and wonderfully made.

~ and ~

In loving memory of
Papa James McCollors

Your smile and love will always be engraved on my heart.

Acknowledgments

I know you've heard it millions of times from authors but it's actually true—the acknowledgments are the hardest part of the book to write. Why? Because you risk leaving out the names of the people who've supported you and the people who you "promised" would get a shout-out in the next book. That's why I'm going to make it easy on myself. You'll see very few names listed in this section, but that doesn't mean I don't have tons of people to thank. It just means that the number of folks who've supported and encouraged me are too numerous to list.

If no one else ever had their name called it wouldn't matter as long as I could thank **GOD** for everything. You know what they say—"If I had a thousand tongues I couldn't thank You enough." I'm always amazed by Your grace and how with Your sovereignty You've strategically ordered my steps all of my life. Sometimes I don't recognize it until I look back at how far I've come. Even at the times when I wasn't faithful, You never left me. Who couldn't love a God like that?!

TO MY FAMILY AND FRIENDS—Some people have drama. We don't. Never have. Never will. I've rested in the arms of your love and support and don't take it for granted the sacrifices you've made as we've watched our dreams grow legs and walk around in this thing called life. Of course my biggest supporter has been my husband, Wayne. I appreciate the times you entertained the kids and let me disappear upstairs or leave the house so I could get some writing done . . . and for the times you called in Mama for backup. It made a lot of difference to have that uninterrupted time when I didn't have to stop to make snacks, pour cups of juice, or sing and play patty-cake. Thank you for the mornings I awakened to breakfast cooking to start my writing day. No one will ever top your scrambled eggs. To my cousin and one of my best friends— Tamiko Reid (aka Meek!). We've been separated by miles but we'll always be close in heart. Thanks for always being available to step up and take care of my business when I come home to Greensboro, NC. By the way, Jayce has Tyler to play with and it's time for Reagan to have her close girl-cousin, too! I know you'll laugh at that one.

TO THE MOODY PUBLISHERS & LIFT EVERY VOICE TEAM—This is our fourth book together and I think it will be the best yet. From my first release, *A Heart of Devotion*, you all have shown your devotion to me. I think I've said this in every book, but thank you for believing in my vision. I don't take it lightly that you trust that the Moody name and reputation of integrity will be represented well within the pages of my books.

TO MY SISTERS AND BROTHERS OF THE LITERARY PEN—Each of us have been given a unique gift and it's up to us to make an impression on the world that nobody can erase. It's our job to keep well-written, quality books on the shelves that our children can be proud of. I never want my children to have to hang their heads low when asked what their mother writes about. Three authors in particular this past year have helped me keep this goal and others in mind as we walk out this literary journey. Victoria Christopher Murray, Sherri Lewis, and Rhonda McKnight—wrap these pages around your neck and consider yourself hugged. To the Anointed Authors On Tour (www.AnointedAuthorsOnTour.com)—one of these days we're going to write a novel based on our literary travels. And to my other author friends (the list grows daily)—let's continue to hold each other accountable. Now get back to writing—after you finish reading this book, of course!

TO MY AGENT—Sandra Bishop of MacGregor Literary. I expect that great things are going to spring out of our new business relationship. I think we took the time to till the ground a little and plant the right seeds even before the ink was put on the page for the contract. Thank you for believing in me and keeping me focused on my career strategies and goals. Your work doesn't go unnoticed.

BOOK CLUBS—Now this may get me in trouble (didn't I say earlier that I wasn't going to list names?), but I couldn't resist adding a small section of some of the book clubs who've supported me. I used my brain and my calendar to spark my memory. If you're not listed, let me know and I'll add you in the next book (for real!). Thanks to the following book clubs: Sukari Harris & Pass The Book, Stephanie Thomas (WXEZ 94.1), Narrow Path, Empowered Book Club, LYLAS, A Good Idea & Mocha Moms, Chavis Library New Book Lovers, Girlfriends Reading Circle, SPIRIT Book Club, Women of Character, Walk Into Destiny, Oak Cliff Bible Fellowship, Circle of Friends II, Cover to Cover, Queens Book Club, Rachel & Leah Retreat, Brown Suga, Sistahs Cross My Heart, Global Impact Christian Ministries, Second Saturday Book Club, Circle of Sisters, Sistahs in Harmony, Sistahs In Conversation, Virtuous Women, New Birth Singles Ministry, Redeeming Love Women's Ministry, Marsha's Book Bytes, Healthy Hearts, and Boys Who Dare. Whew! Try saying that three times fast!

FAITHFUL READERS—And last but not least . . . to the faithful and new readers of my novels. Yes, I ultimately write to please God before anyone else, but I write for you, too. It's my job to entertain you so that you stay up a few extra hours to read even though you know you should be asleep. It's my mission to make you think how your life might measure up to some of these characters I write about. And it's my purpose to nudge you closer to God's heart.

Let me hear from you. Drop me a line at Tia@TiaMcCollors. com, visit my home on the web at www.TiaMcCollors.com, or find me at my vacation spot at www.myspace.com/TiaWrites. I swing through there every now and then.

God's love and mine,
Tia

Chapter 1

Anything worth having is worth fighting for. And you need to decide if you're going to fight for your man."

Sheila Rushmore's best friend, Cassandra, barked the words almost like it was an ultimatum. Sheila agreed with her. Sort of. The problem was that Sheila wasn't sure who or what she was fighting with. Ace had been her man for the last two years. They'd never had a problem. Nothing more than the disagreements and miscommunication that an average couple would have anyway. Until now.

He said nothing was wrong. But womanly instincts told Sheila that Ace was pulling away. There was something building a dividing wall between them. Slowly, brick by brick. When they were together lately, his thoughts seemed afar off instead of on her like they used to be. Something—or someone—was keeping him from the ultimate commitment that Sheila wanted—marriage.

Sheila was more than ready to jump the broom over into marital bliss. After two years of enjoying Ace all to herself, she'd start trying to have a child. Right now, Ace said that he was perfectly content with the two teenage daughters he already had. Of course, Sheila believed, that would change once they were joined in holy matrimony. As long as she was pregnant by the time she reached the defined high-risk pregnancy age of thirty-five, things would be great.

Something in Sheila's gut had always told her she'd have a son. She'd raise him to be a responsible, God-fearing man like Ace, not the good-for-nothing man like her older brother had become. The more Sheila thought about it, maybe she would hold off having a child just in case it brought more pain than joy. Her brother's lifestyle had etched wrinkles across her mother's face long before it was time. Having a child could be postponed, but a husband was another thing.

Sheila turned up the temperature on her ceramic curling iron. "That would make sense if I knew what I was fighting," she told Cassandra, who had turned her attention to Sheila's armoire. Sheila parted her hair into small sections. Ace would be arriving before she knew it, and she wanted to look like a flawless diamond amidst a rack of costume jewelry.

Cassandra slid a gold bangle on her arm and twirled it around her wrist. Both of the women's cheap jewelry had been tossed out when they decided to step up their game. No more living by the mantra "fake it 'til you make it." It had become "do whatever you need to do to get it."

Except when it came to one thing. The diamond engagement ring. As far as Sheila was concerned, she should've had a rock on her ring finger by now. She was smart, educated, and didn't have three kids hanging on her dress hem to drive Ace away. She wasn't a missionary, but she wasn't a downright heathen either. Her motto

"I'm wearing what I have on," Sheila said, pushing back the closet door so she could look in the mirror hanging on the inside of it. "Black is always sexy and I don't want to overdo it."

Cassandra took the red dress back out of the closet. She draped it across her curvy silhouette and stepped in front of Sheila. "There's no such thing as overdoing it."

Sheila retreated to the bed and slid on her pointed toe pumps. "I'm officially ignoring you now. I need to get ready," she said, fastening a gold pendant cross around her neck. She didn't plan on using a dress to lure Ace. She just needed to use her feminine power in another way. Find out what was really bothering him and tend to his needs. She always wanted to be the one Ace ran to when he needed a place to lay his head.

Cassandra interrupted her thoughts. "Since I'm being ignored, I'm leaving," she said, picking up her Coach purse—the one she'd convinced Sheila to give her after she'd borrowed it for a date with Hinton. "And if you're not going to use this dress for its intended purpose, it's going with me. Hinton invited me to a birthday party of one of his coworkers next week. I'm sure it'll be a bunch of investment bankers and their stiff wives. This dress will bring a little excitement to the night."

Sheila walked Cassandra to the door of her high-rise apartment, lighting a few of her candles along the way. She wanted romance to welcome Ace at the door. After being with his teenage daughters all weekend, he'd appreciate some time to relax before they left for dinner.

"Candles won't help you keep a man," Cassandra said. "You've got to do better than that."

"Bye, Cassandra."

Cassandra opened the coat closet and pulled out her leather jacket and a folded shopping bag. "I'm just saying. Are y'all still on that celibate kick? That's probably what's wrong with him. It doesn't take a rocket scientist to know that a man has needs. God made them that way."

"Bye, Cassandra. And don't worry about what goes on behind our closed doors. Ace isn't going anywhere." Sheila said it more to convince herself.

"As long as you have a plan." Cassandra saluted her friend then turned and marched down the hall like there was a crowd of admirers watching her exit. She didn't bother to stop when she looked back over her shoulder and said, "Call me when you're ready to go to war."

Chapter 2

Lynette Bowers had no intention of falling in love with her ex-husband. Not four years ago after the final divorce papers were signed, not two years ago when he started dating again. And definitely not now. So why was her heart feeling like it did seventeen years ago when she first realized he was *"the one"*?

Back then, Lynette was a free-spirited Spelman College junior and Scott "Ace" Bowers was the level-headed Morehouse senior whose effortless charm had swept her off of her feet. First came love, then came marriage, then came two little girls in the baby carriage. But Lynette didn't expect the part of the story where the Mama and Daddy got too busy for each other because of their careers, and they kept butting heads about almost everything, especially how to raise their children. She didn't remember the verse where the parents decided they'd be happier apart than they were together, and their daughters would be added to the statistics of children being raised in a single-parent household. First came love, then came divorce.

From the chaise lounge in her living room, Lynette watched Ace's black BMW slink against the curb like a prowling black panther. No, this was not love Lynette was experiencing now, she decided. This was temporary insanity.

"I've got to do something about this," Lynette said to herself. Either it was PMS or some other hormonal imbalance. Either way, she was thankful there was medication for both.

Ace had recently traded in his practical Volvo sedan for a sportier car that screamed midlife crisis, even though Lynette thought he was at least ten years away from that episode in a man's life.

As always, Ace never parked in the driveway when he picked up or dropped off their daughters, Carmen and Jada. Maybe it was an attempt to respect her personal space in some way. Lynette had never asked. Whatever the reason, it was probably also why he rarely stepped past the front foyer or the formal living room of her home. The same place that was once *their* home.

Since the day they'd decided Ace should move out, Lynette could count on one hand the number of times he'd sat at the kitchen table. And she only needed two fingers to count the other men—besides family—who'd sat there. She was particular about any man she brought into her home, especially because of her girls.

Lynette marked the page of her romance novel with a faded Nordstrom's receipt, then lifted the pinewood tray from her lap and onto the end table. She carefully balanced the meal that had become one of her favorites since kindergarten—a grilled cheese sandwich and a hot bowl of tomato soup. She had barely opened the front door when Carmen rushed in with a cell phone plastered to her ear. Lynette could tell from the excited chatter that the self-proclaimed fashionista had racked up on the latest clothing trends, all at the expense of her father's wallet. Although the private Christian academy the girls attended required uniforms, Friday's attire was left to tasteful outfits at the students'—and parents'—discretion. On that one day each week, Carmen made it her personal goal to be the most fashionable.

Lynette's sixteen-year-old paused long enough to turn around and yell back down to the end of the driveway. Despite the early March chill hanging in the air, Ace and their younger, Jada, were taking their time getting overnight bags out of the trunk.

"Bye, Daddy . . . love you . . . thank you for my birthday presents . . . I'll call you later." Carmen ran her words together like punctuation didn't exist.

Lynette held up a hand to stop Carmen's rush to get upstairs and disappear into her bedroom. "Have I become invisible over the last few days?"

"Hey, Ma. I'll be back down in a little while to show you my stuff," Carmen said.

"Hey, baby," Lynette said, kissing her elder daughter's cheek. "I'll be waiting."

By the names on the plastic and paper shopping bags looped around her arms, Lynette could see that Carmen had persuaded her father to go to the Lenox Square and Phipps Plaza malls. Better Ace's pocket than hers. He'd always had a hard time saying no to them as it was.

Carmen and Jada had their father strung out between both of their pinkie fingers. Carmen could squeeze out his last dime if necessary, and Jada's athletic ability made up for the fact that Ace didn't get the son he'd once hoped for. She guessed it was still a possibility for him though.

While Lynette had no one, Ace had Sheila. From what Lynette had seen, Sheila was attractive. And from what she could remember, she was a corporate recruiter and about eight years younger than Ace. Sheila had just come into the thirties, and Lynette was close to heading out of them. The odds were in Sheila's favor.

But that didn't matter anyway, Lynette told herself. That was the last thing she needed to be thinking about. Her marriage was history.

"You guys hurry up," Lynette yelled outside. "You're letting all of the heat out of my house." She chuckled at what she said. It was evidence that she was getting older. Her grandmother would've said the same thing. Before she died, Grandma Rosa Mae claimed Ace as her grandson. If he even so much as thought about one of her chicken pies with the homemade golden crust, she'd have one waiting for him when he returned home from flying. If Grandma Rosa Mae had been alive when they were going through their divorce, she would've been devastated. In her eyes Ace could do no wrong, but at the time Lynette could've given her an endless list of why he was failing as a husband. In retrospect, most of the things that seemed so big, now didn't matter individually. It was when all of the infractions were heaped together that their molehill of problems became a mountain.

None of that had mattered to Grandma Rosa Mae. With God's help, she thought, anything and everything could be fixed. Including Ace.

Ace. That fine piece of man coming up my driveway, Lynette thought. Forget wanting to read. She'd been alone at home all weekend. Maybe Ace would want to sit and talk a while. Talk was about the only thing she was allowed to do anyway. That is, if she wanted to "do it right." She'd had four years of "doing it right." You could've never told her that she'd be walking down a road of celibacy again. It was getting hard. Real hard.

Stop it, Lynette. Just stop thinking about it.

Ace and Lynette weren't the typical ex-spouses. They'd remained friends even after the divorce, yet had detached themselves emotionally from their romantic love. They still cared for each other—but were only friends. It wasn't until about three months ago that Lynette started looking at Ace through a different set of eyes.

She'd been having one of *those* nights. The kind of night when she thought about the possibility of being single forever and surviving the empty nest once the girls were off to college. She prayed—nearly begged—to God for a husband that she could be friends with like she'd been with Ace when their love was fresh and untainted. Before selfishness and disagreements shook them apart. The next morning after that prayer she'd seen Ace, and that's when the feelings for Ace begin to push their way into her heart again. Didn't God know that Ace wasn't supposed to be the answer to her prayer? He couldn't be.

Because there was Sheila.

Chapter 3

Ace walked inside and took off the cap covering his low tapered cut. His face, however, was scruffy, and at least four days' worth of stubble sprouted across his chin and jawline. He'd let his facial hair grow in over the last few days, but Lynette knew he'd have to shave by morning.

"Lynn?" Ace said it like he'd had to repeat himself several times to snap her out of her daydreaming. He was the only one who she allowed to shorten her name. Lynn. Once in a blue moon, Lynnie.

"Hmm? Hey, Ace," Lynette finally said. "Sorry. Had something on my mind."

"Anything you want to talk about?"

"No," she rushed to say, studying his face. Lynette liked when he wore a beard better than when he had to sport the baby-smooth face required when he was on the schedule as a pilot for one of

Atlanta's major airlines. Facial hair or not, he still looked incredibly handsome today. *Incredibly. It just didn't make sense . . .*

No, Lynette. There was a reason why they'd gotten divorced in the first place. Life was about moving forward, learning lessons, and not repeating the same mistakes.

"Came back with an empty wallet again?" Lynette asked, starting a conversation to distract her roaming thoughts—and eyes.

"Don't I always?" Ace asked. "But I'd do it every day if I had the time. And the money."

Money had never been a problem. Time. That had always been an issue, Lynette thought.

"Well, you've got two months until my birthday, Daddy. So I hope your wallet is stacked again before then," Jada reminded him, popping the gum in her mouth like she was with a group of girlfriends jumping double Dutch by a fire hydrant on a street corner. "I don't really want any clothes, but I've got some other things in mind."

"Please, Jada. That gum," Lynette said. "All that smacking is annoying."

"Sorry, Ma." Jada popped the bubble sitting at the end of her pursed lips, then sucked the gum back into her mouth.

Ace laughed and Lynette knew it was because he was well aware of one of her biggest pet peeves. He knew all the little things about her. If she started over with a new love interest at this point in her life, it would take him a while to learn all of her idiosyncrasies. That alone might send a man running—in the opposite direction.

"You know I've got you, baby girl," Ace was saying to Jada. "You'll have your day, too."

Jada laid her head on her father's chest. Unlike Carmen, Jada hadn't grown out of regularly basking in her parents' affection.

"I won't be able to make it to your basketball game this week," Ace told Jada. He gave her a squeeze and planted his customary kisses between Jada's eyebrows. "I'm taking on a couple of international flight schedules this month so I'll be out of town all this week, at least."

"Yes, I remember," Jada said, wiping her forehead. "And be careful with my skin, Dad. Please."

Puberty had recently dotted several small pimples on Jada's forehead for the first time, and she had started a new skin-care regimen to retain her previously flawless mocha skin.

"What? My lips are clean." Ace pulled Jada closer so he could examine the small breakout. "They actually might help these three little friends you've got staring back at me," he teased.

I could use a little bit of that help, Lynette thought. She felt a warm rush on the inside, and it wasn't from her tomato soup that was growing cold on the end table.

That's what I get for reading that book. Lynette had never been one to get caught up in the television soap operas, but her guilty pleasure had been the occasional romance novel like the one she'd been reading this weekend. As soon as Ace left, she was headed straight to her bedroom to read the entire Bible. Twice.

Jada snapped her fingers. "I'll be right back, Daddy. Let me wash my face and then I'm gonna get you one of my basketball pictures." She dashed up the steps, but not before throwing her arms around Lynette's neck and kissing her cheek.

"Is she serious? Is she really going to wash her face first?" Ace asked.

"She's very serious." Lynette held up two fingers. "Soaps up twice, rinses twice."

Ace sat on the settee in the foyer. "Other than three bodies of walking estrogen in the same house, how are you doing?" he asked, rubbing his knuckles across his stubble.

If Lynette didn't know better, she'd have thought Ace was checking her out. The sweatpants she was wearing were comfortable, but it wasn't like she was hidden under a shapeless mound of fabric. It hugged her body just as nicely as it had the curvy model on the website.

Lynette tapped Ace's leg and he scooted over so she could sit beside him. "I can't complain," she said. "I take that back. I could, but I won't. I just have to remind myself that like the terrible twos, this too, shall pass. This teenage drama."

"You're probably overreacting, Lynn," Ace said. "Give the girls a break sometimes."

There he goes, Lynette thought. Why waste her breath? She'd done that for ten years and Ace was always the one who pointed the issue back to something *she* must've been doing wrong. She was the hand of discipline and his hands would swoop down to his daughters' rescue.

Carmen and Jada were only separated by two years in age, and about six pounds in weight. There were days when they acted like the angels Lynette tried to raise them to be, and others when she felt like someone had switched her children under her nose and given her disrespectful clones. But Ace didn't see that part. Not before they'd gotten the divorce, and definitely not now. Now it was worse. Sometimes she felt that he tried to make it up to the girls because their parents' marriage had fallen into the world's statistics and outside of the values they tried to instill in them.

"All you have to do is call me if they get too out of hand," Ace said. "You know that."

Lynette nodded, though she already knew what he'd do. Nothing. "So far I've been able to handle everything," Lynette said. But what she *couldn't* handle was thinking about Ace and his relationship right now.

Lynette wondered if Ace would marry Sheila. She really didn't want to know, but she felt compelled to ask. It had been at least two years ago when Ace first approached her with the subject of his growing relationship with Sheila. He'd talked to her about how it would affect the girls. Asked her if she thought it was too early for the girls to see him with someone else. They'd had the "talk" with the girls together, and he and Sheila's relationship took off once Ace knew the girls were comfortable with the idea.

But Ace had never asked Lynette how it would affect *her*. Frankly, he wasn't obligated to. So she took it like a big girl and got over it. Yet many times she'd questioned God as to why it seemed the man was always able to move on and find love so quickly, while the woman lived her life for and through her children.

"Well how about you?" Lynette finally asked. She couldn't be scared to face reality. "How's Sheila?" *There. She'd done it.*

"She's good," Ace said, looking at his watch like he suddenly remembered he had somewhere to go. "We're going out tonight."

Sting to the heart. "Special occasion?" Lynette asked. *Like dumping her? Because if I'm alone, the least you could do is be alone, too,* Lynette wanted to say.

"Anniversary. According to her calendar. You know how y'all are."

Anniversary? Stab to the heart. "Oh, so she's hanging in there." Lynette raised her eyebrows. "How long has it been? Two years?"

"Good memory."

"You call it memory. I call it keeping tabs on the woman who's around my girls."

Ace shook his head. "You know I rarely mix my time with the girls with anybody else, unless it's family. Sheila has never been an exception." He added, "Even though she's a good woman."

Ace didn't know that his words were turning the dagger. *God, me and You are going to have to have a long talk tonight,* Lynette thought. *Because there are some feelings that You're going to have to take away. Because I've never looked at this man before and felt like I wanted to cry.*

26

Chapter 4

Ace never had a problem talking to Lynette about his relationship with Sheila, though he didn't make it part of their regular conversation. His comments about her were quick. Nothing deep.

But Ace picked up on the change in Lynette's countenance when he'd said Sheila was a good woman. He couldn't read exactly what she was thinking, but then again, she'd said she had something on her mind. If she wanted him to know, Lynette usually wasn't one to hold anything back.

Ace unzipped the top of his coat. As usual whenever the temperature dropped to anywhere below the sixties, Lynette had the house roasting inside. And he could tell she was having a kindergarten flashback again. He could smell the lingering scent of toasted bread and melted cheese. She'd probably warmed some tomato soup, too.

Lynette smiled at him. It was forced and unmistakably fake.

"I appreciate you keeping the times with your daughters special," Lynette said. "And I know they appreciate having you to themselves, too."

"No problem," he said.

At least somebody appreciated it, Ace thought, because Sheila still had problems with it. Sheila wanted them to be one big happy family—minus Lynette of course. She had never been married and didn't have any children—though he knew she wanted to be a wife. *His* wife. And eventually a mother. To *his* children. A few months after they'd started dating, Ace was quick to tell her that he was done with bringing children into this world. He couldn't see starting over with a baby when Jada was already twelve at the time. He'd have to find another way to make his contribution to replenish the earth. Plant some trees or something, he'd joked to Sheila that day.

Sheila had treaded lightly around the subject since then. She probably thought she could change his mind. But little did she know, there was no way that was going to happen.

Lynette patted Ace's knee. "Sheila's a smart woman. She'd better hold on to you tight if she doesn't want somebody else to snatch you up."

"Somebody like who?"

"That's a good question," Lynette said, scratching her temple. "Because you're getting up there in age and a whole lot of these women don't want old men after a while. Unless it's just to be their sugar daddy, of course."

"So now you wanna be a comedienne?" He chuckled. "Keep your day job."

Lynette's genuine smile returned. It was the one that had made him stop and turn around to meet her when he was on Spelman's campus with some of his Morehouse brothers. She was so beautiful. Even their dissolved marriage couldn't change that. But almond-shaped eyes and soft lips can't keep a marriage together.

And what was up with Lynette touching his knee. Or maybe

it was more of a pat. Any other time he wouldn't have noticed, because that was the kind of person Lynette was. Her hands talked more than she did when she was in a conversation.

But today's touch was different. And it scared him. Not her touch necessarily, but his internal response to it. *Or maybe it's the way she's wearing those sweatpants,* Ace thought, relishing the quick moment he could get an undisturbed look at her. She was relaxed, her eyes closed and her head resting back against the wall. Then she opened them. He didn't have time to act like his gaze had been focused somewhere else.

"Why are you looking at me like that?" Lynette asked.

Her eyes hadn't been closed all the way, after all. He was straight busted.

"I'm not really looking at you," he lied. "I was just looking in your direction."

"Lost in thought, huh?"

"You can call it that."

"What are you thinking about? Sheila?" She sat forward. "You're not popping the big question tonight are you?"

"What? What made you ask that?"

"It *has* been two years. At our age that's more than enough time to know if you're going to marry somebody."

Ace sat up too. Lynette and Sheila were starting to sound like the same recorded message. "I wouldn't take a step like that unless I'd talked to Carmen and Jada about it. Marriage is a serious decision."

"Tell me something I don't know," she said. "And we both know it's not easy, either."

"No it's not," Ace agreed. "But it is what you make of it."

Lynette was leaning back against the wall again. This time he looked a little harder to make sure her eyes were closed. Above her head hung the first piece of art she'd splurged on when they were married. The original piece—painted by a local female artist—was an impressionistic depiction of a woman protecting her seed. A closet artist herself, Lynette always tried to support beginning artists. But even the best artist couldn't transcribe to canvas the beauty—inside and out—of the woman sitting under it. The glow on her face was more alluring the longer he looked at her.

He turned his head. He'd gotten too many looks in already. He tried to focus on something else.

Sheila is waiting for me. What's taking Jada so long to get her picture?

Music suddenly blasted from somewhere upstairs, breaking the comfortable silence he and Lynette had been sitting in. On the radio, some teenage crooner—Ace couldn't keep up with them all—was whining about his naive version of love and relationships.

That boy doesn't know a thing, Ace thought. *He hasn't experienced the half of it.*

The day Ace had opened the final divorce decree, he'd wondered if he should've fought harder—for them. The thought had never crossed his mind again. Until now. *What if . . . ?*

No. He still loved Lynette, just not in that way. He loved her as the mother of his children, as the best friends they once were, and as the amicable friends they were now. Just friends. They had moved on with their lives and both of them were happy.

Moments later a slammed door muffled the music.

"Here you go Daddy," Jada said, coming downstairs and handing him a five-by-seven photo of her dressed in the red and black uniform with a basketball balanced on her knee. "You can add that to my wall of fame at your house."

"You got it, baby girl," Ace said. Relieved to escape his thoughts, he stood up and tried to flick off the white paste Jada had dotted on top of her miniscule pimples.

"Stop, Daddy," she whined, holding his hand away. "This is serious business."

"You're too young to have business." Ace put on his hat, and flipped up the collar of his coat. "You guys be good. I'll call you when I get back."

"All right, Daddy." Jada pulled on Lynette's arms to help her mother to her feet. She wrapped her arms around Lynette's waist. The older Jada got, the more Ace noticed an even more striking resemblance between them.

"Okay, Lynn. Call me if you need anything and I'll get back to you as soon as I can," Ace said, opening the front door.

He looked back. The glow that was on her face—almost a light—seemed to shine more intensely. The foyer's chandelier was off. This light he was seeing wasn't man-made.

"I need to get out of here," Ace said aloud to himself, for one reason to his daughter and ex-wife for another.

Now.

Chapter 5

Ace's twenty-minute ride to Sheila's place near downtown Atlanta was absorbed with thoughts of Lynette. Finally, he took it as a sign from God that he needed to pray for her. Why else would Lynette be entrenched in his mind at a time when he was going to celebrate with his woman?

So Ace followed God's urging and prayed. Then he turned on the radio to try and drown out his thoughts until he pulled into the gated apartment complex on Piedmont Road. He punched in Sheila's gate access code, and turned into the first set of luxury apartment homes.

Some reprieve from his thoughts came when Sheila opened the door.

"Hey, honey," Sheila said, falling into his arms as soon as he stepped inside.

Ace wrapped his arms around her and squeezed thoughts of

Sheila back into his heart and mind. The scent of her freshly shampooed hair mingled with her signature Dolce & Gabbana Light Blue fragrance welcomed him. She held him equally as tight.

"Oh, it takes an anniversary for me to get a welcome like this," Ace said, his face still buried in her full, chin-length locks.

"Don't even try it," she said, softly pushing him away. "Let me blow out all these candles and we can go. I wanted us to sit down and relax for a while but you're late. Shame on you." Sheila gave him a flirty smile.

Watching Sheila made Ace remember why he'd been so attracted to her. Her looks would draw the eyes of most men, and her elegance and intelligence got the approval of women who admired seeing other sisters who carried a royalty about them.

Ace had long let go of his expectations of having a perfect woman. Marriage had shown him that he wasn't perfect, and he couldn't expect anybody else to be. He appreciated Sheila for trying to meet his expectations, but at times he wished she'd try to please God more than him. A few months after meeting, he'd invited her to church. She always attended willingly and noticeably enjoyed the service. But Sheila wouldn't go to church without him, which meant she rarely went. Most Sunday mornings Ace wasn't back in town. And when he was, he usually took the girls to worship with him. Ace knew her relationship with God wasn't about having perfect attendance at church, but he also knew that hearing the preached Word from a pastor like Pastor Bailey would change her life.

One of Ace's first gifts to Sheila was a red leather-bound Bible. He hoped it would encourage her to dig a little deeper to nurture her spiritual life. They'd shared that same Bible the last time they went to church together about a month ago. Most of the pages were still as crisp as the day he'd given it to her.

Sheila had her favorite lineup of televangelists that she liked to watch on Sunday mornings. And there was nothing wrong with that. Even Pastor Bailey had a broadcast that aired on the local cable network. Ace just wanted Sheila to give as much attention to her inner woman as she did to her outer woman. But she was growing. A little slowly, but that had to account for something.

"Let me grab something from my bedroom," Sheila said. "I'll be back in a minute."

"Hurry up. You're going to make us late. Shame on *you*," he teased.

Sheila added an extra twist to her walk as she walked down the short hallway leading to her bedroom. Sconces lined the wall now where there once used to be an arrangement of diamond-shaped mirrors. Sheila was always adding something new to her décor. Ace thought she watched too many home decorating shows and subscribed to too many fashion magazines. How she spent her money had been a heated topic lately, but Ace had no problem bowing out. It was her money and she was entitled to spend it however she wanted to. The problem would come if *her* money ever became *their* money. Or *his* money, *their* money.

Ace knew he didn't deal with his money with a closed fist, but he wasn't going to let anyone squander away his savings for the sake of fashion. He already had Carmen to deal with.

Ace knew Sheila was getting impatient—or maybe it was eager—about getting married. He wasn't ready to give her his last name. It's not that she didn't deserve it. He'd even looked at engagement rings the last time he'd taken in his watch to get serviced. Sheila didn't know that. That was about three months ago. His stomach churned that day he was in the jewelry store. He'd known it wasn't time.

Ace had the typical excuse in his head. *It's not you, it's me.*

Sheila had never tried to replace Lynette, nor had she uttered a bad word about her. For one thing, she'd been given no reason to. There were a few times, however, when Sheila admitted she'd had to fight a tinge of jealousy because Ace had never hidden the fact that he remained friends with his ex-wife.

Sheila accepted it, but that didn't mean she was 100 percent comfortable with it. However, it had been that way between he and Lynette long before Sheila was in the picture.

"Are you ready?" Sheila asked, her laser-brightened teeth encased in pink-glossed lips. She clicked on the soft light under the lamp on the living room end table. A picture of the two of them at her job's Christmas party last year seemed to glow under the lamp's spotlight.

All that night, Ace had heard about what a nice couple they made. Nobody directly asked the question hanging in the air. *"So, when are you two going to get married?"* But he could tell they wanted to know by the way they hinted at him always being at their future events. He endured the night of office politics disguised as a holiday celebration, and fed Sheila's questionable colleague, Clive, with a long-handled spoon. That man always looked like he was up to something.

Sheila picked up her keys. "Okay, I'm ready for real, now."

Ace slid Sheila's red overcoat over her arms, then pulled her into his chest again. Her breathing was slow and relaxed, like she was exactly where she wanted to be. It seemed *she* knew for sure.

"I never thought having the man of my dreams would feel this good," she whispered. "It's been a great two years, Ace. I can't see myself with anyone else."

"Me either, Lynn."

Ace suddenly realized what he'd said, but not as quickly as Sheila had. With the look of shock and hurt in her eyes, Ace saw her expectations for a romantic night flicker out. It was going to be a long—and silent—night.

Chapter 6

The silent treatment.

It was supposed to make Ace feel guilty, but it was making Sheila mad instead. Ace went about his normal, good-natured self—singing in the car, chatting with the young hostess at the restaurant. Probably not even thinking about the fact that he'd call her by his ex-wife's name.

He'd apologized, but for Sheila, that wasn't enough. She'd carried her attitude the entire car ride to McCormick and Schmick's. It was one of their favorite places to dine when they'd first started dating, but this evening was already dampened—not only by the light drizzle that had started, but by Ace's stupid slip of the tongue.

"How long do you plan on acting like a child?" Ace pushed away the plate that used to be heaped with a salmon penne dish, minus the hazelnuts. He finished his tea and motioned for their waitress to bring him the dessert tray.

"First of all, you know I'm all woman, so don't try to bash me with your snide comments." Sheila took her napkin off of her lap and put it beside her plate. "Second of all, I think I'm entitled to be angry. You called me by another woman's name." She was irritated enough to toss her uneaten lobster in his face, but she wasn't that kind of woman anymore. She'd leave that kind of drama for Cassandra.

"It wasn't just any old woman. It was my ex-wife. My friend. And it was an honest mistake. She was the last person I'd talked to before I got to your house."

"And evidently you were still thinking about her."

Sheila pushed away her plate. Ace didn't say a single word in response. That was worse than anything he *could've* said.

And it could only mean one thing. Lynette *had* been on his mind. Probably still was. Sheila's plan to pout had backfired. He was probably thinking about how Lynette was more of a woman and wouldn't act so immature.

"I'm sorry." Sheila reached out for his hand. Ace hesitated a moment, then put his hand on top of hers.

Truce, she thought. *For now.* But it was a mistake she wouldn't soon forget.

"So can we enjoy the rest of the night?" Ace asked.

"Done."

"And you'll come cuddle up beside me instead of leaving my jacket to keep me warm?"

Sheila got up from her lonely side of the table. She drew the curtain closed in their private nook, then slid in the booth beside him, into the crook of his arm. Then it hit her.

Sheila was so mad that he'd called her Lynette, that she'd forgotten that this may be *the* night. He'd brought her to one of their favorite places. He hadn't taken off his sports jacket all night. It could only be because her round brilliant diamond with pear-shaped side stones was waiting for her in its coveted Tiffany box.

"Bring those pretty brown legs closer, girl. I've got a long week. I need some thighs beside me."

Sheila was more than happy to. Lynette may have had his mind for a minute, but now, Ace was with *her*.

"Don't start something you can't finish, Mr. Bowers. And you know the rules."

"Yeah I know the rules. I made sure we had them, remember. But rules are made to be broken."

Sheila reared back to get a good look at Ace's face. He didn't flinch. Looked at her straight in the face like he truly meant what he said. He was always the strong one . . . she was the one who felt like she was in heat.

"Stop playing, Ace."

This time the silence between them was a teaser.

"Are you serious?" Sheila asked.

"Sit back and relax. It's our special night."

The waitress came to clean the table and at the same time, Sheila cleared away her grudges. Cassandra didn't know what she was talking about. She couldn't let Cassandra keep planting those seeds of doubt about her relationship, just because she didn't have a steady man as committed as Ace.

Sheila turned her cheek upwards toward Ace so that he could kiss her. She didn't even complain about that prickly beard that she wanted him to shave off. Ace seemed to breathe her in. Maybe, there wasn't anything to fight about after all.

Chapter 7

"Just tonight, honey," Sheila purred. "It's our special night. Remember what you said about the rules? Well I'm ready to break them." Sheila dropped her coat on the back of the love seat. She wanted, however, to peel off the rest of her clothes and leave a trail from her front door to her king-sized bed. Like they did in the movies.

But this was no movie. Her reality was a relationship with no relations, and despite all the stuff Ace had talked at the dinner table, it didn't look like he was going to back it up.

"If we open a door, it's going to be hard to close it. You know that. We've been down this road before." Ace sat down on the couch. He still had his coat zipped high to his chin as if he didn't plan on getting comfortable.

Sheila had never known a man who had such willpower—not with her anyway. Everyone said the way to a man's heart was through his stomach. Before trying to walk this celibate journey that Ace had led her to, she would've challenged that statement. Her way to a man's heart had always been through the bed. Until she realized she'd never had those men's hearts at all. She'd fed their lusts, not their love. And when the relationship was over, the man packed his issues into her oversized emotional baggage.

That's why she was so in love with Ace. He was even-tempered, made her feel secure, and wasn't only interested in her body. Although on nights like tonight, she wished he was. One of them had to be strong in this walk of celibacy they'd decided on. In actuality, the "they" was really "he," because God knows she was weak in this area.

Sheila pressed the button on her coffeemaker. It looked like caffeine would have to do tonight. Ace was already starting to nod on her couch. He'd come out of his coat and propped his head up on one of her zebra-print throw pillows.

She walked over and sat on his lap, letting her legs stretch the length of the couch. Ace awakened slightly and let his arms relax around her waist. She reclined quietly at first, enjoying the steady beat of his heart and their synchronized breathing.

After a while, Sheila couldn't resist the urge to kiss the side of his neck, then nibble on his ear lobe. When his arms tightened around her, she knew she'd found the button. The button that let his guard down.

Passion lit between them. The classic movie scene she'd thought of when they first walked inside was about to play out.

"No. Stop." Ace gently held her hands down, preventing them from massaging his biceps.

"It's okay," she whispered. "God will forgive us, Ace."

"No, it's not okay. Even if He will."

It was wrong for Sheila to pull out a Scripture on Ace at a time like this, but it was her last ace card, so to speak. "The Bible says 'it is better to marry than to burn,'" she rushed to say, praying to herself that she was saying it right.

"Sheila—"

"It's obvious we're burning." Sheila looked at their tousled clothes and wiped the lipstick smeared across Ace's face. "We should just get married, Ace. We don't need a big ceremony. Just the two of us. I'll even go to the courthouse. As long as I have you, I don't need all the other stuff."

"Sheila." Ace's voice deepened like it did when he meant business.

Sheila interrupted him. "It's been two years." She dropped her voice to almost a whisper. "Don't you think I'm worth it?"

"It's not about your worth, Sheila."

"Well what is it about?" She pressed. Her bottom lip began to tremble as she held back the tears. She couldn't let her emotions get the best of her.

"You're trying to start an argument," Ace said.

"No, I'm not," Sheila said, trying to keep her voice pleasant. "I'm starting a discussion. That's what adults do when they're in a relationship. Especially one they've been in for two years."

Ace lifted Sheila off of his lap. He reached for his coat that had been tossed on the floor in the heat of the moment.

"Don't leave, Ace. Not when I want to talk about us."

"We're fine. Stop working yourself up. Enjoy where we are in the relationship."

That was the problem—no thoughts for the future. Sheila went into the kitchen. Her thermal mug kept her coffee warm but she dumped the liquid down the drain anyway.

The entire night was a wash. By this time, she knew that there was no Tiffany box or any kind of jewelry ring box. She'd kept her gift to him in her purse so they could exchange them at the same time, but the only thing he'd given her tonight was a hard time.

"You know what? I'm exhausted. I think I'll head for bed."

Sheila turned off the light in the kitchen. "Unless you plan on coming with me, you should probably go home and get some rest yourself. Your passengers will appreciate an alert captain."

"So you're putting me out?"

"You can stay—if you want to—on the couch. Just wake me up before you leave in the morning."

If Ace stayed, there was no way he'd make it through the night on the couch. By daybreak, she'd feel her duvet lifting and he'd crawl underneath into the warmth with her.

"No," Ace decided. "It's all good. My bed is calling me, too." He picked up his keys. "Are you going to church in the morning?"

Sheila hated when he asked her that. It was like he was keeping tabs on her attendance. "I'm really tired. I'll probably sleep in," Sheila said.

She heard the muffled ringing of his cell phone in his pocket. He pulled it out as he walked toward the door. From behind him, Sheila could see the name that read across the display. *Lynn.*

"I have to be checked in tomorrow morning by ten," Ace said.

If Sheila didn't know better, she would've thought his pace quickened on the way to the door. He seemed more than anxious to leave now.

"I'll call you tomorrow before I leave," he said. Ace pecked her on the lips.

It was a single, dry kiss.

Cassandra's call to action pushed ahead in Sheila's thoughts. The fight for her man was definitely on.

Chapter 8

Ace waited until he was in front of Sheila's apartment building before he called Lynn back.

"What's up, Lynn?"

"Hey. I need to meet you at your house."

What? "Oh . . . okay. What's going on?"

"Don't get your hopes up lover boy." Lynette's voice was playful. "Carmen left her thumb drive in your computer and it has the homework she needs to turn in on Monday. I need to come and get it before you fly out tomorrow, and in the morning we'll be too busy trying to get out of here on time for church."

"It's pretty late," Ace said. He looked up to the seventh-floor row of windows of the apartment building and noticed the silhouette of Sheila standing at her window. Seconds later, the light turned off, leaving Ace to wonder if she was still watching him or had retreated to bed like she'd said.

"Do you need me to bring it to you? Or I can meet you halfway," Ace offered to Lynette.

"No. It'll only take me twenty minutes to get there. I need to get out of the house anyway. I was cooped up inside all weekend."

"All right then. I'll see you in a bit."

And with that quick conversation, Ace's mind went to work again. He'd been so frustrated with Sheila's constant hawking that he hadn't even been thinking about Lynette until now. Now he had to go back to taming his mind again.

Only God knew if Lynette was subconsciously the reason why he couldn't commit to Sheila. Or maybe Kenny would be able to bring some clarity.

Kenny Pope was Ace's friend of twelve years. As their brotherhood grew, Ace leaned on Kenny as a man of spiritual accountability, hence his nickname from Ace, "Pope." They'd met at a chapter meeting of their fraternity, and had done some community service work together at a juvenile detention center. Although they'd attended two different colleges—Ace at Morehouse and Kenny at the University of Georgia at Athens—they'd crossed the gold and black burning sands of their fraternity during the same year. They'd even crossed over into holy matrimony within a month of each other and knew what came with getting married at a young age.

Kenny was a woman's ideal family man. He was a volunteer football coach for the Little League that his eleven- and thirteen-year-old boys played in, and he was the willing car pool driver for single moms balancing children and their other countless duties. Kenny was heavily involved in his family's life and Ace admired him for having the balance that he could never achieve with Lynette and the girls.

Kenny had helped Ace ground his decisions countless times by using prayer and walking him through Scriptures. It hurt his friend's heart when Ace and Lynette decided to divorce. The night of Ace's final divorce decree, Kenny let him crash on his couch, even though he'd had his own bedroom apartment at the time. No questions asked. He knew Kenny could sense that he didn't want to go home alone.

Ace could count on one hand how many people he considered to be a true friend. Kenny Pope was one of them. And he was always an open ear, even at almost midnight on a Saturday.

Kenny's wife, April, answered the phone.

"Hey, April. It's Ace."

"Hi Ace," she said in her usual cheerful voice. If she was asleep, her voice didn't tell on her. "You doing all right?"

"Everything's good. I'm sorry for calling so late, but is Pope home? He's not answering his cell."

"No telling what he's doing. He's down in the basement. You know the king of the castle never answers the home phone. He got that mess from his daddy. Hold on a minute."

Ace laughed. He knew it was true. Kenny was the younger image of his father, Kenny Sr., in looks, character, and personality. The senior and junior Kennys had everything in their relationship that Ace wished he'd had with his. Ace's father had passed down his work drive—the importance of being a provider. He'd failed to show him how to be a husband and a father.

"Whaddup man?" Kenny was a night owl. Most nights he didn't go to bed until at least three o'clock in the morning, and that was only because he wanted to be alert enough to drop off his boys at school if they missed the bus, which they usually did.

"Bro. Sorry I called you so late, but my mind is playing tricks on me."

"What? Give me a little more, man," Kenny said. "You're scaring me."

"I've been thinking a lot, Pope." Ace paused. This was his first confession. His leather car seat might as well have been a couch in a psychiatrist's office.

"About?" Kenny prodded.

"About Lynn."

"Is she okay?"

"She's fine." He blew a stream of air. "Real fine. Looking finer every time I see her as a matter of fact." He thought about those sweatpants she'd been wearing this evening.

"Oh. It's like that?"

Ace could imagine Kenny shaking his head. Then he'd pick at the hairs on his chin like he did when he was about to go into deep thought.

"Yeah," Ace said, feeling like he was breathing better already. It was a relief of sorts to get the secret off of his chest. "Crazy, ain't it?"

"No. Not really. She *did* used to be your wife," Kenny said.

"But now she's the ex. There's a reason for that."

"But there were more reasons she was your wife."

Ace pulled into his garage. "Now you're the one trippin'. You're supposed to tell me that I'm thinking crazy. You're biased toward Lynn but Sheila is a good woman, too."

"Never said she wasn't. But is she a good woman for *you*? That's the real question."

"Come on, Pope. Why do you always have to be so deep?"

"I'm just saying. You called me. I can't help God wired my mind like this. My line name was Professor Pope. I've told you the stories."

"'Bout a thousand times." Ace opened his door and punched in the code to turn off the alarm. "Come on back to this century. It's too late at night to talk about old frat stories."

Ace sat down on his couch and tossed his car keys on the table beside Sheila's present. *Shoot. Sheila's present.* He couldn't believe it hadn't even crossed his mind. He'd made another grave for himself that he was going to have to dig himself out of. Perhaps the heart-and-key-lock charm would help him get out a little faster. It was always "Tiffany this" and "Tiffany that." Sheila had dropped so many hints about opening a blue box—with something that she hadn't bought for herself—that he would've been a fool not to take that drive out to Phipps Plaza.

"So whaddaya going to do?" Kenny asked. "About Lynette?"

"Nothing. I'm with Sheila."

"Man. I've never heard you talk one time like you're trying to make what you have with Sheila permanent."

"That has nothing to do with Sheila. Everything to do with me."

Kenny laughed. "So you're using that old line? You're going to have to find something else to say soon. Sheila's not going to go for that forever."

"Shoot. She's not going for it now," Ace admitted. "The pressure is on my neck man. I can feel the leash clamping down on me." He coughed and sputtered like he was being strangled.

Kenny laughed, but it didn't take him long to snap back into giving his tried-and-true advice. "Only a dog needs a leash, man. As long as you're being an upright, righteous man that's dealing with a virtuous woman you don't have to worry about all that."

Ace questioned whether he could still be considered an upright, righteous man if he was dating one woman, but thinking about another. He cut to the chase. "Lynn's on her way over."

"She's what? Y'all aren't doing that late-night call thing are you?"

"Slow down, Pope. She's picking up Carmen's thumb drive. She needs it for her homework. And little does Lynn know, but she's already got me in trouble one time tonight. I called Sheila by her name."

"No you didn't."

"I did."

"And you're still walking? I'm surprised she didn't cut your legs off at the knee. Women don't play that."

"Tell me about it," Ace said.

"Sheila must be in it for the long run, then."

"Oh, that's not all. I just realized when I walked back in the house that I forgot to give her the anniversary gift."

"And she didn't say anything about it?" Kenny asked.

"Not a word."

"Oh, don't worry. She's sitting on that one. Letting it simmer for a while. You'll hear about it sooner or later."

Ace heard a clicking in the background like Kenny was setting up the balls on his pool table.

"Seriously, man," Kenny continued. "All I can tell you is the same thing I tell you about everything. Pray about it. Ask God for wisdom, and ultimately for His will to be done."

"You know what? You *do* say the same thing every time."

"I figure if God's Word never changes, neither should my advice."

"That's good enough for me," Ace said. He kicked off his shoes. "If God can't clear up this confusion I'm having all of a sudden, nobody can."

"Why don't you come with me and the family to church to-morrow?" Kenny asked. "My wife's been throwing down in the kitchen all day so we're gonna eat good when we get out."

"Man, I wish. I'm reporting in the morning. I'll take you up on that offer when I get back in town." Ace heard the noise again. Kenny was definitely knocking his cue ball around the pool table.

"That's straight," Kenny said. "Then we need to get back in the gym so you can work off some of this stress. Neither one of those women are gonna want you if your stomach is scrubbing the ground."

Ace rubbed his four-pack—where his six-pack used to be. It was going to take a lot for him to have a stomach that spilled over his belt. "I'll do that man. The gym has been calling me for some time anyway."

"And don't let Lynette stay at your house too long. You know the flesh gets weak late at night, and if she was looking fine to you earlier today, you can imagine how she's going to be looking to you tonight."

"If that's the case I might need to throw the thumb drive out the window when I see her drive up."

"One day and she's got you feeling like this? I might have to bring my wife in on this prayer assignment," Kenny said. "You can't play with my wife. She'll pray until you and Lynette are standing at the altar again."

With Kenny's statement, it was like Ace felt a warmth move across his body. It brought with it a sudden rush of peace. He hadn't felt something like it in a long time. "Later, Pope," he said, hanging up.

The night-lights in Ace's hallway and a lamp in the guest bedroom were automatically set to come on at dusk. Being away from home so much, it was a precautionary measure to have them and his other security lights outside. The girls called the lights lining the hallway his personal runway.

Ace disrobed and got ready to put on his pajamas, until he remembered it probably wasn't the appropriate thing to do with Lynette coming over. Instead he pulled on some sweatpants and a grey Morehouse sweatshirt.

By the time Ace shaved his beard and brushed his teeth, he noticed the headlights from Lynette's car seeping through his bedroom blinds. As if on cue that she had arrived, Ace's home phone rang. He picked it up off of the base in his bedroom and looked at the caller ID. It was Sheila. Ace considered not answering, but he knew he had nothing to hide. He and Lynette were taking care of some business related to their children.

"What's up, Sheila?"

"I'm calling to apologize for how our night started . . . and ended. You know I love you."

"I love you, too," he said, his remark punctuated by the doorbell. Not once, but twice, like an anxious door-to-door salesman. He never recalled it being so loud.

"Is that your doorbell?" Sheila asked.

Nothing to hide, he told himself. *I'm a grown man.* "It's Lynn."

Silence.

"She's coming to pick up Carmen's homework."

Silence. Ace listened for her breathing. *Did she hang up?*

"And I'm sorry I forgot to bring your anniversary gift with me. Charge it to my head, not my heart. I left it on the table trying to rush to get the girls home."

Doorbell.

"Why don't I wait on the line until you take care of what Lynette needs," Sheila suggested. "It shouldn't take long."

Sheila didn't sound happy. Not in the least bit.

"A while ago you couldn't wait to get into bed," Ace said, going to the door and trying his best to end the conversation without making matters worse and seeming suspicious. "Sleep tight, okay. It's nothing to worry about."

"We've always been honest with each other, Ace," Sheila said. "Don't let that change now."

This time Ace didn't have to wonder if she hung up.

Chapter 9

Lynette had actually put on lipstick. A shade called *Bronzed Peach* to be exact. She could've sworn Ace had looked directly at her lips when he opened the door, wondering why she'd gone through the extra effort.

She was right. He had keyed in on her lips.

"Looks like you've got another stop to make after you leave here. You've got your lips all glazed up."

"Glazed up? That's a different way to put it." Lynette rubbed her lips together and wondered if she'd overdone it. She should've kept with the Balmex. "I did these lips for me and me alone. There are two things a woman can do that will instantly make her feel better. Put on lipstick and some earrings," she told him.

"I think you did it for me." Ace left her standing in the living room while he went into his office. "You might as well tell the truth, Lynn," he yelled out to her.

"You wish," Lynette said. *I wish.*

Lynette looked around Ace's home. Although she dropped the girls off occasionally for their time with their father, it had been forever since she'd been inside. Nothing had changed since the last time. A drop of Lynette's preference for art had gotten into him, and mounted over the fireplace Ace had one piece that looked like a painting of overlapping of geometric shapes.

Definitely not what I would've chosen, she thought, knowing he'd paid good money for it and that it wasn't a flea market find. If nothing else, it complemented the walls that were painted a soft golden color. If it weren't for the previous owners, every wall would've been painted eggshell white because décor wasn't his forté.

Ace was the walking definition of a type A personality. He was driven by perfection and schedules and it used to drive Lynette up the wall. To do something spontaneous was a stretch because he liked order, whereas Lynette was down to go with the flow. She didn't mind a house that looked like a home—a few things out of place. Stray tennis shoes in the den or a few days worth of mail left on the breakfast bar until she felt like looking at it. Ace couldn't stand it if things weren't where they were supposed to be. His home was still proof of that. She knew his shoes kicked off by the couch wouldn't be there by the time he went to bed.

Two pictures of Carmen and Jada were in identical frames on the middle of the end table. A leather magazine holder on the floor beside the couch held his business magazines stacked perfectly— in order by month she was sure. The set of car keys were on the coffee table where he always liked to keep them. Right beside the Tiffany box.

Tiffany box?

It could only be for one person. The box looked too big to hold a ring, and besides, Ace had already said that he wasn't proposing right now. Lynette wished she could pick it up and give it the shake test. Since there was no guarantee that she wouldn't get caught red-handed, or in this case, blue-handed, she decided to go to the next best source. Her girls.

They would know. And maybe it was wrong to think, but she hoped they hadn't helped pick it out. That was too much to handle.

Ace walked back into the living room and handed her the Hello Kitty key chain that was hooked to Carmen's thumb drive. He also slid a check into her hand.

"I don't need it," Lynette said, and tried to give it back to him.

"It's for the girls."

"You already gave me money for the month," she said. They'd never had a formal child support order. She hadn't ever considered getting one because Ace contributed over and above what the state would've mandated.

"Put it away in their savings. Something is bound to come up with school or something."

Ace wouldn't take the check back, and for a moment, their hands touched. Lynette wondered what would've happened if she intertwined her fingers with his. Would he somehow absorb the feelings she was having, or would he shut her out? But she would never know.

Because there was Sheila. And now there was that stupid Tiffany box.

Chapter 10

Sheila waited for the overworked and squeaky arm to rise so she could pile into the parking deck with the other Monday morning commuters. If it wasn't for the ever-growing debt she amassed trying to keep up with these folks, I'd quit this job today, she thought.

She couldn't wait until she was Mrs. Sheila Bowers. The first Mrs. Bowers made a critical mistake, from what Ace had told her about their past. He hadn't called it "critical," but that's the way she saw it. Lynette was all into building her practice as a pediatric dentist. Who in the world would put looking into the mouths of screaming kids in front of their husband? But Sheila wouldn't risk losing a marriage or anything else to her career. It was simply a way to pay her bills. Yet sometimes her paycheck was barely doing that.

Sheila had hoped Ace was going to call her back last night after Lynette left. He didn't. And she didn't call him either. She didn't want to seem as insecure and desperate as she felt. Instead, she said a prayer that nothing would happen, and watched home-improvement show reruns on cable until she drifted off to sleep.

This morning Sheila woke up wishing she hadn't been trying to be so tough. Now Ace would be gone all week on international flight assignments and she'd have to wait for days before she could see him in person. They'd finally get to exchange anniversary gifts and everything would be back to normal.

Sheila's Bluetooth earpiece chirped in her ear. "Answer," she said to the voice-activated technology. Since she knew Ace wouldn't be calling because he had to report this morning, there was only one person it could be.

"Hi Cassandra," Sheila said.

"Girl, where you been? I called you all day yesterday."

"I went to church," she lied. Actually, the only reason why she'd stepped out of bed when she did was because she had to eat and go to the bathroom.

"I know y'all stay in church for a long time, but I didn't literally think it was *all* day. That's why I'm a faithful member of Bedside Baptist."

"Church was in the morning." Sheila pulled into an empty space and turned off her car. There were enough exhaust fumes already tainting the city air. "The rest of the day I rested. Had some me time." That part was true.

"You're a bore," Cassandra said. "You need to have a life outside of Ace."

"I do."

"Well it's a boring one. You're too young to be acting like an old married woman, especially since you don't have a ring yet." Cassandra paused for a second. "Or do you? Because I know if you'd gotten one I hope I would've gotten a call by now."

"We haven't exchanged gifts yet. We're waiting until Ace gets back in town."

"Uh-hum," Cassandra murmured. "Well let me tell you what I cashed in on this weekend."

Sheila didn't have a ring, *yet*. Cassandra was right. But she'd have one by the end of the day. The blue topaz and white gold ring beckoned to her from the jewelry store every time she walked by on her way to the Nordstrom's shoe department. At lunchtime she was going to the Lenox Mall to return a pair of pants she'd been using as an incentive to lose weight, but too many high-calorie restaurant meals and early morning four-dollar lattes had spoiled that plan. So until Ace decided it was time to present her with an engagement ring, she'd treat herself to the jewelry she wanted and deserved.

"Look," Sheila said, interrupting Cassandra's rundown of her shopping spree with Hinton. "I need to go. I'll call you back at lunch."

"Make sure you do. They work you like a dog up in there. You need to hurry up and get that ring so you can turn in your notice."

Sheila didn't want to hear another word about a ring. "Talk to you later, Cass," she said, rushing her friend off the phone. No more reminders that her dream to be Mrs. Ace Bowers was delayed again.

Sheila and Cassandra had grown up together battling the streets in their tough southwest Atlanta neighborhood. On one side of the railroad tracks, corner drug deals were more common than the weekend vendors selling bags of fruit at the stoplights. Less than ten miles away and about a five-minute ride on the MARTA public transportation system was Sheila's first dream—college. Cassandra moved from California to Atlanta to live with her grandmother right before their seventh-grade school year started. Together, they decided to chase what they saw as the "good life" instead of getting caught up in the perils of their neighborhood. Sometimes they fell short on the promise not to get involved, but for the most part, they kept their hands clean.

After graduating from Clark Atlanta University with big dreams and even bigger student loan liabilities, Sheila and Cassandra put their paychecks together and squeaked by while trying to live in the midtown Atlanta luxury that didn't match their purses.

Sheila had bounced around at several companies over the years until she finally landed the job as a junior corporate recruiter at J. Morrow Corporate Recruiters. Finally, she'd been able to move into her own place and dump Cassandra as a roommate. Six months later, she'd met Ace.

Sheila opened the glass and steel doors on the sixteenth floor of the building that housed her work office and was greeted by the front desk receptionist, Nancy. Nancy was using a steady hand to draw a meticulous line of lip liner around her imaginary lips. She filled it in with cherry-red lipstick that was way too bright for her complexion.

"Good morning, Nancy. How was your weekend?"

"I didn't move a limb," Nancy said, sliding the phone's headset on top of her over-teased hair. "Mark wanted to go out on the boat, but it was way too cold for me. I didn't want to do a single thing."

Nancy was as sweet as she could be and looked more fitted to work at a country store selling baked apples instead of at a downtown Atlanta office.

"It was a relaxing one for me, too," Sheila said. "Sometimes we need a lazy day."

"Ain't that the truth."

Sheila picked up a copy of the *Atlanta Journal–Constitution*, and headed down the hall to her office. *See*, Sheila thought to herself. How was it that a receptionist who probably made half her salary could afford a boat? It wasn't just about keeping up with the Joneses. It was about the Nancys, too.

Clive Alston was one of the nicest looking fifty-something men that Sheila knew. His tailored suits and monogrammed shirt cuffs screamed distinction. Sheila was proud to have an intellectual brother hold such a reputable position at the company. It could be stressful, but Clive was even-tempered and confident. Sometimes too confident. He knew what—and who—he wanted. Which was one of the reasons why Sheila tried to stay clear of him, unless it was business related. And above all else, he was married. She'd met Clive's wife, Gina, at the company's Christmas party. She was as put together as he was, maybe even more. And from what she heard, she was a cutthroat attorney.

"Good morning, Sheila," Clive said, carrying a mug of steaming coffee.

"Hi Clive," she said, unlocking her door.

Clive—and his cologne—followed her inside.

"Mmm. You're wearing that suit. And I mean *wearing*," he said.

"Gina and I are about the same size. You should check out the racks at some high-end boutiques." Sheila opened the blinds behind her desk. "Your wife would appreciate an unexpected gift."

"My wife gets surprises all of the time. In fact, she gets whatever she wants, whenever she wants. Is that your case with . . . what's his name? Andy?"

Sheila rolled her eyes. "You mean, Ace. And he's more than good to me."

Clive walked closer to her desk. "I'm still waiting to see the ring. See how good of a man he really is."

Why was everybody else so stuck on a ring? "Rings don't make a relationship," Sheila said, dropping the newspaper into the in-box on the corner of her desk. "That's obvious."

Clive's wedding band looked like it belonged on the ring finger of an NBA championship basketball player. It was huge and typical for a man that had an overbearing presence like her colleague.

Clive laughed like her comment didn't phase him. He was who he was. Always had been; probably always would be.

"I'll see you at the eleven o'clock meeting," Clive said. "Rich is buying lunch so we're going to be there for a while. Conference room B."

"Thanks for the reminder. Now scat. I've got work to do. There are some of us who actually work for our paychecks."

"I don't work for my money," Clive said, his cockiness rolling out on his words. "My money works for me." He walked toward the door. "If you ever want to take some advice from me you'll get to that point, too. Some things are about job security."

Did he know something she didn't know, Sheila thought, flipping through the files on her desk. Even though corporate recruiting wasn't what she wanted to do the rest of her life, she'd been trying to work her way up to at least a senior recruiter. But she felt stalled.

Granted she was late sometimes and didn't consistently go above and beyond the call of duty, but she did what was required. That's what they were paying her for. Being at the company for almost three years should've counted for something. However, seniority hadn't been a deciding issue when they promoted her colleague, Danita, to a senior recruiting position even though she'd been there just over a year.

Sheila fought to keep her eyes open during the meeting . . . something about some accounts they could possibly be losing in the future. Unless it was about her future with Ace, she couldn't care less. She looked at her watch, hoping Ace had called and left her a message while she was in her meeting. She would've checked her BlackBerry if it hadn't been for Clive watching her every move.

Five o'clock came and went. Then six o'clock. At seven-thirty, Sheila called the security desk for an escort then packed her belongings. Even though it was still light outside, her building had recently had some instances with strangers roaming through the building after normal business hours. The building's manager sent out a notice for all employees—especially the females—to exercise caution when they worked late.

Clive was at the receptionist area when Sheila walked out. His necktie had already retired for the day and his starched sleeves were rolled up to his elbows.

"I didn't know you were still here. I thought your office door was closed," Sheila said.

"It was," he said. "I was shutting out the distractions so I could get some work done. My wife hates when I bring the office home."

Sheila looked at her watch. Clive lived in Woodstock, at least a forty-five-minute drive home. "By the time you get home it'll be time to eat, go to sleep, and start the day all over again in the morning."

"My day doesn't even begin until nighttime. You know what I mean?"

Sheila didn't even ask what he meant. Clive could twist a conversation too many different ways.

The elevator doors slid open and a security guard stepped off. More like bounced off. Jamal was always upbeat, and was the kind of guy who could convince a burglar to return items to his victims, then repent of his evil ways.

Clive raised his eyebrows at Jamal. "I can walk you to the car," Clive offered.

"That's okay. I'm in safe hands. Right, Jamal?"

"You know it," Jamal said. "They've got me strapped with a trusty nightstick." He hit his side.

"Then I'm sure we'll be just fine," Sheila said.

Jamal lifted his nightstick off the hook at his waist. He twirled it between his fingers before handing it to Clive. "Look on the end of my stick."

"Isaiah 54:17," Clive said, inspecting the length of the black piece of wood. "Which says what? I'm a businessman, not a preacher man."

"No weapon that is formed against you will prosper."

Sheila opened the door. "That's why *he's* walking me to the car."

"Trust me," Clive said. "If somebody rolls up on you, baby girl, you're going to need more than a nightstick and a Bible verse."

Jamal didn't let Clive ruffle his feathers. In fact, Sheila couldn't recall a time when there wasn't a ten-inch-wide smile plastered across Jamal's round face. Jamal flung open the door for Sheila and escorted her—and Clive—into the elevator. Jamal worked the part-time four-to-nine shift at the security desk to help him pay for some of his college expenses. Most young men his age were into girls and clubbing, but Sheila could tell Jamal was different. She'd walked up on him a number of times with his head buried in one of his schoolbooks. Not far away from it was his Bible and his CD player where he constantly played his gospel CDs or one of his pastor's sermons.

Sheila imagined Jamal was a lot like Ace was when he was younger. Ace had such a strong foundation in his relationship with God, something Sheila wished she had. But with her past—the stuff she'd tried to bury—she didn't see how even a loving God could actually forgive her and never think about it again. The sea of forgetfulness—or whatever that pastor on television had called it.

Sheila knew how hard it was for her to forgive somebody who'd wronged her. Like her pothead brother, Devin, who found her social security number and used her information to open an account for a gas station credit card. If it wasn't for her mother calling—crying and begging her to help get him out of trouble whenever he was locked up—she would've written Devin off three years ago. If she and Ace had a child—especially a son—he'd never be like her brother. She'd make sure of that.

Chapter II

There was never a dull day in the pediatric dentistry offices of Drs. Lynette Bowers and Tonia Singletary. Typical days usually brought in children whose wild antics had chipped off a tooth, or some other mild emergency. Between routine cleanings and exams, there were cavities to be filled, and that in itself was always a showdown between the staff and the anxious child who was terrified of needles, or even the sight of the laughing-gas mask. Lynette was glad the workweek was over.

Lynette had forewarned her best friend, Audrey Landers, that there were to be no matchmaking attempts at the party this evening. Tonight, Audrey was to focus solely on celebrating her husband's fortieth birthday, and not trying to connect two supposedly lonely souls in an attempt at sparking love.

"If the Bible says that a man who 'finds a wife finds a good thing,' how are you going to be found if the only place you go is home and church?" Audrey had asked on more than one occasion. She always pressed Lynette to get out more.

Lynette wanted a God-fearing man, but she felt like the men at her church saw a scarlet letter across her chest when they looked at her. Not only was her uncle the pastor, but it was the church where she'd grown up, and the place where she and Ace worshiped for so many years. Evidently the eligible men there considered her untouchable ground. That left her male family members, and the men she'd known so long that they were practically brothers. So zilch was going on behind the doors of the sanctuary. That was fine. She wanted to focus on worship when she was at church, not trying to prevent her mascara from smearing if she wanted to let loose and have one of those good soul-cleansing cries.

Besides, Lynette thought, love wasn't that easy. She'd had to learn the truth about love the hard way.

Lynette turned the heat up another notch in her car. Once the sun had set, it had become nippier outside than she thought. Technically, spring didn't come in until the end of March, and the weather reminded her that winter was still upon the city. The heat from the vents blasted in her face and Lynette enjoyed it without anyone in the car complaining that they were about to pass out.

Lynette had left the girls in the capable hands of each other, knowing that one would quickly out her sister if it meant saving her own behind. Lynette had her cell phone attached to her hip in case of any irresolvable arguments or emergencies, but didn't expect either. At the time she'd walked out the door nearly twenty minutes ago, Carmen and Jada's imaginations had been swept into one of the three movies she'd rented. They were bundled up together underneath the oversized fleece that they always shared on lazy family nights, with a chicken supreme pizza on one side and a hamburger pizza with extra cheese on the other.

There was one thing about her girls. They had the common sibling-rivalry spats every now and then, or could forget their home training and smack their lips when they were agitated, but she never had any big trouble from either of them. A stern look or word from Lynette usually snapped Jada back into place, but it took a little more to deal with Carmen. Sometimes, she could be hardheaded. She got it honest though, Lynette knew.

But it had been a good week with no clashing of wills or PMS-induced battles in the house. As exhausted as she was, Lynette could've stayed at home tonight, but she had no intention of staring at her girls or the four walls. She'd actually been looking forward to the birthday bash all week. She simply needed to get out of the house for some mature adult conversation and entertainment —no cavities to fill, no thoughts of Ace.

Lynette parked on the curb in front of the Landers' house, pulled on her wrap, then scurried out of the car. She joined a hand-in-hand couple on the porch waiting for someone to come to the door. After a second ring, Audrey finally answered.

"I'm sorry," Audrey said. "I could barely hear the doorbell over all the noise. Come, in. Get out of the cold. I was hoping it wouldn't be so chilly, but you know how the weather can be this time of year." Audrey planted a kiss on the cheek of all of her arriving visitors. "One day you're in short sleeves, and the next day you about have to wear a fur."

"No," Lynette said. "You're the only one who'd gallivant around Atlanta in March with a fur on."

"Jealousy doesn't look good on you," Audrey said. "I'll let you borrow one of mine," she said, winking at the couple who'd arrived at the same time as Lynette. Audrey held on to Lynette's arm. "Everyone's in the den and the kitchen," she told the others. "And you can hang your coats in the hall closet if you'd like."

Audrey bit into one of the Spanish quiches on her plate. "Don't act like you're guests here. You know where to go," she told the couple who were still connected to each other like one of them would run away.

Audrey looked at Lynette from head to toe while she popped the last piece of quiche in her mouth. "Looks like you came with your own matchmaking plans," she said. "I forget what you look like when you get all dolled up instead of wearing that boring white coat or those scrubs with all those frogs and smiley faces on them and what not."

"Don't start," Lynette said, coming out of her wrap. "But I do look good, don't I?"

"You must've gotten help from the girls, because I *know* you didn't put together all this fabulousness by yourself," Audrey said.

"Girlfriend, I was born with all this." Lynette playfully flung her hair over her shoulder.

Audrey stepped back so she could admire Lynette's silhouette, accentuated in a black knit sweaterdress with a hem that fell just below her knees, and knee-high leather boots that hugged her calves. Most days Lynette wore her hair pinned back out of her face so that it wouldn't get in her way while she worked on her patients. Tonight, she'd let her hair loose because she'd felt like letting loose, too.

Earlier, Lynette decided to fight Friday lunchtime traffic and dip by the mall and pick up an eye shadow and lipstick from the makeup counter. She almost made it out with only two items, but the makeup artist at the counter looked so radiant, but natural, that Lynette bought everything she needed to duplicate the woman's look. She ended up leaving with a full bag including the free purse-sized bottle of lavender body mist.

"Shoo. Get back to Kirk and stop acting like I'm some exhibit at the zoo," Lynette said. "I can mingle on my own. I'm a big girl."

"All right, already. And just so you know, there are some fine, available, God-fearing men up in here," Audrey said. "I made sure of that. But I'll let you find them for yourself."

"Thank you for the update. And I'll do just fine enjoying myself. Alone, if necessary."

"Tootles." Audrey disappeared in the direction of the hum of the old school R&B music and conversation.

On the way to the den, Lynette passed the room that the Landers used for their extensive library and office. A display of paintings set on easels caught her eye. Their house was like a second home to her, so Lynette wandered into the room to take a look.

Although the track lighting was on its dimmest setting, it was enough for Lynette to admire the meticulousness of the artist's work. Her amateur work that she attempted some weekends paled in comparison.

Lynette forgot about her mix-and-mingle promise to Audrey until the lights in the library brightened and a well-dressed man, seemingly in his midforties, walked in. His low-cut beard was sprinkled with grey and his hair was cut with the precision of one of the models on the hair coloring kit box for black men. In some ways, he looked like Ace.

The intruder to Lynette's private moment asked, "Are you the art critic in the house tonight?"

"I wouldn't call myself a critic. I'm not that deep, even though I have a few original pieces in my collection."

"Me, too. More than a few actually," he said, stuffing his hands into his pants pockets. He stepped back as if he needed to see a wider perspective of the canvases.

They stood in silence for a few moments. Lynette glanced at him every now and then. He was clearly at least four or five inches over the six-foot mark in height, and it was obvious, even wearing a turtleneck and sports coat, that he did something to keep his frame lean. His hands were still in his pockets so Lynette couldn't see if he was one of Audrey's invited prospects for the single ladies at the party.

"So *you're* the art aficionado?" she asked cautiously, not really wanting to interrupt him, but desiring more conversation. Lynette hadn't met many men who were art collectors.

"You can say that."

"Then you must know what's going on in here."

"From what I know, Kirk said he wanted to do an art showing for a local artist. The artist is supposed to talk a little about his work sometime later."

"That should be nice." Lynette pointed at the canvas in front of her. "I definitely want to hear about the artist's inspiration for this piece. It's fascinating."

"I couldn't agree with you more. And there's always a story behind every work."

Lynette threw her wrap over her arm. "I wonder if these pieces are for sale."

"Of course. Have you ever heard of an artist passing on a sale of one of their pieces?"

Lynette nodded. "You've got that right," she said, propping her hand under her chin. All of a sudden, she found herself trying to look cute, and prayed she looked as impeccable as the woman at the makeup counter.

She was glad she'd put in the extra effort for her mini-makeover tonight. She hoped her confidence and self-esteem shone through past her blushed cheeks and that this man—or any man for that matter—could see that she was genuinely a good person. As a woman of faith, she desired to live a life that was pleasing to God. She didn't like to disappoint Him. That's why it took her awhile to get over the fact that she'd gotten divorced. But she'd finally forgiven herself, and knew God had forgiven her the moment she asked. He'd blessed her in so many ways. And Lynette prayed her next blessing came with testosterone and biceps.

Lynette stole a glance at the man who'd now walked over and started adjusting a few of the pictures on their easels. Lynette added a few things to her prayer request. It would be nice if the blessing was at least six feet tall, with a six-pack, and a six-figure income.

"This one would be perfect for my living room," she said,

hoping the conversation would lure the handsome stranger back into conversation. "That is, if the artist hasn't gotten too ambitious with the price."

He walked over and gave her a smile. She noticed that he had a small chip on his front tooth but if she hadn't been looking at him so closely, she never would've seen it. "I'll make sure you can take it home," he said. "We'll negotiate."

Lynette should've known. "All this is you?"

"All me."

He extended both of his hands toward hers and sandwiched her hand in between his. No ring, she noticed.

"Frank Stanford."

"Lynette," she said, purposefully giving no last name. It had become a habit. The Internet was way too informational when you didn't want it to be. She didn't have anything to hide, but the idea that someone could do research on you in the confines of their home was a bit eerie.

"So you'll tell me the inspiration behind this piece I've been looking at, Frank?" Lynette asked, catching the flirtatiousness in her voice. It had been four years, but she was quickly getting the hang of it.

"If it takes all night." He turned his head and lowered his voice as if someone else was in the room. "Especially if she's serious about buying it."

"Artists are usually so serious. This one's got a sense of humor," Lynette said, talking to her invisible friend, too.

Lynette and Frank heard a murmur of voices moving in their direction. Audrey and Kirk were directing the guests into the library. Audrey, being the over-the-top hostess that she loved to be, faded out the other music in the den, and turned up the jazz music in the library. Unless they'd told you, a person would never have guessed that the customized speakers were built to look like books on the bookshelves.

Kirk motioned to Frank from across the room. Her best

friend's husband was effortlessly handsome and equally as kind. Kirk was the kind of man who sent Audrey to Lynette's house for weekend female bonding, and paid for a traveling masseuse to massage their cares away—if only for a sixty-minute session. Growing up in a house with a mother and three sisters, Kirk knew the importance of sisterhood.

"You plan on staying for a while, right?" Frank asked Lynette as the crowd of Kirk's friends and business associates swarmed into the room.

"Definitely. I'm usually the cleanup assistant, anyway," Lynette said.

"Good. We'll reconnect before the night is over. It's been nice talking to you Lynette," he said, then went to the corner of the room with Kirk.

After a brief introduction by Kirk, Frank talked about the inspirations for his paintings. He was charming and articulate, and the ladies Lynette knew to be single were definitely captured by the way he presented himself. Including her. She tried not to wear the look of fascination that was the common thread across the faces of a few of the saved and single women who were probably praying for a man just as much as Lynette had been lately. She knew at least three of them—Tangela, Portia, and Truda.

But one woman in the crowd stood out as much as the revealing red dress she was wearing. She'd taken no regard for the chilly temperatures and the low-cut back that stopped almost at her waistline. She looked to be in her early thirties, and even from across the room, Lynette could tell she was up to something.

Every few moments, the woman slinked through the crowd until she was little more than an arm's length away from Frank. She acted overly interested in what he was saying, but even when he turned to describe one of his paintings, her eyes never left *him*.

"Every one of my pieces is inspired by dreams that God gives me and then I try to translate them into art. It's also why each painting is named after a Scripture." He walked over to the one Lynette had been admiring. "This one," he said, stealing a glance at her, "is titled *Fearfully and Wonderfully Made*."

When Frank turned away, Audrey put her hand on Lynette's shoulder. "Well, excuse me," Audrey whispered.

"Don't start. You knew what you were doing," Lynette whispered back.

"I didn't do anything. This is Kirk's setup." Audrey had traded the plate of appetizers she had earlier for a champagne glass of sparkling white grape juice. Lynette knew it was nothing more, even though a strawberry had been slit and perfectly perched on the rim. Several other people in the room were holding similar glasses.

"You said you've been praying that a man would find you. Don't try to hide now," Audrey said, noticing two ladies who'd put on their coats and were heading toward the door. She handed Lynette her glass and tipped out to walk out her guests.

Frank was still talking about some of his inspirations when Audrey returned.

Lynette said, "Need I say that I'm not trying to be with just any man. Number one, he needs a relationship with God. That alone will keep a whole lot of drama out of my life." She handed Audrey her glass back. "You know the rest of my list so I'm not going to get into all that."

A woman standing in front of them looked back over her shoulder.

What did this woman think this is? A prayer vigil where we can't talk? Lynette lowered her voice more. She was not trying to have anybody involved in her love life—or lack thereof.

"Sorry, Jackie," Audrey said to the woman. "Why don't you move a little closer so you can hear over our big mouths," she said. Audrey jabbed Lynette in the side once the lady turned back around.

"Honestly, I can't vouch for the man," Audrey continued. "I

only met him about a month ago and we've only talked a couple of times. I can't cosign on his character so any moves he makes will be on you."

Why not be open to meeting new people? Lynette thought. *If Ace can meet Sheila in the airport, is it a stretch to think I can meet somebody at a birthday party? We have at least one thing in common with our love for art, and his work is God inspired. According to him, anyway.*

Once his presentation was over, Lynette watched how easily Frank drew people into his world. She was confident her sale wasn't the only one Frank would make. She watched to make sure no one else was making a play for the painting that she'd already claimed. After he'd quoted that Scripture like the poetry it was, someone else was sure to vie for the purchase of it.

Ms. Red Dress was standing so close now that it seemed Frank was wearing it instead of the woman. A man who seemed perturbed about the woman's actions walked over, whispered something in her ear, then walked away again. Her expression morphed like she was ready to spit venom, but she retreated away. But not before Frank had handed her a business card. She slipped it into her purse without the other man noticing.

"Who's your friend in the red dress?" Lynette asked.

Audrey knew exactly who she was talking about because her friend didn't even change positions to get a good look.

"I know we haven't always dressed as tastefully as we do now, but do you think a friend of mine would be marching around here with her goods out? She came with one of Kirk's colleagues. Hinton, I think. That man needs Jesus, anyway."

"Don't start acting up. You know God's going to get you later and then you'll be calling me asking me to pray with you about your mouth."

Audrey laughed. "Well, I'm not interested in talking about that chick, anyway. Let's get back to you and Frank. It won't hurt to get

71

to know the man. Put him on a ninety-day probationary period like they do when a person's hired for a new job."

"Ninety days? It won't even take me that long."

Frank looked their way like he knew he was the subject of their conversation. He winked and Lynette felt herself blush.

"He *is* a cutie," Audrey said. "He can't compete with my hubby, but he'll do for you."

Lynette's mouth dropped. It was a good thing she knew her best friend was full of jokes in the name of love. "I'm definitely putting you at the top of the prayer list tonight. I'll probably fast for you, too, because you're in dire need of a breakthrough."

Kirk called for Audrey. He'd been cornered by three of his frat brothers who were threatening to take him out back for forty birthday punches.

"I'm going to save my man. I haven't given him his *real* birthday present yet and I need him to be in tip-top physical condition."

"You're disgusting," Lynette said.

"No. I'm married," Audrey said, brushing through the crowd like there was a six-foot-long, silk cape flapping in the wind behind her.

Seeing Lynette alone, Frank broke away from the people around him and came back to her side. "So if I remember correctly, you were checking your calendar to let me know when I could take you out," he said.

Two blushes from one man in one evening. Lynette considered this day one of his probationary period.

"For some reason I don't remember that conversation," Lynette said. Even though Ms. Red Dress had occupied herself with tasting the spread of appetizers placed strategically around the room, it seemed like she wasn't going to let Frank get too far out of her peripheral vision.

"I always have to keep an ace up my sleeve," Frank said.

Lynette fiddled with the tennis bracelet on her wrist. *Ace. Why in the world did he have to say that name?*

Chapter 12

The overworn baggy jeans and hooded black sweatshirt did nothing to detract from Frank's handsomeness. He backed his grey Chevy Tahoe to the top of the driveway, then slid Lynette's painting out of the back so he could ease it into the house. Its beauty was covered by brown paper held together by painter's tape, and it wasn't until Lynette helped Frank strip the protective covering that she remembered why she couldn't resist dipping into her savings for it.

"Where did you say you wanted it?" Frank asked, looking around the living room.

The walls were tastefully painted in the hues of autumn leaves, making the perfect backdrop for her current collectors' art. When she'd decided to repaint the walls, she'd compared so many paint swatches that the shades all started to look the same. On the day she was about to postpone the home decorating project, she decided on what turned out to be the perfect combination of shades. It was her decision and her decision alone. It was a gift, so to speak, to herself after the divorce.

Lynette looked around the room for a moment then pointed to the area above the chocolate brown leather couch. "I'm going to move that one to the den and put your piece here."

"In the prime location." Frank turned his Atlanta Falcons hat backwards. "I'm honored."

"You should be," Lynette said, as Frank helped her remove the current piece from the wall. "My parents bought me this one for Christmas about seven years ago."

Ace, she remembered, had clued them in to it. He'd fallen short in other ways, but he always knew which studios to visit when it was time to purchase artwork for her.

Lynette's naked eye had correctly judged the dimensions of *Fearfully and Wonderfully Made.* When Frank steadied it on the prehung hook in the wall, it looked like it was sized for the space. The funny thing was that it was easier for Lynette to choose art on first sight for her home, than it had been for her to choose the appropriate—yet seemingly unplanned—outfit for Frank's visit.

Thursdays were usually Italian night, and spaghetti was on tonight's dinner menu. That meant cooking in baggy yoga pants and her church's breast cancer walk T-shirt with the stretched neck. Not exactly the picture she'd painted for Frank when they'd first met last Friday. So a pair of jeans, brown leather boots, and a chocolate V-neck sweater later, she was standing over the stove stirring chunky vegetable pasta sauce and dropping in sliced pieces of turkey sausage. A person would've thought she had three heads by the way Carmen and Jada looked at her.

"You're going somewhere, Ma?" Jada had asked.

"No. Someone's dropping off a painting that I bought."

Carmen opened the pantry door and dug her hand in a box of vanilla wafers. "Someone that you need to put lipstick on for?"

"I'm grown. Don't worry about my lipstick. Worry about your homework," Lynette had said, and shooed the girls out of the kitchen and back upstairs until dinner was done.

After sucking down their dinner, Lynette knew they'd retreat separately into their bedrooms like they always did. Carmen would gab on the phone until Lynette put an end to it. Jada would try to beat her high score on online sudoku or solitaire, then draw comic book characters in her sketch pad. And Lynette would pretend like she wasn't anxiously waiting for Frank.

She'd stressed over the ensemble she was going to wear, all so that she would look like she *hadn't* put it together. And here Frank was, looking like he'd been working in the back fields out in South Carolina somewhere.

"It's amazing how a little change can give you a new outlook," Lynette said, admiring how the picture brought out the gold tone of her accent wall.

"Speaking of change. I need to go home and get these clothes off. I was helping one of my brothers move today and time got away from me. I don't usually deliver paintings to my clients looking like I've been scrounging around in the back of a dump truck."

That's good to know.

"You don't look that bad," Lynette said, now glad that she'd gone the extra mile anyway.

"That bad? So there's still hope for me yet."

"Yes, there's hope." Their eyes seemed to be having a private conversation until Lynette ended it.

"Is there enough hope for you to come to my showing tomorrow night?" Frank asked. "It's downtown off Peachtree Street. They have a jazz band on Fridays, too."

This was another one of the countless times Lynette had to put her children before herself. Not only was there Jada's game the next day, but the girls had already challenged her to a game of Scrabble. Not a big event to most, but it was about the time they spent together. She wouldn't cut out on them. Hormonal teenage girls were a lot less forgiving than the young girls they used to be. Back then, Mama could do nothing wrong. These days it seemed, everything Lynette did was either wrong or embarrassing.

"I'm sorry. Jada's championship basketball game is tomorrow evening and there's no way I'd ever miss that. Then we've got other plans afterwards. You have to have kids to understand how they look forward to the small things."

Frank lifted his cap and readjusted it on his head. "My son is only four, but I've learned a lot about the importance of keeping promises. If *he* doesn't remind me, his mother does." He shook his head as if he'd recently thrown out the white surrender flag for one of those battles.

A four-year-old son? Maybe he's not as old as I thought. Lynette wouldn't have guessed Frank to be younger than forty.

Frank never mentioned having children even though Lynette had talked about Carmen and Jada at Kirk's party. She couldn't mark a strike against him, though. Frank wasn't required to divulge all of his personal information during one conversation . . . and especially to a woman who, by every definition of the word, was a stranger.

"I couldn't imagine having a four-year-old at this time in my life," Lynette said, trying to prompt him to tell her his age without her asking.

"It's definitely not an easy thing," he said. "But it makes me stay in shape so I can keep up with the little man. He can run through a room like a cyclone. I've never seen anything like it."

"He'll appreciate it in the long run. He won't have to say his Daddy is an old man," Lynette teased, pushing it a little further.

"When he's ten, I'll be fifty-one. I'll be ancient in his eyes, already," Frank said.

He's forty-five, Lynette calculated quickly. She was about to turn forty so at least he was in her acceptable range. She knew she wouldn't rob the cradle by dating anyone younger than thirty-seven, and she preferred not to date a man who was more than six years older than she was. But forty-five? She could work with that.

Frank stooped down to pick up the paper and tape that they'd stripped off the painting. The paper crackled as he crumpled it into his chest. "What about grabbing something to eat one Sunday morning? Not this week, but next. About ten-thirty or eleven."

The hope of being asked out on a date was nonthreatening when it was in Lynette's mind. But now that she saw Frank's persistence, she second-guessed about whether she was ready. She instinctively glanced toward the staircase to see if one of the girls were peeking around the corner. They used to have a habit of hunkering down and listening to Ace and Lynette's private conversations and heated arguments.

Only knowing a man for a week wasn't long enough to accept a date. *Was it a date?* Ace was the last person she'd dated, and surely the rules had changed since then. What would the girls think?

The hesitance in Lynette's mind must've been written on her face.

"Let me walk out with a little ego left," Frank said, turning his hat so that it covered his eyes.

Lynette held out her hands for the trash. He handed it to her, but held on to his end until he'd pulled an answer from her.

"Okay. Why not?" she finally decided. How else would she know if he'd last past the probationary period?

Lynette's lips cracked into a smile. She had to do something for herself every now and then, and this would help her turn off the screen in her head that kept playing Ace's face and voice. Praying for him didn't abate her feelings, it only intensified things. Lynette convinced herself that it was a temporary attraction and her mind —and heart—would be back to normal in no time. Whatever normal was.

Perhaps Frank could help her do that.

Ace would be back in town next weekend. All of the most important females in his life—Carmen, Jada, and Sheila—would be waiting for his time and attention. Now, Lynette would have someone waiting for her, too. Even if was just for the day.

"So where would you like to go?" Lynette asked again, pushed by the realization that Ace would probably go straight into Sheila's arms.

Chapter 13

Lynette shook her head. She'd debated on whether to tell Audrey that she was going out with Frank, but knew her friend would find out through Kirk anyway. Keeping it a secret would only fuel Audrey's suspicion that something was indeed brewing between Lynette and the urban Leonardo da Vinci. He'd told her that by night he brought his dreams to life on canvas, but by day, he was a landscape engineer.

Through her earpiece, Lynette could hear the soft panting that accompanied Audrey's cool-down on the treadmill. Every day without fail Audrey could be found in her exercise room with some high-tech watch on her wrist that could monitor heart rate, calories burned, and probably perform a body scan if necessary. The television was turned on to a courtroom reality show, and a Bluetooth earpiece was clamped on Audrey's ear. Lynette had seen it a thousand times.

"No," Lynette rebutted Audrey's comments. "It's not a love connection. It's brunch."

"Whatever you want to call it is fine," Audrey said. "I'm just glad you're doing something with someone of the male species."

Lynette turned on the side street that led to the Legacy Christian Academy. A few students lingered outside near the gym entrance, but other than that, most people were probably inside waiting for the tip-off for the championship basketball game. Jada was a first-string guard and she always looked for Lynette from the moment she stepped on the basketball court.

That's why Lynette hated that she was running late. She liked to be sitting at half-court on her customary third-row bleacher before they announced the starting line-up. The stands were probably packed by now.

"You make me sound so desperate sometimes," Lynette said as she eased over a speed bump in the school's parking lot.

"No, sweetheart." Audrey let out a tired sigh. "Never that. But you *are* excited about the attention from Frank. Tell the truth."

Lynette didn't let out a peep. She'd talked to Frank at least once a day since he'd delivered the painting, and each time she learned a little more about him. His son, Eric, was his only child and had ironically been born on Frank's birthday—June 22. Also Ace's birthday. God truly had a sense of humor.

"Tell the truth," Audrey pressed.

"I'm sure we'll have a nice time. But other than our love for art, we seem to be total opposites."

"Opposites attract. And you can't deny the giddy smile I know is smeared across your face right now. I can hear it in your voice."

Yes, the smile was there, Lynette thought. But it didn't linger. Not with what she'd just seen.

"Girl, I've got a situation. I'll call you later," she told Audrey, not saying or waiting for a good-bye. Lynette slowed down to a crawl and pulled into an empty parking space that could camouflage her car, but not block her view.

Even at a distance there was no mistaking Carmen's girlish sway, yet for a moment Lynette hoped it wasn't her, walking hand in hand with a boy Lynette didn't recognize. He towered over Carmen by a head and shoulders length. It was the perfect height for her to be able to lay her head on his chest. And she did.

Lynette sucked in her breath. Then . . . then her baby girl looked up into that boy's face and let him kiss her. It was a short peck. Over as fast as it started. But a kiss nonetheless. Then another one.

Lynette could've rammed the gas and jumped the curb, but her common sense came forward to question whether she was over-reacting. Then parental emotions took over.

No. She wasn't overreacting. Carmen knew better than to parade around with this public display of affection. At barely sixteen, she was still a child—yet a child who knew better. To make matters worse, she was gallivanting around her esteemed Christian academy.

God, You might want to flash a lightning bolt of warning across this sky before I get to her.

Lynette might expect—though not accept—this behavior from other hormonal teen girls. If Carmen was acting this way in sight of the people outside, there was no telling what secrets were behind the brick building of Legacy Christian Academy.

Not only was it improper, but it was downright embarrassing. Lynette sped around to the circular driveway in front of the school, and blared the horn to stop the lovebirds' stride. She could imagine the anger on her face spoke more than the words she'd have to say. She'd heard the phrase used that a person's blood was boiling, but this time Lynette felt it. And if she could see herself, she was sure steam was spouting from her ears, too.

Carmen moved faster than a pig about to be turned into bacon, as Lynette's dad would say. She hopped in the front seat and slammed the door, probably hoping to shut out any embarrassing outbursts from her mother. Carmen stared straight ahead, ignoring the boy whose initial look of alarm had now transformed to a look of concern.

Lynette let the silence in the car weigh on Carmen's conscience. She found another parking space and opened her door, still having not uttered a word. The anticipation of what was to come had Carmen glued to the seat, and her eyes to the floor.

"I'll deal with you when we get home," Lynette warned. She outlined her instructions in a steady voice like she was dictating a grocery list for the natural foods store. "You'll walk in the gym," Lynette said, "and sit beside me the entire game. You won't move, not even to go to the restroom, because it seems you've had a memory lapse that you actually *do* have some home training."

As another hurried set of team parents rushed into the gym, the rise of applause and screaming spectators escaped. Lynette wouldn't be surprised if the uproar was in response to one of Jada's calculated three-point shots.

"Let's go," Lynette said. "I'm missing the game out here fooling with you."

Carmen followed Lynette into the gym. Most of the game, Carmen busied herself with her science and social studies homework until the final buzzer screamed to announce the end of the game. It would go down as a debacle that the Legacy Christian Academy Titans heaped on the St. John Eagles.

Jada led the victorious team in their signature chant and dance step around the logo painted in the middle of the gym floor. She was still basking in the glory of the win when their coach released them to the locker room. She ran over to Lynette before going to get her duffel bag.

"Mama, do you realize I had a triple double today? My first ever."

Lynette shone like the championship trophy the team had

been presented. "I saw you do your thing," she said. Thanks to Ace, Lynette was up on basketball terminology and even knew what a triple double was.

Jada noticed Carmen still sulking on the bottom bleacher. Carmen's friend Macy had tried to strike up a conversation with her, but left confused when she didn't get a response or even so much as a courteous smile from Carmen.

"What her problem?" Jada asked, squirting water into her mouth. A drop trickled down her chin and Jada wiped it off with her forearm. Lynette would've preferred that her younger child act a little more ladylike at times, but she didn't bring it up. It was minimal compared to what she'd seen outside.

"Leave her alone, Jada," Lynette said.

Jada's head coach, Coach Tatum, approached them with a smile as wide as his moon-shaped face. It was evident by his swollen midsection and flabby arms that his peak athletic days were behind him. However, he hadn't lost his skills, passion for the game, or desire to see the girls he coached succeed in basketball and life.

The occasional bead of sweat escaped from its hiding place in the coach's thick black hair, and rolled down his forehead. Coach Tatum swiped them away with a dingy white towel from his back pocket.

"I think there's a future with the WNBA right here," he said, patting Jada on the shoulder.

Lynette brushed Jada's sweaty bangs off of her forehead. "She definitely did an exceptional job today. I think she's due a feast for a queen," Lynette said, knowing that the first thing Jada would want to do when they left was eat. She was always famished by the end of her games, and although Lynette wasn't a fan of restaurant buffets, that's usually where they ended up.

"A feast at the least," Coach Tatum said. He wiped his forehead again. "Ms. Bowers, can I speak to you in private for a second before you leave?"

A win tonight. Exceptional grades. What's Coach Tatum about to spring on me? One issue a day is enough.

"Sure," Lynette said, looking at Jada. Jada's face was a question mark, too. "Go get your things, Jada."

Lynette followed Coach Tatum to the corner of the hardwoods that wasn't overrun with students and teachers.

Now his sweat seemed to drip more than the small, damp towel could soak. He tried to give Lynette a pleasant smile, but it ended up looking more like he'd had a taco with black beans for lunch that was starting to upset his stomach.

"This probably isn't the proper time to ask you this question . . ." Coach Tatum started.

Oh, Lord.

". . . but I was hoping you'd give me the honor of letting me take you out sometime."

Lynette could tell it wasn't something he did all the time, because the poor fellow looked like he was about to pass out. She hated to have to crush him on his championship day after she knew the team's win had given him the extra confidence he needed to approach her in the first place.

"I'm flattered, Coach Tatum," Lynette said.

"David," he said. "We should be on a first-name basis by now, anyway."

It seemed his confidence rose half an inch. And she was about to smash it back down.

Lynette cleared her throat.

"David, I don't make it a practice to form any kind of personal relationships with my girls' teachers or coaches. Keeps things clean and simple that way. Do you know what I mean?"

The rejection caused more sweat to bead on Coach Tatum's nose. He looked embarrassed that he'd stepped out of his introverted box and asked. A runaway basketball bounced their way and

84

Coach Tatum caught it. As quick as his hands touched it, his self-esteem peaked again.

"Is there anything I can do to change your mind?" he asked, hopefully.

Lynette admired his tenacity. "When you're a single mother, some decisions are made for you, especially when there are girls in the picture."

Coach Tatum tossed the ball to the student assistants who were rounding up stray equipment. "You can't blame a brother for trying," he said.

"That you can't." Lynette waved for Carmen and Jada to head toward the exit. "Have a good evening, Coach. I mean, David. And congrats on the championship. You deserve it just as much as the girls."

Lynette had had quite a day. First there was Frank. He'd left a sweet message on her work voice mail that welcomed her the first thing this morning. Then there was the man who tried to pick her up at the gas station by offering to squeegee her front windshield. Now Coach Tatum. Lynette followed the girls out the exit door and to the car. The same could be said about weather, drama, and men. When it rained, it poured.

Chapter 14

Jada couldn't wait for her dad to call so she could tell him about their championship win and her record-breaking game. On the way home and at Golden Corral, she'd commentated on practically every play. But Carmen still didn't have much to say. Until she was behind closed doors with Lynette.

With swollen eyes and tear streaks dried on her face, Carmen pleaded with Lynette. She was a pitiful sight to see and Lynette almost wanted to cry herself.

"Please don't tell Daddy. I promise it won't happen again. It's only been that one time that we even held hands." She looked away when she said, "And that was my very first kiss."

Lynette doubted that. Her daughter seemed to forget that she'd been sixteen once. When Lynette thought she could try to act grown at fourteen, it had been her father who quickly reeled her back into reality. That time it had been her father's surprise appearance when he'd been on his way to the concession stand during the football game at her school.

At least Lynette had waited until they'd got home to blow up. But Walter Morehead didn't. He'd caught Lynette hugged up with a boy named Rodney and it had taken almost two weeks for the gossip about her dad's tirade to die down in the halls of her high school.

"Please don't tell, Daddy," Carmen said again.

Lynette couldn't help but think that Carmen was using reverse psychology. She probably *wanted* Lynette to tell Ace. His punishment—if there was any—rarely fit the crime. Carmen probably wanted her father to convince Lynette to reduce her sentence.

When they'd first arrived home, Lynette followed Carmen to her bedroom and immediately began unplugging every piece of technology she had in her room—the television, telephone, MP3 player, all of it. She'd given the proverbial speech about being a young lady, respecting your body, and having a standard so that young boys did the same. It wasn't the first time they'd had this talk, but applying it in the midst of peer pressure was another thing.

Although Ace was active in his daughters' lives, these were the kinds of things Lynette hated to deal with alone. As she sat on the edge of Carmen's bed, Lynette realized one thing as a mother. She was more hurt than she was angry.

"Mama, please," Carmen said.

"I don't think you realize how much you've disappointed me," Lynette said. "But I'm not the main person to be concerned about. It hurts *God's* heart when His princesses don't honor themselves."

Carmen's eyes widened. "I'm not having sex, Mama. I would *never* do that until I'm married. You've got to believe me," she said, the tears washing her face again.

"Like I just told you, Carmen. Sex doesn't just happen. Sometimes it's a series of little events that lead up to it. Everything seems innocent. Then you do a little more . . . and a little more. And sex isn't the only way you can dishonor your body."

Lynette didn't want to think about it. She knew even a child who'd grown up in the most disciplined, Christian household, with the most loving parents could make mistakes. Unfortunately, she'd seen it before and it had happened in her own family. If only she could hold her daughters under her protection forever. But when she wasn't there, God would be.

"Don't make any plans for after school or over the weekends for the next month," Lynette said. It wasn't as harsh of a punishment as she'd expected to give or probably that Carmen expected to get. But Lynette thought about how many times her Father had shown her mercy. In fact, God gave her new mercies every single day.

"Yes, ma'am," Carmen whispered weakly, knowing she'd gotten off easy. Any other time she would've offered other suggestions for her punishment.

Lynette left her daughter to sit in silence. She'd probably let her use her techie gadgets in a week or so, but she wasn't compromising on letting Carmen hang out with her friends.

Lynette retreated to her bedroom. She'd purposefully made sure it was a place of solitude and serenity. Her favorite thing to do was cuddle up inside the cloud of pillows on the king-sized bed. She had a small Bose portable CD player on her nightstand that she used to play the worship music that serenaded her to sleep at night, but other than that there was nothing else to distract her. In the past, she and Ace had so many arguments in this same room. That was part of the reason why she couldn't tolerate any noise there. As far as Lynette was concerned, the bedroom was supposed to be used for two things. One of them was sleep. The other she didn't have to worry about until she had a ring on her finger and a husband by her side.

By the time Lynette finished getting herself together from the draining evening, Ace had finally called the girls. Jada launched into a play-by-play reenactment of the basketball game before passing the phone off to Carmen. Lynette could tell that Carmen's eyes still held the silent plea to keep her indiscretion between mother and daughter.

Lynette still hadn't made her decision after Carmen and Jada's brief conversation with Ace. She took the cordless phone into the laundry room to sort the clothes in the packed laundry baskets. She appreciated the weekly help of the housekeeping service that kept her home tidy the way she liked it, but she didn't like the thought of someone handling her dirty clothes. Looking at the high stacks, she decided that she may have to add the chore to Carmen's punishment.

"Hi, Ace."

"What's up, Nettie?" he said, with a chuckle in his voice.

Ace's voice put a smile across her face. "Oh, we're going there, huh?" Lynette laughed. "How's Grandma Toot, anyway? I need to call her this week before I get on her black list."

Ace's grandmother, Grandma Toot, had always called her by the Southernized nickname, from the first time they'd met. Said she looked like a "Nettie," instead of that proper name, Lynette. Whenever they'd visit Grandma Toot, Lynette seemed to take on the persona of Nettie—helping the eighty-six-year-old shuck ears of corn and shell peas from the small garden she still tended in her backyard. It was a change going away from the bustling city to Griffin, Georgia—a town where the fair in the grocery store parking lot was the highlight of the week.

Grandma Toot never missed sending Lynette a card for her birthday, Mother's Day, and Christmas, at the least. All of the cards had a special prayer penned in Grandma Toot's shaky and barely legible handwriting. She always ended them by signing, "God's love and mine."

A few years prior, Ace had taken the girls to Griffin during summer break. They'd called Lynette pleading in desperation to come home because there was no cable and their cell phones couldn't get coverage. Not to mention, they only had computer access by going to the library where the librarians would kick you off if you exceeded the time limit.

"Maybe I can get the girls to go down for spring break," Ace said. "Grandma Toot would love to see them."

"Not likely they'll do it without being tied to the hood of the car," Lynette said. "Besides, we're supposed to be going to New York."

"Carmen's idea?"

"Of course. Who else?" Lynette shoved a load of whites in the front-loading washing machine.

"Things all right with the girls?" Ace asked. "I hope you've taken your Superwoman cape off for the night."

"Yes. It's on the hook until the morning," Lynette said. She thought about the drama that had ensued earlier with Carmen. Her motherly compassion convinced her to keep it to herself.

"So Jada had a big night, huh?" Ace said.

"Yeah. She really did her stuff. You would've been proud."

"Man, I wish I could've been there."

"I'm glad you weren't," Lynette said, separating all of the jeans from the basket designated for dark clothes. "You can be very loud and embarrassing when you want to be. They would've carted you right out of that gym."

"I'm entitled to get a little rowdy every now and then when I'm not working. I always have to maintain my composure as the trusty pilot so I won't scare the passengers."

"Oh, it's not just because you're trying to be so sophisticated. You know the TSA don't play."

"Which means if I get put off of my job, you'll have to take me in."

"No, sir. You better call Sheila for that," she teased. "I don't take in strays."

At one point—even as early as six months ago—Lynette

would've said that and meant it. But that wasn't the case now. This thing her heart was doing right now was ridiculous. She didn't know how else to explain it. They'd been able to talk about anything —more so after the divorce than when they were married. But Lynette didn't plan for anything about what she was feeling now to travel from her heart to her lips. And why did she have to bring up Sheila's name in the first place?

Lynette let out an audible sigh, but didn't realize how loud it was until Ace asked, "You all right?"

"Just tired," she said. *Keeping myself from falling in love with you is starting to turn into a full-time job,* she wanted to say. Instead she answered, "I've got a full patient load tomorrow because Tonia isn't going to be in the office."

"Another escapade with her man of the month?"

"Leave Tonia alone," Lynette said, defending her business partner of seven years. "She's calmed down. A lot. People can grow, you know."

"That's good to hear," Ace said. "She could only be around a woman like you for so long before some of your virtue started to rub off on her."

He really needed to stop with the compliments. "It's been seven years. I'd hope I was able to do something by now. I was starting to wonder if my little light was shining as bright as I thought it was."

"It definitely shines. You don't have to worry about that," Ace said.

Stop it, Ace. "When it's all said and done, I believe God will have His way in her life," Lynette said.

Ace had always found Tonia's ways and insights on relationships amusing. She was adept at her career and business decisions, but made all the wrong choices when it came to relationships.

"Yep. Time has a way of changing a lot of things," Ace said.

He sounded like he was reflecting on something, Lynette noticed.

"Things you wished you'd done," he continued. "Things you wished you hadn't."

"Is this leading to some kind of personal confession?" Lynette asked. She felt her heart in her throat. *I shouldn't have asked that question.*

"You're the one sighing and all that," Ace said. "Got something you want to tell *me*?"

"No. You?"

"No."

Both seemed to be at a loss for words. Lynette had to do something before her confessions dropped out of her mouth faster than she could control them. She'd learned the hard way that words were hard to take back.

"Well, I'm off to bed," Lynette said, hurrying off the phone. "We'll talk to you later. Be safe."

"You, too. Tell the girls I love them," Ace said.

Lynette hung up the phone. The longer she listened to Ace's voice, the worse it got. And the sad thing was that he had no idea.

Lynette went to bed with too much on her mind for her to relax. Praying had helped, but some of her thoughts refused to take a backseat to her desire for sleep. She started reading a novel, then remembered why she'd decided to keep those kind of romance books on the bookshelf and away from her bedside. In fact, one of the women at church was trying to build a library at the women's restoration house where she worked, so Lynette decided to donate them to a worthy cause.

Lynette went into the sitting room located off of her bedroom, packed her collection of romance novels in a cardboard box, then crawled back into bed. She read a few pages from a woman's devotion, prayed, read her Bible, then prayed some more. And some more.

She called her mother and listened to Claudette Morehead

talk about the updates from the committee who was working on the women's retreat. Lynette was currently serving as the vice-chairperson for the special retreat they were having for the single women, but it sometimes felt she didn't have the enthusiasm for it that she should. She was one of only two women in the group who'd been married before. And although she was by every definition of the word, single, Lynette hadn't connected with the other women. They were usually anxious about being married, and Lynette thought they were sometimes more invested in the thought of being married than in the work that actually went behind it. Marriage was work. Hard work. When Lynette was truthful and shared the realities of sacrifices that marriage required, she started to feel unqualified. Who was she to talk about the aspects of a successful marriage?

Yet, she'd stayed in the ministry because that's where God had her for the time being. But now, trying her best to listen closely to the heart of what He desired for her, Lynette knew this year might be her last. That was more than fine with her. She would use her time to be more involved in Carmen and Jada's lives. The last thing she wanted to do was be a grandmother, Lynette thought, wondering if she was overreacting and if things weren't really as a bad as they seemed.

Lynette picked up the phone to call Audrey. It was eleven o'clock, but she'd get over it.

"Why are you calling me this late?" Audrey said, though Lynette knew she wasn't mad. "You know I need my beauty sleep."

"I'm sure you've got some hours to spare. You're like the woman in Song of Solomon. All that."

"That I am. And thank you for buttering me up. You must want something."

Lynette hit her with the question that she knew would make Audrey throw off the covers and sit up against the back of her mahogany sleigh bed.

"What should I do if I think Carmen is thinking about doing it?"

"Doing what?" Audrey said.

"*It*. You know."

"*It?* As in relations? As in what's only going to go down with her after she's married and no time before?"

Lynette could see Audrey now. Wagging her finger in the air. "Yes. That *it*." Lynette turned off her bedside lamp and scrunched herself up under the covers because Audrey hadn't wasted any time in diving headfirst into the conversation. These conversations with Audrey always started out with one intention, but blossomed out in so many directions by the time they hung up the phone. These late-night conversations had replaced the pillow talk she used to share with Ace in the early years.

Audrey had shared Lynette's tears, laughter, dreams, and failure. They could talk about anything, but Lynette wasn't ready to tell her the thing, or rather person, that had been keeping her up at night—Ace.

Chapter 15

Ace lifted his pilot's bag into his trunk then waited until the defrost cleared his windshield. The warmth from his heated leather seats made it harder to stay awake. He could've stayed right there in the parking lot and slept. There was probably some button he could push to make this thing give him a massage. His new toy was like his personal concierge on wheels; he'd added all of the amenities, except the GPS system that he now regretted not getting. A man who flew planes should drive the closest thing to a Boeing 747 on four wheels.

It was the kind of car fit for a bachelor. Ace had talked himself out of buying the car three times before. He was the practical type and not one to splurge on big purchases. He finally got to the point where he didn't consider this a splurge. He worked hard and made sure the numbers wouldn't throw his budget under.

Lynette had teased about it being his early-midlife-crisis car, but Sheila loved it. Anything that screamed rich was her kind of thing.

Ace revved the engine and leaned his head back against the headrest. Sheila had already called and was waiting for him at The Flying Biscuit Restaurant. But the only thing Ace wanted to see was the inside of his closed lids.

He and Sheila lived on opposite sides of town, but he could tell Sheila wanted to see him today. Sooner than later. Usually after coming off of a flight rotation, he preferred to be alone so he could rest. It wasn't that Sheila had to be entertained, but it was too much of a temptation to have her cater to him like she wanted. When he was tired, anything was liable to happen.

But Sheila had said she'd had a rough week at work with her micromanaging supervisor, and an even more trying night after a one o'clock a.m. call about her roguish brother. Devin had landed himself in jail again. Her mother was giving her a hard time since she'd refused—at Ace's suggestion—to help post bail. This wasn't the first time Sheila had been asked for a "loan" and like the other times Ace was sure this wouldn't be paid back either.

As Ace joined the few cars on Interstate 285 North, he noticed that most everyone he passed looked like they were going to or coming from church. Men donned suits, women wore their suits saved for Sunday morning worship, and children sat in the backseat with their faces scrubbed free of their breakfast and glistening with an extra dollop of Vaseline.

Checking his speed, Ace tapped the brake. This morning wasn't the time to get stopped for a speeding ticket. The car glided so smooth at eighty-five miles per hour, he hadn't realized how fast he was going. He was in a rush to eat, then go home. An hour. Ace would give Sheila an hour and his next smooth landing would be on the runway to his bed.

He wouldn't be surprised if one of his brothers from church had slipped a copy of Pastor Bailey's sermon today into Ace's mailbox. Sometimes the worst thing about having such an erratic schedule was that he couldn't attend worship service on a regular basis. Fortunately for Ace his church's media ministry provided CDs and MP3 downloads of all of Pastor Bailey's sermons. If he had a package waiting for him, Ace would play the sermon and let it minister to his spirit while he slept.

Because of his hectic schedule, he cherished his moments of rest. He remembered the time—about three weeks after his divorce from Lynette—when he'd been unable to sleep. While he wanted to attend church where they'd worshiped as a family, the wounds were too fresh and he didn't want it to be an uncomfortable situation for her or the girls. The next Sunday morning, Ace had gotten in his car and prayed for God to lead him to a church where his spirit could find rest. Less than three miles away from the apartment he'd been staying in at the time, he felt a pull to turn into the parking lot of Grace Temple. He'd been there ever since. It was an older church, full of seasoned mothers who wore white every third Sunday and held missionary meetings once a month. But Pastor Bailey was a young man, and despite his age, they respected the call on his life. The congregation—at least most of it—was open to embarking on innovative ways to serve their community and fulfill the Great Commission.

Ace held on to the things that were stable in his life. He had to. With rising airport security, an unstable economy, and constant talks of pilot strikes, something or someone had to be stable in his life. God was that someone.

Ace tuned in to the AM station programmed in his car stereo. It wasn't a secret that Ace was a fan of quartets. Grandma Toot was the reason for that. During the five years he lived with her from six to eleven years old, it seemed they were either at church services or quartet concerts more than they were at home. He liked the concerts the best because they always had food in the church fellowship hall afterwards. In addition to that, Ace couldn't wait for the weeklong vacation Bible school in the summer. For some reason during that week, Grandma Toot let him do whatever he wanted.

In the open fields behind Grandma Toot's house, he'd stretch out under the sun to watch the cumulous clouds morph into bears, faces, and trees while he waited for a plane to fly by. Ace marveled at the power of a machine that could leave behind white jet streams to paint the sky. He wondered how something that weighed so much could defy gravity.

When he asked Grandma Toot, she'd had two answers. One was, "God gave people brilliant minds to build things like that." The other was, "Check some books out from the library and write me a report."

Grudgingly, he checked out an armful of books and sat at the kitchen table. Before he even turned the pages of the first book, he wished that he would've kept his mouth shut. But then he was pulled into the pages and wanted to read every book he could find about airplanes. He asked for model airplanes for Christmas and birthdays.

"Don't you want something else?" Grandma Toot always asked him.

"Yes," he said, one morning when he was watching her clean collard greens. "Make that two airplanes."

Grandma Toot had said that only God could put it in a little boy's heart to fly that close to the heavens, so she encouraged him every step of his career.

Ace cruised into the turning lane and took a right into the restaurant parking lot. He turned off the radio and before he could step out of the car, he turned to meet Sheila's radiant face at the closed window. He couldn't help but smile. Whenever he returned home, she always acted like he'd been away for months. It was the way she looked at him, like he could do no wrong. Sheila wanted him to be the perfect man, but he thought he was far from it.

Sheila opened the door for him and practically yanked him out.

"Thank you for coming, baby. I know you're tired, but I couldn't wait until tomorrow to see you."

"I'm glad I came, too," Ace said, pulling her into an embrace and a kiss that he knew she was waiting for. Her body melted into his. At times like this when Ace knew he was missed, sleep didn't seem as important.

Ace finally pulled away. "Let's get inside," he said, when it started to drizzle.

"Uh-huh. Before we get frozen together. Which isn't such a bad idea," Sheila said. Her voice cooed like a lovebird.

Today's sacrifice was worth it, Ace thought. With delay on top of delay, this was the best he'd felt all week.

Then he saw *her*.

Chapter 16

Lynette noticed Ace's car from the moment he pulled up. His front vanity plate would always give him away. He'd had the same symbol on the front plate of all of his cars since he'd first gotten his pilot's license—a black tag with a red ace symbol like that on a playing card.

Lynette looked around to see if there was another table near the back that she could slip to, but more patrons were starting to come inside, most likely indicative that worship service at a nearby church had ended.

She'd been the one who'd chosen the table by the window. And why? *You know, God,* Lynette thought. *This isn't funny.*

She'd watched Ace and Sheila. Hadn't been able to look away. They were wrapped in each other's arms, seeming to care nothing about the damp weather. She'd watched him kiss her. He'd initiated it. It was something she'd never had to see before. His lips pressed into hers brought a lump up into Lynette's throat.

Lynette had felt a pain like a double-edged sword stab through her heart again. She shouldn't have watched them. Maybe it wouldn't be hurting so much.

She chased her hurt down with a sip of warm green tea. Ace had moved on and was in a thriving relationship. Lynette would make herself be happy for him. And she'd be happy with where *she* was in life. She was only thirty-eight, and love was surely still within reach.

Lynette wasn't foolish enough to shake her fist at God, but she wondered why God had chosen her to pray for Ace. Granted, he *was* the father of her children. And it wasn't like she thought she was the only one who sent up petitions to heaven for him, but he'd been heavy on her spirit for the past few days. Seeing Ace and Sheila together, Lynette figured it must've been for her to pray for her ex-husband's relationship. If she was willing to pray for their success, then surely God would bless her with a thriving relationship, too. Wasn't that how it was supposed to work?

Lynette looked at Frank. He was leaned against the bar waiting for his name to be called. In a few moments, he would unknowingly brush past her ex on his way to bring her the order of spinach and artichoke quiches. She wondered if they'd give the universal head nod between brothers when they shared the brief moment in time in the same space. If things worked in Lynette's favor, she might be able to enjoy her brunch without having to acknowledge Ace or Sheila's presence.

Lynette soon found out the odds weren't in her favor, especially since Ace and Sheila were making their way toward her table.

"So you made it back?" Lynette stood to greet them. To her own ears, her voice sounded shaky, but it couldn't have been more unsteady than her weak knees.

"Not too long ago," Ace said. "After we eat I'm going home and crash."

"I remember those days," Lynette said, with a brief reminiscing that she didn't intend to share aloud. "Couldn't pry your eyes open with a crowbar."

Evidently Sheila wasn't having any trips down memory lane. "Good to see you again, Lynette," she cut in. "It's been a long time."

Maybe I should've acknowledged Sheila first, Lynette thought. That would've been the cordial thing to do. But seeing Ace up close and personal again had made Lynette forget what she'd expect from the "ex-wife" if the high-heeled shoe was on the other foot.

"Nice to see you, too. That's a sharp coat," Lynette said. She meant it sincerely. While Lynette's fashion and style definitely weren't lacking, there were some people that were suited to wear things like the red and gold coat Sheila was wearing.

"Why thank you," Sheila said. "I couldn't walk out of Neiman Marcus without it."

Lynette noticed how Sheila slipped her fingers between Ace's. The crossing of Lynette and Sheila's paths were few and far between. Other than the first time they'd been formally introduced at Ace's suggestion, they'd only seen each other three or four times. Once Lynette had dropped the girls off at Ace's house, and Sheila was supposed to be headed out the door in a rush for a hair appointment. Funny how the appointment didn't seem as urgent once Lynette arrived, and Sheila had lagged around until Lynette was in her car and "safely" pulling out of the driveway.

"I'll let you get back to enjoying your meal," Ace said to Lynette.

"Yes," Sheila added. "And we'll eat so we can hurry and get home. I'll make sure my Ace gets plenty of rest."

My Ace? She's going a little overboard to stake her claim, Lynette thought. "Good," Lynette said. "And I'll keep the girls at bay for a while so he can do that."

Frank approached the table with his and Lynette's brunch in hand. Frank pulled out his chair and tried to fit comfortably into the space that was left when he wedged his chair against the one of the woman sitting behind him.

"How are y'all doing?" Frank said. "Good luck finding somewhere to sit and eat in this place."

"Uh . . . Frank, this is Ace," Lynette said. "And his friend, Sheila." *There's no need to go into the ex-spouse spiel right now.*

Frank turned sideways so that he could stand back up to shake their hands. Though Frank had salt-and-pepper hair and slightly more mature features, one thing was clear. A stranger who didn't know any better would've thought he and Ace were brothers—or at least close cousins on the limbs of a family tree.

Is that the reason I think Frank so attractive? Lynette thought. She'd thought they looked alike before, but now that they stood side by side, the resemblance was undeniable. *It's not just Frank's looks,* Lynette convinced herself. *I'm drawn to his intellect and our similar interests. Right?*

Sheila smiled like she was relieved that Lynette was preoccupied with another man. Ace's face showed no emotion. It had always been hard for Lynette to read his face anyway. It was one of the best attributes a pilot could have—being cool in the case of an emergency. Or in this case, not showing that he even cared a lick about whether Lynette was out with another man.

"What's up, man?" Ace said, slipping easily from the dialect of the man wearing his pilot's uniform and into his brother-man-to-brother-man language.

"It's all good," Frank said, before taking his seat again.

"Frank's an excellent artist," Lynette said, as if she had to fill the dead air that was left floating between them. "I bought one of his pieces to put in the living room."

"An artist? Oh you've definitely got her hooked," Ace said.

Lynette couldn't tell if Ace's comment was supposed to be a joke or not. He still had that same nondescript look on his face. Lynette looked at Sheila. It looked as if she were pressing to make her fake smile seem real.

"I remember Ace telling me one time that you were all into art and things like that," Sheila said. "You two should get along great, then. How long have you been seeing each other?"

Lynette spread a napkin across her lap and picked up her silverware. Sheila was digging for information that wasn't anyone's business.

"Now Sheila, don't come trying to sweet talk to get a good deal on a painting," Lynette said, knowing that her comment had nothing to do with Sheila's question. Nevertheless it worked, and seemed to send them a signal that they should be on their way. Lynette couldn't stand to keep watching Sheila rubbing her hand up and down the side of Ace's arm. It was too much. *God, why? Didn't I pray enough for them?*

"I'll take a Gucci purse over a painting anytime. No offense, of course," Sheila said, then turned to Ace. "Let's order, honey. I'm famished."

"Take care," Ace said. "Tell the girls I'll call them tomorrow when they get out of school."

"All right."

Lynette forced herself to enjoy the rest of the brunch. The date. Whatever it was supposed to be. It's almost like she didn't breathe until she saw Ace and Sheila leave the restaurant. They'd arrived in two separate cars, but she couldn't help thinking about them together going back to Ace's house. Sheila had said she'd make sure he'd get plenty of rest. *My Ace,* she'd called him.

"I'll be back in a minute," Lynette told Frank, excusing herself to the women's restroom. She needed to get herself together. She walked into the last stall and locked the door. That's when the tears flowed freely. All she wanted was a loving relationship, and it seemed that God kept putting Ace's relationship in her face.

Lynette already surrendered. She'd told God that she'd do whatever He wanted her to do. It wasn't easy for her to pray for Ace in this situation. She knew God was ultimately in control over her life if she'd just let go. She thought she had. Wasn't a divorce the obvious sign that she'd let go?

Lynette inhaled deeply—in through her nose, out through her mouth—until she could feel the tension start to ooze from her body. On the way back to her table, she watched Frank from afar. She followed his wandering gaze to a table near theirs where two women were sitting. One of them turned and seemed to notice Frank watching. She smiled, opening up the option for Frank to approach her if he wanted.

Lynette didn't give him a chance. What he did when they weren't together was his business, but when she was in his presence, *she* was going to be the main attraction.

"Are you all right?" Frank asked, when Lynette sat down and blocked his view. "I didn't know whether to send somebody in to check on you or not."

"I'm fine," she said. "Just dealing with some things women sometimes deal with," she added. That was a sure way to stop the questions.

"So the man you introduced me to earlier—the pilot. Is that your cousin or something? One of my homeboys used to be interested in getting his pilot's license. For leisure, though."

"Oh, I know him well, all right," Lynette said. "Ace is my ex-husband."

Frank pushed his seat back. The table behind him was finally empty, which meant he now had room to stretch his legs. "And you two still talk like that?"

"Of course. We have children together."

"I can't believe his woman would go for that. My son's mother catches an attitude anytime she even thinks I might have somebody in my life, and we haven't been together for almost three years. If it wasn't for Eric, I wouldn't even talk to her."

Lynette shrugged. "Sheila has no choice but to go for it. Thus far, she hasn't disrespected me and I haven't disrespected her."

"How about her and your girls?" Frank asked, stacking their empty dishes on top of each other.

"They don't spend that much time with her. When Ace is with Carmen and Jada he gives them all of his attention."

"For now. But if your ex and his woman ever get married, that might change."

Who's he to put his two cheap cents in? Lynette thought. "I doubt it."

Frank lifted his eyebrows in doubt. "That chick was holding on to him for dear life. She looks like she'd fight to the end if she had to."

"And she'd lose," Lynette said, confidently. "Because Ace wouldn't put anybody in front of his daughters."

"Even his wife?"

"Even his wife."

"So that must be the reason why you all broke up?"

Frank's question caught Lynette by surprise. She'd emerged from the restroom with intentions to make the most out of a first "date" in a long time. She'd refused to let Ace take over the moment, especially since he wasn't even here.

"Ace is a good man," Lynette said. "We had our problems, but that was between us. Nobody's perfect."

"You're defending the brother like you still want to be with him," Frank said.

Lynette took her jacket off the back of her chair and draped it over her shoulders. She wasn't about to let this conversation go down another road. "Are you here to learn more about me or about my ex-husband?"

"Unless he's trying to get back with you before I even get a chance to know you, I could care less about your ex-husband," Frank said.

"Good. And if we go back to trying to pull any skeletons out of the closet, let's deal with some of yours."

"Where do you want to start?" Frank reared back in his chair. "Like you said, nobody's perfect."

Chapter 17

Walter and Claudette Morehead's brick ranch home sat amidst oak trees, elms, and Lynette's childhood memories. Her parents relished the friendships in their settled community, although the surrounding neighborhood in the southwest DeKalb County wasn't thriving like it used to be when they'd moved into the family home in the early eighties. Every shopping center had at least three abandoned buildings that used to house businesses owned by people in the community. But they'd fallen to the emergence of new shopping districts and discount retail giants that were built a ten-minute driving distance away. The attendant at the corner gas station did his job behind a bulletproof glass, and the parking lot to the gas station had become a setup for the weekly vendors selling everything from animal-print rugs to red roses in buckets and knock-off black art.

The Moreheads saw the treasure in the community for what it

"once was" and didn't have plans to move. Ever. Especially since they were into retirement. Besides that, the Moreheads valued traditions, memories, church, and family.

Once family, always family, Claudette always said. Of course, that included Ace. Whenever he was in town during holidays and family functions, Claudette made sure she left him a message letting him know he was welcome to come over to eat. His visits grew fewer and far between once he started dating Sheila. Once, Lynette had even suggested he bring Sheila over to her parents' during a Labor Day cookout. It never happened. Now, Lynette was glad it hadn't. She couldn't see Ace's girlfriend meshing into their life and making one big happy family. Some folks could do that. She wasn't one of them.

Lynette pulled into the grassy patch behind the carport. The walkway leading up to the screened-in porch was currently only lined with small mounds of potting soil. But Lynette knew an array of flowers that could compete with a spring rainbow would soon sprout courtesy of her mother's green thumb.

She stepped onto the porch, welcomed by the smell of deep Southern fried chicken. She tapped on the door leading to the kitchen and her mother greeted her with the face and attire of a wannabe celebrity cook with a show on a local cable station. Claudette dusted her flour-covered hands on her overwashed apron before unhooking the latch.

"That was a quick meeting," Claudette said. "I didn't expect to see you until about three or so."

Meeting. That's what Lynette told her mother about her brunch with Frank. She'd kept it from the girls and her parents right now for obvious reasons, especially because her mother would turn into a relationship counselor.

Lynette sat down at the kitchen table, where she regularly feasted not only on meals, but advice. She wished she had someone to help her make sense about Ace. His face. His voice. His scent.

All of it was on her mind during the entire ride over to her parents' house.

Lynette contemplated again about calling Audrey, but she wasn't sure how Audrey would react. On one side, she'd probably sympathize with her and hold her hand while she got over this new hump. On the other hand, Audrey would probably want to slap her and ask her why she was putting herself through this when Ace had a woman and had gone on with his life.

Then there was her mother's approach. Claudette's first question of course would be if it was Lynette's lonely flesh talking, or had she heard something from God. But Lynette had already asked herself that question.

"So what's been going on with you?" Claudette asked, as if her seventh instinct—the one mothers are automatically blessed with —was speaking to her and dropping her hints about the conversation going on internally with Lynette.

It's already time for me to go. Her mother could wear down her walls before Lynette realized what was going on.

"Work and the girls. Same old, same old."

The wooden kitchen chair squeaked as Claudette eased down into it. Not from her mother's weight, but merely from the fact that Lynette's father liked to hold on to everything until he'd gotten the maximum use out of it—even if it meant twenty years.

"You need a hobby or something," her mother said. "You're pushing close to forty and that's supposed to be the new twenty, you know?"

"Tell that to my thighs," Lynette said.

"You got those from me. Some generational things just won't change. Not even with prayer." Claudette laughed and her eyes squinted so far back into her head that Lynette could barely tell they'd been there.

Claudette got up to turn off the collards simmering on the stove. She stirred the pot of lima beans that was heating along with a fresh turkey leg and the automatic seasonings that had been cooked into the crevices of the pot over the years.

Returning to the table, Claudette asked, "Carmen's been unusually quiet. Makes a lot of difference around here when she's not yapping away on that cell phone."

"Yes. Well she's been on punishment so she can't talk on the phone."

"Jada told me. Sassy mouth?"

"I wish it'd been that easy. But we're working it out. I was going to let up on her after a week but she was acting too funky around the house. It's been two weeks, not a lifetime."

"Unless you're a sixteen-year-old."

Lynette needed some weight off of her shoulders. "Mama, do you know I caught her—"

As if on cue, Carmen walked into the kitchen.

"Hey, Ma," she said. It was the first smile her daughter had given her all week. Either she'd finally dropped her attitude or she was playing interception on a conversation she thought was about to happen.

"Hey, Carmen," Lynette said.

The phone mounted near the refrigerator rang. It shrilled too loud for the small house, but Claudette kept it loud for her husband. He refused to accept that his hearing wasn't what it used to be. Lynette and everybody else grew tired of arguing with him. She guessed when his entire world went silent, he'd finally believe it.

By the third ring, Lynette realized her mother wasn't going to answer because she was too busy adding salt to a shaker. And Carmen wasn't taking any chances putting a phone up to her ear—not if it meant inadvertently adding more time to her punishment.

Lynette got up and picked up the phone. "Hello?"

"Lynn?"

"Ace?" *Why, God? Can I get a simple answer to a simple question?*

"Yeah. I was calling for the girls. Neither one of them are an-

110

swering their cell phones, and I knew you . . . I mean, they . . . would probably be over to Mama Claudette's house."

"I thought you said you weren't going to call them until tomorrow."

"I got home and couldn't sleep."

Seems Sheila couldn't keep her promise or her man, Lynette, thought. *I shouldn't be thinking things like that. It's just plain ugly, and God doesn't like ugly. I need prayer.* She tried to keep the smirk from spreading across her face but she could feel it moving on it's own.

"Lynn?"

"Oh. Carmen is standing right here," she said. "Hold on for a minute."

"Lynn." Ace's voice trailed from the phone receiver.

Lynette put the phone back up to her ear.

"You didn't tell me you were seeing anyone," he said.

"I'm not really," she answered, wondering why he cared.

"So ol' boy was just a business associate?"

"I didn't say that either."

"I'm glad to see you getting out, that's all I was trying to say."

"I don't tell you everything," Lynette said. *That was obvious.* All of a sudden it perturbed her that he was surprised to see her out of the house with a man. He'd spent two years with Sheila and now all of a sudden he can't believe she had a life outside of her office and the girls.

"Who do you want to speak to first?" she asked, steering the conversation away from her personal life.

"Carmen if she's still standing there," Ace said.

"Hold on a second," Lynette said. She handed the phone to Carmen.

Lynette kept her ear on the conversation her daughter was having with Ace, just in case he was trying to drill her for information.

Lynette pretended like she was looking at one of her mother's

111

Good Housekeeping magazine recipes that she'd posted up on the refrigerator. *It's not fair, God. I want to move on and be happy. I don't need to deal with any lingering feelings for Ace. I'm not one to try and rush You, but if You could let me know what's going on quick, fast, and in a hurry, I would definitely appreciate it.*

When she felt like the girls' conversations with Ace had nothing to do with her, Lynette wrapped a drumstick in a piece of wheat bread. Since she was destined to have thick hips, it didn't matter anyway. She might as well enjoy it.

Chapter 18

Lynette had a life. Finally. And for the last two weeks it had been a very good one. Sometimes life was about taking chances. She'd read that morning in her devotional that it was supposedly aerodynamically impossible for a bumblebee to fly because of the weight of its body compared to its wings. No one had ever told bumblebees that, so they just flew. So that's what she was doing. Just flying and not caring much about the other buzzing that was going on around her.

If Lynette didn't let herself get distracted by the small things, she'd finally be able to focus on doing things that made her happy, and look at the blessings instead of the insignificant things that seemed to be going on.

Bzzz. Two of the dental hygienists had called in sick on the same day from fighting a twenty-four-hour stomach bug that seemed to be going around. It was an inconvenience, but she was thankful they decided not to come into work and pass anything along to the other staff or her patients.

Bzzz. Jada had waited until the last minute to tell her about an awards banquet they were having for the basketball team. She'd prefer to know about these things a week in advance, but Jada had a feeling she was being awarded the MVP award.

Bzzz. Frank was ten minutes late picking her up for lunch, but at least she hadn't stayed in her office eating apple slices and chicken salad on honey wheat bread and listening to her "Master Italian in a Month" audio tutorial CDs. Because another thing that would make her happy was taking a sabbatical to Italy and letting her parents deal with Carmen and Jada so that she could go away and be refreshed. When in Italy, do as the Italians do.

If Lynette wasn't worried by the thought of being retained by the Italian police, she'd lie on her back and enjoy every stroke of the beauty from the Sistine Chapel, following the fingertip of the depiction of God on the creation to every scene of angels around it.

Frank wasn't a Michelangelo, Lynette thought, but he was a genius in his own right.

Following a lunch of turkey panini sandwiches from a nearby deli, Frank took her on a personal showing of his paintings that were being showcased at the Woodruff Arts Center. He'd included some of the pictures that were on display at Audrey's house as well as some of his earlier work. Lynette had to give it to him, he had a talent for conveying the Scriptures in a way that made it seem like God was orchestrating his hand with each stroke. Her own dabbling in watercolors looked like a kindergartener had done it if you compared it to Frank's. She'd told him so.

"You never told me you were an artist, too. I thought you only collected pieces."

"Can you blame me? I'm an amateur with a capital A," Lynette said. She walked further down the hallway to take a look at the last piece being displayed. Her feet were throbbing in the pumps she'd brought to work to change into. After being in loafers all morning, her left foot, especially, was protesting.

"Ever taken any art lessons?" Frank asked.

Lynette laughed. "If you count watching that guy with the Afro on television who paints all the nature scenes, then yes. He's the only art teacher I've had."

"I bet if someone *personally* showed you some of the techniques you'd get it down in no time."

"Are you volunteering?"

"For a small fee," Frank said, opening the door for her as they walked out of the gallery and to the curb where he'd parked his SUV. "It'll cost you another night out with me."

Lynette let Frank help her into the passenger seat. "I think I can afford that," she said before he closed the door.

Lynette felt the vibration of her cell phone from her purse. It was probably Kym checking to see if she was getting close to the office. She'd hired Kym because of her administrative skills and the glowing reference letter from the dentist office she used to work at before her husband's job transferred him from Nashville to Atlanta, but sometimes Kym's type A personality could be overwhelming. Lynette looked at her watch. She would be about ten minutes late, but the lone hygienist that was there today would get started on any waiting patients.

Lynette looked at her cell phone. It was a good thing she was a passenger and not the driver because she may have slammed on the brakes and jumped out in the middle of the street. She could only count this as another distraction, another thing trying to buzz in her ear and take away the great time she'd had at lunch with Frank. That was the only reason she could think why Ace would be calling her right now.

No. I'm not doing it. I'm not answering the phone so he can have me up crying and praying tonight while he's whispering sweet nothings and mushy talk to Sheila and telling her how he can't wait to get home to see her.

Lynette dropped the phone back into the bottom of the purse.

"I hope you had a nice time," Frank said. His seat was pushed back so far from the steering wheel that she couldn't see how he managed to drive. Why was it that men thought the driving seat was the closest thing they had to a recliner when they were on the streets?

"I did. You're very talented."

"Appreciate it."

"And I'm going to hold you to those lessons," she reminded him.

Frank pulled the down his sun visor, then reached for his shades. "I can teach you some things for sure. Let me know when you're ready."

He looked over at her, but Lynette couldn't see his eyes anymore. She didn't acknowledge his comment, although his tone said there was more than painting pictures behind those words. Even the most spiritual man could slip up and let his testosterone talk for him, so she'd let Frank have one free comment before she put him in his place. If he didn't know, he'd soon find out—Lynette was not the woman he wanted if he was looking for a saint on Sunday and a loose woman from Monday through Saturday.

Her romance novels had been dumped off and she had no plans on acting out any of the scenes from those books until she'd stood before God and united her life with the man He'd chosen for her.

Ten minutes later Frank pulled up in front of the medical professional building. The timing couldn't have been worse. Lynette wished the tint on Frank's windows was as dark as the lenses of his shades. Maybe then, Tonia wouldn't have seen her. Tonia waved at her so hard that Lynette swore Tonia's hand was about to break off.

"I'll call you," Frank said as he eased against the curb.

That was the open-ended way Frank always said things. Lynette noticed that he sometimes left things open so he wouldn't back himself up into the corner with a promise. That call could be tonight, or next week. But she'd wait. If Frank truly wanted to take her out again, he'd make it sooner rather than later.

"All right," Lynette said, and opened the door before there was the awkward moment when he expected a kiss. *He has to be around longer if he wants to touch these lips,* she thought. "Be good."

"So I see you've been keeping secrets," Tonia said, bumping her car door closed with her hip.

"Please. What's done in the *dark* is a secret. I have nothing to hide. It's one o'clock in the afternoon." Lynette grabbed an armful of dry cleaning from Tonia. "What's all this stuff anyway? You aren't packed yet?"

"Yes. But a woman needs her options."

Tonia had been talking about her upcoming ski trip for over two months. According to the flyer Tonia had shown her, it was a weekend packed with late-night fire chats, old-school parties, mix and mingles, and of course, skiing. Forget the fact that Tonia had never set her size-six feet in ski boots before.

"It's a ski trip, not a fashion show," Lynette said. "And it's going to be a bunch of fake snow."

"When's the last time you've been on a ski trip? A singles ski trip at that."

"You need to stop," Lynette said. "You lived in Florida most of your life. I bet you've never even seen snow."

Tonia laughed. "I've seen it before."

The sliding doors of the building glided open. "On TV," Lynette teased. "If this trip is anything like the singles events I've been to, then it's going to be a lot of women looking at each other. Only this time, you'll be roasting chestnuts by an open fire."

All of this talk about singles reminded Lynette that she had a meeting about the singles retreat scheduled for tonight. She didn't see why they couldn't meet after Sunday worship service like most of the other ministries.

"You're just jealous," Tonia said. "I told you to come with me. But it looks like you've got your hands full." She pushed the button to the third floor where their pediatric dentist suite was housed.

Beyond the exam rooms and behind their closed office doors, they'd shared more than dental X-rays and business partner meetings. Never married and no children. Divorced with two daughters. There were always stories to tell and tears to cry.

Lynette and Ace had only been divorced a few months when she and Tonia decided to merge their individual practices into a larger dental office. From that point on Lynette's business had become her husband, and if she was truthful, it always had been.

Lynette unlocked the suite door. Kym was in the receptionist area, buds from her iPod stuffed in her ears. Although the practice closed an hour and a half every day for lunch, Kym rarely left. Instead she brought her lunch to work. As a single mother who lived with her own mother, she always said it was the only peace and quiet she got. And to Lynette's relief, there weren't any patients waiting after all.

Lynette and Tonia waved at her, then Lynette followed Tonia into her office. She hung the dry cleaning on the back of Tonia's door.

Her partner had two large suitcases plus a small carry-on unzipped and lined up against the wall for final inspection.

"So you've finally got a guy friend?" Tonia asked when she closed the door. "It's about time. And why didn't you tell me?"

Lynette smirked but Tonia was too busy digging in her bags to notice. Tonia should know why Lynette had kept it to herself. At forty-one and with a history of failed relationships, she wasn't the best person to entrust too much information to when it came to relationships. Even though Tonia longed for a good man, she'd always been convinced that her looks, success, and high standards had been a liability in her relationships instead of an asset. Lynette had to give it to her though. Tonia never stopped trying.

"Friend is too strong of a word," Lynette finally said. "I don't throw that term around loosely."

"Okay, well-l-l-l . . ." Now Tonia was writing memos to herself on sticky notes and posting them across the top of her desk.

Lynette would give the basics. There wasn't much more she could offer than that. Like Audrey said, it was nice to have someone of the male species to talk to besides her dad. And Ace. Until she could clear her mind of this foolishness about him, she had to look at him in a different way. Only as her children's father.

"Well?" Tonia dumped the contents of her purse.

"I met Frank at a party that Audrey threw for her husband. We first hit it off because we both have an interest in art. Uh. What else? He owns a landscape business, too."

"And he's cute, too. I couldn't see him real well, but he looked like he has at least half of his teeth," Tonia said.

"You're full of jokes," Lynette said.

Tonia threw away a handful of old receipts and gum wrappers, then started to reorganize the inside of her purse. "I had to do a double-take, too. For a minute I thought it was Ace. They look a lot alike, but I guess you realize that."

"Ace has been history for the last four years. It's time for something new."

Tonia snapped her fingers in the air and wiggled her hips. "That's why I'm going on this ski trip. I need to expand my territory. Meet somebody new who can handle all of this," she said, her hands now above her head like she was modeling for a magazine. "Speaking of somebody who *couldn't* handle all this—do you know one of my exes had the nerve to call me last night? Duane. Talking crazy.

Acting like he was still in love. How his eyes had been opened and he realized what he'd missed out on."

Lynette shifted in the wingback chair across from Tonia's desk. Maybe God was speaking to her with Tonia's lips.

"And what did you say?"

Tonia zipped up her overstuffed makeup case and tossed it in her check-in luggage. "I told him, 'I don't make the same mistake twice.'"

And Lynette didn't plan on doing it either, no matter what her heart was saying.

Chapter 19

I don't think there will be much of a fight," Sheila was telling Cassandra. "I thought I'd told you that we ran into Ace's ex-wife a couple of weeks ago and she was out with another man. That was the best thing I could've seen all day. I think God set it up to show me that I didn't have anything to worry about."

Sheila wiggled her toes as the manicurist rubbed a brown sugar scrub on her feet. When Cassandra offered to treat her to a manicure and pedicure this morning she didn't hesitate. It was time for a fill-in anyway and Sheila was starting to feel bad that she was going to have to skip her MasterCard payment this month. At least now she could send in half of the minimum payment and put aside some money so she could eat for the next two weeks. The first paycheck of the month always left her strapped. It was the one she used to pay her rent, car payment, and car insurance.

"What did Ace do?" Cassandra asked. She was wrapped in a

fluffy white cotton robe while she waited for her hot stone massage.

"What do you mean what did he do?" Sheila said. "He was the gentleman that he always is. He spoke to them and then we went to our own table to eat." Sheila slipped her hands in the warm gloves that the manicurist held out to use for the paraffin treatment. "Do you know she tried to bring up what Ace used to do when they were together?"

"And you let her get away with it? She was trying to play with your head," Cassandra said.

"Actually I assured her that I would take good care of him."

"Well your version of taking care of your man and my version are two different things. You can count on that."

"Stop going there, Cassandra. I know what you're talking about. Most men don't care anything about what God wants them to do. They just want to sow their wild oats anywhere. If Ace doesn't want to have sex then I think that's an honorable thing."

"If you say so," Cassandra said, using the knuckle of her finger to turn on the massaging chair so that she wouldn't smudge her freshly painted French manicure.

"I say so," Sheila said. It was honorable, she thought. And frustrating. And old-fashioned. "So anyway," she continued, "Lynette's man should keep her plenty occupied just in case she gets lonely and starts thinking a little too much about Ace. The guy—I forget his name—is an artist."

Cassandra turned off the vibrating chair and sat forward in excitement. "Oooh," she crooned. "Speaking of artists. I forgot to tell you about a cutie I met when I went to that party with Hinton. He's an artist, too, but he's *not* a starving one."

"And you picked up this man while you were there with Hinton? Unbelievable."

"He's not officially on my team yet, but a girl always needs options. I asked for his business card that night. I've been thinking about getting some pieces for my apartment."

"Who's going to buy it? Hinton? I know *you're* not going to invest money on anything you can't wear."

"You're just jealous," Cassandra said. She bent down to get a close look at the design that the pedicurist was painting on her big toe nail. "As far as I'm concerned, why should I spend my money if there's a man who's more than willing to spend his?"

There was some truth to Cassandra's statement, Sheila thought. Although Sheila was barely keeping her head above water in her massive ocean of bills, she could at least say she could take care of herself if she needed to. She was just tired of doing it. But Cassandra had always relied on her physical assets and gullible men—and doing a good job at it.

Sheila couldn't remember the last time Cassandra had held the same job for over six months. Considering her record of jumping around companies, it was a wonder that anyone ever hired her. Her lot in life was not to be an administrative assistant, Cassandra always said. She usually complained that her undergraduate bachelor's degree in business administration was nothing but a piece of paper and another way for the government to take the money she worked for by loaning students money they knew they couldn't pay back.

Once Cassandra had asked Sheila about working at J. Morrow with her, but there was no way she was going to have them work at the same place. Sheila tried to keep as much of her personal business out of the mouths of her business associates as she could. But if Cassandra worked there, *everybody* would know *everything* about her.

An attendant approached them with a tray of miniature blueberry muffins and wine flutes filled with cranberry juice.

"Perfect timing," Sheila said, instructing the spa attendant to set her items on the side table. "I haven't eaten breakfast this morning."

"It won't hurt you to miss a few meals," Cassandra said. "I've seen you from the back side and it's not the way it used to be."

Sheila rolled her eyes. She knew she'd put on a few extra pounds but it was nothing a few days of walking on the treadmill fitness center of her complex couldn't take care of.

"You know maybe you could find a better way to say things sometimes," Sheila suggested.

"That's what friends are for. To tell you the truth. When you've known each other as long as we have then you shouldn't have to sugarcoat stuff. And you, my sister, need to drop about ten."

"I'm going to pray for you," Sheila said, chuckling off the hurt. But she really meant it. Sometimes Cassandra didn't realize the things she said to people could be hurtful. Or maybe she did. Because Cassandra had thick skin and wasn't moved by much, Sheila thought her friend figured everyone else was the same way.

Cassandra wanted Sheila to be the same thirteen-year-old timid girl she'd been when they met. Cassandra was a lot bolder than she was. She usually called the shots and decided which kids they'd hang out with in the neighborhood. If Cassandra didn't like them, then Sheila couldn't like them. Sheila had parted ways with Kenya, her best friend from third to seventh grade, because Cassandra thought she was ugly and plain and the reason why some of the boys never wanted to be seen talking to them down at the park.

"You should listen to me," Cassandra said, interrupting Sheila's thoughts. "Ace probably sees so many women getting on and off of his plane. And those stewardesses, too. You need to make sure he remembers he's got a good and fine thing at home."

Listening to Cassandra had gotten Sheila in trouble on more than one occasion.

Even after they made a pact not to be caught up in the ruckus that their neighborhood was known for, Cassandra was always willing to push the envelope. She had a thing for Sheila's brother, Devin, and would go out of her way to get his attention. Of course,

Devin had no interest in Cassandra, but he used the crush to his advantage and convinced Cassandra to make "runs" for him. In return, Cassandra got the attention from him that she craved and about five dollars that she'd spend as soon as she got the chance.

Summer break was usually the best time of Sheila's life. Her mother left the house for work long before she'd cracked open one eye. She could eat three bowls of Fruit Loops if she wanted to and didn't have to listen to her mother scream about how she was loading up on sugar. And although she had to put up with Devin sometimes, for the most part he kept clear of her and chose to hang out with his "homeys."

It was one of the days when hot steam rose from the asphalt streets and it was impossible to walk farther than the mailbox and not have sweat trickle down your back or collect like raindrops on your forehead. Sheila would have preferred to stay in her room with the door closed so she could soak up the air conditioning from the unit in her window, but a knock on her door changed all that.

Devin didn't give Sheila time to open her bedroom door before he barged in. "Give me your book bag," he demanded her and Cassandra. Those were the code words he always used when he had a run he wanted Cassandra to make. Cassandra was lying on her stomach on Sheila's bed. She was using a Q-tip dipped in fingernail polish remover to clean up the polish she'd smudged around her cuticles.

"I don't have my bag, today," Cassandra said. "My grandma took it because she saw all of the makeup in it that *your* sister said would look cute on me."

"Where's yours, Sheila?"

"No. You're not using my bag," Sheila had protested. "I don't want it getting messed up."

Devin opened her closet door and snatched the bag off of the hook it was hanging on. "Nobody is going to mess up your stupid bag," he said. "Don't y'all want ten dollars?"

Cassandra swung her feet around and was standing up beside Devin before he could get any words out of his mouth. "I do. I've been wanting to buy Janet Jackson's *Control* cassette. That song is my jam," she said, rocking her hips from side to side. A little too much. Devin hadn't even given her a second look.

"Well, tell Sheila to stop whining like a baby and go with you to take care of some business," Devin snarled.

They went but it wasn't Cassandra who carried the jean book bag that day. It was Sheila. And for the sake of fashion—Cassandra complained that the book bag didn't match her outfit—Sheila ended up spending the night in juvenile detention.

The Atlanta police had been watching the house for over two months, and Sheila and Cassandra were regular visitors. They never went inside. They knocked on the screen door three times, and after a hand reached out for the book bag, they sat on the porch steps and waited until the same hand threw the book bag back outside. That day, Sheila picked up the bag and hooked it around her arms. And by the time she walked to the end of the block, the police had picked her up.

It took one night in juvenile detention and a stint of court appearances to convince Sheila that she wasn't interested in a life of crime. Even today she hated to think about it.

Sheila gently touched her fingertips to make sure the polish was completely dry. It was time for her to leave. She'd timed out the morning so she could get in her manicure and pedicure, but still have time to get dressed before Ace arrived to pick her up. They were finally going to spend all day together. Well most of the day. He'd promised Carmen and Jada that they could come and spend the night at his house again. She realized they were his children, but sometimes Sheila wished either she could take precedence over them, or that they could do things together with the girls.

Ace was too protective over his time with the girls. When they got married, that was going to have to change, Sheila thought. He couldn't always steal away for outings with them and leave her alone to count down the minutes until they returned. That was not the way to keep a happy home.

"It's time for me to go," Sheila told Cassandra. "Thank you for treating today. I owe you one," she said, hoping Cassandra wouldn't ask her to return the favor anytime soon.

Cassandra peeled the paper off of one of the small muffins and nibbled the top layer. She was scheduled to have a full day at the spa and Sheila knew she'd take advantage of every amenity and perk the staff offered.

"What are you and Ace doing today?" Cassandra asked. "Reading Bible verses together so you can keep your hands off of each other?"

"If you were standing in a doorway right now, I'd close the door in your face," Sheila said.

"No you wouldn't. You love me way too much for that. I've always been your girl through thick and thin. Literally."

That had become their motto when they entered the ninth grade. "Thick and thin," they'd say, then pound their fists together like they were the African-American version of the Wonder Twins and needed to activate their powers. And the power to change what? They were still living the same paycheck-to-paycheck lifestyle. The only things that had changed were their geographic location and the prices of their toys.

A diamond engagement ring wasn't a toy by any means, but Sheila was still going to get one. That would shut Cassandra up.

Chapter 20

Ace threw up a three-pointer. It swished through the basket without hitting the rim and barely seemed to touch the net.

Kenny rebounded the ball and threw it back to Ace, who'd moved to another position outside the three-point arc. He released another shot that coasted in the air just as smooth as the last.

"I see you're getting your game back," Kenny said. He was waiting for a miss so he could get a chance at the ball, but Ace hadn't missed yet in eleven shots.

"Getting my game back?" Ace said. "I never lost it." He covered his eyes with one hand and shot the ball with the other. It clanked against the rim.

"See what happens when you get cocky?" Kenny said, running after the loose ball. He took a few layup shots before stepping to the free throw line. "So let's get to the real reason of why you got me out of bed at eight o'clock on a Saturday morning to come and shoot hoops."

Ace had called Kenny to meet him at his church's gymnasium. Pastor Bailey had given him the key and the permission over two years ago to use the gym anytime he wanted. Ace used to have more time to work out and shoot hoops, but Sheila had replaced the moments he spent with his barbells and his Spalding.

He'd taken Sheila to the gym once when they first started dating, but her impatience affected his game. Not too long after that, she'd turned the tables on him as he became the spectator while she seemed to try on every piece of clothing in the mall. He'd never asked her to wait on the bleachers again, and she didn't torture him by making him sit outside fitting rooms. It was an understanding they had.

Much like the understanding that he and Kenny had that neither one of them would rush the other when he had something to discuss. For that reason, Kenny didn't pressure Ace to give an answer until he was ready. Ace didn't start to reveal his heart until one of Kenny's shots fell short and Ace had the ball back in his hands.

Ace gripped it. Rubbed the bumpy surface. He slammed the ball against the hardwood and it catapulted back into his hands.

"There's no use kidding myself," he finally said, lobbing the ball into the air. He let it fall to the ground and bounce a few times on its own before he stopped it. "I'm in love with Lynette," he said, sinking a shot from the foul line.

Kenny retrieved the ball and passed it back.

"I saw her out last week with another man and it hurt me," Ace said. He swallowed the lump rising in his throat. "Hurt me to my heart, Pope. I haven't felt like that since the day I opened the divorce decree."

"Are you sure she was kicking it like that with him? Maybe it was business."

"Doesn't matter. The fact that I saw Lynette with somebody else and it hurt me means I still love her. It made me think about what she may have felt the times she saw me with Sheila in the beginning."

"Has Lynette ever said anything that made it seem like she was upset?" Kenny asked.

"Not a word. It's been two years for me and Sheila so Lynette could probably care less about me. Or about us." Ace dribbled the ball back and forth between his legs.

"So what are you gonna do?"

Ace shrugged. He picked up the basketball, twirled it, then balanced it on his index finger. It whirled around in a blur. That's how his world was feeling right now—in a blur.

"Man, you don't know how bad I feel right now," he said. "Sooner or later I'm gonna have to end my relationship with Sheila."

"Better sooner than later," Kenny said.

"Some women don't take things like that so well," Ace said, letting the ball drop to the hardwood. "I've told you the story about Monique Jacobs. Ain't no doubt Sheila will probably go through the ringer. And that's not because I think I'm all that. I just know she has her insecurities. Heck, we all do."

"You and Sheila weren't meant to last," Kenny said matter-of-factly.

"Now you say something." Ace jogged over to get the ball, which had rolled under the bleacher. He tried for a layup, but missed.

"I said it in so many words plenty of times. You heard what you wanted to hear," Kenny said, defending himself. "You're a grown man that has to make and live by his own decisions."

Ace threw the ball to Kenny. His friend's spiritual eyes saw much more than his natural eyes.

"What did you see?" Ace asked. "I'm all eyes and all ears right now. Dead serious."

"You got wrapped up in a woman you weren't equally yoked with. She looks good, she's young, and she'll go to church with you when you ask. But that's about it." Now Kenny was the one sinking the shots. "She's there when you want her to be and she doggone near worships the ground you walk on. But . . ." Kenny paused. "Do you know how I can tell you didn't plan on making her your wife?"

"I'm listening."

"It may have been a subconscious thing, but you've never let her too far into your world."

"My world is work and the girls."

"Because that's what you ended up making it. It's been what? Two years you've been with Sheila and I can count on two hands how many times I've seen her and me and you live in the same zip code."

Kenny had a point. Subconsciously doing something didn't make it any less true. The first time he'd introduced Sheila to Kenny and April there seemed to be more silence than conversation during dinner. The Popes—especially the boys—were used to Ace's former life . . . and former wife. When the children started to ask too many invading questions, April had shooed both of them upstairs to their rooms.

Ace never expected Sheila to replace the relationship that April had cultivated with Lynette, but not even a slight connection clicked between April and Sheila. It hadn't extended beyond being cordial. And since Lynette and Ace's divorce, April and Lynette didn't converse as much as they used to. Their husbands had been the common link between the two. After it was broken, it was awkward to try and piece back together.

Ace sat down on the bleachers and stretched out his legs. He leaned forward, trying to touch his nose to his knees. "Do you think it's possible to love two people?"

"I guess anything is possible. And I hate to say it this way, but in a situation like this somebody is always going to be the front-runner."

Ace knew without a doubt that Lynette was clocking in at first place.

Kenny unlaced his basketball shoes and changed into a pair of run-down tennis shoes that had seen better days. "You've got some decisions to make, man. And more than that, you've got some conversations you need to have. Even if things aren't rectified with Lynette, you still owe it to Sheila to be honest, especially since you know in your heart that you don't plan to take the next step with her."

"I hate to hurt a woman like that," Ace said. "I wish I could stay away from seeing and talking to both of them until I can get my mind cleared." Ace picked up his towel and wrapped it around his neck. "That's easier to do with Lynette than with Sheila. I'm supposed to pick Sheila up at lunchtime so we can spend the day together until it's time for me to pick up the girls."

Kenny picked up the windbreaker he'd worn into the gym. It had the Greek letters of his fraternity embroidered across the chest. The brotherhood he shared with Ace went far beyond the fraternal bond—it extended to their hearts.

"If this is God leading you back to Lynette—and I think He is—then He'll give you the right words to say to Sheila," Kenny said. "Because Sheila needs to be loving God as much as she's loving you. You can be a lot of things to her, but you can't be her God."

Chapter 21

Ace had been lured. He and Sheila had started out looking at birthstone pendants for her mother's sixtieth birthday. Now they were at the display case for diamond engagement rings and wedding bands.

"Now this is one of my favorites." The saleswoman pulled the ring from the case and balanced it between two fingers. Her teeth looked like she'd just left a laser-bleaching session. They shone as bright as the diamond. But still not as brilliant as Sheila's face.

"Oooohhhh, that is nice," Sheila said.

Ace could see her fight the urge to slide it on her finger. He inched his way to the Movado and Bulova watches before the women could reel him in with the bait.

After ten minutes and no interest from Ace, Sheila seemed to have gotten the point. Her voice and face had lost all signs of enthusiasm.

"I'm ready," she said, holding a small white bag with her mother's gift.

"All right." Ace looked at his watch. "You'll have to ride with me to get the girls. I told Lynette I'd pick them up by six."

"Oh . . . okay."

Sheila was clearly surprised, Ace noticed. He'd never taken Sheila to Lynette's house. That was a line he wasn't ready to cross. The other he tipped across once in a blue moon—the one of including Sheila in his plans with Carmen and Jada. Yet no matter how he explained his reasoning, Sheila always made a push for more time with the girls.

Today was no exception.

"So what are we doing tonight?" Sheila asked as they pulled up to the stop sign at the cross street near Lynette's house.

We? Here we go again, Ace thought. "After I drop you back home, me and the girls are going to the movies. Have some father-daughter bonding time."

"That's been your excuse for two years. I'm over it." Sheila pouted. "Tell me the real reason why you never want me around them."

Ace wheeled into Lynette's subdivision. He honked the horn at Phil, one of his former neighbors. No matter the weather, Phil was always outside doing something to beautify his yard or the exterior of his house. Years ago, Phil had been the one to landscape the front of their home so that Lynette would have more than a bouquet of flowers as a Mother's Day gift—she'd had an entire yard full.

"Why, Ace?" Sheila pushed.

"We've had a good day," Ace said to her. "Don't ruin it."

He flipped open his cell phone and called inside. It was better if he didn't see Lynette today. Even though they'd talked, he hadn't had to see her. Not seeing her made it easier for him to disregard his feelings until he was able to make a move.

"Hey. I'm outside," he said when Lynette answered. "Can you send the girls out?"

"Sure," Lynette said. "You don't want to come inside?"

Ace felt Sheila watching his every move. It was like she was looking for a reason—a smile on his face, a gleam in his eye, anything—to start an argument.

"Maybe next time," he lied. He didn't know if he could take it.

"Okay, then. I'll see you when you get back. Take care of my babies."

Was that a hint of disappointment in her voice? "Always," Ace said. And Lynette hung up.

Carmen and Jada rushed out of the front door. Four days' worth of clothes, magazines, and techno gadgets rolled behind them in their monogrammed suitcases. And from the look on their faces, they were visibly thrown off from seeing Sheila sitting in the front seat.

Ace got out of the car, loaded their bags in his compact trunk, and waited for them to squeeze into the backseat. Then he did what he said he wouldn't do—he looked toward the house. He knew he shouldn't have. Ace knew Lynette would be standing there, in the window or the doorway, until they pulled off. But surprisingly she'd walked out on the porch.

He didn't even acknowledge her when she waved, but he noticed how the glow still hovered over her, beckoning his heart. She looked like she was dressed for an evening out, and he wouldn't be surprised if it was with old boy from the restaurant. Ace climbed into the car and closed the door to his thoughts of them being together.

"So, ladies," Sheila said, turning around to look at the girls. "I think your dad should treat you to a little spa treatment. All I have to do is make a call to one of my hookups and you can have the royal treatment this evening. How about it?"

Jada answered quickly. "Not my thing. By the time I get through with basketball practice it'll be chipped off anyway."

Ace glanced in his rearview mirror at Carmen. He knew it

135

wasn't an offer his fashion-minded and high-maintenance daughter could refuse.

"I *could* use a paraffin treatment about now," Carmen said. "But I thought we were going to the movies tonight."

"We are," Ace said. He didn't even know what a paraffin treatment was, but he didn't see a reason why a sixteen-year-old should get one anyway. "Maybe we can do something tomorrow. We'll see."

Although Sheila didn't say a word, she made sure he knew she wasn't happy about it. Not a word passed between them until Ace walked Sheila to the front door of her apartment.

"You can't keep me out of their lives forever," Sheila said, turning her key in the lock. "If we're going to be in a relationship, sooner or later, they'll have to know me as more than 'their daddy's girlfriend.'"

"They have a mother, Sheila."

"You don't have to tell me that. I'm not trying to take Lynette's place. I couldn't if I tried. It's obvious." She looked him straight in the eyes and didn't blink.

It was the second piece of bait Sheila had thrown out tonight. Ace wasn't going to take this one either.

"Give the girls time," he said in a voice that wouldn't flare up Sheila's anger. Or his.

Sheila opened the door and stepped inside. She turned to face him, her body blocking the entrance. "I'm starting to think *they're* not the ones who need the time," she said, crossing her arms to block off any attempt for affection.

Ace kissed her forehead anyway, then headed for the elevator. He didn't have time for petty arguments. He wasn't in the mood. "I'll call you before I go to bed," he said without turning around.

"Don't bother. I'm going to relish my time. Alone," Sheila said.

Then came the slam. When Ace looked back, he didn't see the vision he'd seen when he looked at Lynette.

He saw a closed door.

Chapter 22

There's a first time for everything. Lynette and Ace's first kiss on the steps of her dorm. Buying their first home together. The birth of their first child. Ace bringing Sheila to their house—she meant, *her* house—today. Some firsts she could do without.

Lynette had intended to walk outside to speak to Ace since he wasn't up for coming in. She needed to see him. To see if the feelings were still there.

She hadn't had to step far outside to see Sheila conveniently tucked in the front seat of Ace's car. It was the spot usually claimed by whichever girl made it to the car door first.

Lynette touched up her lipstick, then ran a comb through her hair. *I could use a rinse to get rid of some of these stray greys,* she thought, studying herself in the master bathroom mirror. It would give her hair and her skin a boost. Since she was into trying new things, why not? Why stop with Frank as the only new thing in her life?

Lynette turned out the light and went to the den to wait for Frank. Tonight held yet another first. It was the first time she'd let Frank pick her up from her home for a date. A date. She was fine with saying that word now.

Lynette's ego had kicked in when Ace honked the horn for the girls to come outside. After seeing Sheila in the car, she'd purposefully walked out on the porch so that Ace—and Sheila—could see that she was dressed to *live*. She didn't like to say dressed to kill, because any man in their right mind would want to stay alive when she was looking as good as she was right now. Tonight, Ace would know that she wasn't wrapped up in oversized sweats and cuddled up in the arms of her love seat. She had plans.

It was obvious that Frank was interested in her and Lynette was enjoying the time she spent seeing and talking to him. With both of their busy schedules, it was hard to coordinate going out, but this weekend both of them were without their children. Frank had shown himself to be a gentleman and well rounded.

The doorbell chimed. And prompt, Lynette added to her list as she opened the door.

There was an extra squeeze in Frank's hug tonight. Before Lynette knew it, she'd given him a quick peck on his cheek.

"You look nice," Frank said, trying as discreetly as he could to soak her in. He wasn't as discreet as he thought he was.

"Thanks," Lynette said. She picked up her purse and wrap. "I'm ready if you are."

Frank's cell phone rang and it irritated Lynette that he actually answered it. She couldn't make out the shrill ranting that was coming from the other end, but it was evident that the person wasn't happy.

"I can't deal with that right now," Frank said, turning his back as if that would prevent Lynette from hearing his words. "You're his mother. If you use your mind I'm sure you can figure it out. You know . . . that little thing inside of your head."

The screaming continued, and it seemed to be getting louder. Lynette was getting a headache just thinking about the drama.

"No, I'm not coming. I'm busy," Frank said.

Lynette went into the kitchen and left Frank standing in the foyer. She didn't want to be drawn into anyone else's issues. She couldn't imagine what she would do if her relationship with Ace was that stressful.

No. No thought of Ace—in any way—was going to be allowed tonight. She stood at the breakfast bar and flipped through the latest issue of *Gospel Today* magazine until she heard Frank's conversation end.

Lynette walked back into the foyer. "Ready?"

Frank had been the picture of cool when he'd first walked into the door, but the conversation with his son's mother had frazzled his demeanor.

"Eric is sick," he said. "He only has a cold but his mother blows everything out of proportion. She's acting like the boy's got pneumonia."

"Things that are small to us can make little ones pretty irritable," Lynette reasoned.

"His mother is the one that's irritable."

It was almost like he growled the words and Lynette knew immediately that his attitude wasn't what she wanted to be around tonight. If she had to choose between Frank's arms and the arms of her love seat, the La-Z-Boy would win.

"You know what? Maybe you should go and get your son," Lynette suggested. "We can postpone. It's no problem."

Lynette thought he took the offer too quickly.

"Are you sure?"

"Positive." Lynette secretly wished she hadn't given away her entire collection of romance novels. If she wanted romance tonight, she was going to have to find it in the pages of the Song of Solomon. She needed to spend some time with God tonight anyway. The day had gotten away since her early start this morning, and she'd jumped into full gear without even praying. If she'd done that first, she probably would've canceled their date and saved Frank the gas.

Frank rested his hand on the doorknob before he walked out. "I'll make it up to you. You know how it is."

"I definitely do," Lynette said, dropping the wrap from her shoulders. "I hope Eric feels better soon."

"Me, too," Frank said, backing out onto the porch landing.

It was the second time Lynette had watched a man drive away from her house this evening. She decided to stay dressed up while she ate dinner alone. It wasn't the dinner at Rays on the River that she'd expected to have tonight, but a frozen meal could be what you made it.

She scooped the Salisbury steak, manufactured mashed potatoes, and square fudge brownie onto a dish sitting on top of a gold leaf charger plate. And instead of drinking the water from the twelve-ounce bottle like she usually did, Lynette poured it into a champagne glass from the curio. It was one of the crystal glasses she and Ace used on their wedding day. They'd used them once a year on their anniversary, but she hadn't touched them since their divorce. Now, she didn't see any reason why they should stay closed up behind glass. After all, someone had paid for them with hopes that they would bring lasting memories.

And they would. Life was about building new memories, and tonight she'd look back and recall how she chose to spend time with her first love. God.

Lynette ate her dinner, relishing the silence. It was amazing how God's still, small voice could be heard so much clearer without the daily distractions and unnecessary household noises.

She felt revived, and she didn't have to fly across the world to Italy to make it happen.

"But if You're taking requests, Lord, I still won't mind that trip," she said, tucking a list of things and people that she wanted to pray for into her Bible. "Lei è il mio primo amore," Lynette said, surprising herself that her Italian audio-learning CDs were enhancing her foreign language skills so easily. "You are my first love."

Chapter 23

It was the perfect Saturday to take Carmen and Jada to the spa. Ace rarely got up early on the days he didn't have to work, so Sheila knew it was safe to spring her surprise at ten o'clock.

She'd packed her cooler in the car specifically to carry the strawberry-banana smoothies from Henry's Sandwich Shop down off of Auburn Avenue. A peace offering of Ace's favorite breakfast enchilada was bagged up tightly with a secure place on her front passenger seat.

Sheila knew she'd overreacted last night. She'd had to deal with her mistake all night. She hardly slept, yet she didn't call Ace. Sheila knew him; the time wasn't right. He'd needed at least until this morning to calm down, and she'd needed the time to deal with her insecurities.

Ever since Ace had called her by Lynette's name, something had shifted in their relationship. Twice she'd asked him, "What's wrong between us now?" Both times he'd said, "Nothing."

Sheila's cell phone rang. She looked at it and decided to ignore the call from her mother. She wasn't in the mood to hear about any of Devin's drama. Or maybe today would be the day she whined about how she was the only one of her friends without grandbabies. And from the looks of things, it may be longer before her mama was a member of the Grandmother's Club.

Ace avoided the engagement rings like marriage was a curse. If that was the case, then maybe Lynette wasn't her problem after all. Who in their right mind would want to go through torture with their ex-spouse for a second time?

As she stepped out of her car and into Ace's driveway, Sheila hooked her purse and the cooler strap over her shoulder. The bottom of the brown bag of breakfast enchiladas was still warm. Before ringing the doorbell, she listened for a moment to see if she could hear any voices inside. She rang the doorbell after she heard outbursts of laughter. Evidently everybody was in a good mood.

Ace opened the front door still dressed in plaid pajama pants and a Morehouse alumni T-shirt. Sleep was still in his eyes and his voice was groggy. Sheila wanted to believe that exhaustion was also the reason for the annoyance on his face, but she had the feeling his face still would've looked like that if he was bright-eyed and bushy-tailed.

"What are you doing here, Sheila? Why are you doing this?" Ace whispered.

Sheila didn't know what to say. Her plan seemed silly now. At six o'clock this morning, it was a good idea. Evidently she'd cried away some of her common sense last night.

"I don't know," she finally managed to say. "It seemed like a good idea at the time. But now . . ." Her words left her.

Over Ace's shoulder, Sheila saw Carmen skitter past, headed toward the kitchen. Then the aroma hit her nose—bacon. Turkey bacon, for Ace of course. And the sweetness of buttermilk biscuits.

"Daddy," one of the girls yelled. "Come do the eggs before the bacon gets too cold."

Jada appeared at Ace's side. "Hi, Ms. Sheila. You came to eat breakfast with us?"

Ace moved back and opened the door wider so Sheila could come in. But she didn't feel welcome.

"I'll make some more bacon," Jada said, seemingly unaware of the uneasiness in the room.

Sheila forced a tight smile so her lips wouldn't quiver. "Oh no, I'm not staying," she said, holding out the cooler pack and brown bag. "Just dropping off these smoothies and some breakfast enchiladas."

"Oooh, thanks," Jada said, running her hand across the warmth of the bag holding her unexpected breakfast treat. "Now Daddy can chill out and not have to cook our eggs. 'Cause you know he makes the bomb eggs. Ms. Sheila, you're the best."

Tell that to your father, Sheila wanted to say. She looked at Ace. His look toward her had softened, but it still made her feel less than five inches high. "No problem, sweetie," Sheila said to Jada. "You guys have a good time with your dad, okay?"

"We always do. See you later, Ms. Sheila. Maybe we'll spend some time with you another day."

Ace had told Sheila that although she was the youngest, Jada had such a mature way about her. Though unintended, Jada's remarks made Sheila feel like she'd tried to barge her way into their lives. Make a family. But she didn't want to be the girls' mother. She simply wanted to be their father's wife.

Jada left Ace and Sheila alone at the door. Ace pulled Sheila's arm so she'd step inside.

"I just need you to understand," Ace said.

Sheila conceded. "I do now." She'd make herself let her relationship with the girls grow slowly. But that wouldn't be the case with Ace. Soon Sheila would make him believe that it was time for their relationship to go to the next level.

Before walking back to the car, Sheila gave Ace the kind of kiss that would keep her on his mind all day. *We'll be together. And I'll do whatever it takes.*

Chapter 24

When the girls were at home, Lynette would pay for peace and quiet. No petty bickering. No muffled music behind closed doors. No rummaging through the refrigerator twenty times in one hour. Just calm. Like it was last night.

Now, other than the occasional hum of the ice maker turning on, it was completely silent.

And Lynette couldn't stand it. She'd slept late, read her Bible, and prayed longer than she'd done in a long time.

Silence welcomed unwanted thoughts to her mind. Thoughts that made her wonder if Sheila was acting as surrogate mother to her children right about now. It was a rare occasion for Ace to have the girls and Sheila together. But rare didn't mean never.

Lynette showered and dressed. There was no need for her imagination to run wild. Her girls would give her the full report about everything when they returned home. Until then, she'd see if

Frank wanted to catch a matinee since their plans had been rerouted last night.

"Hello?" Irritation dripped from Frank's voice when he answered the phone. His attitude hadn't changed overnight.

Lynette almost hung up. She hadn't expected Frank to carry his tensions into another day. "I caught you at a bad time?" she asked.

"Who is this?"

"Who do you want it to be?" Lynette said, returning his snappiness. She caught herself. She'd been in the posture of prayer that morning and she'd already let another person's attitude cause her to react instead of respond. She needed to go back and read in her devotion about the bumblebee. Frank had definitely been a *"bzzz"* the past couple of days.

Frank's tone changed. "Lynette? I'm sorry. There's a lot going on with Eric, and his mama is doing her best to make my life miserable. Can I call you back?"

"We'll catch up on Monday," Lynette said. As far as she was concerned, he'd ruined his chance for the day. "I'm headed out of town for a few days."

"Everything okay?"

"Early birthday celebration," Lynette decided on a whim. She had no idea where. Before a few seconds ago, she didn't even know she was going anywhere. *Estrogen can sure cause a woman to make spontaneous decisions,* she thought.

"Please . . . go ahead and take care of your business," she told him. *Also known as your baby's mama.*

"Happy early birthday, Lynette."

"Thanks," she said, then hung up and called her mother. "You think Daddy can stand to be alone for a couple of days?"

Maybe the silence hadn't been that bad, Lynette decided. Claudette's excited chatter hadn't stopped the entire ride to the

Château Élan resort. Lynette knew the update on everybody's children and grandchildren. But once Claudette dove into her report on the recent deaths and obituaries she'd saved in her top dresser drawer, Lynette had to make it stop.

"Mama, please. We're going to celebrate another year of *life*. Can we keep our conversations about people in the land of the living? I'm not planning on crossing the chilly Jordan anytime soon."

Claudette flipped up the sun visor mirror. She'd been surveying her overplucked eyebrows. "I guess you're right. There are better things to talk about," she said, fixing her hair pins to hold her hair behind her ears. "Like you. You need to talk about anything?"

Me? Falling in love with Ace again would be a good start.

Lynette veered off Interstate 85 and onto exit #126 for Château Élan. Seeing the French country design of the winery and resort made her life feel less complicated already. She tossed the idea around about taking a sabbatical to France instead of Italy.

But right now, a Swedish massage was the first thing on her list. She needed to knead away the stress and drama. Forget she had responsibilities. Forget about Frank and his baby-mama drama. And as much as she could, Ace too.

Lynette checked in and was led to the room where she and her mother would be staying for two days and one night. The bay window looked out onto a lake that was surrounded by a canopy of trees. The only things missing were a path of red roses leading to the Jacuzzi tub, and a chilled bowl of chocolate-covered strawberries. And a man. But *she* had her mama there. Self-pity overshadowed Lynette's excitement and she'd only been in the room for fifteen minutes.

"It's amazing how you can be so close, yet so far from home," Claudette said. She'd already changed out of her clothes and into a white plush terry cloth robe from the closet. "Are you sure we have to leave tomorrow? We should check out on Monday instead. God doesn't expect me to have perfect attendance at church. I'll already be missing church anyway and I don't have a thing to rush home for. Your daddy will survive."

"What?" Lynette could've passed out across the king-sized bed. "You used to make it seem like I'd go to hell if I wasn't at church every time the doors opened. Why do you think I slept in most Sundays when I went away to college?"

"The past is the past. No need to look behind you." Claudette pulled back the comforter on the king-sized bed and inspected the high-thread-count sheets.

In a place like this Lynette doubted her mother would find the crumbs or miniscule stains she was looking for, but that didn't stop Claudette from doing an examination of the linens and an even closer scrutiny of the bathtub.

"My goodness, it's nice in here," her mother said.

Lynette was glad she'd brought her mother along after all. Claudette was the kind of person who found joy in the simplest things.

"Me and your daddy need to come back here. Maybe we'll come for our anniversary."

"You should," Lynette agreed. "My treat."

"Oh, we'll definitely come. Especially if you're gonna bless us with it."

Lynette would give her parents the world if she could—and if they'd let her. The only thing the Moreheads seemed to be worried about was making sure Lynette and the girls were happy. But above all else, they lived to honor God first, then each other.

It would seem with such a godly example of marriage before her all of those years, marriage would've been the last thing Lynette would've failed at. But it was the first.

Success followed her through education and to her career, but it had failed in its job to maintain the happily ever after.

The thoughts were coming again. Ace. Their marriage. Her desire for him. Standing on the balcony of the fourth floor spa suite with her mother, Lynette made a tough—and scary—decision. Actually, she didn't make the decision of her own accord. In a soft urging last night, it was one of the things she felt God had planted in her heart. She'd have to tell Ace that she thought they deserved a second chance. And she had to do it soon.

Chapter 25

Château Élan had been everything Lynette had expected and more. But it was Tuesday now and she was back to thinking that there was a first time for everything. However she didn't like the way this "first" was playing with her mind.

Instead of the alarm clock, she was wakened by a hesitant, then persistent, knock on her bedroom door. Before she could give them permission, Carmen and Jada entered with their version of a spectacular breakfast on a silver serving tray. It was an assortment of things that didn't require that they turn on an electrical appliance. Blueberry muffins. Fruit. Strawberry-banana yogurt. A granola bar. Orange juice.

By midmorning, Lynette had been stuffed a second time with scones and an edible fruit arrangement from the staff, and poor Frank had attempted to apologize for his behavior by sending a vase full of sunflowers and a balloon bouquet. It put a temporary smile on her face.

But that would all change if she received a birthday call from Ace. Even after the divorce, he'd never failed to be the first one to wish her another blessed year, even if it meant calling at midnight. The morning was halfway over and his customary first call had turned into the first time he *hadn't* called. Like Lynette had said days ago when he'd brought Sheila to the house . . . some firsts she could do without.

Lynette did so much better talking to Ace over the phone than she did seeing him in person. In person, she was a coward. She'd proven that last night when he dropped the girls off after picking them up from school. Lynette was supposed to be revealing her heart, but she'd stammered through even their routine. *Drop the kids off. Tell them to behave. See you next time. Let me know if you need anything.*

Lynette made up some nonsense about being tired and it seemed as if Ace was doing all he could not to make eye contact with her. She hated that their relationship was becoming a series of awkward exchanges. Was this how it was going to be if Ace married Sheila?

Lynette pulled the hygiene mask from her mouth and peeled off her latex gloves.

"We're all done sweetheart," she said to the glassy-eyed girl reclining in the dentist chair. It hadn't taken long for Lynette to fill the two small cavities, but she saw the shoulders and neck of her patient relax as she sat upright.

"See, that wasn't so bad, was it? I told you I'd be very careful, didn't I little Miss Joelle."

The numbed side of the girl's face barely let the words get out. "It was okay," she said, gently patting the side of her jaw.

"You promise to brush and floss at least twice a day?"

Joelle nodded her head, her face looking as if she'd regretted every piece of candy and sweets she'd ever touched.

That promise might last until the Novocain wears off, Lynette thought. A low beep chirped into Lynette's interoffice earpiece before Kym's voice came through.

"Excuse me, Dr. Bowers. I have Dr. Walton from the girls' school on the line. She's holding on three."

"Tell her I'll be there shortly," Lynette said, leaving her patient in the capable hands of one of the hygienists and hurrying to her office. A call from the assistant principal during the middle of the day couldn't come with good news.

Lynette closed her office door behind her and prayed this was about something that wouldn't bring her birthday to ruin.

Once they got past the greetings, Dr. Walton didn't waste any time.

"I'm sure you know I don't call my parents at their jobs unless it's pretty serious."

"Yes." *Just get to it.*

"Ms. Bowers, one of our teachers found Carmen skipping class. She was sitting out in the back student parking lot in the car of a young man who doesn't attend our school."

Lynette was stunned into silence. The thoughts of what could've been happening in that back parking lot ticked through Lynette's head. *I'm gonna kill her. Well, maybe not kill. But I'm gonna hurt her real bad.*

Dr. Walton continued. "This is very out of character for Carmen."

Lynette found her voice. "I'm just as surprised as you are. Surprised, disappointed, and angry. Very angry," she admitted.

"I'm sure it won't make you feel any better to hear that she needs to be picked up from school as soon as possible."

Lynette sighed. *Why, God?*

Dr. Walton continued. "Since this is her first infraction, I'm

153

only suspending her for half a day. But she'll have in-school suspension for the next two days."

"I understand. Where is she now?" Lynette asked. *Probably somewhere crying her eyes out and praying that God would spare her life.*

"Sitting outside of my office."

"And the boy she was with? Jail?" Lynette chuckled. She had to laugh to keep from crying. Where had she failed?

"I feel you," Dr. Walton said, connecting with Lynette for a moment as one mother to another. "He was escorted off of school property."

"Thanks for the call, Dr. Walton. I'll be there shortly."

Lynette looked at her desk clock. *Eleven-fifteen.* The clock was encased in a mahogany case. One side was the clock, and the other was a monogrammed frame displaying a picture of her girls. Her innocent girls.

Lynette unlocked her purse out of the bottom drawer, then found her colleague. Tonia was dealing with a pint-sized tot who all but welded his mouth shut so Tonia couldn't perform an exam. There was no telling how long she'd been trying to pry it open, but there was no sign of impatience on her face. The child's mother—on the other hand—looked exasperated. Her mouth clenched tightly too while she tried to keep the child's head from moving.

"I hate to disrupt you, Dr. Singletary. But can I see you for a minute?" Lynette asked.

"Sure. Taking a break might do us all some good," Tonia said, leaving her patient time to rest for his second round.

Lynette lowered her voice in the hallway. "I need to go to Carmen's school and handle . . . a situation. Can you take over my patient load? I only have three more before lunch."

"Of course," Tonia said, eyebrows raised. "I can tell by the way you said that, this *situation* just might have muscles and an Adam's apple."

"You talk like a woman with experience dealing with teenage girls."

"No, I talk like a woman who gave my mama drama. It's just hormones; it'll be all right. She'll get over it soon. Look at me—I turned out fine."

Lynette smirked.

"Don't say a word," Tonia said. "Go deal with your fast behind child."

"Oh, I'm going to deal with her all right," Lynette said.

Lynette walked outside to an unexpected spring shower and had to run to her car. As soon as she got to the driver's side, her foot landed in a puddle that formed courtesy of a large hole in the asphalt. Water soaked her shoe and the hem of her pants. "Happy Birthday to me," she grumbled.

Chapter 26

As much as Sheila hated coming to her job, the reality of possibly losing it made her more than nervous. The credit card companies could care less about unemployment. They wanted their money—even if it was only the minimum payment—no matter what.

She was already on a rotation schedule when it came to paying those pesky collectors. They always seemed understanding when they first got her on the phone, but their snaky heads raised and they could spit some fiery venom as soon as Sheila said that she didn't have any money to send them that month. That was not the way she wanted to live the rest of her life.

"Right now we're not sure which positions will be cut. That's at least a month away. But I felt we owed it to you to let you know what was coming down the pipeline. Most of us have families to take care of. Or at the very least, bills." Richard chuckled nervously, but there was no way to end the tension from his announcement.

Sheila shifted in her seat. She still didn't know how she was going to address her debt with Ace when it was time. Hopefully by the time he proposed, she could knock down the debt enough so that her charging habit wasn't a complete embarrassment.

Sheila was so busy calculating the bills in her head that she didn't realize she'd zoned out of the meeting until it was over and everyone started to leave their seats. A few of her associates filed out like they'd been sentenced to walk the plank. At least three of the top executives who were sure their positions were safe from the reduction were chatting like the announcement didn't affect anyone in the room.

Clive was one of them. Clive timed his exit with Sheila's and followed her into her office. Sheila couldn't see him, but she could feel his presence.

Clive was one of the decision makers. She needed to stay on his good side. That way, she could leave J. Morrow on her own terms. When Ace brought his loving wife home.

"Would you like to go out for lunch?" Clive asked.

"Why not? I could use something to eat right about now."

The look on his face showed that he wasn't expecting her to accept. He loosened his tie and slid it over his head. "Meet you downstairs in ten minutes," he said before she could change her mind. "I'll get my car and pull it around front. I think it's still drizzling out."

"That's fine. It gives me time to send out a few follow-up e-mails."

Sheila directed her attention to her computer, purposefully ignoring Clive. He was standing at the door soaking her in like part of his mission was unfolding with success. Sheila's face grew warm as a herd of her colleagues walked by. She wondered if they noticed how Clive was eyeing her. If Cassandra had her chance with Clive, *she'd* be the one to make *him* blush. But that would be a meeting that would never happen. Sheila would see to it. Cassandra was aggressive and bold, but probably not as crazy as Mrs. Clive. She'd heard the watercooler talk.

"You can go away now, Clive," Sheila said, trying to concentrate on the twelve new e-mails that had popped up in her in-box since the time she'd been in that dreadful meeting. She didn't actually feel like going to lunch, but it was all about the survival of the fittest. If she had to sacrifice an hour at lunch to keep her job during the first round of cuts—to keep the creditors at bay—then she'd do it. But Ace would never know. From the moment he'd met Clive at the Christmas party last year, he'd called him a shady character.

Sheila sent as many e-mails as she could during the ten minutes before she walked downstairs to meet Clive. She knew that she'd have to turn into a robot in order to place some of these applicants into corporate positions. J. Morrow didn't care about her. They cared about results. Their goal was to increase their bottom line.

As promised, Sheila saw Clive's Jaguar through the double glass when she stepped off the elevator. She also saw Jamal, whom she knew usually didn't arrive until around three or four o'clock.

"What are you doing here?" Sheila asked.

"Catching a few extra hours," he said. "One of my professors is out of town so he's sending us our assignments via e-mail. I was blessed to get a call that Rod needed some time off, because I needed some more money for my pockets," Jamal said, opening his laptop case. "And I can still get my work done."

"You're so committed," Sheila said. At his age—and even now —she could think of tons of other things she'd rather be doing besides work.

"I try to be. I know most people think I just sit here watching the monitors and escorting people out to their cars, but I enjoy what I do. I know God has me on a temporary assignment here, and when He's ready to move me to my next place of provision, I'll know I'm done."

"That's a good way to look at it," Sheila said. She noticed that

Clive had gotten out of his car and had opened the passenger's door. Jamal noticed, too.

"I know you work with him, but you should keep things strictly business," Jamal said. "He's the kind that if you give him an inch, he'll take a mile."

Or two, Sheila thought.

"It bothers me that he's a married man, but he doesn't respect women," Jamal went on to say. "He looks at them like they're a piece of meat."

Right now I'm not looking for respect, I'm looking to keep my job until I'm the one to turn in my notice, Sheila thought.

"Thanks for looking out for me, Jamal," Sheila said, leaning over the security desk to give him an innocent hug. Jamal was the kind of brother she wished she had in her life. She would trade in Devin for Jamal any day. "You're going to make an astounding husband one day. Any woman would be proud to be your wife."

"That's the best compliment I've gotten all week," he said. He rubbed the tiny hairs that had sprouted on his chin. "Usually the women just talk about how cute I am," he teased.

His chin hairs were so short and fine that he could've shaved them and Sheila would've never noticed. It was like the face of a twelve-year-old had been put on a body almost twice its age. He *definitely* didn't have the physique of a twelve-year-old boy.

"You're too funny," Sheila said, and headed toward the door. "If you were a little older and I didn't have a man, I might have to give your lady friends a run for their money."

"Friend," he yelled after her. "There's only one. And she'll be my one and only forever."

Sheila slid into the Jaguar's front seat and Clive closed the door. How could a guy in college be so sure that he wanted to marry his girlfriend, and Ace—a forty-year-old grown man with an excellent job—not be ready to put a "Mrs." in front of her name. There was something wrong with that picture. Very wrong.

Chapter 27

Lynette talked to herself the entire ride to Legacy Christian. "I have enough on my plate than to have to deal with this foolishness," she said, walking into the school. She scribbled her name across the visitor's sign-in sheet, then immediately turned to see Carmen perched at the end of a bench outside of Dr. Walton's office.

An invisible rod ran down the middle of her back, forcing her to sit as erect as the Junior ROTC cadets that carried the flag at the basketball games. Puffy bags rimmed Carmen's eyes. *How long ago was it that I saw this same pitiful face?* Lynette thought.

Lynette silenced her fury until she signed Carmen out and left Jada a message not to wait for her sister after school. When their feet hit the sidewalk outside, Lynette let loose.

"So you accomplished your mission to humiliate and embarrass yourself . . . and me . . . and Jada twice in one month?"

"That's not what I was trying to—"

"And if you want to act like you're grown, be disobedient, or come in my house crying if you get pregnant, then I can save my money sending you to private school and send you to school with the hoodlums."

"Mama, I'm not—"

"And after we had that talk and you begged me not to tell your father." Lynette could've replayed every sentence from that night. She beat herself up. Maybe she'd been too easy on Carmen because her punishment hadn't been enough to scare her straight.

Lynette paused under the flagpole where the students and teachers sometimes gathered for prayer and reflection. She needed both right about now.

"I'm disappointed in you." Lynette let it sink in. The four simple words brought the tears back to Carmen's eyes. "And you *will* give me that boy's number."

Carmen's eyes bucked wide in horror.

"And I'm calling your daddy, too," Lynette added. "He should get home sometime tonight."

It looked like Lynette would talk to Ace tonight after all.

Chapter 28

Ace always hated seeing either of his girls cry, but it was evident that Carmen had been doing little else than that. Still, he was livid. Caught skipping school with some knucklehead? He'd let her off easy on a lot of things, but this wasn't going to be one of them. Ace had always told Lynette that she didn't have to be the strong arm of discipline, that he could do it. And he had—in his own way. It was something the two of them never agreed on because they had two different philosophies about disciplining children. It was one of the areas they'd skimmed over when they were in marriage counseling. He guessed each of them thought the other would give in when it actually came time that they'd have to use the concepts in the books they'd been assigned to read about raising children. If only he'd known.

Lynette subscribed to the idea that a spanking was the best option when getting their children back in line. But Ace was a talker.

He thought his scolding and the children's tears could work the same kind of result.

"You're not here with them all the time like I am, Ace," Lynette had complained countless times. He was rarely at home then, but it wasn't because he hadn't wanted to be. There were certain sacrifices he was making so that he could provide for his family. It was too late when he realized that providing for them, and being there for them, weren't the same thing.

Carmen descended the steps slowly, as if touching one the wrong way would detonate another blast from one of her parents.

"Hey, Daddy," she said, sulking. Carmen stopped in front of him. He opened his arms to let her know that even though he was upset and disheartened, his fatherly affection was still there for her.

"What's going on, baby girl?" Ace asked, taking her hand and leading her to one of the chairs at the kitchen table. "Tell me what's really going on, because your daddy can't believe your mama had to call me with this nonsense."

Carmen sat down and tucked her legs under her backside. She looked so petite and vulnerable, and definitely not like an incorrigible child that was about to be scolded for choosing to do what she knew better than to do.

Carmen put her head down on the table. Ace didn't say anything; he just watched her shoulders quiver and listened to the sobs she was trying to muffle.

Ace felt like he was under inspection. Lynette was leaning against the breakfast bar watching them. Her arms were folded across her midsection and it looked like this situation had pricked her last nerve. She hadn't said anything to him since the sentence she'd welcomed him inside with. He'd said, "Hi Lynn. Regardless of all of this I hope you had a happy birthday."

And she'd simply answered, "Hey, Ace. I'll go get Carmen."

No, stay here with me, he'd wanted to say at the time. But she'd stomped upstairs and sent down their oldest child. Now Lynette was watching *him*. Seeing how he was going to handle this situation with his daughter.

Ace looked out of the open kitchen window that faced into the backyard. The plantation shutters were folded open, and had it not been a blanket of darkness outside, he would've been able to see the perfect framed view of the spacious backyard. There was a wooden swing set and playhouse that of course the girls were now too old to enjoy. But when he'd had it installed for them, they couldn't get enough of telling him how he was the best dad in the world. They'd even drawn a certificate for him and signed it in their own version of cursive handwriting.

The Royal Empress tree that towered behind the play set had grown three times as fast as the girls, boasting both its explosion of purple blooms that added to spring's first aroma, and the memories of impromptu family picnics under its shade. Those were the good days.

How did they get *here*?

In hindsight, maybe they weren't ready for marriage at such a young age, him at twenty-three and Lynette at twenty-two. It was the summer she graduated from undergrad. Back then, they had no doubt that their love would last forever. The problem came when they grew more passionate about their careers than they did about their marriage. And after their family started to grow, having children brought as much stress as it did pleasure.

Ace looked at Carmen. She'd sat up in the chair and dried her eyes, but she wouldn't look in his direction. Instead, she played with the soggy, crumpled ball of tissue in her hands. He reminisced about how he'd marveled at how tiny her hands looked when they brought her home from the hospital. Now her fingernails were painted with a light polish and her pinky nail had some kind of flower design on it. Times had definitely changed.

Even though he saw them on a regular basis, it still seemed like time was getting away from him. Carmen was sixteen, and in two years, she'd be leaving home and getting a taste of the outside world without her parents' constant scrutiny.

"What can I say?" Ace said. "You're too old for me to give you a spanking and send you up to your room. That's not going to solve a thing. I can even take away your cell phone and all those other gadgets, but that's not necessarily going to make you make the right choices."

Carmen was finally looking at him. She'd lost her chubby cheeks to a more slender face, and he couldn't remember the last time he'd seen her with ponytails.

"That's what part of life is about," Ace continued. "Choices. And the choices you make—whether right or wrong—can change your life in an instant. For better, or for worse."

Ace glanced over at Lynette and saw that she was nodding her head in agreement. It caused him to relax, to know that she was by his side in this.

"So this weekend, you're going to study about choices. I want you to get your Bible and write a report about three people who made bad choices and the consequences they had to deal with. And do the same with three people who made good choices."

"Yes, sir," Carmen whispered.

Lynette was standing behind him now. He could feel her presence, but it caught him off guard when she put her hands, ever so gently, on his shoulders.

Carmen looked up at her parents. "I'm sorry," she said. "It won't happen again. I'll do better."

"Yes you will," Ace said. "We're all going to do better. I'm sure both me and your mother made choices that we wish we could take back. But the good thing about it is that God gives us *more* than second chances. Do you believe that?"

"Yes, sir," Carmen answered.

Lynette sat down at the kitchen table with them. "Me, too," she said.

It was only there for a second, but Ace caught the faith in Lynette's eyes.

Was she hoping that they'd have a second chance, too? He felt the Holy Spirit's presence in the room. Kenny had been right. He was going to have to be honest with both Sheila and Lynette. And the time was drawing near.

Chapter 29

Sheila hated times like these. When she couldn't get in touch with Ace her mind always kicked into overdrive. She scanned the news channels to make sure there was no word of plane crashes on the route he was flying.

When they'd first started dating, her nerves could barely take it. Six months into their relationship, Ace brought her a sterling silver bracelet with a small charm shaped like an airplane. He'd written a Scripture on the box top—Psalm 91:1–2. There were few Scriptures she knew by heart, and that wasn't one of them. But Ace recited it to her like he'd had it committed to memory since his childhood days with his grandmother. Sheila hadn't had the privilege of meeting Grandma Toot yet, or eating one of those sweet potato pies that he raved about.

Sheila looked up the Scripture—highlighted in her Bible—whenever she needed to calm herself. "He who dwells in the secret place of the Most High shall abide under the shadow of the Almighty," she said. "I will say of the Lord, 'He is my refuge and my fortress; my God, in Him I will trust.'" It wasn't working tonight.

If Sheila hadn't tried to muscle her way into spending time with Carmen and Jada, she probably wouldn't be feeling like this. Things had been stacking against her over the past month or so. Being called Lynette. Being ignored at the jewelry store. Her sad attempt at family time.

Sheila flipped the channel away from the news. Crime. The country's economic woes. The unveiling of crooked politicians and CEOs. The news was the last thing she needed to watch at a time like this. She finally landed on a Christian television network where one of Atlanta's preachers was delivering a sermon about faith.

All this time, Sheila thought, she'd been thinking of schemes to keep Ace. But maybe faith was the way.

"You've got to see yourself possessing what you believe God for," the preacher was saying. "Then as an act of faith, you start preparing yourself for it."

The camera scanned the parishioners, some standing, nodding, and waving their hallelujah hands in the air.

Sheila closed her eyes. It wasn't hard to see her and Ace together. She already knew how she could incorporate the furnishings from her apartment into his home. It was already the perfect size. Four bedrooms. Two and a half baths. It would still be a few years before both Carmen and Jada were off to college, so surely they'd want to keep their current rooms, for now. But Ace's office could easily be transformed into a nursery.

Sheila smiled. *Yes. I can see it. J. Morrow can have my job; I don't want it anyway. My only job will be to be Mrs. Scott "Ace" Bowers. I'll have faith. Ace will call me as soon as he can tonight. And Ace will ask me to marry him soon.*

Sheila drifted off to sleep with the image of her life with Ace in her head. It had been a long three days without him, and he was due home at any minute. Pot roast, potatoes, and steamed asparagus were arranged on their wedding china, and on the table decorated with candlelight. Anxious to see his face, Sheila ran to the door as soon as she heard the garage door whining shut. She opened the house door to see Ace. And standing beside him . . . Lynette.

Sheila jerked out of her nightmare and sprang forward in the bed. She reached for her cell phone on the nightstand. Her call to Ace's cell phone went directly into his voice mail. Again.

Sheila threw off the covers and frantically dressed, pulling on a pair of jeans and a button-down shirt over her silk camisole. This wasn't because of any flight disruptions. There was only one place her man could be.

Sheila had stored the general vicinity of Lynette's house in her memory. She'd found the subdivision after backtracking from only two or three wrong turns. From there the house was fairly easy to find, and she'd remembered that it was a two-story, four-sided brick house. But then again, nearly every house in the affluent neighborhood was. She was depending on the streetlights to help her spot the custom-designed mailbox post with the "B" on it.

Lynette had never changed back to her maiden name, for whatever reason. Maybe it was her way of holding on to Ace. Sheila shielded her eyes and face from the upcoming bright headlights. She'd bought the cherry red Lexus to gain attention, but now she wished she had a black car to hide her in the night. After the car passed, she crept slowly down the quiet street, looking at the row of houses on the right. Things were beginning to look familiar.

Sheila didn't recognize Lynette's house by the "B" on the mailbox post. She didn't have to. There was no mistaking Ace's car parked at the top of the driveway. The security light against the house made it easy to see his personalized front tag. Sheila pulled against the curb, one house away, and on the opposite side of the street. From what she could see, the house seemed dark except for a light illuminating from a single window on the second floor.

Was it Lynette's room?

Too many questions pounded Sheila's mind and pushed out a rainfall of tears from her eyes. She'd never felt hurt and anger so powerfully at the same time. She wanted to rev her engine and slam into the front grill of Ace's man toy. But she also wanted to collapse into the passenger's seat and cry her eyes out.

But what now? She'd found the answer she was looking for, but now wished she hadn't.

Sheila waited for at least ten minutes, hoping Ace would come out. But he didn't. And his cell phone was still forwarded into voice mail. She'd already tried calling three times.

When Sheila couldn't take it anymore, she decided to leave. Playing private investigator was Cassandra's thing, not hers. She drove to the end of the street, did a U-turn, and rode by the house slowly. There was still one light on upstairs. And there was no sign of Ace's impending departure.

"God, please send my man out of that house," she said, wiping away a new stream of tears. "You gave them a chance and it didn't work out. Now it's my turn. Don't I deserve it?"

Passing the house, Sheila looked back one last time. The mystery behind the lighted room taunted her. She couldn't so much as see a shadow in the window.

Sheila found the subdivision entrance with no problem. It wasn't until she pulled out onto the main street that she felt an awkward pull to her car. Then a strange knocking. She took her foot off the gas and coasted to the shoulder of the road.

"Please, God. No," she said, panicked. Her car note was too high for this luxury vehicle to conk out without warning. Sheila beat herself up for not keeping up its proper maintenance, but imports weren't too cost efficient. Sadly, the repairs were going to hit her purse for more than she had, and way more than it would've been to keep it maintained in the first place.

The electronic gadgets failed to give her a warning. Or at least she thought. She looked at the panel and realized she'd been too wrapped up in her mission to find Ace to notice the yellow gas-tank warning light.

Chapter 30

Sheila woke up Ace before his alarm could. Since he parked his car in the garage, she didn't know if he was even home. She'd tried to call him again this morning. But once again, she met with his voice mail instead of his voice. He wasn't even answering his home phone. She hadn't slept all night, and it showed in the creases of worry and tear streaks under her eyes.

She considered walking inside with the key that Ace had given her for emergencies, but now of all times she couldn't remember the alarm code. It was too early in the morning to awaken the neighbors and cause a scene with dispatched police officers in the event that he wasn't home. Ace answered the door by the time Sheila rang the doorbell for the third time.

"What? Sheila? What are you doing here?" Ace was wrapped in the Sean John bathrobe she'd bought for him.

Sheila fell into his arms. She temporarily forgot about what she'd seen last night. She was just relieved to see that he hadn't spent the night at Lynette's house. That his arms were around her instead of around his ex-wife.

"When I couldn't get in touch with you I was so worried," she said. Her voice was muffled into his shoulder. "You were supposed to call me when you got in."

"Baby, I'm so sorry. I got caught up in dealing with an issue with Carmen. Why didn't you call my cell?"

"I did," she said. "Over and over. But it just went into voice mail."

Ace closed and locked the front door. He pushed away Sheila's uncombed bang and wiped his hand down the tears drying on her cheeks. "I must've turned my cell phone off by accident. My mind was somewhere else. I didn't mean to scare you like that."

Sheila fingered the airplane charm on the bracelet. "I was a nervous wreck. I just can't imagine losing you." She meant that two ways, and the words started the tears again.

"I've always told you not to worry about me. There are more accidents on the roads than there are in the air. It's closer to heaven up there," Ace said.

He laughed, although Sheila could tell it was a tired one. It had to be about six-thirty in the morning. Just in case Ace had been home, Sheila had picked out a freshly dry cleaned suit and thrown some toiletries into her travel bag so she could get dressed from his house. If she had her choice, she wouldn't even go to work. But lying awake last night, she'd had nothing to do but think. She'd work her relationship with Clive to her advantage, but she still needed to stay on top of her game. She needed to stash as many pay checks as possible until she figured out how to shovel through this financial mess she'd heaped on her life.

Sheila told Ace, "I just need to lie down for a little while." She still hadn't let go of Ace, now holding on to his hand.

She let him lead her into his bedroom. He folded back the

covers on the side of the bed that was still made up. She crawled into the coolness of the sheets, but when Ace crawled into bed and turned his back to her, Sheila scooted over until she could feel his body heat. This was the place where she should be. Here. Her and nobody else.

Ace would never know that her insecurities had pulled her out of bed last night and had her staked out by his ex-wife's house. He pulled his covers up to his neck and she knew he'd be asleep in no time. He was a person that could fall asleep seconds after his head hit the pillow.

Sheila rested her cheek on the back of his shoulder blade until Ace finally turned on his side to face her.

"Are you going to work?" he asked.

"Yes. But I'm not sure how long that'll be happening."

His mouth stretched wide in a yawn. "What do you mean by that?"

"Richard told us yesterday that they have to do some layoffs."

"Never would've expected that."

"You and me both."

Ace pulled her closer to him. "Don't worry. No matter what happens, God has your back."

Sheila closed her eyes. She didn't want the moment to end. The image she'd had in her mind last night was replaying. Like the preacher said, she had to activate her faith to see them together.

"I love you, baby. And I've always got your back, too," Sheila told Ace. "Forever."

Sheila leaned in to kiss him. He was slow to return her kiss at first. But as her passion ignited, Ace's followed. But this time, unlike the other times, neither of them put the fire out.

Chapter 31

Sheila left Ace's place with a smile on her face, but under his countenance was guilt. He knew God would forgive him for what had happened, but the conviction was thick. Even before he closed the door, Ace realized it had happened because his defenses were down. Putting a celibate man in the bed with a desirable woman like Sheila was a recipe for sin. He didn't even want to tell Kenny about this one. First, he tells his best friend that he's in love with his ex-wife. Last night he thinks that it's time to come clean. Then this morning, he sleeps with his current girlfriend, who shouldn't be his girlfriend anymore in the first place.

What kind of man did that make him?

A confused one, Ace thought, closing the door once he could no longer see Sheila's car. His heart was at a crossroads, and it was only fair to everyone involved that he make a decision. He'd just told Carmen that life was about choices. Now Ace had to take his own advice.

Ace changed out of his pajamas and into a T-shirt, shorts, and basketball jersey. He pulled out the set of gymnasium keys from where he kept them on a tack in the closet. The slight pungent smell coming from Ace's laundry basket reminded him that he needed to wash the clothes from his last visit to the gym with Kenny. He went to his laundry room and dropped the basket on the floor.

During the years he'd spent with Grandma Toot, she had picked a Scripture for Ace to memorize and recite each month for children's Sunday. With Grandma Toot, he never forgot a Scripture, because she didn't just make him remember it for one week. She made it applicable to his life.

That's why he'd never forgotten James 1:8: "A double-minded man, unstable in all his ways." At Grandma Toot's he was the man of the house and it was up to him to take care of the manual labor. And when a job was too complicated for him, he had to find someone else with more expertise.

Grandma Toot lived her life according to God's Word. Even today, she still had the large-print Bible open across the coffee table in the formal living room. A plaque hanging near it beside a row of family pictures read, "As for me and my house, we will serve the Lord."

When Grandma Toot learned of Ace and Lynette's divorce, she'd simply said one thing. "What God has joined together, let no man put asunder. You and Nettie made a vow before God. And that's all I'm going to say."

Ace knew what Grandma Toot would say if he told her about his dilemma now. "Go back to Nettie. Y'all have those children together, and unless one of y'all is beating on the other, or doing wrong by having relations with other people, you can work it out."

"Well, Grandma Toot," Ace said. "Things aren't always that simple. Especially not now."

Chapter 32

Lynette had been out of the dating game for a while. She guessed that's why she thought some of the games may have changed, but evidently they hadn't. She'd never had to chase down a man, and she wasn't going to start now. Frank had yet to reschedule their dinner date, and Lynette was still waiting for the private painting lessons he promised every time they talked. And it had been four days since their last conversation.

She threw out the theory that something terrible had happened to him. There was only one word to describe it. Trifling. At forty-five, you'd think Frank would be over that stage by now. Ace had never played relationship games with her, even though he could've tried to pull off clandestine relationships with her other Spelmanites like some of his Morehouse frat brothers. Ace was focused when he knew what he wanted, and he'd passed on the same characteristics to Jada.

Jada couldn't stand to see her C grade in history among the other As and Bs on her progress report. It was the only reason Lynette agreed to give up her Saturday morning and drag Audrey downtown to the Martin Luther King Jr. exhibit with her so that Jada could boost her grade with an extra credit project. Instead of focusing on the more prominent civil rights leader for her work, Jada wanted to research King's wife, Coretta. She was equally as important to the movement as far as Jada was concerned.

In Jada's own words, "You can't have a great man like that unless you have an even greater woman."

Lynette had taught her girls to shun mediocrity as a lifestyle, so Jada's comment alone made Lynette want to fulfill her daughter's request. Jada always went the extra mile. For her project, she decided that she couldn't settle for photographs and the descriptive copy from the historical site's brochures, or even articles from the Internet.

Jada wanted to take her pictures firsthand, and even dress up like the first lady of the civil rights movement to give her report. But Lynette had drawn the line when Jada requested they get a life-sized cut-out of Dr. King made so that she could stand beside him during her presentation.

Jada fished the digital camera from her backpack and snapped away at the exterior of the building. Before entering the MLK Visitor Center, Lynette's future journalist of a daughter had even approached a few of the visitors with the camcorder, and asked them how the Civil Rights Movement had affected their lives, and how they thought Mrs. King had contributed.

"Your child is exceptional," Audrey said, furiously tapping her fingers across her BlackBerry. "I wish I had as much drive as she does. I'd get a lot more done in my life."

Lynette yanked the BlackBerry out of Audrey's hands and put it in the tote bag beside her. "Today your best friend is going to be *me* and not that little portable computer. Your thumbs should be tired of all that typing."

"All right, all right," Audrey said. "Evidently you're in need of a little sistah love."

"I'm glad you can see that," Lynette said.

"So tell me what's been going on with you? With you and Frank to be more exact. You haven't given me an update in about a week."

"Here's the update." Lynette sliced her hand in front of her neck. "Frank's cut."

"What? That was quick. It didn't take him long to get a pink slip." Audrey loosened the strings of an accessory bag that she'd pulled out of her purse, and replaced the gold round studs she was wearing for a pair of sterling silver hoops.

"Those earrings are cute," Lynette said, before jumping back into her reasons for giving Frank the ax. "Besides the fact that Frank has some baby-mama drama in his life, he's been AWOL. I can just sense that something's not right. He didn't return my calls or my text messages so I kicked him to the curb."

"Safe landing, my brother," Audrey said. "You know what I say. Life's too short to play and waste time. Move on."

"You didn't say that when Ace and I were having trouble," Lynette reminded her.

Audrey pulled her sunglasses down onto her nose. "You can't even put those two in the same category. Ace was your husband. And your baby daddy. Frank was a temporary fixture."

"You got that right," Lynette agreed. She watched a family coming toward her on the brick walkway. The father carried the younger of the two girls on his shoulders, and the older girl held her mother's hand, a Hello Kitty purse swinging on her skinny shoulder. That had been Lynette's life on the weekends when Ace wasn't on call and didn't end up being pulled away at the last minute. As a reserve pilot back then, he'd had to leave when the airline called, regardless of what was happening at home. Ace did what he had to do. She did, too. Unfortunately at the time, her priorities weren't with supporting her husband and selflessly building her family into a strong unit.

That was then. This is now.

Audrey jabbed Lynette's arm with her elbow. "You're going silent on me. Tell me what's going on."

"It's nothing."

"So now you want to act like I'm a stranger? I know you."

Lynette watched the husband lean over and give his wife a kiss. The woman wiped off the lipstick smudged across his lips. *I'm not going to cry. I'm not going to cry.*

Audrey pushed past the surface and seemed to read the words written on Lynette's heart. "It's Ace?" she asked.

"It's Ace." Lynette sighed.

"He's not tripping, is he?"

"No, *I'm* the one tripping."

"Are you giving that man a hard time? It must be some drama with his chick. What's her name?" Audrey snapped her fingers. "Sheila."

"The only drama with Sheila is that she's with Ace," Lynette said. "And that's not her fault. It's probably mine."

Audrey pushed her sunglasses back to the top of her head, using them as a band to tame her hair that was being blown about by the slight wind. "I need you to give me a little more so I'll know that I'm right about what I *think* you're trying to say right now."

Lynette stared at her friend. "And you think *what?*"

"That you've been thinking about Ace again in *that* way."

"*That* way?"

"The way a man loves a woman."

"Yes," Lynette said. It was the first time in a while that Lynette had stunned her friend to silence.

Audrey crossed her arms over her midsection. "So what are you going to do?"

"Live my life," Lynette answered. "I can't go adding drama to somebody else's life because I'm having this sudden resurgence of feelings. It wouldn't be fair to Ace or Sheila. Besides, all of this might pass over."

Lynette didn't believe a word she was saying. It was not going to happen. Nothing was passing over. God had awakened Lynette too many nights for her to think this would blow over like a summer thunderstorm. There was going to be some rumbling and a few lightning strikes by the time it was over. And Sheila would probably wish one of those lightning bolts would strike Lynette.

"You got a word from God. I can tell," Audrey said. "Don't try to run from it or you'll be like Jonah and get thrown in the belly of a whale." She laughed. "And trust me, you don't want to be up in there."

Jada walked over to where Lynette and Audrey were sitting. She powered off the digital camera and handed it to her mother. "I'm ready to go inside," she said. "That is if y'all are finished with your grown folks' business."

Lynette reached out to swat her on the backside, but Jada's youthful quickness was no match for her mother. "I've got your business," Lynette said. "Let's go."

By the time they'd walked with Jada through the Kings' historical birth home, their stomachs were grumbling loud enough to hear. The food and shopping at Atlanta's downtown Atlantic Station beckoned Audrey to eat and to find a new dress for her sorority's upcoming ball.

After Jada ran off to find food that better suited her taste, Lynette and Audrey snatched a table by a window so they could partake in one of their favorite extracurricular activities—people watching. In seconds, Audrey could weave an engaging story about people as they walked by. Lynette always told her she'd missed her calling as an author and should've been serving up *New York Times* best sellers instead of working as a business consultant.

Audrey shook her head and Lynette figured that her mind was ticking away like clockwork. Lynette's back was turned to what Audrey could see so she waited for her friend's creative commentary.

"I know nothing beats godly discernment, but a woman's instinct runs a close second," Audrey said.

"Huh?" Lynette was stumped.

"You were right to give Frank the ax," Audrey said. "Turn around and take a look out the window."

Chapter 33

There was no wonder that Lynette's phone calls or e-mails weren't being returned. Frank had someone else who was taking up his time. She guessed he'd figured out that he couldn't balance his business, artistic endeavors, *and* two women without letting at least one thing slip through the cracks. In this case it was Lynette.

"See. That's some mess that I can do without," Lynette said. "God is so good. He'll show you exactly what you need to see." She slid her chair back. "I'm going to go speak. Let him see I know the game he *tried* to play."

"Shake him up a little bit," Audrey said in agreement. "You have to do that to those players every now and then."

"Exactly."

"I'm staying in here at my front-row seat," Audrey said. "I wish they served popcorn here."

Lynette walked out of the door and directly into Frank's path.

Once she got closer to him, she realized that the woman wrapped around his arm was the same one from the birthday party Audrey had thrown for Kirk. All the inching and slinking to get close to Frank had paid off for Ms. Red Dress, and Lynette hoped the woman thought Frank was worth it.

"Hi, Frank," Lynette said, flashing her entire set of pearly white thirty-twos. She was smiling, but not because she'd caught Frank with another woman. They weren't married or seriously dating, so technically he had the right to go out with whomever he chose. This smile was a silent thanks to God for answering so many of Lynette's prayers. God didn't want her to waste her time, or get caught up with someone who wasn't worth it.

If it wouldn't have caused her to look like a purebred fool, Lynette would've taken a praise break right there in front of the two of them.

Frank looked almost as stunned as Audrey when she'd heard the news about Lynette's love for Ace. This would be a day to remember.

"Hi, Frank," Lynette said again. "Nice to see you." She turned to Ms. Red Dress. "And you, too. I believe I remember your face from Kirk's birthday party."

Ms. Red Dress held her wrist out and adjusted a gold bangle bracelet, acting as if she was bored at the thought of having a simple conversation with Lynette. "I'm sorry. I don't believe I know a Kirk," she said.

Frank seemed to have found his voice. "Kirk Landers. I had the art showing at his house and Lynette here purchased one of my pieces. *Fearfully and Wonderfully Made*, I believe it was."

"Something like that," Lynette said, deciding whether she should dish out some additional information to make Frank squirm. He was trying to get off easy.

"Oh, okay." Ms. Red Dress held out her hand like she expected Lynette to kiss it.

Lynette gripped her hand into one of the strong business handshakes that she'd been taught during college to use at job interviews. The kind with power. The kind that showed a person you were someone who meant business.

Ms. Red Dress snatched her hand out of Lynette's firm grip. Lynette had probably put a bit more pressure than she intended to. *Sorry about that, God. I think I got a little carried away.*

Enough was enough. Lynette had had her entertainment for the day. She'd done what she had to do to let Frank know that his calls—if he'd ever planned on returning hers—were no longer welcome.

"You two have a good day," Lynette said, then went back into the restaurant to do what she'd come to do. Enjoy time with her best friend.

"You're way too nice," Audrey said. "I don't know what you said, but I thought I was going to get a good laugh."

"I might have thought about it back in the day, but true godly women don't behave that way," Lynette said, smiling. "At least not today. Frank caught me at a good time."

"Or at least we try not to act up," Audrey said. "If it wasn't for the Holy Spirit, I would've gotten myself into some situations, if you know what I mean."

"Do I? We don't even want to take that walk down memory lane."

"Sea of forgetfulness. And I'm so glad about it. Makes me want to treat myself," Audrey said.

"You treat yourself for waking up every morning," Lynette said.

Audrey was nearly a professional shopper and negotiator. Lynette had seen her skills at work more than one time when they'd traveled to New York for a weekend shopping outing. Audrey liked high-quality items, but she didn't believe in paying inflated prices. By the time she left the store, Audrey could make a salesperson feel like they owed her money for taking the item off of their hands.

Audrey stood up. "You're right. I don't take any day for granted because you never know what the next day holds," she said. "And when we were walking over, I saw a cute little shoe named grace, and another named mercy that I've got to take home with me."

"Wait a second," Lynette said. She stopped Audrey before she set out as a woman on a mission to do some damage in the stores. "I want to reward myself with a cone of strawberry cheesecake ice cream."

"And a double scoop of chocolate Ace," Audrey joked.

"Don't say that," Lynette said. "I've been staying away from him as much as possible. The last couple of times he's picked up the girls, I've sent them out the door before he could barely get out of the car. And both times I wasn't there when he brought them back."

"And what has he said?"

"Nothing."

"That's not even like the two of you," Audrey said. She hooked her arm through Lynette's. "He knows something is going on."

"I was hoping he didn't."

"Oh, he knows. And the only reason he's not saying anything is because *he's* feeling something that he's trying to hide too," Audrey said. "All I know is that you can't run forever. One of you is going to eventually have to say something."

Lynette knew she was supposed to be the one. "Me and God are going to have to work this out another way," she said, reaching for her ringing cell phone that was clipped to the front of her purse. She knew Jada would probably be checking in soon to tell her that she'd finished eating and was going to find somewhere to spend the rest of her birthday bounty.

But it wasn't Jada. It was the double chocolate scoop.

"You're not going to believe this," Lynette said, handing the phone to Audrey.

"It's Ace?" Audrey asked.

"It's Ace."

Audrey pushed the phone back into Lynette's hand. "What are you giving the phone to me for? Answer it. God didn't waste any time with that one."

Lynette tried not to look at the eager expression on Audrey's face. It was like they were high school best friends waiting for a call from one of their crushes. "Hello?"

"Hey, Lynn. Are you busy?"

"No. Just out with Audrey. We took Jada out this morning to get some things together for her history project." *Why am I feeling so nervous?*

"Oh. Tell Audrey I said hello. And to keep you out of trouble."

"Audrey, Ace says hello. And that *I* should keep *you* out of trouble," Lynette said, twisting his words around.

"Hi, Ace," Audrey sang, loud enough for Ace to hear. "Long time, no speak." Audrey dropped her voice to a whisper. "Did you know your ex-wife has fallen back in love with you?"

Lynette covered the phone, although there was no way Ace could've heard what she said. There was a rumbling of background noises on his end of the phone.

"I don't want to keep you," he said. "I was calling to see if you could bring the girls to the airport on Monday evening at about six o'clock. I'm going to have a layover for about three hours and I wanted to eat dinner with them."

"Dinner? That shouldn't be a problem. I'll let them know."

"And you might as well stay, too. No sense in dropping them off and having to come back for them."

Okay, now I'm really going to pass out. "All right. That should be fine. We'll make plans to be there, but if anything changes give us a call."

"Thanks, Lynn."

"See you Monday."

Audrey said, "See you on Monday? What's that all about?"

Butterflies were fluttering in Lynette's stomach. "Ace wants me to bring the girls to have dinner with him at the airport. And he told me that I might as well stay and eat with them."

"Hopefully you'll have your nerve up by then."

"I'm not telling him anything, Audrey. Pretend like I never told you anything, okay?"

"Not going to happen. You told me because deep in your subconscious you wanted me to believe with you. You wanted somebody to tell you that you're *not* crazy and that maybe you made a mistake when you signed those divorce papers."

"You make me sick," Lynette said.

"The medicine I'm giving you is good for your soul," Audrey said. "You can thank me later. As a matter of fact, I'll put it on your tab because I give you a lot of advice and I haven't charged you yet."

"You keep acting up and I'm not bringing you out in public again," Lynette teased.

Lynette opened the door to the ice cream parlor. A bell on the door rang like they were entering a country café positioned at the intersection of two dirt roads. The smell inside could only be described as sweet. This ice cream wasn't going to be good for her thighs, but it was definitely going to find satisfaction in her stomach.

"But what about Sheila?" Lynette asked once she had double scoops balanced in a waffle cone. "I'm not trying to be the source of anyone else's heartache. And then you forget that Ace may think I've lost my mind. How is that going to make me look?"

"All you can do is put Sheila and Ace in God's hands. Number one, you're not some malicious woman trying to steal somebody's man from them. And as far as Ace is concerned, I'd rather you talk to him and know where he stands, than to not say anything and carry around a 'what if' for the rest of your life."

Easier said than done, Lynette thought. She had unshakable and unstoppable faith in so many things, yet this situation with Ace was testing how much faith she truly had. But she knew one thing—the true test would come on Monday.

Chapter 34

One obnoxious trucker had been riding Lynette's bumper for the past two miles. At this rate, she could've walked to the airport faster than this. She concluded that there must've been an accident somewhere down the road that she couldn't see, because there was no way a Monday evening should have this much backup.

Through the rearview mirror, Lynette could see Jada squinting down at her text book. Neither of the girls had spoken much since she'd picked them up. Jada had complained about the "tons of homework" she'd needed to finish before she got home so she wouldn't miss any episodes of tonight's reality show line-up.

Carmen on the other hand, couldn't hold a decent conversation with a human being because she had the earbuds of her iPod stuffed in her ears.

"You should probably put on your glasses, Jada," Lynette said.

"I forgot them at home," she said.

"You didn't lose them, did you?"

Jada smacked her lips. "Ma. As much as I hate those things, I know I can't see my work without them. Plus, I don't plan on paying for another pair out of my savings. One time was enough for me. That's why I wish I could get some contacts."

"When you're sixteen."

"Why is that always the magical number for everything? When I turn sixteen, I bet you'll say when I'm eighteen, and when I'm eighteen, twenty-one. I'll be a little old lady still waiting for my contacts. I'll probably be blind by then." Jada turned in her lips and smacked them together like she was missing two rows of teeth. They shared a laugh.

"For one thing, that's not going to happen because I plan on you being out of my house by the time you're twenty-one," Lynette said. "I'll give you time to graduate from college at least."

"You just want us out so you can be free and do what you want. Maybe you'll find a man and run off and get married in Hawaii or somewhere."

"Now that's a thought," Lynette said, although she'd rather it be Italy than Hawaii. She'd been listening to her Italian audio tutorial CDs during the ride until the girls begged her to turn them off.

Jada was doing a better job at daydreaming than she was doing at finishing her homework. "And when you get ready to fly off with your fiancé, Daddy will be piloting the plane," Jada said. "And when the plane lands he'll get off and come running after you and fall on his knees and beg you to come back to him. But your new man will be begging you, too. Now that would be funny."

Lynette pushed Jada to go further with her story. *This could prove to be interesting.*

"And what about Ms. Sheila?"

"What about her? Daddy could write her some kind of Dear John letter and leave it on her door. She'd probably do all of that mushy crying and stuff, but she'd get over it soon. And find her another man," Jada said.

She sounded so convincing, Lynette thought.

The rush-hour traffic finally broke free, but Lynette never saw the remains of an accident as she expected. There was even less congestion the closer she got to the airport, and they were able to find a parking space in a section of the deck where they could walk directly across the walkway and into the building.

Before the airport's increased security measures, Lynette used to prefer going upstairs to the south terminal to eat on those few occasions when she and the girls met Ace during layovers. They were nine and seven years old then, and trips like those were more exciting than school field trips in their eyes. As long as they had chicken fingers, fries, and a fruit punch, life was good.

But teenagers were a different story. Carmen and Jada had different culinary tastes and definitely different attitudes.

Lynette had made Carmen take off her iPod and that was just one of the reasons why Carmen had an attitude. People always said that a daughter pays back her mother for everything she did to her own parents when she were growing up, but Lynette was almost sure she didn't give her parents as hard a time as Carmen had been giving her lately.

Carmen groaned. "We're not going to be here a long time are we?"

"Why? You don't have anything else to do but sit and watch television or talk on the phone. You don't have any homework, remember?" Lynette said.

Carmen smacked at her lips. "Gosh, I was just asking."

"No. You were asking with an attitude. A very bad one, at that. It wouldn't hurt if you would try to be more pleasant to be around or I can give you something to be mad about."

Jada fanned her hand in the air. "Amen to that, Mama."

"Shut up, Jada," Carmen said, boring a hole through her sister with her eyes slit like daggers.

"You shut up," Jada said. "You're the one with the—"

"Both of you keep your mouths shut. I'm not trying to hear any of that right now," Lynette fussed. She left her daughters standing in front of one of the airline's self-service kiosks.

Not one to like to disappoint her mother, Jada caught up with Lynette and put her arm around her waist.

"Sorry, Ma."

Lynette knew that Carmen wouldn't apologize now, but by morning, she would've had time to think about her attitude. She was good for writing notes, or calling Lynette's office phone during the night and leaving a voice mail that Lynette would hear once she arrived at work.

Once the preteen years had hit her household, Lynette had decided she wasn't going to drive herself crazy with their emotional ups and downs. She believed in disciplining their children, but she also knew she didn't have the strength and energy to fight every battle. From the time they were born, she'd been teaching them God's ways. That's why she knew that God could be a better parent than both she and Ace put together. When things got tough—and tougher—she left them in God's hands.

It was funny how Carmen's attitude from moments earlier melted away when she spotted Ace.

"There's Dad. Over there," she said, quickening her steps.

Ace was standing near one of his airline's check-in counters chatting with a representative. When he noticed his daughters, he shook the man's hand and walked away with his arms open, welcoming Carmen and Jada into his embrace. "How are my queens doing?"

"Good, Daddy."

"And I'm hungry. No, make that famished."

"Let's eat, then. I'm starving, too," Ace said, turning to Lynette. "Thanks for bringing them out, Lynn. I hope traffic wasn't too bad."

"It was a little tight coming through downtown, but it got better."

"You're staying, right?"

Why was he looking at her like that? "Yes," Lynette said. The butterflies were back. She'd thought all night about how she'd bring up the subject, and whether it was even the appropriate time. It wasn't a conversation she planned on having in front of the girls, so Lynette couldn't see how it would work out that they'd have any private time. It was the airport for goodness sake. Not exactly her definition of a romantic atmosphere.

The pedestrian traffic inside the airport was as crowded as it had been on the interstate. In courtesy, Ace made room for an elderly woman to pass them. She shuffled past, holding on to the hand of an attentive young man who was watching her every step.

"Are you sure I can't get you a wheelchair, Grandma?"

"Oh no," she protested. "God gave me the activity of my limbs and I'm gonna use them as long as they'll move. Even if they don't move as fast as y'all young folks. Ain't that right, sir?" she said, turning to Ace.

"Yes ma'am," Ace said.

"So you fly one of those big old planes? I see you're wearing one of those fancy uniforms," the woman said.

Although her shoulders were slumped over in age, there was a certain strength about her. Lynette could see it in her eyes and smile, both rimmed with wrinkled lines of wisdom. She reminded Lynette of Grandma Toot.

"Yes ma'am, I'm a pilot," Ace said.

"God be with you. I still don't know how those things stay up in the air. I hold my Bible in my lap the whole time I'm up in the air."

"Yes ma'am," Ace said. "That's a good thing to do."

"You know you can't go wrong with God's Word. And doing what He says. Obedience is better than sacrifice."

193

God was using the mouth of an elderly woman—who had more days behind her than she had in front of her—to speak to Lynette.

"Yes ma'am," Ace said again.

The woman's grandson took her purse from her and put it on his arm. To see a young man do that was a true act of love, Lynette thought.

The woman gripped her grandson's forearm. She looked at Lynette with a twinkle in her eye. "I can tell you've got a good husband and that he takes care of his kids," she said. "My Jesse did the same. He's gone on to be with the Lord now, but my children and grandchildren still take good care of me."

She looked back at Ace and the girls with the admiration. "You make sure you take good care of your girls," she said, shaking a teasing finger bent with arthritis at Ace. "All three of them."

Ace looked at Lynette when he answered her. "Yes ma'am."

Ace scanned the food court for the first empty table that would be abandoned by rushed travelers. He snagged one with only three chairs, and borrowed an extra seat from a nearby table.

"I know you all are hungry, but I want to give you something first," he told Carmen and Jada.

He opened his pilot's jacket and produced two ring boxes. Carmen, always one to favor jewelry, opened her box first and took the ring off of the soft bed of felt.

"Oooh, Daddy," she said, sliding it on her finger with no hesitation. "This is nice. I need to get my nails done this week. That'll really show it off."

"I'm glad you like it."

"I like it too, Daddy," Jada said. "But I probably won't wear it every day. I don't want to lose it during basketball practice and stuff."

He took the ring out of Jada's box. "You don't have to wear it

194

every day. But I want you to know what it means when you do look at it."

Lynette leaned over to Jada and wrapped her arm around her daughter. They were gold rings, dainty and the perfect size for their fingers. Three hearts were intertwined on the ring—a big heart in the middle, and a smaller one on each side.

"The heart in the middle represents you and the love you should have for yourself. The two on the outside represent the love from me and from God."

Evidently, Carmen's incidents with the boy at school had uncovered Ace's sentimental side, and Lynette was thankful. She'd always had a good father in her life, so she knew what it meant for a daughter to feel her father's love. Having her father as an example in her life kept her from hooking up with what her dad calls "those knuckleheads." Even during her short rebellious stage, she still knew right from wrong. But she came back around, just like Carmen would do.

Carmen held out her hand so Lynette could take a closer look. "Nice," Lynn said. "Very thoughtful, Ace."

Lynette could tell the girls were trying to be patient and relish the moment, but because they hadn't eaten since lunch at school, their stomachs were probably speaking louder than their emotions.

"They're not going to last much longer without fainting," Lynette said. "You better set them free."

Ace reached into his pocket for a wallet, handing them each a twenty dollar bill. Lynette knew he wasn't expecting any change, and she knew the girls weren't going to offer it.

"Let me take my multivitamin while it's on my mind," Lynette said. "I missed it at lunch." She pushed down the child-resistant cap on a small bottle of vitamins. "After you hit thirty-nine it seems like you need a little extra help with energy," she joked.

"I don't know what the inside of your body is doing, but the outside looks as good as you always have," Ace said.

195

"Thank you," Lynette said. She slipped the pill into her mouth, swallowed it dry, and tried to think of something else besides revealing her heart to Ace. She tried to pretend there was something more interesting to look at in her purse.

When Lynette looked up to ask Ace if he wanted to go ahead and get his dinner, she caught him staring at her. He didn't look away, and his gaze almost caused her to melt. Lynette felt her face grow warm and flush, and Audrey's words came back to mind. Somebody was going to have to say something sooner or later. *Should I?* Would she be the one to change their destiny or would . . .

"Lynette," Ace said. "It's no secret that our relationship has been a little . . ." He searched for words, "unusual, lately."

Lynette nodded. Her head was the only part of her body that wasn't frozen.

"Part of it's probably my fault. I've been fighting something," Ace said.

She felt him. Literally. He was resting his hands on top of hers now.

Ace took a deep breath. "I've had this fight on the inside because . . ."

A peace descended on Lynette. She knew what was coming.

Chapter 35

If Cassandra hadn't been with her, Sheila was sure she would've collapsed to the floor. There was Ace. Locked in a gaze with his ex-wife. Everything inside of Sheila imploded, but she had to take her frayed nerves and transform them into nerves of steel in front of Cassandra.

I won't crack. I won't break down.

Ace hadn't mentioned a layover. Now Sheila saw why. It was fate that Cassandra had called Sheila to pick her up after a trip she'd taken to see somebody in New Jersey. She still wouldn't say who. But coming to the airport was the last thing Sheila had wanted to do. Her bed was calling her, not the two hours of traffic she'd endured getting to the Hartsfield-Jackson Airport. Only to see this. She wanted to shake her fist at God and ask why. Why did things like this always happen to her?

Sheila closed her eyes. Hoped she'd been mistaken. But Cassandra confirmed it.

Cassandra stopped midstride, not caring who was behind her and that she'd stopped the steady stream of rushing passengers.

"I know that's not Ace. Look. Is that *your* man?"

Sheila didn't have to take another look. "That's him," she said, drumming up her courage at the same time.

"And he's with that woman from the party. I just saw her on Saturday when I was out with Frank." Cassandra snapped her fingers. "Lynette."

"Are you serious? You met Lynette? That's Ace's ex-wife."

Cassandra's jaw dropped. "What?"

Sheila thought back to running into Lynette at the restaurant eating brunch with a man. "Frank is the name of that new guy you're seeing?" she asked Cassandra.

"Yes. Which reminds me. He still hasn't called me back."

Sheila was ignoring whatever Cassandra was talking about. Her mind started clicking. She couldn't remember for sure whether the man she'd met with Lynette was named Frank, but she was about 90 percent sure. That was more than enough.

"So what are you going to do about your man?" Cassandra said. "He's staring in that chick's face like he wants to lay a deep kiss on her lips and she doesn't plan on moving away. Look at her."

Sheila saw it. She didn't need the extra commentary.

The tears threatened to come again, but Sheila grabbed Cassandra's hand, at the same time, grabbing some of Cassandra's attitude.

But the front didn't last for long. Sheila thought she could be strong, but here she was sobbing in front of a stunned Ace and Lynette.

"Ace? What's going on here? I thought we were always honest with each other. I asked you . . ." Sheila's tears fell faster. "I asked you if there was anything wrong . . . and you . . . you said nothing."

Ace held up his hand. He stood up and put a hand on her shoulder as if she would lose her mind and pounce on somebody. It was a good thing he did. She didn't know who she wanted to jump on first—him or Lynette. They were probably equally as guilty.

"Sheila, calm down. Don't—"

"Calm down," Cassandra blurted out. She could escalate an argument in seconds. Her high-pitched voice climbed another octave whenever she was mad. Sheila wiped away her tears. The scene was bringing stares from the surrounding tables, and Lord knows she didn't want airport security involved.

"You've got some nerve," Cassandra said, stepping up beside Sheila. "You're up in here all cozy with another woman looking like you want to take her home."

"This 'other woman' is my ex-wife. Lynette brought my kids out to see me because *I* asked her to."

It was apparent that Ace was irritated that Cassandra had even tried to force herself into his business. He was never a big fan of Cassandra, but Sheila knew he tolerated her because she was her friend. Cassandra's neck-rolling was only making things worse than they already were. Sheila wished she could disappear. No, she wished this wasn't happening at all.

Sheila didn't know what made her turn to Lynette, who was sitting calmly as if this whole thing had nothing to do with her. And here Sheila was—with Cassandra—making a fool of herself.

"Why would you try and take away the man who means everything to me?" Sheila asked. Her voice cracked, but she was speaking loud enough that only those at the table could hear. "You had your chance, but you thought something was more important than your marriage," she said. "I've never caused you any problems."

Lynette stood up, picked up her jacket, and looked Sheila square in the eyes. "I'm here for my girls who are entitled to spend time with their father whenever *they* want to and whenever *he* wants to. I'm not going to stoop to you and your friend's level by causing a scene."

Carmen and Jada walked up, each with a bag of food in one hand and a drink in the other. They looked just as astonished, and from what Sheila could see, a little uncomfortable.

Like any protective mother would do, Lynette rushed to get the girls out of the unfolding dramatic scene. "Come on girls, let's go. Say good-bye to your dad. You can see him later this week. I'll make sure of it."

"Lynette, don't go. Please sit down. I can handle this," Ace said.

Handle this? Since when did I become a "this"? Sheila thought.

"He has no respect for you girl," Cassandra said in her other ear. "Let's go."

They all stood in a circle, wondering who would make the first move. Despite what Sheila had seen, it wasn't that easy for her to walk away from a two-year relationship that she'd poured her heart into.

Lynette seemed to be rethinking whether she should shield her girls or allow them to stay with their father. Ace had an arm around each of his daughters. He looked at Sheila, and then at Lynette.

Lynette was the first to speak. "Let's go, girls," she said, then walked away.

Carmen and Jada looked at their father, then followed their mother, who had already pushed past the crowd and was heading toward the south terminal exit.

Ace went after them, dodging the maze of scattered chairs in the food court to run behind her. He'd left Sheila standing with Cassandra.

"I wouldn't even fight for him," Cassandra said. "Bump what I said. He comes with two kids, a baby mama, and he's not even servicing your womanly needs—if you know what I mean. Find yourself somebody who wants you. It'll make your life a whole lot easier."

Ace's actions had said what his words didn't. He'd left her standing there, and to most women, the embarrassment may have been enough for her to wash her hands of the relationship. But nothing about Sheila's life had ever been easy. And it wasn't going to be easy to let go of Ace. She had no plans to.

Chapter 36

Lynette. Please wait. Lynette."

Ace had already called Lynette's name three times, but she didn't bother to turn around. Whenever he called her Lynette instead of Lynn, she knew he meant business. She just wanted to make it to the parking deck as soon as possible so that she could get home to the safety of her bedroom and cry this out.

In between Ace's pleas were a string of "Mama, stop," and "Mama, what happened?" coming from the girls. Lynette finally stopped when she felt a hand grab her elbow. She turned around to face Ace with Carmen and Jada behind him. Both of their eyes were glassy, and Lynette knew if one of them started to cry, the other would follow suit.

Lynette let Ace guide her to an area away from the crowds.

"Girls, can you wait over there while I talk to your mother?" Ace said.

They both seemed hesitant. Carmen's arms were crossed in defiance, and the emotional Jada looked like she would be the first to drop a tear if she tried to say a word.

"Obey your dad," Lynette said.

They sulked their way to the area for unclaimed baggage, but kept a watchful eye on their parents. Lynette knew that with the girls watching, she couldn't let her expressions speak for her.

She steadied her emotions. "If it's not about the girls I don't think we should talk. Sheila seems to be a good woman, and she's right. She's never caused me any problems." Lynette paused, thinking about the years when they were in love. And then the years when it all fell apart. "And we had our chance."

"What about second chances?"

Lynette couldn't believe her ears. She'd wondered for months what it would feel like if Ace ever spoke those words. Nervousness. *How could we ever start over?* Hope. *Does he really mean that?* Anger. *Why didn't he fight harder the first time?*

Lynette adjusted her purse strap on her shoulder. "Now's not the time for this. We're standing in a crowded airport and you expect me to talk about something that will change our lives in a major way. I can't do this. Not now."

Lynette looked over at Carmen and Jada. Jada was still watching them, but Lynette noticed a slight scowl on Carmen's face. She followed her daughter's eyes. There was Sheila. She was watching Ace and Lynette, too, and looked like she wanted to fall apart. Ms. Red Dress stood behind her with a glower on her face to match Carmen's. Ms. Red Dress looked like the boxing coach on the side of the ring, prompting her boxer to get back in the fight. But Sheila wasn't budging.

"I'm leaving, Ace," Lynette said. "I need to get the girls home."

"When can we talk?"

"I don't know. When I'm ready, I guess."

Ace bowed out like he didn't want to pressure her too much.

Lynette could tell by his eyes that he had so much else to say. She also saw the confusion that he felt in his heart, but the hope he had as well. But the biggest thing Lynette felt, was his love. It was an undeniable force that made it almost impossible for her to walk away. It took her back to the night of their engagement on top of Stone Mountain.

Ace had never been a natural romantic, but when he tapped into his creative side, Lynette always appreciated his extra effort. He'd given her a handwritten invitation the night before to a sunset picnic. Ace picked her up from her parents' house with the two blankets he'd instructed her to bring. They didn't talk much on their ride there because the love songs on the radio spoke for them. They held hands as they climbed for the peak of the mountain. Lynette had taken the climb several times before and each time complained the entire way about her throbbing thighs. But that evening it didn't seem taxing at all. She was breathless when she reached the peak, but it wasn't from the climb. Ace pulled a setup out of the duffel bag that could've easily duplicated a candlelight dinner at a restaurant. As the sun began to set, he asked for her hand in marriage. He'd said that he wanted to spend the rest of his life with her. That night—like right now—she could literally feel his love.

Lynette motioned for the girls to come over. They moved faster than she'd seen them move in a long time, and immediately slid under their father's arms.

"I'll make it up to you, baby girls," he said, and kissed each of them on their foreheads. "We'll go out to eat at the Varsity when I get back in town."

Carmen looked over her father's shoulder to the direction where Sheila had been standing. She was gone. "Just us, Daddy," Carmen said. "Nobody but us."

"And Mama, too," Jada said.

"Yeah. That'll be okay. Mama, too," Carmen agreed.

"Let's go girls," Lynette said. She reached out and they took her hands. She squeezed their fingers and walked out of the exit.

Lynette's ear had been pressed close to the heart of God. He'd told her that her life was going to change soon. Lynette didn't know exactly how or when. And it scared her. But above all else, she had to protect her children. They'd been through so much already.

Carmen waited until they got in the car before she questioned Lynette. "Why was Ms. Sheila there anyway?"

"I don't know," Lynette said, reaching out to pay the parking deck attendant.

"She's always showing up when she's not supposed to. Like that time she tried to bring us breakfast at Daddy's house and he'd already told her the night before that he wanted to spend time with us by himself."

"Oh, really," Lynette said, knowing that she only needed to show a little interest for her girls to tell the rest of the story. And they did.

Jada chimed in. "She wants us to be one big happy family." Jada leaned forward from the backseat to kiss Lynette's cheek. "But she'll never be my mama."

"I don't think she wants to be your mother," Lynette said, trying her best to stay unbiased.

"But she wants to be Daddy's wife so bad. I can tell," Carmen said.

"I think Daddy wants to be with Mama," Jada said, talking directly to her sister like Lynette wasn't chauffeuring them back home. "I can tell."

"Divorced people don't get back together," Carmen said, opening up her fast-food bag and spreading her dinner across her lap. She chewed a mouthful of an oversized burger. "Daddy might marry Ms. Sheila and forget all about us, anyway. That's what Tasha's daddy did."

"Your Daddy would never do that. He'd never forget about you."

"I don't think so either," Jada said.

"All I know is that the male species is always messing something up, so don't be surprised if it happens," Carmen said.

"That's no way to talk," Lynette said. "You're too young to think like that anyway."

Carmen shrugged her shoulders. By the time they arrived home, she'd stuffed her earbuds back in her ears and crawled back into her teenage world where the only things that mattered were fashion and music.

"I wouldn't care if you and Daddy got married again," Jada said. She'd kept the conversation going almost the entire ride home. "I know Ms. Sheila is his girlfriend, but she's not his wife so I think all is fair in love and war."

"What?" Lynette responded, chuckling. "You act way too old for your age."

"Mature, Ma. The word is mature." Jada picked up her glasses from the kitchen table and sat down with her history composition book. "With God, all things are possible. Isn't that what you always tell me?"

Chapter 37

Even the best makeup concealer couldn't mask Sheila's under-eye bags. Nancy had commented all week that she looked overworked and tired. Since the day after seeing Ace at the airport with Lynette, Sheila had put in overtime at work, staying behind closed doors until she was the last person to leave. At around nine o'clock, she called the concierge desk for a security escort. All week, Jamal had come to walk her to the car. Sheila used to have a good time talking to Jamal. He had a way of cheering anyone up. But even he hadn't been able to break her out of the slump.

Being at home alone made things worse, which is why Sheila clocked in extra hours at work. She had steered clear of all communication with Cassandra—phone calls, text messages, e-mails. Her friend only made things worse and planted negative comments in her head. Sheila didn't need any help with that. Her mind did enough of that on its own.

Sheila heard a tap on her office door. At least thirty minutes before, she'd check the hallway and seen that all the office doors were closed and the lights off. She sat still, not wanting to make a sound in case it was a criminal with the audacity to announce his arrival. Quietly, she lifted the phone off of the receiver so she could call downstairs.

"Sheila. It's Clive. Open the door." He wiggled the doorknob. "Are you all right?"

Sheila got up from the desk and unlocked her office door. "I thought everyone was gone. What are you doing here?"

"I came back to get my laptop. My wife had a networking dinner with her Toastmasters group so I decided to do some work from home." Clive had changed into a pair of jeans and a green Polo shirt. Even in casual clothes, he looked like he'd slid his clothes out of a bag of dry-cleaned garments.

Sheila turned her back to him and went back to her desk. For the last two hours she hadn't been doing any work at all. She'd been shopping on the Internet. In between purchases she'd written a poem about love. How it had the power to hurt and bring joy.

"I've been worried about you this week," Clive said. "You haven't looked like yourself."

For a moment Clive looked like a concerned uncle, instead of the sneak Sheila had always known him to be. Besides Nancy, he was the only colleague who'd shown any concern about her all week. Sheila could only imagine what the others had been running their mouths about in the break room. She'd been on the flip side before, guessing what personal problems a colleague was trying to hide.

"I'm okay. Just dealing with some personal things." She laughed it off. "You know how women can be. Emotional about the smallest thing."

"I doubt a small thing would have you strung out all week."

"That bad, huh?"

"And the last thing you want to do is bring a lot of emotion to work. Especially not at a time like this."

Sheila had tried to forget about the impending layoffs, but one comment from Clive had added it back to her already heavy heart.

Clive took a seat in the chair across from her desk. "I know man troubles when I see it," he said. "It's written all over your face. And trust me, it ain't pretty."

"Thanks," Sheila said. "I appreciate the compliment."

"Bad timing for a joke," Clive said. "I apologize. Let me make it up to you. Let's go get a drink."

"I don't drink. You know that."

"Well at least get something to eat."

Eat? Sheila hadn't been able to do that in the last four days. Funny how heartache worked better than the Atkins, cabbage soup, and all the other trendy diets combined. She hadn't even been able to indulge in her daily cup of chocolate latte.

"I'm really not hungry, Clive."

"Don't tell me you just want to go home. Cry yourself to sleep until your man comes to his senses?"

"If I so choose," Sheila said, knowing it was the last thing she wanted to do. It was either that or wait by the phone or walk around with her cell phone clipped to her hip all night. Ace had only called her twice after the incident at the airport but she hadn't answered because Cassandra had convinced her that she was playing the weak, desperate girlfriend if she did.

"Sometimes you have to make a man sweat," Cassandra had said. "He'll appreciate you more."

Stupid advice. Ace had only called once more since then, but left a message on her office voice mail. All he'd said was that they needed to talk. Even though Sheila had tried, she hadn't been able to reach Ace. If only she could talk to him . . .

"So are you coming or not?" Clive stood up. "You deserve better." He picked up his laptop case and walked toward the door.

Sheila noticed that a small grey patch of hair in the back of Clive's head seemed to have spread over the past month or so.

Sheila made a mental note to call her beautician in the morning to schedule a touch-up to her roots. In fact, she was going to call the aesthetician, Emille, for a facial massage, too. If she didn't feel fabulous, the least she could do was look it.

"Why not?" Sheila finally said to Clive. "I'll come. What will it hurt?" She picked up her purse to leave, not bothering to hibernate her computer or organize her desk for the next day.

When she saw Ace again—which she prayed would be in the next couple of days—he would see all that he was missing. And he'd never look at Lynette like *that* again.

Chapter 38

Ace didn't wish his situation in life right now on any God-fearing man. He hated to know that he was in the hearts of two women, and neither one of them deserved to be hurt. But in the end, someone would be. Including him.

Some men would covet his position, and play with the women's hearts. But Ace had learned the hard way that there was nothing like a woman scorned. A woman like Monique Jacobs. Monique had turned out to be as vindictive as she was beautiful. If it hadn't been for his freshman crew at Morehouse blowing up his head and convincing him that dating two women was what true "playas" did, he never would've gotten a taste of reality. During his first year of school, he parked his car at his cousin's apartment complex, but that didn't save it from the brick through the windshield. Or the two flat tires.

Monique made a lasting impression on his life, and oddly

enough, made him a better man. So when he met Lynette in front of McAlpin Hall he knew he had to come correct. He never dreamed on that day that they would marry, divorce . . . and end up here.

Ace had tried to call Sheila before he boarded the plane that night, but she didn't answer. Because of Cassandra, no doubt. All he wanted to do was explain himself to her, but the more he thought about it, he surmised that only a coward would have a conversation like that over the phone. So he left her a message at work, hoping by the time he got home that she'd be able to talk to him with a rational mind and that Cassandra wouldn't be coaching Sheila in her ear.

On the other hand, Ace hoped someone *was* talking to Lynette, and he preferred that person to be God. Lynette was a praying woman; Ace knew that. He just hoped God was telling Lynette the same thing that He was telling him. They were supposed to be together again. He didn't know how. And he didn't know when. But God was an expert at working out all of the particulars.

Of course, if Lynette flew to the side of Audrey, Ace still had someone on his team. Audrey was the kind of friend that every husband prays his wife will have. Caring. Steadfast.

The last time Ace had personally talked to Audrey was when his girls spent the weekend with her and he'd had to pick them up while Lynette was out of town for some kind of conference for pediatric dentists. No doubt, he still had the phone number saved in his cell.

Audrey answered on the first ring.

"Couldn't wait to talk to me, huh?" Ace said. "I bet you knew this call was coming."

Audrey sounded confused. "I'm sorry. I think you may have the wrong number."

"Audrey, it's Ace." She didn't say anything, like it was taking her mind a minute to compute why in the world her best friend's ex-husband would be calling her.

"Ace Bowers."

Audrey laughed. "I know who you are, Ace. It hasn't been *that* long."

"Good. I take it you're doing all right."

"Great, actually."

"And how about Kirk?"

"Oh, he's still kissing the ground I walk on," she joked.

"I guess some things don't change," Ace said. She was still the same good, ol' Audrey.

There was an awkward silence for a moment, and Ace knew Audrey was waiting for him to fill it.

"Hmm. Have you talked to Lynette lately?"

"Earlier today," she said.

Silence again.

Audrey's answers were short. She wasn't going to give Ace anything without him working for it.

"No. I mean have you *talked* to Lynette. Did she say anything about me?"

"You're asking me to break the code, and you know I can't do that," Audrey said.

Okay, I'm getting somewhere. That was Audrey's way of saying yes, Ace thought. He took a deep breath.

"Look, I know you know everything that me and Lynette went through. I'm just asking you to throw out all that stuff from back in the day and give me a clean slate."

"You know Lynette was never the kind to bash you. Of course, she had her moments, but she never painted you in a distasteful light. But when it comes down to it, I'm all about protecting my sister and making sure she's not hurt. Again."

"I can't promise that I'll never hurt Lynette. But I can promise that I'll never do it on purpose." From the silence on the other end of the phone, Ace didn't know if it was the right thing to say to a woman, but he was only entitled to tell the truth.

"I've been trying to call Lynette for four days and she's not answering or returning my calls."

"She'll talk to you. Eventually," Audrey said. "In my opinion, one of the first things you need to do is make sure you put some closure on other things. Other people. You know what I mean."

"I'm waiting to do that now," Ace said.

He'd finally made it to Sheila's condo and saw that her car wasn't parked in the designated space for her unit. He pulled into a guest space in an area where Sheila probably wouldn't notice him immediately. Like Audrey said, he needed to put closure on their relationship before he could even talk to Lynette. It needed to happen tonight, so he didn't need Sheila running the other way. They needed to face each other head-on.

By the time he backed up into the guest parking space, Ace saw Sheila's car pull up to the gated entryway. As the black wrought iron gate swung open, he took a deep breath. This wasn't going to be easy.

"All I want is for Lynette to ask God what she's supposed to do," he told Audrey. "Please tell her that. That's all I ask from you."

"I will," Audrey said.

"Thanks, Audrey," Ace said, turning off the ignition. "I have to go now."

"It'll be all right," Audrey said, in a voice that sounded more relaxed than it had since she'd picked up the phone.

Ace prayed she was right. Sheila was pulling shopping bags out of the trunk as he approached. He called her name softly so as not to startle her.

Seeing Ace seemed to startle Sheila anyway. The look on her face was ambivalent . . . like she didn't know whether to run into his arms or bolt away from him.

Sheila didn't speak. But she cried.

Ace was careful in his actions. His concern for her made him want to embrace her until she could get over this sudden change in their relationship. He hadn't wanted it to happen like this. It would've been better if they'd been slowly weaned from each other. Weaned? How odd did that sound?

Ace walked over and stood on the curb, feeling it was better if he waited for Sheila to come to him. He didn't know what to do with himself. He shoved his hands in his pockets and watched her putter around with things in her trunk.

"I'm sorry," he said. "I never meant for anything like this to happen."

"I asked you a million times what was wrong," Sheila said, now standing beside him. "You always said nothing. You acted like I was crazy for feeling what I was feeling."

"But I—"

"But you lied," Sheila said, raising her voice. Her tears fell faster now. Even they seemed to stream down with anger. "I saw how you were looking at Lynette. And the sad thing is that I don't know if you've *ever* looked at me like that."

Ace knew nothing he said could change the image burned in Sheila's mind. Women didn't forget things like that. Moreover, he couldn't deny *the look* and everything that came with it.

"I'm sorry," he said again. It was the only thing to say that made sense at the time.

Ace took a cautious step forward and peeled the shopping bag handles out of her hands. She let him. Sheila walked past him and inside to the elevator. They stepped inside with a couple who couldn't wait until they got behind closed doors to express their affection for one another. When the woman noticed Sheila's tear-streaked face, she seemed to pull back from her beau, but not before glaring at Ace.

He wanted to plead his case to her. Debunk the myth that men were dogs and had no regard for women's feelings. He cared for Sheila. That's why he was here.

Sheila stepped off when the elevator stopped at the seventh floor. She unlocked the door to her condo, not waiting to hold it open for Ace. He went inside, pushed the door closed with his foot, then set the bags down on the coffee table. With a possible layoff looming over her head, Ace thought shopping was the last thing Sheila needed to be doing. There was no way he'd mention that now.

Ace could see the rise and fall of Sheila's chest, like her heart was pumping her up for her response.

"So you're in a relationship with Lynette now? Things are back like you always wanted? Must've been why you always steered me away from marriage. Because you were using me."

Sheila must've been waiting to come inside before she let it all out, Ace thought.

"That's not true, Sheila. I didn't use you."

"Well, what do you call it?"

"Look," Ace sat down on the end of the couch. "Lynette and I aren't in a relationship. As a matter of fact, she's not even talking to me right now, and I—"

"Oh, so you've been calling her?"

Ace realized he was digging himself a hole. He held his forehead in his hands. "I'm confused about a lot of things right now. I'm just asking you to—"

"Oh, you're not confused," Sheila said. "When Lynette walked away at the airport, you went after *her.* You might have thought *you* were confused, but doing that made things very clear to me."

Ace couldn't argue with her. He ran his hands down the side of his face. He looked over at Sheila. She was doing everything she could now not to look at him, but he saw the tears running down her face again.

"I don't even know what to say," he confessed. "Nothing I say will make a difference right now."

Sheila walked over to the couch and stood over him. "Unless

you say you're willing to give us a chance. There's a reason why you divorced Lynette. What makes you think things will be different with her now?"

One of her tears fell on his hand.

"I don't know, Sheila." It was a dumb thing to say. Not sufficient at all for a time like this. At that moment Ace realized that if he walked away from Sheila, then things may not work with Lynette at all. He could very well end up alone.

It was a chance he had to take. He had to go with his heart. Then again, the Bible did warn about following the heart. *The heart is deceitful and wicked. Who can know it?* What if his heart was deceiving him?

Ace stood up and was surprised when Sheila laid her head on his chest. She wrapped her arms around his waist. Instead of letting his arms hang at his side like steel, he put them around her, but they didn't convey the same emotion that she was feeling. Her arms said, *"Please stay."* His said, *"I'm sorry."*

Ace pulled away. "I have to go now."

Sheila lifted her arms from his waist to his shoulders. She rubbed her hands on the back of his neck, then tried to pull his lips to hers.

"Don't," Ace said, lifting her arms up.

Sheila looked dejected at first, but then her face twisted in resentment. "Go ahead." Her voice almost sounded like a sneer. "You'll be back. But I can't guarantee I'll be here. I'm an attractive woman. It's not like men run the other way when they see me."

"Do what you need to do, Sheila. God's going to have His way," Ace said.

Sheila picked up her shopping bags and walked down the hallway toward her bedroom. Ace waited to see if she would come back out, but after a few minutes she didn't. He closed the door behind him.

Chapter 39

Sheila was definitely going to put Ace's words into action. "Do what you need to do."

She'd invested too much of her time and love into building a relationship with Ace. She didn't plan on making it that easy for him to walk away. As much as she hated to admit it, she knew Ace wasn't the kind of man who would hurt her on purpose. But that didn't make matters better.

The more Sheila thought about what probably contributed to him leaving, the more her insides boiled. Cassandra always messed things up for her, then walked away without any blemishes. Not this time. If Cassandra hadn't hooked up with Frank, then Lynette would still have a man in her life. Which meant she wouldn't have given Ace the time of day and Ace would be begging Sheila for forgiveness. *He* would be doing what he needed to do to make things right with her.

Well this time, Cassandra was going to fix it.

Sheila hammered her fist three times on Cassandra's apartment door. It echoed through the hallway and probably sent Cassandra's neighbors scrambling to call 9-1-1. Let them. This wasn't the nine-to-five workplace Sheila. This Sheila wasn't beyond pulling out her street history if she needed to. And she needed to.

"Sheila?" Cassandra yelled through the door. "What in the world is wrong with you?"

Sheila could see Cassandra's eye pressed in the small peephole.

"Open up," Sheila demanded, like she was an FBI agent making a drug bust.

"Not until you calm down," Cassandra said through the door. "I'm not opening a thing until you act like you have some home training."

Sheila inhaled a deep breath and blew it out through her mouth. There weren't many times that Cassandra didn't do what she said. And if Sheila didn't calm down enough to make Cassandra open the door, it would be a wasted trip.

"Okay, Cassandra," she said in a voice that was ten decibels less than the first demands she'd screamed. "Please open the door. I need to talk to you."

"Can't it wait?"

"If it could wait, do you think I would've showed up at your apartment?"

The lock clicked. Cassandra opened the door.

"This is bad timing, you know," Cassandra said. "But I'm going to let you in since you're looking all crazy and what not."

Cassandra's living room was furnished with a chocolate brown leather sectional that took up most of the walking space. When they'd lived together in a larger space, the couch didn't look as massive as it did now. Cassandra had an affinity for cheetah print fabrics, and in Sheila's humble opinion, she'd taken the accessorizing with the print a little too far. A rug in the middle of the floor. Lampshades. Two throws strewn across the back of the sectional. Sheila felt like she was in a zoo.

"I need your help and you don't have a choice in the matter."

"Listen at you getting all bold and what not," Cassandra said.

"I need you to help me get Ace back," Sheila explained. "You know that fight-for-your-man speech you gave me at first? Well, you're going to be my coach. I've put too much of myself into him for him to walk away."

If she'd been standing before someone else, Sheila would've cried. It wasn't the time for that, and she didn't want Cassandra to think that Ace had reduced her to a weakling.

"So he left you for his ex?" Cassandra asked.

"I'm assuming."

Cassandra shook her head like she was a disappointed parent. "I told you to always have options."

"You're the reason I'm in this predicament anyway."

"Why is that?"

"Because you hooked up with Lynette's man and now she doesn't have anyone to preoccupy her time or her heart. That's why."

"How was I supposed to know I had the same taste in men as your man's ex? I mean, your *ex-man's* ex," she said, running her bare feet across the cheetah-print rug.

Sheila's anger simmered. "You're going to help me."

"You haven't *prayed*?" Cassandra asked sarcastically. "With all that praying Ace had you do so you could keep your hands off of each other, you should've been sending up some prayers that he'd stay with you."

Cassandra was clueless. Sheila had never been the kind to discuss the intimate moments she'd had with men, but at least she had something that could shut Cassandra up for a change.

"I'll have you know, Ace and I did share a wonderful experience together. And because we didn't do it all the time, it made things more special."

A vindictive smile smeared across Cassandra's face. "What do you need me for? Think with your pretty little head, Sheila. That's your plan, right there. Give it a couple of weeks and play the pregnancy card. His ex is not going to want to deal with him, especially if she knows that you two slept together, and definitely not if she thinks he has a baby on the way."

"How am I supposed to pull that off? Sooner or later he's going to know that it's not true."

"It takes at least three months for a woman to start showing, anyway. By that time, he'll be doting over you so hard that he'll forget all about his ex-wife. Before things go too far, you can fake like you lost the baby. And we can do some other things in the meantime."

Sheila was getting nervous. She wasn't sure what else Cassandra was going to come up with, but this scheme was going to play hard on Ace's emotions. "I don't want to bring something back on myself," Sheila said. She'd always thought that what goes around, comes around. "Karma," she told Cassandra.

"Do you want Ace back or not? You're just giving him a situation to help him see how much he really loves you and how his ex-wife is *not* going to stand by his side."

"What about doctor's appointments and all of that?"

"Ace is hardly in town, anyway. Give him your own updates. It's not like he's going to run and check behind you."

That was true. Ace would probably take her word for it. Hopefully.

Cassandra didn't seem phased at all by Sheila's request. She'd rattled off the pregnancy plan like it was one she'd devised and carried out for herself. Sheila didn't doubt it.

Sheila thought she heard a rush of water coming from Cassandra's bedroom. She listened for a few more seconds and knew unmistakably the shower had been turned on.

"I told you this was a bad time," Cassandra said, picking up one of those throws and wrapping it around her midsection like it was a skirt.

"I know that's not who I think it is," Sheila said. "Tell me it's not."

"Okay, I won't tell you."

"You owe me more than this pregnancy plan," Sheila decided. "Lynette needs to think she's seeing signs from the heavens that she needs to stay away from Ace."

"So you're trying to play the hand of God?"

The words hit Sheila in her stomach. At that moment, her stomach felt like a million butterflies were slapping their wings against each other. Sometimes her conscience could get the best of her. That's why it would work best if Cassandra's fingerprints were on this plan, and not her own.

"I'm not playing anything. You are," she said, hoping by saying it aloud that God would charge this to Cassandra's bill only.

"I have no problem with that," Cassandra said. "What's the ex's full name?"

"Why?" Sheila started to panic. She hoped Cassandra wouldn't take things to an extreme. "Why? Are you going to hire a hit man or something?"

"Girl, no. Ace really did affect your head. Do you think I would chance putting all of this beauty behind bars? I don't think so. I just need her information so I can shake her up a bit."

Okay. Shaking a person up was fine. "Lynette Bowers."

"Bowers? She kept her married name?"

"I said the same thing to Ace one time," Sheila admitted. "He said it was for professional reasons and so that she wouldn't have a different last name than her girls. But that's not something we need to be worried about right now."

"Exactly," Cassandra agreed. "Worry about getting her out of the picture."

Chapter 40

Ace tossed, fighting the covers and his thoughts. He prayed. God wouldn't let him sleep, so Ace was awake through the night. He knew he'd heard God correctly. In the stillness of the night, it was easy to discern His voice. In this case, God was definitely taking the foolish things to confound the wise. Why else would a forty-one-year-old man go and talk to his ex-wife's parents? It sounded like such a juvenile thing to do, but who was he to argue with God.

Mama Claudette had always been an early riser, and Ace didn't think things could've changed that much. By eight o'clock, she was usually dressed, had already drank her cup of strong, black coffee and read the morning newspaper—that unlike most, she still had delivered to her front door. And if the weather was cooperative, she'd work in her small flower garden or tend to the plants on the back porch.

So Ace didn't hesitate to call her at eight o'clock after finally forcing himself to get two hours of sleep.

"Good morning," Mama Claudette said.

"Good morning, Mama Claudette," he said. "This is Ace."

"Let me pinch myself and see if I'm awake," she teased. "I haven't gotten a call from you in so long."

"Don't do me like that, Mama," he said. "I'm sorry."

"Well if God can forgive a person, I can too."

"Yes ma'am," Ace said. "And after all that, I have to confess that I'm calling you with selfish motives."

"Now what would that be?"

"Actually, I was hoping I could come by this morning."

"I'll tell you like they've been saying at my church for years. My doors hang on welcome hinges."

"So I'll see you in an hour?" Ace hoped her morning was free. He was already dressed and only wanted to make a run to the dry cleaners and drug store before heading to her side of town.

"That's fine," Mama Claudette said. "Have you eaten yet?"

Ace had already checked his bare refrigerator. The only thing in there suitable for breakfast was an orange and a container of blueberry yogurt that had expired three days ago. He'd planned to go grocery shopping before it was time for the girls to come over again. "Not yet," he admitted.

"Lord, I've already eaten breakfast and I'm thinking about what I'm going to cook for lunch. Come on and get you something that'll make your stomach happy."

Happy wasn't the word for it. Ace's stomach was ecstatic. Mama Claudette had laid out a spread to rival any chef's country breakfast. Ace couldn't pay for a meal like this, and he didn't remember the last time he'd eaten so much. It was the kind of food that called for a nap afterwards. Ace always had a light but fulfilling meal whenever he had to fly. He couldn't stay awake past take-off with a meal like this one.

Mama Claudette hadn't asked about the reason for his visit yet. She was scooping hash brown casserole on his plate faster than he could eat it. When he forked the last bite of scrambled eggs into his mouth, the screech of the back porch door announced his ex-father-in-law's arrival.

Pop Walter was wearing a navy blue Windbreaker outfit with dirt stains on the knees. He pulled off the cap that covered his thinning and receding hairline.

"What do we have here?" He pounded Ace on his back, then tossed his cap on one of the kitchen chairs.

Ace stood up and shook Pop's hand. "How are you doing, sir? You look like you've been out doing some work."

"Me and some of the other deacons did some yard work at the church." He looked at Ace's empty plate and the other dishes and empty pans in the sink that were left over from breakfast.

"Shoot. If I can get breakfast like this when you come over then you need to come every day."

"Now you know you need to stop," Mama Claudette said. She opened the refrigerator door and poured her husband a glass of orange juice, then handed him a small orange pill from a prescription bottle.

"If nobody else eats, you know you eat. And you eat good, too."

Pop rubbed his stomach. "Anybody can look at me and tell that." He pulled out a kitchen chair and pushed the lace placemat out of his way. He took a minute to find the local news section of the newspaper, before he directed his attention back to Ace.

"So why does my wife have you stuffed like a turkey at my kitchen table? You on your way to flying one of those missiles?"

Ace shared a chuckle with his former father-in-law. The conversation didn't seem so intimidating when Ace thought just he and Mama Claudette were going to be there. Pop's arrival had changed things. When it came to the women in his life, he was very protective. It had taken Ace a few months to break through his nonchalant exterior when he'd first started dating Lynette. But once Pop realized Ace had honorable intentions with his daughter, he became like a second father—rather like Ace's first father. Unfortunately after the divorce, their relationship had become more cordial. Man to man—there was no disrespect.

"So?" Pop said, folding the newspaper in half after he'd skimmed the first few pages.

All of a sudden Ace wished he could rewind the day and wait until Pop wasn't there . . . staring him in the face like he was an officer and Ace was a suspected criminal.

Mama Claudette broke the tension by coming behind Ace and rubbing his shoulders. It made Ace think about what Lynette had done the night he had to have the talk with Carmen. There was approval in her touch, and Ace knew that Mama Claudette knew what he was about to say.

"I was hoping I could talk to you all about Lynette," Ace said.

"Lynette?" Pop pushed his chair back and crossed his arms over his ample stomach. "What's going on with her? I just talked to her last night and everything seemed fine."

"It's more so about me. And Lynette. Together."

"Together?"

Mama Claudette let out a sigh. "My God, You're so good," she whispered, shaking her head.

Pop looked at his wife like she'd been withholding a secret from him. "One of y'all needs to tell me something."

"I'm finding out things from Ace the same time that you are," Mama Claudette said. "But I've got a heavenly Father who tells me things, too." She pointed her finger skyward. "And He's been whispering some things in my ear that are happening right before my eyes."

Ace was relieved. He could always depend on Grandma Toot and Mama Claudette to confirm something he was concerned with in his spirit. At that very moment, looking at Pop didn't seem so daunting.

"There's actually no 'us' yet, but I'm hoping it will be ... again."

"So you're telling me you want to get back with my baby?" Pop asked.

"Yes, sir."

"And what makes you so sure she wants you back?" His mouth was a tight line across his face.

"I'm not sure. But I'm willing to take the chance. What do I have to lose?"

"Another woman for one thing," Pop said. "I thought you had a lady friend for a while. At least that's what the girls told me."

"We're not together anymore," Ace said quickly. He shifted in the chair.

"Since when?"

Ace thought about it. He wasn't sure when his relationship with Sheila was officially declared over. This conversation was about to take a nosedive. He looked over at Mama Claudette, hoping she'd offer some help. Nothing.

"I don't see how you can jump out of one relationship and right back into another." Pop leaned forward. "I don't want my daughter being some kind of rebound woman."

Ace couldn't blame Pop for his concerns. They were all very legitimate.

"What does Lynette feel about all this?" Pop asked, not waiting for Ace's response.

Mama Claudette moved from behind Ace and sat at the chair beside him. He thought she was coming to his rescue, but she still didn't say anything. When Ace looked at her, he saw an unassuming smile on her face.

"I haven't talked to her."

Pop was dropping questions before Ace could finish his sentence. "Have you tried?"

If only he knew how much, Ace thought. "Yes, but she won't talk to me right now."

Ace took it upon himself to recount the incident at the airport since he was sure Pop would drill it out of him sooner or later.

"You and Lynette got yourself to this point. By getting divorced, I mean."

Ace took a drink of his juice and wiped his brow. Sometimes Pop gave pills that could be hard to swallow.

"Divorce isn't what I wanted for you all in the first place," Pop continued.

"Yes, sir. I wish I would've . . ." Ace shook his head. The last thing he wanted to do was cry, especially in front of Pop. *Man up,* he told himself. "I hope God will let me make it right."

"You've got to do more than hope. You've got to believe it. And you've got to put some action behind it."

Ace looked his ex-father-in-law in the eyes. He needed to know he'd do right by his daughter. This time forever.

"Yes, sir. I believe. And I'm prepared to do what it'll take."

Mama Claudette stood up and pushed in the kitchen chair. She cleared the table and set the dishes in a sink full of sudsy water.

"God will let you make it right, and Lynette will, too. She might be scared, but who can blame her?" Mama Claudette ran the dishrag across the table and counters, swooping the crumbs into her hand. "God is dealing with her right now. I'm not a gambling woman, but I'd put money on that."

"Long as it's not my offering money, woman," Pop said, rearing back on the legs of the chair. "I don't want to have to put you out."

Mama Claudette lifted the cordless phone from its cradle on the wall. "I know that's not gonna happen," she told her husband. "I'm the only woman in the world that wants you," she said, dialing a phone number. "Besides, I've spent too much time training you and I've almost got you like I want you. That's forty-two years of hard work that's not going to go to waste."

Pop stood up and pulled his wife into an embrace. He kissed her round cheek. "Neither one of us are going anywhere, so stop all your yapping," he said. He extended his hand to Ace as a sign of support. "I'm with you. God be with you, too." He chuckled. "Especially with my daughter."

With that, Ace watched him gather his things and leave a trail of dirt that fell off his shoe soles as he walked down the hall.

"Lynette," Mama Claudette was saying into the phone. "Call me when you're on the way home. I want to come by and drop something off. I have a special delivery."

Ace was already feeling better. He knew Mama Claudette would deliver more than just a package. She was going to leave some sound advice with her daughter, too. And if Ace had his way, some serious prayer as well.

"Thank you, Mama Claudette," he said, once she'd hung up the phone. "I appreciate you talking to Lynette for me."

"Oh, I'm not going to do the talking. You are."

Chapter 41

Ace wasn't usually the kind of man to have people step in and handle his business. But this wasn't the usual case. Mama Claudette wouldn't do anything that God hadn't led her to do. And if Lynette's heart had really grown rock hard toward him—impenetrable to his love—there was no way Mama Claudette would allow his ego to get crushed. Besides, if anyone could melt a cold heart, God's love could.

"I can see why you like this car," Mama Claudette said. "It rides so smooth that you can't tell how fast you're going." Mama Claudette peered over at the odometer and Ace instinctively lifted his foot off the gas pedal.

Mama Claudette began to experiment with the buttons on her seat. "Of course you're probably going to have to trade it in. Those girls' legs grow longer by the day."

"We'll take it one day at a time," Ace mumbled.

Ace couldn't think that far ahead. He'd been fighting doubt over the last few hours since Mama Claudette had made the call. It was funny how those thoughts of doubt started to creep in when he was alone. To help the hours of the day pass quickly, Ace had driven all over the city like he was a tourist who'd never stepped foot in the state of Georgia. Before coming back to the Moreheads' home, he'd spent time in the parking lot of a church down the street. He'd driven to a nearby park and shot hoops on the basketball court. Then he'd found himself leafing through greeting cards at the corner drug store, hoping someone had written something that could translate the feelings in his heart to words on a page.

Nothing.

His words would have to be pure, not manufactured.

Ace sat at the stop sign for a few moments before turning on the street to Lynette's house. He used to sit at this same spot when they were going through tough times—wondering if he should go home or turn and ride around until he was sure Lynette was asleep. Sometimes sleep was the only thing that kept them from arguing.

Once again, Ace was at a crossroads in more ways than one.

Mama Claudette didn't say a word. In fact, it seemed she wasn't paying much attention to his hesitancy, but was busy putting stamps on a stack of envelopes she'd pulled from her purse.

Ace took a deep breath and turned left. He pulled into Lynette's driveway and parked his car on the side of the house. He hoped neither Lynette nor the girls had seen them drive up. The element of surprise would work in his favor.

Mama Claudette reached out for his hand, giving it a little squeeze.

"It'll be fine. Say whatever God gives you to say. You can't be fazed by Lynette's initial reaction and what you *think* is on her mind."

"Yes, ma'am," he said, soaking in her advice. He wondered if the words applied if Lynette slammed the door in his face. He'd gotten that a time or two from her before.

Ace tried to use Kenny's advice and stay away from constantly replaying what had happened in the past.

He opened his door then went around and did the same for Mama Claudette. He let her lead the way to the door, then purposely stood away from the view out of the peephole.

Ace heard Lynette's voice before the door opened.

"It's your grandmother," she said to the girls. "I've got the door, you finish your homework."

"Mama?" Lynette said, turning the latch.

"Yes, it's me. I know you can see me through that peephole."

As many times as Ace had stood on the front porch landing, he'd never been this nervous. He was about to get the answer to the question he'd been asking himself for months. Ace hoped it would be what he wanted to hear.

Lynette opened the door.

Chapter 42

Lynette didn't see Ace immediately. Her mother gave her a kiss on the cheek as she scooted by her. That itself was a surprise. Kisses were reserved for birthdays and extremely sentimental moments.

Ace stepped into her view and Lynette realized the reason for her mother's kiss. It had said, *"I'm sorry. I had to do it. You'll thank me later."*

Ace stood so still that he looked like one of the decorative cement lions that sat guarding both sides of the doorway.

He looked at her. She looked at him.

Lynette heard her daughters' voices talking to her mother upstairs, leaving her alone with Ace. Putting her back where they'd been before Sheila had walked up at the airport.

"So you're the special delivery?" Lynette asked with a slight smile. She stepped aside so he could come in.

"According to Mama Claudette."

Lynette led Ace to the sunken den area. She's expected him to sit on the love seat facing her, but he shared the couch with her instead.

"I was going to call you tonight," she said, truthfully. Conviction had reminded her how she'd felt when Frank had avoided her calls. "It wasn't the most mature thing to dodge your calls and ignore your messages, but I had to shut everybody out. I've had quite a few things to think about."

"I hope one of those things was *us*," Ace said, his eyes hopeful.

"Yes," she said. It was the only thing. But there were so many layers to that word, "us." Each time she peeled one back, she exposed another part of her heart. Lynette had cried about what they once were—good and bad. About what they were now. And at possibilities of what could be. Or if it even *should* be.

Lynette sat up straight and tried to put on a professional air. "Nothing is worth talking about if you're still with Sheila."

"Sheila and I aren't together."

"I'm not trying to be your rebound woman."

"You sound like your dad. There's nothing rebound about this."

He talked to my father, too? "Well you need to go through a detox or something. How do you think you can leave a relationship you've been in for two years and try to rebuild something with me? If that's even what you want."

Lynette stood up and walked over to the fireplace. She had to put some distance between them. "We're making a lot of silent assumptions about *us*," she said, making her fingers into quote marks.

"I talked to Sheila yesterday. I had to put some closure on it."

"And it's over just like that. No drama? No tears?"

"Of course there was, Lynette. But I'm not here to talk about me and Sheila. I can't say she's not ever going to call me and talk about getting back together. I can't say she can turn her feelings off like a light switch. I can only speak for myself."

"So you've turned your feelings, emotions . . . your love . . . off

234

". . . just like that?" Lynette walked around the perimeter of the room. God was making her face this situation in person instead of hiding behind the telephone.

God, protect my heart, Lynette prayed. *I'm mad right now. He went ahead with his life, and now he thinks he can come back into mine on a whim. I thought it was what I wanted. But is it really?*

Ace hadn't said anything. He had his head down between his hands, and it seemed like he was praying just as hard as she was. He didn't look up until she sat back down beside him on the couch.

"Talk to me," Lynette said. "I want to know what you want."

Ace turned toward her, and once again, they were back in the bustle at the airport. God kept taking her back there, like He was telling her they needed to confront the things that made them grow apart in the first place. Their careers. His travel.

"I want you," he said, with a certainty in his voice.

Lynette exhaled.

They'd come full circle. The last time they'd sat together on this couch was when they'd had a family meeting to tell the girls that Ace wouldn't be moving back in. The painful memories rushed back in for Lynette. They'd put off the discussion at least three times in an effort to protect the girls. First, there was spring break. Then they'd decided to wait until after Jada's birthday. Then, they postponed the talk because Carmen had to get her tonsils out.

On the day they decided that they couldn't delay any longer, even the clouds seem to hang lower in the sky. Although the earlier part of that week had been ideal spring weather, that Wednesday's weather was overcast and gloomy. Ominous clouds rolled over the city soon after Lynette picked the girls up from school and they'd barely made it into the garage when the sky opened up. Instead of pushing them to do their homework as soon as they walked in the door like she usually did, Lynette let them watch television. While she watched them from the stool in the kitchen, she realized that this day would be one that they'd unfortunately never forget.

When Ace rang the doorbell, it seemed to take a hundred steps for Lynette to get to the front door. Seeing their father, the girls jumped up and ran into his arms. He led them to the couch, and began the talk that would change who they were as a family. Tears fell from everyone's eyes that night and Carmen's and Jada's appetites seemed to walk out with Ace when he closed the door. Without dinner, they climbed into Lynette's bed and she held them until morning.

"Did you hear what I said?" Ace asked. "I want *you*. I want us to have a second chance."

"All of this is too sudden," Lynette said.

"It's not sudden. In fact, it didn't happen soon enough. I know what God spoke to me, and I know He's been speaking the same to you, too. Are you willing to take a second chance?"

Although they'd been physically apart, it was starting to feel like God had still grown them together. The closer to Him they'd become, they'd built a foundation for "them."

Lynette could hear Carmen and Jada upstairs talking to their grandmother. She wasn't just answering for herself.

"What do you want me to say?" Lynette said.

"Say yes. I want you to say yes," Ace said as a single tear rolled down his cheek.

Time stood still.

Chapter 43

Yes," Lynette said, before her emotions and her mind's trip to the past could talk her out of it.

Ace stood and pulled her to her feet. They held in an embrace and it felt so much like their wedding day, except there were no spectators. This moment—as scary as it was—had been reserved for the two of them alone.

Time began again. "I'm scared," Lynette admitted. "I don't know what this all means. I don't know how we're supposed to pick up the pieces."

"We're not going to try and put any pieces back together," Ace said. "Let's start from a new beginning and with a whole life that we can build together. Not fragments."

Lynette suddenly felt the urge to explain where she was in life. "I'm not the same person that I was four years ago. And I must admit, I've grown used to doing things on my own. And doing it all my way, and you too, I'm sure. How are we supposed to handle that?"

"One day at a time," Ace said.

Joy rose in Lynette's belly. She started laughing. "And you had the nerve to bring my Mama over here? Now that's a desperate man," she said.

"No. Your mama brought *me* over here," Ace said. "And you can call me desperate if you want to. Because I was. And if being desperate can help keep you this time, then I'll carry that title with honor."

Lynette sighed. In her mind, their history was trying to steal their moment. "It's not going to be easy," she said. "We've got some issues we need to work through and it's going to take some counseling."

"I agree. And I'll go for as long as it will take," Ace said. "But let me tell you one thing that I'm sure of. This won't be a long process."

"You sound so sure."

"I *am* sure," Ace said.

"You have to be if you talked to both of my parents. Is there anyone else I need to know about?" Lynette asked.

"Kenny. But that should be no surprise to you. Just like I wouldn't be surprised if you told me you've been talking to Audrey. Because I know you have."

"Did she say something to you?"

"I told you. Me and God have been having some serious discussions. It's nothing like hearing from God so clearly late in the midnight hour. If He won't let you sleep, it's usually because He's got something to say."

"I've got my own set of bags under the eyes that will say 'Amen' to that," Lynette said.

A shrill of laughter came from upstairs. Hearing the music turned up so high, Lynette could imagine that her mother was either twisting up the words to some of the girls' favorite songs, or she was doing her trusty two-step dance.

"What about the girls?"

"It will be a transition for them, too. But God's got us, Lynette. I have faith in that," Ace assured her. He twined his fingers into hers. "Don't trust me on this one," he whispered. "Trust God."

Lynette looked up into Ace's eyes. She knew they shared the same concerns over putting their hearts on the line again. But at least she wouldn't have to walk around for the rest of her life wondering what could've been.

Ace answered her innermost thoughts. He used a finger to lift her chin, then kissed her. On the cheek. Softly. Then tenderly on the lips, as if doing so any harder would make her shatter into a million little pieces.

Chapter 44

Ace hadn't answered Sheila's last three calls or text messages. She'd given him five days to see the error of his ways on his own, but it looked like she was going to have to remind him of what he'd lucked up on by meeting her. Ace had said plenty of times that she was a blessing in his life. How did that change so fast? If Sheila could convince him to come over so they could talk, she felt sure that she could change his mind with one conversation.

Sheila opened up her trunk and added another shopping bag to the other bounty she'd collected during her lunch break. If Ace wouldn't come to her, she'd go to him—armed with all of his favorite things. The salesperson at the Christian bookstore helped her pick out a devotional for men. She knew he kept one in his flight bag that he'd been carrying since she'd known him, but it was one that Lynette had given to him when they were still married. She'd seen the inscription in it before. This one was new and crisp, and written by one of the prominent preachers she always saw on television.

Then there were the jars of his favorite Dole All Natural fruit that she would position perfectly in front of the two books of word and logic puzzles. Pilots needed to keep a sharp mind, he'd said. But Sheila's favorite gifts were the three Armani ties. She could picture Ace wearing one to church, and she'd go with him in an outfit that perfectly coordinated with the tie of his choice. He'd appreciate the ties, but probably not as much as he was going to be impressed by the portable GPS system. That was the thing that would seal the deal. He'd mentioned more than once that he should've added the amenity to his car. Now he wouldn't have to.

To top it off, Sheila planned to write him a love letter like she used to do when he had to fly out internationally and be away from her for a few days. In it, she'd tell him that they could travel the world together. She would give him the love that he deserved— now and forever. Sheila would give herself. All of herself. Whatever made Ace happy.

Sheila tossed her Louis Vuitton clutch on the passenger's seat and threw her car in reverse. She'd spent all of her lunch hour running errands and needed to get back in the office before the one-thirty meeting that Clive had called. If the highway construction workers had taken a break and the downtown street lights were timed right, she could walk in the building with five minutes to spare. She hadn't had time to eat. Her appetite was still virtually nonexistent, but she'd come to look at it as a blessing. The three pounds she'd lost over the past week was what she'd needed to get back into most of her suits without having to squeeze into the breath-constricting body shaper she'd bought.

"You are kidding me," Sheila screamed, when she noticed that the free-flowing traffic had come to a complete halt. She immediately reached into her clutch for her BlackBerry and called Clive's office phone. When he didn't answer, she sent him a text message.

SORRY. STUCK IN TRAFFIC. BE THERE ASAP.

Sheila scrolled through her messages, praying that she hadn't missed the message alert and that Ace had finally sent her a response to her call. There wasn't a message from Ace, but there was one from Cassandra.

MY FIRST TASK WITH "THE EX" IS COMPLETE. SHE'S GOT A SURPRISE WAITING FOR HER.

"Oh no, what in the world did she do?" Sheila said aloud, hitting the speed-dial number for Cassandra.

"You got my text message, huh?" Cassandra said when she answered the phone. "I've completed my first task so I hope you're working on your end with Ace."

"What do you mean your first task? What did you do?"

"I slit her tires."

Sheila braked so a merging car could squeeze in front of her. She didn't know what the driver's hurry was. They were all stuck. "You slit her tires? Are you serious?"

"Yes."

"How did you do that?"

"I looked up her office on the Internet and staked out her building." Cassandra said it like it was something she did every day.

"How can you stake out a building in broad daylight? No," Sheila shook her head, not believing what she was hearing. "How could you *slit tires* in broad daylight?"

"Don't worry about how I take care of my business. You make sure you're taking care of yours."

Sheila thought of the bags in her trunk. "I am. I'll talk to you later," she said, as she inched closer to her exit.

Sheila started to feel bad. She had no idea what kinds of things Cassandra had planned, but at least the tires were replaceable, she rationalized. It's not like Lynette didn't have the money to take care of it. As long as Cassandra didn't inflict any bodily harm on anyone, then these small acts of revenge were forgivable.

The usual ten-minute drive had sucked twenty-five minutes out of Sheila's day. All heads turned toward her in sync when she tipped into the conference room.

"Nice of you to join us," Clive said, between the PowerPoint slides he was reviewing.

"Traffic," Sheila explained. "I sent you a text message," she said, uncapping her Montblanc pen. As she rolled the leather high-back chair closer to the conference table, her ringing phone interrupted Clive's presentation. She pushed the button to silence the ring tone, and noticed that it was Ace returning her call.

Shoot, she thought to herself. There was no way she could leave the room without Clive taking pleasure in embarrassing her in front of her coworkers. She'd already overheard her name once that week at the watercooler. Sheila didn't care. That would change soon. In fact, in an act of celebration for her renewed relationship, she'd entice their sweet tooth with a box of fresh Krispy Kreme Donuts in the morning.

The icon popped up on Sheila's screen symbolizing that Ace had left a message. Right about now Clive could make any comment that he wanted. Nothing could douse the feeling of euphoria welling up inside. Sheila was ready to make up for the days she'd been without Ace. She'd study her Bible more and go to church more regularly—even when Ace was on duty and couldn't go with her. He'd see that she could be a blessing again.

Sheila felt an upsurge of energy the rest of the day, and by the time she was ready to go home, her appetite had returned. And so had Clive.

"What do you do? Wait until you hear me leaving so you can walk out at the same time I do?" she said, surprised at the flirtation in her voice.

"You would only be so lucky, little girl," Clive said, eyeing her like a piece of devil's food cake.

"What?"

"You need to stay on your game," he warned. "You've been fore-warned that staff reductions were on the horizons. Now is not the time to be irresponsible and do things like come late to my meeting."

"I sent you a text message when I couldn't get you. I thought that would suffice."

"Look at the big picture, Sheila. It's not all about coming correct with me. People take note about all the little things. Big people in big places."

Sheila looked at her watch. She'd prefer to be on her way out the door so that she could get refreshed for when Ace called her back. She was sure he'd want to come over, or if he was too tired, she was more than willingly to take the trip out near Camp Creek to see him. He'd left hope for her in his message.

Hi, Sheila. I got your voice mails but I've been on duty. I'll call you tonight when I get home. Hope you're doing okay. All right. Talk to you later.

"Do you have somewhere to go?" Clive asked.

"Home would be nice," Sheila said. "And possibly some other places."

"Would one of those other places include going to dinner with me?"

Sheila resisted the urge to roll her eyes. "No, Clive."

"You owe me one, and you don't even know it," he said. "Don't forget it."

Sheila couldn't entertain whatever Clive was insinuating. *I do everything in my power to forget everything about this place as soon as I close my office door,* she thought. *And Clive always wants to add to my stress.*

"I'll see you in the morning, Clive," Sheila said.

"If I were you, I'd be the first person in the office," he suggested.

Sheila ignored him. She had to get ready to see Ace tonight. And when he saw her, he would forget there had ever been a Lynette. Ever.

Chapter 45

What do you mean, no?" Sheila asked, plopping down on her couch. "Why are you doing this to me, Ace?"

"I'm not doing anything to you, Sheila," Ace said from the other end of the phone line. "I'm helping you to move on. If we see each other, then it'll make things harder for you."

"Harder for me? This is all for *me*? After two years it seems like you'd have some hurt somewhere in your heart."

"Of course I do. This wasn't planned. But I realize that you can't wallow in the past when you get to a point that you have to move on."

Sheila wasn't happy with the way this evening was unfolding. She found a bottle of ibuprofen in her purse and popped two pills. "Well you have to convince me this wasn't planned," she said, "because it seems like you're moving on too easily."

Ace didn't respond. Silence was never a good thing when talking to Ace. It usually meant there was some truth to her statements.

"You've moved on," Sheila said. "And I know it's with Lynette. There's no telling how long you were planning to launch your game plan. Why don't you just admit it?"

Sheila heard Ace moving around in the background. It sounded like he was rambling around in the pantry to find something to eat. This conversation meant nothing to him. She'd come home and taken a bath with cucumber and green tea shower gel and coated her skin with a moisturizing lotion of the same scent. She'd slipped on her perfect pair of jeans with a soft pink camisole tank top and made sure his signature basket was flawless. She'd even written her love note to him on monogrammed stationery and spritzed Dolce & Gabbana Light Blue on the matching envelope. And Ace . . . was looking for food.

Sheila tried another tactic. "You have some things over here that you need to pick up."

"Like what?"

"I can't name everything that you've left over here in the last two years, Ace. I'll put them in a box and you can come pick them up."

"If I don't remember what it is then I probably don't need it. I don't mind if you want to donate the things or throw them out. What you do with the stuff is up to you."

"Are you sure?" she asked.

"Positive. Sheila, I need to go," Ace said. "I have some things to take care of before I hit the sack."

"Give me a call tomorrow," she said. She needed to keep some line of communication open with Ace. She realized that she couldn't bombard her way back into his life; it had to be a progressive effort.

"I won't be doing that, Sheila," Ace said. "I can't. It'll be easier this way."

"Evidently you don't know how this is affecting me or else you wouldn't say that," she said, playing on Ace's compassionate side. If the guilt card was the only thing she had to play, she'd slap it on the table. And Sheila made sure he heard her heavy sobbing. Ace needed to know what she was going through and she wanted him to carry it with him long after they hung up the phone.

"Sheila." Ace's voice was softer now.

Sheila didn't answer him until he called her name a second time.

"Yes?" she said, sniffing her nose. Soggy wads of crumpled tissue were at her side and she'd almost made it to the bottom of another box of Kleenex.

"Would you like for me to pray with you?"

"Yes," she said. She *did* need prayer. Ace's prayers had always had a way of calming the rocking of the boat on the stormy seas of life she'd had to endure. He'd always come to her rescue. And right now, she was willing to take his hand and walk out on the water together. If her tears couldn't get to him, she knew God's voice would.

God, please tell him to stay, Sheila said in a silent prayer.

"God I come to You on behalf of Your child, Sheila. Above all else she needs You now. Sometimes things happen in our lives that we don't expect, but there are no surprises to You. Help her to see that there's not a man—not even me—that can complete her. In Jesus' name we pray. Amen."

These weren't the words she wanted to hear, and she was sure these weren't the words God wanted Ace to say.

As soon as Ace finished the prayer, his phone beeped with another call.

"Hold on a second," Ace said.

See, he does *want to talk to me,* Sheila thought. *He's just trying to play hard to get. He wants me to stick around so that he'll see that I'm truly committed to him.* Sheila got up and went into the living room. It was spotless and staged like it was a model home. Although she couldn't eat when she was dealing with a situation, she usually had urges to clean. She'd scrubbed the kitchen counters and

247

backsplash with a green-friendly cleanser she'd ordered off of an infomercial the other night when she couldn't sleep. The stainless steel appliances sparkled like they'd done when they'd first arrived on the truck from the appliance store.

"Sheila?" Ace clicked back over to the line and the calmness he'd had in his voice after their prayer had left his voice.

"What's wrong?" Sheila said in a panic. If Ace needed her, she'd be there before he could hang up the phone.

"Do you know anything about Lynette's tires being slashed?"

"What? Why would I slash Lynette's tires? I have better things to do with my time."

"It seems funny that she's never experienced anything like that before."

"Ace." She called his name like he was a child being reprimanded by his irritated mother. "I didn't slash Lynette's tires."

"I hope you wouldn't stoop that low," Ace said. "Because if you did, then I'm glad that our relationship ended when it did. It may take a while, but the wool will always fall off of a wolf in sheep's clothing."

Ace had never in their time together spoken like that to her. It was like another person rose up in him when he thought that someone had wronged Lynette. Sheila didn't like that he'd spit words like fire toward her, and she hated that he was so obviously protective of his ex-wife.

"Don't try to accuse me of doing something I didn't do," Sheila said.

"I apologize for accusing you if I don't have any evidence, but I don't apologize for what I said. Because I meant it."

Sheila calmed herself down. Her hands were beginning to shake. She couldn't let Ace hang up the phone with dissension between them.

"I'm sorry that Lynette's property was damaged. I hope she's able to take care of everything without too much trouble. I can imagine that was a big inconvenience, especially with having to deal with the girls and all."

"It's taken care of now," Ace said.

Sheila relaxed. It seemed that he wasn't as worked up as he'd been moments before, and at least her words had calmed him down. He'd been like a volcano about to erupt.

"I have to go now," Ace said. "Take care, Sheila. Everything will be fine."

"You promise?" she asked.

"No. But God does." Then Ace hung up.

Sheila turned on the television. At least she hadn't lied. She hadn't touched Lynette's tires, and she had no control of the things Cassandra decided to do. Sheila's assignment was strictly with Ace. And despite what he'd suggested earlier, she had no intentions of putting his things out for Friday morning's trash pickup or dropping it off at a donation center. When he came back, he'd appreciate that she could see past his rash decisions. She closed her eyes the way she'd done after that pastor's sermon on faith; and she envisioned them together again. After a long flight duty, he'd return home and she would be waiting for him. Unlike the last nightmare that had interrupted her dream, Lynette *wouldn't* be there.

Sheila's face lit up. She thanked God for suddenly reminding her of another reason why Ace wasn't serious about them breaking up forever. He didn't ask for the one possession that made the biggest difference in their relationship. On the day he'd given it to her, Sheila knew she was more than another phone number in his cell phone. He'd given her the thing that bachelors coveted more than their cars. The key to his house.

Chapter 46

Lynette's roadside service had taken care of her slashed tires before the last patient walked out of the door. Thankfully, it was already arranged that the girls were being picked up by her mother so they could attend Bible study. They were having a nontraditional worship service for the youth and part of the service included a virtuous girl's fashion show that Carmen had helped coordinate, and a step show that Jada was going to participate in.

Her mother was shocked that only Lynette's tires had been slashed in a parking lot full of cars—and in the middle of the day at that. Just like Lynette, her mother had pointed her finger at Sheila.

"She didn't seem like the kind of woman who would do something like that," Lynette said. She'd been sitting behind her closed office doors during lunchtime and asked Tonia to bring her back a sub sandwich from the local deli.

"True character isn't revealed in the good times; it shows up when life is tough. You've never had anybody do something crazy like that, and believe me, it wasn't a random act."

"I know that's true, Mama. So what am I supposed to do about her?"

"Call Ace," she said. "She's his problem."

"If she slashed my tires then she's *my* problem," Lynette said.

The idea of the entire act infuriated Lynette. When she'd first seen her rims sitting on the asphalt surrounded by lifeless lumps of rubber, she had to make a conscious decision not to curse.

Ace hadn't been able to control his anger and withhold his words in the same way. When he told Lynette that he had Sheila on the other line, her first emotional reaction was anger.

She thought Ace had said he'd put closure on their relationship, so she didn't understand why he had to talk to Sheila for any reason. Then her emotional reaction quickly switched to insecurity. It wasn't simple to dissolve a two-year relationship with one conversation. She should've known that Sheila wouldn't bow out and retreat to the corner.

Lynette came to a realization at that moment. The fight she should've used to keep her marriage together the first time may very well be what she may have to use to put it back together this time. And her winning blow to knock out the enemy would come through prayer.

Lynette could either react to the situation like Sheila wanted her to, or she could respond to it. She chose to respond. *This* time, she'd swat this little distraction away like the gnat that it was. She'd fly like that bumblebee and not care or worry about what others did or had to say about the situation. *This* time. God help her.

It was at least ten minutes before Wednesday evening Bible study was supposed to start, and Lynette was content sitting in her car to unwind from her busy day. She turned off the rush-hour gospel mix that the evening DJ had serenaded her with during the drive and sat in complete silence. Until the tap on her window. It was Kelly Rush.

It wouldn't have surprised Lynette if Kelly had been the first person to arrive at midweek Bible study. Her last name was fitting to her personality, and Lynette had never seen a time when Kelly's feet—and mouth for that matter—weren't moving eighty-seven miles per hour. Even though she could be worrisome, Lynette had to give it to Kelly—she was faithfully committed to the ministry.

Lynette let down her window.

"Lynette, I'm so glad I spotted you," Kelly said, with the remains of a red and white peppermint bouncing around in her mouth. "I've been sitting in my car trying to work out the workshop schedule for the single women's retreat. I know we're supposed to relax and have a good time, but we need to refresh ourselves spiritually, too."

"You're right," Lynette said, leaning her head back against the headrest. She hoped that Kelly would take the hint that she could use some relaxation right now.

"We still have a few minutes before Bible study starts if you want to go over this now," she suggested, and waved her yellow file folder in the air.

Kelly took it upon herself to go around to the passenger's door. Lynette hit the lock and bid farewell to her ten-minute power nap. Then again, this could be a good thing. If she took care of her duties now, Kelly wouldn't hound her about another meeting for at least two weeks.

The retreat was actually going to be an astounding weekend event, especially since Kelly had infused it with her bubbly personality—there was the Big Hat Brunch and the Divine Diva Dinner to name a few events. Lynette felt guilty that she hadn't put as much into the planning as she should have. Her contribution was to teach a short session about dental health and how your teeth played a part in a person's overall physical health. But by the end of the ten minutes, Kelly's excitement had rubbed off on her and Lynette volunteered to facilitate a pajama chat session with the ladies.

"One minute until seven." Kelly stacked her planning sheets into her folder and shoved it in her shoulder bag with her pink Bible. "We better get inside."

"I'll be inside in a minute," Lynette said, as she heard her cell phone ringing. "Thanks for being so organized, Kelly. That's a gift that you should use all the time."

Kelly's face beamed. "Now that's confirmation from God," she said, "because I was thinking about starting a virtual assistant and personal concierge business."

"Go for it," Lynette encouraged. "I'd hire you."

"I'm going to hold you to that." Kelly pushed the car door closed with her hip and headed toward the church. She waved excitedly at a member who was wrestling a Spiderman action figure out of the tight clench of her toddler son's hands.

Lynette picked up the cell phone, hoping it was Ace who was calling her. That would've been the perfect punctuation to end her day. But instead, it was a call from Frank.

"He's got to be kidding," Lynette said to herself, turning her cell phone to silent. She tossed her phone in the glove compartment and opened the car door. She felt an unexpected tug on the door as she started to step her foot out. Lynette turned. She braced herself to land an upper hook to the jaw in the name of self-defense. Slashed tires were enough for one day.

"Whoa," Ace said, stepping back. "You looked like you were about to knock my head off."

"I was prepared to do so if I needed to," Lynn said, relaxing her shoulders. "You shouldn't roll up on a woman like that. Especially one that's had her tires slashed today."

Ace held out his hand and helped Lynette out of the car. She never thought she'd see the day when they would be standing on the same church grounds again. Mount Pisgah was where they'd grown together as a family. It had been Lynette's church since birth, and half of the congregation was comprised of her aunts, uncles, and cousins—distant and close. During her and Ace's separation and impending divorce, it was hard to go through the dissolution of her marriage when it was so obvious to her family. It was like the 800-pound gorilla that parked itself beside her on the purple-cushioned pews on Sundays. They didn't want to disrupt her worship experience with talk of her domestic problems, yet they didn't want to seem like they didn't care.

It was an unspoken fact that Ace had been sorely missed. She could imagine that heads would turn when he walked in the sanctuary. That is, if he was coming inside.

"Are you coming in or did you come by to check on me?"

"Both. Is that okay?"

"Of course," Lynette said, glad that she'd taken a change of clothes and her toiletries bag to work. Her entire perception of herself had changed since she and Ace decided to work on their relationship. Lynette found herself making the extra effort to pamper herself, even on rushed weekday mornings.

She wondered if it had anything to do with the fact that Sheila always looked so impeccable whenever Lynette saw her. How was she supposed to compete with that? She most certainly couldn't do it wearing Minnie Mouse scrubs and a lab coat on a regular basis.

Ace was dressed in a pair of jeans—Lynette knew he'd asked for medium starch at the dry cleaners—and a striped button-down shirt. *Talk about looking good,* Lynette thought.

"I thought maybe we could talk to the girls together after service," Ace said. "I know they're having their special youth service in the community room tonight. Jada told me."

"You want to talk to the girls, *here?* At church? Ingenious."

Lynette chuckled. "Corner them in a place where they're sure to be on their best behavior."

"We're going to need all the help from God we can get. But like I told you before—and I truly believe it—God's got us. And honestly, I don't think the girls are going to have a hard time."

"That's my prayer," Lynette said. "Sometimes with them and their hormonal teenage stages you don't know what you're going to get. Especially with Carmen."

"Don't expect the worst. Expect the best," Ace said, opening the doors leading into the vestibule.

The faithful few who attended midweek Bible study were already settled in the sanctuary. As was customary on Bible study nights, someone was appointed to recap Sunday's announcements before praise and worship began. Lynette expected Ace to turn down the right side hall and head to the community center so that he could sit in the back and secretly enjoy Carmen and Jada's performances. But he didn't.

"You're coming inside the main sanctuary?" Lynette asked.

"Isn't that what you're supposed to do? I didn't drive all this way to sit in my car."

"You know we're bound to get some looks as soon as we open these doors?"

"These are your kinfolks," Ace said. "Let them get all their looks in now because this is a picture they're going to have to get used to seeing again."

Lynette blushed. It was nice to feel special and desired again.

Lynette walked inside and she and Ace took their seat on the same pew as her cousin Corinne. She could tell Corinne was trying to restrain herself from running around the church with her hands in the air. Corinne had always said that she never believed that it was meant for Lynette and Ace to get divorced. "You'll get back together one day," she'd told her once.

Back then Lynette had rejected even the thought of it. She didn't believe it then, and she could barely believe it now. She should have, though.

It's happening, she thought. Lynette opened her Bible and the pages fell open to the page she'd bookmarked last night before falling asleep. She'd been studying one of her favorite Scriptures, Jeremiah 29:11. "For I know the thoughts that I think toward you, says the Lord, thoughts of peace and not of evil, to give you a future and a hope."

Ace scooted over closer to Lynette and stretched his arm along the back of the pew.

"Did I tell you how good you look tonight?" he whispered. "Smell good, too."

"Keep your eyes and your nose to yourself," she whispered back.

Corinne pushed a folded scrap of paper into Lynette's palm. Lynette opened it and saw a smiley face and the words, *Ain't God good?*

Lynette stuck the paper in her purse. She looked over at Corinne and mouthed the words, "All the time." Last night Lynette had been reading about her future and hope. And this evening, she was sitting beside them.

Chapter 47

Ace felt like he'd never left Mount Pisgah. From the time he'd pulled into the parking lot of the church, a feeling of *home* had overtaken him. It was like God wanted to welcome him back—a prodigal husband—and let the first person he saw be the woman that he wanted the most. Lynette.

Ace admitted that things were moving fast—he was responsible for that. But once he knew he'd heard from God and once Lynette said yes to a second chance for them, he hadn't seen much reason to take things slow. True, there was counseling to be done, but other than that, nothing else was holding them back.

Ace balanced his Bible on his knee. He'd been soaking in every word from Pastor Neil like he needed it to breathe. He feasted on the Scripture, savoring the life it had given to him. Pastor Neil was a wonderful pastor, and an even more wonderful uncle. Ace knew him as Uncle Sanford, but whenever they were on church grounds, he always addressed him as Pastor Neil as a sign of respect.

Just like Lynette said, plenty of questioning looks had come his way. Yet there weren't any sneers and no one slit their eyes at him. Instead, there were smiles of approval and even a wink or two from the elderly women on the Mother's Board who'd noticed him when he went to place his envelope in the offering plate. Ace couldn't help but glance at the pulpit to see Pastor Neil's reaction. He did a double take when he noticed Ace, and the expression on his face said, "Hallelujah."

It had been intimidating to talk to Pastor Neil years ago when his marriage was on the rocks. Since the pastor was also Lynette's uncle, Ace sometimes felt his mouth was bridled and he couldn't fully express his frustrations with Lynette. Ace had been a more selfish person then. But like Lynette said, they were coming together as the people they were now and not as the ones they'd been.

Ace was a better man. He was confident of that. But the only person who'd probably argue the point was Sheila. His concern for her couldn't have been more sincere. If he looked at the situation through her teary eyes, he could see why she felt like she'd been dumped at the wayside with no regard for the two years she'd spent with him. He didn't want to see himself as insensitive when he knew that ultimately, her tears couldn't last forever.

Sheila would move on. There would be a man for her whose heart didn't end up longing for someone else. She'd have her dream of a husband and eventually children. It just wouldn't be with him.

After the benediction, Ace was briefly swarmed by some of the members—most of them Lynette's cousins. They didn't directly question the story behind his presence, but Ace knew they'd taken their assumptions to Lynette. Stolen glances. Tight embraces and whispers in Lynette's ear. At least the transition back to his church home would be an easy one.

Pastor Neil walked up with his Bible tucked under his arm. Wednesday nights were extremely informal and tonight he was wearing a pair of black jeans and a hunter green Polo shirt with the church's logo embroidered on the left pocket. Pastor Neil was equal to Ace in height, but years of enjoying the soul food that the Neil women were famous for—topped by his wife's skills in the kitchen—had made him a much rounder man. But the feature that surprised most people was his hazel eyes. No one else in his family had acquired that trait, and it was often joked that God gave him those eyes so that he could see what others couldn't see.

"If I wasn't in the house of the Lord I might think my old eyes were playing tricks on me," Pastor Neil said.

Ace reached out to shake Pastor Neil's hand, but the elder man nearly yanked Ace's arm out of the socket as he pulled him into a hug. His monstrous arms nearly squeezed the breath out of Ace.

"I give you permission to pinch me if you need to," Ace said. "But your eyes see as good as they always have."

Ace knew his attendance wasn't a complete surprise to Pastor Neil. Ace had personally gone to him when he decided to switch church homes. Pastor Neil had sat behind his cherrywood desk in the church study. On one side of his desk were three different translations of the Holy Bible and on the other were the study tools and resources he used as God led him to prepare his sermons. "You'll be back. Back in the church and back together with Lynette. What God has joined together, let no man put asunder."

Ace had walked out with doubt that evening, but sure enough the words Pastor Neil spoke were as clear as the cross hanging above the altar.

Pastor Neil gripped Ace's arms and shook him as if to rough him up a bit. That was the Uncle Sanford coming out of him.

"Yes, sir," he bellowed. "It's definitely you." He looked at his watch. "My wife's not feeling too well and I told her I wouldn't stay at the church all night so I have to go. But I expect to see you again soon."

Ace stuffed his hands in his pockets. "It'll be next Sunday before I can make it back because I'm about to fly out. But if Lynette is all right with me coming then I'll be here."

"I'm sure she'll be fine. If not, by the time I finish with her she will be," Pastor Neil said. "I have to take off my clergy collar and deal with her with an uncle's love sometimes."

Lynette walked up by her uncle's side. "You were born to be a pastor. You never have known how to whisper," she said, looking around. "Where's Mama and Daddy?"

"I think they're at home dealing with the same little bug that's got my wife in the bed tonight. You know how those nasty stomach viruses can be. And they can come out of nowhere."

"They didn't even call and tell me," Lynette fussed. "I wonder how the girls got here."

"I went and picked them up from Claudette's house after she got them from school." Pastor Neil sat a brown cap on his head. He'd worn the same style and color cap ever since the day Ace met him, and he always covered his head before he stepped outside, no matter the weather.

"I'll wait and call them in the morning," Lynette said, "so they can get their rest tonight."

Everyone had already made their way to the adjoining vestibule. Weekday Bible study was usually over by eight-thirty so that the people who needed to be at work the next morning wouldn't have an excuse to skip out. It wasn't like the time after Sunday services where the deacons had to shoo people out of the church so they could start to lock up. Tonight, the church building and the parking lot would soon be empty and dark.

"I better go and get the girls," Lynette said. "Sometimes they tend to forget they have school in the morning and I need to make sure they did all of their homework."

"Actually, I was still hoping we could have our talk with them," Ace said, then turned toward Pastor Neil. "Can you give us a few minutes to talk to the girls? We haven't told them there's about to be some changes in their lives. Again."

Pastor Neil dug into his back pocket and handed Ace a set of keys. "Stay as long as you want to. I'm counting on you to lock up, then give the keys to Lynette. I'll get them before Sunday, or if not, I've got plenty of spare keys."

"Thanks Uncle Sanford," Lynette said.

"Yes. Thanks," Ace said. "I just didn't want to put our talk off another day."

"And it looks like you won't have to put it off another minute either," Pastor Neil said, as the girls flung open the doors leading into the sanctuary.

"Daddy!" Jada squealed, then covered her mouth. She knew better than to yell inside the church, but it seemed the unexpectedness of seeing her father had overridden her respect for God's house. "What are you doing here?" she asked, right before a solemn expression replaced her excitement. "Is something wrong?" She looked at her Uncle Sanford.

"No," Lynette rushed to say.

"I—we—need to talk to you guys about something," Ace said.

Carmen leaned against the arm of the back pew. She was carrying an extra purse that was overstuffed with the CDs that Ace assumed she'd used for their fashion show. She was a lot like him in that she enjoyed music. And although she preferred contemporary gospel, she wasn't opposed to listening to some of her grandmother's Shirley Caesar when the mood hit her.

"Why do we have to talk here? Can't you come to our house, Daddy? Everybody is already gone, and—"

Lynette cut her off. "Sit down, Carmen. We're talking here because your dad said so."

"Yes ma'am." Carmen surrendered without another word.

Ace and Lynette sat on the pew in front of their children. He cleared his throat. "Your mama and I wanted to talk to you because we believe that God is putting our family back together."

Jada jumped forward in the pew. "You mean you're going to get married again?" she said, like she could already see herself as a maid of honor. "I knew something was happening. I just knew it. After we saw Ms. Sheila at the airport that day, I could tell she was kinda upset about something, and—"

Ace shut down her chatter by holding up his hand.

"I know this seems to be happening fast. Things don't always take a long time when God puts His hands on it."

"This is the best thing that's happened to me all year," Jada said. "Even better than winning the basketball championship. I can't wait. Can you, Carmen?"

Carmen looked shocked beyond words. There was rarely a situation where she didn't offer her opinion, but this seemed to be one of them.

Ace continued. "When something like divorce happens, it leaves behind a lot of emotional pain. Not just for the man and woman, but for their children, too. Even though me and your mama have always been friends, there's probably still an amount of hurt left in our hearts. Only God can mend us back together and help us heal as a family."

"If you get back together this time, what happens if you want another divorce? That's too much drama," Carmen said, shaking her head.

Ace listened to her heart and not to her words. She was speaking out of fear. Her thoughts of their marriage had been shaped by her parents' past anger, and it was going to be hard for her to see past that.

Lynette's voice was calm and soothing. "I've always told both of you that if you ever felt like there was a time that you couldn't trust me, or anybody, then you could always trust God. You know how to pray and you know how important it is for you to have your own relationship with God. Your dad and I want you to pray for us and for our family as a whole, the same as *we're* going to do," she said, placing her hand on Ace's forearm.

"I can definitely do that, Mama," Jada said.

Jada didn't seem swayed by the experiences from their past. Ace knew she'd heard more than young ears were intended to hear. Jada was ten years old when things seemed to plummet from bad to worse overnight. But Jada seemed to be walking in a childlike faith.

Lynette stood up and walked to the pew where the girls were sitting, squeezing past Carmen's legs so that she could sit between her daughters.

Ace treasured the sight before him. It was true that most times a person didn't know what they had until they let it slip away. But this time around, Ace would have an intense grip on his family and the promise that God had given him.

"We need you praying for us too, Carmen," Lynette said. She pulled her daughter's head down onto her shoulder.

Ace noticed the first reluctant tear fall down Carmen's face.

"I'll pray," Carmen said as she cried. "These aren't sad tears." She wiped her face with the sleeve of her jean jacket. "I'm crying because I'm happy."

Ace wanted to freeze the moment in time, but he knew that they had to continue to move forward. Because the best was yet to come.

Chapter 48

Sheila was one prayer away from heaving a brick through Lynette's windshield. She'd expected her SUV to be in the safe haven of her garage, but tonight of all nights, it was parked exactly where it needed to be for Sheila to smash the window and have time to jump back in her car before Lynette or anyone else in the neighborhood could wake up and realize what had happened.

Would it make the situation with Ace better? No. But it certainly would make *Sheila* feel better.

Sheila prayed for a sign. Something to tell her not to do it. Something to tell her that she shouldn't be the kind of woman she used to watch on those worthless talk shows. Something to warn her that this was the kind of thing she should leave in Cassandra's hands.

"Give me a sign, God," Sheila urged, hoping she'd see something in two minutes.

Sheila leaned over to the floor on the passenger's side and gripped the brick. This was not the time to drive a bright red coupe, but she had no other option. At three o'clock in the morning, there shouldn't be any witnesses anyway. This was the kind of neighborhood where financial stresses like she had didn't keep people awake through the night.

Sheila opened the door and crept out into the night. She'd already calculated how close she could get to the house before the motion light activated. Based on where she needed to stand, she had to give an extra hoist to the brick so that it wouldn't fall short and nick the hood instead of landing on target.

The two minutes passed without a sign.

Sheila threw the brick.

Just as she thought, Lynette's car alarm blared, cutting through the neighborhood's silence. She didn't expect the headlights to blink too, but they did, and the security motion lights shone brighter than Sheila expected.

Sheila ran to her car, jumped in, and sped down the main street. She'd double-checked her gas tank this time so there was no chance that she'd be caught with an empty tank. There was no way she could explain to Cassandra how the same situation had happened in the same place. If she had to follow her brother's footsteps and be hauled off to jail, it wouldn't be for landing a brick on the bull's-eye on the windshield of the car of her man's ex-wife.

Sheila breathed a sign of relief once she was on the highway. She normally wasn't the kind of woman to do that kind of thing. Then again, evidently she was. But it felt good—overwhelmingly good. But if Sheila had to go back and do it all again, she wouldn't have thrown that brick. She would've thrown *two*.

Chapter 49

Lynette perched her feet up on the ottoman cushion that matched Audrey's cream papasan chair. Audrey's home was so different from her own. With two obsessively clean adults, there wasn't a fingerprint to be found on anything glass, and although there was wooden trim and crown molding framing most rooms in the house, a speck of dust couldn't find a permanent home for long. Lynette knew Audrey before she married Kirk, and she didn't recall her friend being this tidy. A spouse's ways—both good and bad—had a way of rubbing off on the other.

Kirk was a disciplined numbers-crunching man. A lot like Ace. It was a characteristic that worked well for the business the Landers shared. Kirk was an investment banker by trade, but he was just as involved in Audrey's consultant business—drumming up business for her through all of his contacts. Their motto was to plan and work hard in their early years, so that they could play just as hard in their later years, if not before.

Audrey had invited Lynette and the girls over for Sunday dinner, and afterwards the girls had disappeared downstairs in the family entertainment room with Kirk. Lynette always had to pry them away from the air hockey table when it was time to leave, because they always seemed to have an interminable championship tournament going on.

Audrey let up the shades on the screened-in porch. Though a springtime chill had caused them to put on sweaters this morning, the rays soaking through the room's skylight had left it comfortably warm.

"I knew it was a possibility, but I didn't know if it would become a reality," Audrey said, after Lynette had given her the latest update on her and Ace.

"It's definitely becoming one," Lynette said.

"It's so unreal that you've got the ex slitting your tires. I still can't believe that mess. And I can't believe you didn't call and tell me when it happened."

"Because I know you have the tendency to get worked up, and the more you focus on the negative things in your life, it seems the bigger they become. Besides, there's no proof that Sheila actually did it."

"You don't always need proof. You've got discernment. That gift from God alone overrides any evidence."

"You sound like my mother," Lynette said.

Audrey picked up a plastic watering can and trickled water across the ivy plants accenting the room. It was her intention to bring the feeling of outdoors inside, and she'd accomplished it. Lynette could even smell the fragranced air fresheners that were plugged in inconspicuously around the room. She knew the scent. It was called Rain Shower.

"I might sound like your mother," Audrey said, "but you sound like bad dialogue out of a movie script and you're playing a naive blond who doesn't believe the sky is blue even though she's looking at it."

"Did you have to put it like that?" Lynette asked.

"Yes. So what now?"

"With Sheila?"

"With everything," Audrey said.

"Well, I don't have time to worry about Sheila and her foolishness. Unless she does something to threaten the well-being of one of my children then I plan on ignoring her. She wants me to react. And I refuse to do it. I'm too old to play those games."

"It seems like she should be too," Audrey said. "We both know that age has nothing to do with maturity."

"Tell me about it. Frank was too old to be trying to play the field, but *he* didn't seem to realize it."

Audrey sat down and draped a throw across her bare feet. "Frank was a distraction," she said. "God didn't even let you get into him before He ripped that away." She zoomed her hand in the air like it was a makeshift plane. "God knew Ace was flying up on the horizon."

Lynette noticed how a ring on Audrey's finger caught the light and bounced it back in her direction. "Is that a new rock?" she asked, getting up to get a closer look.

Audrey held out her hand so Lynette could admire her upgraded diamond ring. "I thought your anniversary was in November. What's the special occasion?"

"Love is the occasion," Audrey said. "I've got that man wrapped around *all* of my fingers." She wiggled her fingers then held her hand at arm's length so she could admire it herself.

Lynette smacked her lips. "Kirk is the only man who can handle you," she laughed, knowing that Audrey was equally as smitten with her husband. They were always trying to outdo each other.

"I know your marriage isn't perfect," Lynette continued. "But there are things that Ace and I could learn from you. If the two of you can commit to sitting down with us and telling us how you handle communication in your marriage, that would be a true blessing in our lives."

"If I can be of help in any way then I'll do it. And I know Kirk won't mind either. Let us know when."

Lynette heard the thundering of feet that sounded like her girls were coming up the side steps from the basement. "It's like a herd of elephants whenever they're over here," she said.

"Your girls are more than civilized," Audrey said. "It's my husband that reverts to his childhood when Carmen and Jada come over."

"Anytime Jada especially is around Ace or Kirk, the introverted little girl disappears. Carmen is a little too prissy for Jada's taste and she gets tired of her sister trying to do a makeover on her."

"The oldest sibling always thinks they run things."

"I know nothing about siblings. You know both Ace and I were only children. We're both used to getting our own way," Lynette said. "I must admit it. I wouldn't mind if Jada acted a little more feminine sometimes. She won't even carry a purse. She'd rather carry a basketball."

"Leave the girl alone, Lynette. She enjoys being who she is. When she finally starts paying attention to boys you're going to wish you could turn back the hands of time. Let her stay a little girl as long as possible. There's no need to rush her."

Audrey was right. Lynette needed to hold on, because there weren't any more children in her and Ace's future. Jada wasn't exactly a baby, but sometimes she clung to Lynette's side like she was. During some evenings, Jada would join Lynette in her home office. While Lynette tapped away on her laptop, Jada would drag in her beanbag and slump down into the lifeless mass to unravel the solutions of the word problems from her advanced math class. Fortunately for Lynette, math was one of Jada's strongest subjects.

She'd gotten her skills from her father. Anything with numbers was Ace's forte. Lynette couldn't wait to have him back home. And it wasn't just because he could handle numbers.

Audrey interrupted her thoughts. "You have a look on your face."

"What kind of look?"

"*That* look. Like you have Ace on the brain."

Lynette didn't try to hide her giddiness. "I do. He's been gone since Thursday morning and it seems like it's been forever."

"Oh, you've got it bad," Audrey said. "When does he get back?"

"Tuesday," Lynette said, detecting a whine in her own voice. She reached for a tortilla chip from the bowl Audrey had sitting on the table. She was still full from the Mexican cuisine Kirk had decided to cook for them, but she dunked the chip in the chunky salsa anyway.

"Are you going to make it?" Audrey asked her.

"I've been making it for four years without him. I think I can hold out another two days."

Audrey shook a finger at her. "When he gets back home you two may very well need a chaperone."

"Tell me about it," Lynette said. "You're laughing, but I'm serious. Since we already know each other in *that* way, it makes it even more of a temptation."

"You might want to keep the girls around you at all times. If nothing else, it'll remind you to set an example for them."

"Good idea. Because Lord knows I don't need to give them anything to work with. Especially, Carmen."

"Speaking of Carmen, how's she doing with that boy situation? She was acting like a different child sneaking out of class and what not," Audrey said.

Lynette didn't want to think about it. She hadn't seen the boy again or heard that Carmen was talking to him on the phone, unless she was doing a superb job at hiding it.

270

"I think Ace and I scared her half to death when we threatened to call the boy," Lynette said. "I knew Ace wouldn't do it, but I guess Carmen didn't want to risk the humiliation and whatever else she thought her father might do."

"Who was that kid anyway?"

"Some boy she met at the mall when I let her go with her little group of girlfriends. I know I can't watch over her twenty-four hours of the day, but sometimes I wish I could. When I think of the kinds of temptations that children face these days, it makes me want to lock them up in their rooms until they're thirty."

"Why? Then they'll come out and still make mistakes. To a certain extent you've got to let them live their lives so you'll get to the point that you can trust their decision-making skills," Audrey said. "It's true that they should learn from some of your mistakes, but every now and then, they're going to make some of their own."

"I didn't want one of her mistakes to come in the form of a baby." Lynette shook her head at the thought. It made her stomach flutter. Her teenage cousin had unfortunately experienced teenage pregnancy after having sex one time—or so she said. One time. One weak moment. That's all it took to make a person's life change forever.

"All you can do is pray that God keeps them covered."

"Sometimes I pray so much for them that God probably gets tired of hearing my mouth," Lynette said.

"Oh, I doubt that," Audrey said.

Lynette put down the chips when she realized she was being driven to eat by her concerns, and not by hunger. She wiped her hands off on a napkin and settled back into the ottoman. "Counseling. Prayer. One day at a time," she said to Audrey. "That's how the Bowers family is going to make it this time."

Audrey sat back in her chair and folded her legs under her. "Girl, I have a confession to make."

"See I'm all in a spiritual moment and you're about to knock me off of my cloud. 'Fess up," Lynette said.

"When you first told me about your revived feelings for Ace, I was talking a good game, but in my mind I was thinking that you had bumped your head. Real hard."

"You and me both," Lynette admitted.

"All I could think about was all you'd gone through and I didn't want to see you hurt again because it took so much out of me to see you crying all the time. I was praying that you wouldn't walk back into the same pit, then have to claw your way out. But you, Lynette, are showing me faith in action. You're willing to put all of your insecurities and fears aside so you can let God's will be done in your life. I know you said you wanted to glean some things from me and Kirk, but your life is teaching me right now."

"Thank you, Audrey. I mean that," Lynette said, knowing that she had to renew her faith and mind every day.

God was faithful to His word and Lynette was thankful that she had a relationship where she could hear His voice, even when there were times when she was slow to be obedient about what she heard. She was grateful that God was faithful even when she wasn't, and that His love for her was unconditional.

"God is so good," Audrey said, as if she were having the same thoughts as Lynette.

"All the time," Lynette said. "And all the time, God is good."

Chapter 50

The music was so loud that Sheila couldn't hear herself talk. Cassandra acted like she was listening, but it seemed she was more interested in the man that was sitting across from them at the bar. It was supposedly a Monday-night mixer for the young professionals who worked downtown, but Sheila wasn't sure how people could meet and connect if they couldn't have a decent conversation over the music. She would've had a better time eating the leftovers she'd bagged after her lunch out with Clive.

Given some time alone and away from the office, Clive wasn't that bad. He was making her time away from Ace much easier, but once she and Ace got back together, she'd have to go back to giving Clive the cold shoulder.

"I'm telling you, the dream was so real," Sheila said. "I promise you. When I woke up I was panting like I'd really had to run back to my car after throwing that brick through Lynette's windshield."

"You wouldn't even throw a brick in real life," Cassandra said. "You'd be too worried about messing up your nails." She snapped her fingers above her head when the music mix rolled to an old EnVogue hit. "That was my jam," she crooned. "Do you remember our times at the skating rink?"

"You're so rude," Sheila said, pouring the last half of her flavored sparkling water in her glass. "I was in the middle of a conversation."

"I'm tired of hearing about your Ace drama. Okay, at first I said you should fight for your man. And if you really want him, that's what you're going to have to do. But it's been two years, he's got two half-grown daughters that he's hardly ever let you spend time with, and there is no ring in sight. In fact, he's not in sight. He's with his baby mama. Move on."

"It's not that easy," Sheila said. She was tired of trying to explain her feelings to a woman who traded men like baseball cards. Cassandra was always looking for an upgrade, but in Sheila's book, Ace was a product with all of the amenities.

Cassandra turned up the rest of whatever was in her glass and scrunched her face like it had burned her throat. "Well then, if you can't move on, force Ace to make a decision. If he won't come to you, go to him. Don't give him the time to get you out of his mind. That's all I'm saying about that situation tonight." Cassandra stood up and pushed in the bar stool. "I came here intending to have a good time and I suggest you do the same."

Sheila watched her walk away toward the next man who'd probably be swindled into paying Cassandra's rent or at least a portion of her utilities. Sometimes Sheila envied Cassandra's strength. She obviously had her weaknesses in some areas, but she had an unbreakable backbone when it came to dealing with men. But there was one of Cassandra's suggestions that Sheila *didn't* plan on taking. She wasn't going to stay here and have a good time. She'd left Ace numerous messages since last week but he hadn't returned her calls. She had no way of knowing if he was completely ignoring her, or if he was on flight duty. Either way—tonight, she was going to him.

The house was completely dark. If Ace was home, Sheila would've at least seen a hint of movement or light coming from the living room or through the side window of his bedroom. What she was able to ascertain after going inside would help her decide on one of two options. Either she'd leave the basket she'd made for him on the coffee table to welcome him when he returned, or *she'd* be the gift waiting for him when he opened the door.

Sheila looked over her shoulder as she turned the lock to the front door. She wished she still had the extra garage door opener, but Ace had needed it months ago when he had to leave his car overnight at the dealership, and she'd forgotten to get it back. If she could go through the garage door, maybe she wouldn't have the feeling that she was doing something wrong. But why was this wrong? Having a key was the same as having unspoken permission to enter the premises whenever she liked.

Sheila closed the door behind her before the little angel on her right shoulder could convince her to turn around and go back home. She always thought the illustration of an angel on one shoulder and a devil on the other was a funny exaggeration. But now, she was feeling a pull between what was right and what was wrong. She shrugged the feeling off, hit the light nearest the door, then hurried to turn off the alarm. Until that moment she hadn't thought about whether he'd changed the code. She keyed in the four numbers—three, eight, one, four—and the warning beep went silent. She exhaled.

Sheila's heart returned to its normal patter as she gently placed Ace's basket on the coffee table in the exact place that she'd pictured it. When he came through the garage door, it would be the first thing he saw. It would be hard to miss. Before covering the basket with cellophane wrap, she'd included a new frame and an eight-by-ten picture of her and Ace that she'd had enlarged. It would go perfectly with the other picture of them from her company's Christmas party last year that she'd put on his corner end table. She loved looking at . . .

Where is it?

Sheila flipped on the lamp on the end table. He'd probably moved it to a more prominent spot. She walked over to what she called the miniature shrine that he'd set up for photos of Carmen and Jada. Her picture with him was nowhere to be found among Jada's volleyball and basketball pictures. She didn't see it between Carmen's photos from last year's cotillion ball and the one standing in front of Six Flags Amusement Park.

It was gone.

If it has been three days ago, Sheila would've cried. It's possible that she would've shed her share of tears even yesterday to see that Ace was removing the signs of her presence in his life. But tonight she was just plain angry. By removing their picture, Ace had erased the last two years out of his memory. Why was it so easy for men to move on?

Well, she didn't want it to be easy for Ace. Like Cassandra said, *"Don't give him the time to get you out of his mind."* If Ace thought he had a child on the way, she—and the baby—would be the only thing he'd be able to think about.

Sheila walked down the hall and into Ace's office. He'd scribbled some notes on his desk calendar—a doctor's appointment, Jada's basketball game—but there was nothing about his flight schedule. But that wasn't the most important date. She needed to count back to the morning that they'd slept together. Her plan had to be enacted at the perfect time, and if need be, she'd wait in the shadows until the calculations made sense.

Sheila turned off the light in the office, and then went to peek into Ace's room. That's where she found her answer. His pilot's bag wasn't in its usual spot on the side of his dresser. At least she felt better that she wasn't completely ignored, even though she still thought he should've been considerate enough to return at least one of her five calls.

"That's okay," Sheila said. "Soon, he won't get enough of calling me, and Lynette will be feeling his disregard."

Sheila activated the alarm before locking up. On her way to the car, Ace's next-door neighbor, Ralph, pulled into the driveway of his two-story brick-front home. He was a bachelor, too, and always teased that if Ace didn't make Sheila an honest woman soon, he'd make her his bride. It would've been flattering if Ralph wasn't old enough to be Sheila's father and didn't have a rounded Afro that added four inches to his height.

"Are you still taking care of that man?" Ralph asked. "I see he has you coming over to do his laundry while he's out of town," he joked. "It'll be a nice surprise for him to come back tomorrow to a basket of clean underwear."

"The only clothes I ever wash are my own," Sheila said. "And I don't even like doing that."

"Oh, now that explains it. That's why y'all aren't married yet." Ralph threw his head back and laughed.

It wasn't that funny, Sheila thought. In fact it wasn't funny at all.

Ralph pushed the button on his console to open the garage door. "Don't worry. He'll come around. Even if you never lay a hand on his dirty underwear."

You're right, Sheila thought as she opened her car door. *He* will *come around. Even if it has to be with a little help.*

Chapter 51

It had been a long time since Ace felt this free. Everything about his flight duty had been as close to perfect as it could be. There were no delays, the weather was clear, and even the stars in the sky seemed to have added to their shine. A last-minute flight change hadn't delayed his plans to ask Lynette out as soon as he got home. The change had actually accelerated things because he was able to return a day earlier.

"I'm on my way home right now," Ace said, rolling his pilot's bag through the crowded terminal A corridors in the airport. "I'm close to starving so I'm going to grab a bite to eat here first and if you don't mind, come by your house." He couldn't wait until he could say he was coming "home."

"That's fine," Lynette said. "It shouldn't be too late. As long as you're here by about eight o'clock."

"You're putting me on restriction?"

"Yes. Just like I would do any man."

"But I'm not *any* man."

"You're right. And that's all the more reason for us to set our limits. We're not married, remember? Just because we're starting to date again doesn't mean those certain privileges we used to share kick back into gear."

"This is going to be hard," Ace said. "I don't foresee we'll be in this stage for too long."

"For as long as it takes," Lynette said. "This time we're doing it right."

Ace maneuvered through the crowd so he could get to a place with less foot traffic. He wanted to find a place to talk that wouldn't hold up the frenzied passengers behind him.

"You're right. Everything about this time will be right," he said, still knowing that before the year was out, it was highly possible that Lynette would be his wife again.

Ace's stomach rumbled. The taste for a hearty hamburger with all of the fixings was calling his name. He wanted to wash it down with a soda so strong that it made his nose hairs tickle. "I'm going in to get a bite and then I'll call you back. It won't be long. I don't want to take my chances of talking to a closed door when I get there."

"Okay," Lynette said. "Can't wait to see you."

"You, too." Ace went into one of the less-crowded restaurants in the terminal corridor, and found a place at the bar. He'd been sure he wanted a hamburger when he first stepped off the plane, but now seeing other choices like grilled chicken and a pulled rib sandwich, he couldn't make a decision. Ace ordered a Sprite—the fountain kind wouldn't give him the kind of kick he wanted—and flipped the menu over again.

It seemed the restaurant was getting a sudden influx of hungry passengers. The one empty seat beside him at the bar was taken up before he took his first sip of soda. The woman did a little hop as she pulled herself up onto the high chair. She wrestled to steady her carry-on luggage in the small area under her feet, and scrunched up her handbag until it was safe between her lap and the bar top.

"How are you doing?" he asked her. Ace spoke as he always did to everyone that he made eye contact with. His grandmother had taught him to be polite and not to miss a chance to acknowledge another person. It wasn't just the courteous thing to do, it was also a show of respect.

"I'm making it," she answered. "I have to go to New Jersey to take care of my grandmother's estate business." She shook her head. "I'm honored that she left me as the executor, but sometimes dealing with family is more trouble than it's worth."

"It can be like that sometimes," Ace said, and looked up at the three televisions hanging above his head. Three sports programs were broadcasting simultaneously. He couldn't hear any of them, but that didn't matter. He was trying to steer clear of being sucked into a conversation about somebody else's family drama.

"I only got to see my grandmother about three times a year, but it's been one of the hardest four months that I've ever had in my life," the woman said. "She knew she was going home to be with the Lord, though. She called me one night and said that I needed to get up there to see her as soon as I could," the woman said, running her finger down the glass of water that the bartender placed in front of her. "Something told me that I'd better drop everything and heed her words. And I was blessed to spend four full days with her before she passed away . . . holding my hand."

Ace felt guilty for trying to shut the woman out. He may have been the only sane ear that she'd had to listen to her lately, and the least he felt he could do was look at her and not try to watch the basketball highlights and scores.

He looked at the woman beside him. Her perfume consumed most of her presence, and Ace thought she would've looked more attractive if she hadn't camouflaged her beauty with so much eye makeup. He guessed she was trying to accent her almond-shaped eyes with the black eyeliner on her lids, but it took more away from her beauty than added to it. Ace was glad Lynette never tried to parade behind a face full of makeup.

Ace looked for comforting words to say. It wasn't about what he thought about this woman's looks. She was merely looking for sympathy. "When a thing like that happens, God has a way of showing us the more important things in life," he said.

"I couldn't agree with you more." She held out her hand. "Michelle," she said.

"Ace," he said.

"Ahh." A smile spread across her face. "Ace. Pilot. Flying Ace? Real cute."

Ace experienced a moment of déjà vu. There was something too familiar about the scene at this restaurant. When the woman pulled a business card out of her purse and handed it to him, it hit him. This was the same restaurant where he'd met Sheila. Ace downed the rest of his soda in one gulp and set the glass on the cardboard coaster.

"It was nice talking to you, Michelle. I pray everything with you and your family goes well."

"It would be nice if we could keep up with each other," Michelle said, batting her eyes.

Any other man may have jumped at the chance. But the fact that Michelle was that forward with wanting to keep in touch with a man she'd known less than ten minutes spoke for itself. Besides, he knew a temptation when he saw it.

Ace put on his pilot's hat. "There's a woman who already has my heart."

"Blessed woman."

"I'd like to think so," he said, handing Michelle's business card back to her. "Have a good one."

Michelle slid the business card back in her purse and swiveled around in her chair.

Ace knew that his commitment to rebuilding his family might bring increased temptations. Michelle hadn't been the only woman who'd accosted him since last Thursday morning when he'd flown off. In fact, there had been a woman who'd approached him every single day. He couldn't remember their names—he had no reason to.

Ace's first temptress came following his first flight during this week. He was standing at his customary position in front of the cockpit as the passengers lugged off cranky children and their carry-on luggage. She was wearing a blue jean outfit that looked like it had been sewn specifically according to her body measurements. She didn't try to hide the fact that she was interested in him, and had even told one of the flight attendants to inform him she'd wait for him if he wanted her to. "No, thank you," was the return message he'd sent to her.

The next woman that came to mind didn't look like the kind who would openly approach a man. Her hair was pulled back into a tight bun, and she wore small gold hoops with a freshly starched white shirt and chocolate brown slacks. She looked more suited to be a principal at an all-girls high school, but the words she'd said to him could've come from a woman in quite a different profession.

Ace was no dummy. He knew the future waiting for him and he didn't plan on messing that up.

Ace revved his car engine as he thought about Lynette. If her tastes hadn't changed in the last few years, he knew she would love to see him in his pilot's uniform. Even during the days in the past when the space between them was colder than a Colorado winter, there was something about him putting on his pilot's uniform that changed her attitude toward him. But something told Ace he might want to stop by home to change into something else. For both of their sakes. He had every intention on keeping their relationship pure until after they recommitted their vows.

Living close to the airport had its advantages. Ace arrived home in fifteen minutes and planned to change clothes and be headed back out of the door in less than five. Until he saw the gift basket sitting on the coffee table.

Chapter 52

Sheila had been in his house. It even smelled like her Dolce and Gabbana perfume. Ace was furious that she'd had the audacity to enter his home without permission, but more frustrated with himself that he'd forgotten to take the key from her. He'd given it to her as a backup measure so long ago that he hadn't even thought about it. Until now.

Ace dialed Sheila's number from the cordless in the kitchen. He'd ignored all of her voice mail messages and the pleas for him to call her back. He hated that it had to be that way, but he felt it was the best way to help her move on and forget about him. The reason he'd been so patient was that he realized that it was hard for a woman to let go after two years with a man that she thought she'd spend a lifetime with. But this—coming into his house—was too much.

Sheila answered on the second ring.

"So you must've seen your gift basket," she said as soon as she answered. "I know you love it."

"Sheila, you had no right to come in my house." Ace made himself stay calm even though he was raging like a taunted bull on the inside.

"You *could* say thank you first before you start blasting me out," Sheila said.

"I'm not keeping the basket. I appreciate the gesture, but it's not going to change anything between us."

There was silence on the other end of the phone. He thought for a moment that she'd hung up the phone until he heard her sniffles.

"All I want is for it to be the way it used to be with us," Sheila said. "You never gave me the chance to make our relationship better. In case you don't recall, there were reasons why you left Lynette in the first place. What would make you think things would work out now? She's used to being without you."

How many times had Ace heard those same words from her? Sheila was trying to play every emotional card she had, and he wasn't going to be sucked in. He'd considered his and Lynette's different approaches to discipline and rearing their children to have caused a rift in their marriage. He had already thought about how their careers had pulled them in different directions. He'd also had plenty of thoughts about what the rest of his life would be like without her, and he wasn't going to let that happen.

"Sheila, don't make things harder on yourself. I want God's best for me *and* you."

"*You* are God's best for me," she hurried to say.

"I don't believe that's true," he said.

"Did you ever?"

Ace couldn't answer.

"How could you waste two years of my life?" Sheila cried. "I love you, Ace. And you love me, too. I know you do."

Ace had only been on the phone with Sheila for a couple of

minutes and he was already emotionally taxed. "I don't consider them wasted years," he said, ignoring the last part of her comment. "Relationships don't always work out. But in our case, I think we both learned things from each other."

"Like to never trust a man with your heart," Sheila said.

Ace had never intended to hinder Sheila's life with more emotional baggage. "You'll trust again," he finally said. "Trust God, first. Above everything and everybody."

"I thought I did. And look where it got me. Without you."

"It's dangerous to make a man your life."

"Well you weren't thinking about that before," Sheila said, her voice changing from one weeping to someone irritated.

I refuse to mess up my evening. "I can't keep the basket," Ace said. "I don't want to throw it away, so let me know where I can drop it off or when you can meet me to pick it up. And bring my key, too. I have to go now."

"Why? We can meet now. I'm free and it'll only take me a few minutes to drive out to—"

"No, not now. It'll have to be later. I have to go," Ace said. He hung up the phone.

Ace turned his Bose CD player on rotation through six of his favorite gospel artists so that he could lift his spirits. He quickly changed out of his clothes, then walked through the house to see if Sheila might have touched or rummaged through any of his things. All seemed to be undisturbed, but he still felt violated to know that someone had been in his home.

Before Ace left home on his last flight duty, he'd cleared his home of everything related to Sheila. Pictures of them together had gone out with last Thursday's garbage and he'd made arrangements for the Salvation Army to collect two bags of clothing and some other odds and ends that she'd given him. He had intentionally rid his home of her presence, but she'd come and put it back.

Ace turned up the music while he fixed himself a chicken salad sandwich. He'd run out of the airport restaurant so quickly that he'd almost forgotten how hungry he'd been. He lined the top of the meat with potato chips then pressed a piece of wheat bread on top. Lynette used to hate hearing him eat a crunchy sandwich, but once he convinced her to try it, she was eating her sandwiches with a layer of chips, too.

Ace sat down at the kitchen table. Soon, he'd get to share his meals with more than his own thoughts. And he'd get to share his bed, too. That would be more appetizing than any food.

He unclipped his cell phone from his hip when he realized it was nearing seven o'clock. He was about to push the number three button to speed dial Lynette at home, but stopped when he remembered that Sheila's number was programmed in the number two slot. He reprogrammed his phone, removing Sheila from speed dial and changing Lynette's number to the number two slot.

"I hope you're on your way," Lynette said, as she picked up the phone. "Time is ticking away."

"I'm on my way right now. I ended up stopping by the house for a minute," he said. Ace paused, wondered if he should mention Sheila's gift that was waiting for him. He decided to wait. "Do you need me to bring you anything?"

"No. I ran out to pick up Chinese for dinner since I didn't feel like cooking and the girls are upstairs finishing their homework."

Ace turned on his alarm and got into the car. "Have they said anything else about us?"

"Of course they have. Their main concern is whether we're going to move out there with you and if they'll have to change schools. Carmen's having a fit because she's pleading her case that it would be better for her to stay at Legacy since she only has two more years of high school, and Jada's concerned about her basketball career and making sure she stays on first string."

"Which is nothing for them to worry about. Whatever happens to us, I'll be sure their lives aren't too disrupted."

"I agree."

Ace chuckled. "Have we ever agreed this much in the past?"

"Waaaaaaaay back in the day," Lynette said. "It's like we're in the honeymoon phase of a new relationship. And I don't want to be negative, but something is bound to come up sooner or later where we don't agree. That's just life. Give it some time."

Ace wished she wouldn't say things like that. He still had to tell her about Sheila's latest move. "We'll work through anything and everything that comes up. I wish we could say that we always have, but—"

"But we're not going to look backwards. We're going to keep our eyes on the future," Lynette reminded him. They would each have to help the other to focus on the great expectations of their future, and not keep reverting to the past.

"Since you're in my future, the picture is looking mighty fine to me," Ace said.

"You know," Lynette said, "I *personally* don't need anything before you get here, but you might want to stop somewhere and buy yourself some game before you get here."

Ace could hear the cheerfulness in her voice. At least a part of Lynette that he adored hadn't changed—the Lynette that liked to laugh and had her own bit of cute sarcasm.

"Don't quit your day job. I heard it's tough out there on the comedy circuit," Ace said, pulling out of his garage.

Ralph waved him down from his mailbox before he turned out onto his street. "Let me holler at my neighbor," Ace said. "I'll see you in a bit."

Ralph was the unofficially assigned neighborhood watchman. He was the kind of person people hate to have around if they're trying to keep something private, but are grateful for when they need to know what's really going down in the neighborhood. Ace's subdivision and its surrounding area wasn't in an area of high crime, but a year prior there had been a surge of daytime break-ins. Ralph had paid for daytime security for their street out of his own pocket when the homeowner's association didn't approve the addition as a line item in the budget. A month later, the board miraculously gave approval to allow a private security company to occasionally monitor the area during the daytime. Since Ace was away from home often, he was appreciative for any extra set of eyes.

Ralph was a helpful hand, too. During heavy travel times, Ace had been known to voluntarily pick up a few extra flight schedules as long as it didn't go over the airline's allotted maximum number of flying hours. On at least three occasions, he'd returned home to a freshly cut yard and trimmed bushes, courtesy of Ralph. His neighbor refused every dime that Ace tried to pay him for his time, but he gladly accepted a buddy pass the couple of times Ace had offered.

"What's going on, Ralph? You're looking clean as usual," Ace said.

"Gotta keep myself up so I can keep up with the young cats like you," Ralph said. "Man, you've got your woman coming to your house to take care of you while you're out of town. I've got to go to my women's houses. They're the old-school type."

"So you saw Sheila?" Ace said, getting mad all over again.

"Yesterday when she was leaving. I was teasing her about washing your clothes, but you know how the new-school women are. She doesn't seem like one who's into a lot of domestic work. Women these days have their careers on their minds, not the household and children."

Ralph didn't know Sheila very well. She was a career woman now, but she was chomping at the bit for someone to loose her from the corporate world. Someone. *But not me,* Ace thought.

"Ralph, I have to be honest with you. Sheila might be having some problems letting go. I'm not seeing her anymore."

"Uh," Ralph grunted. "I should've known something was up." He straightened the stack of envelopes in hands. "You know women can put up a good front when they want to." He raised his eyebrows. "She wasn't in there tearing up stuff like some kind of fatal attraction, was she?"

"Naw. She didn't pull anything like that."

"Let me tell you what I've learned about women in my sixty-one years," Ralph said. "Don't put anything past them. The nicest, sweetest ones can spin their heads around in a quick minute if you make them mad enough."

"God knows I don't want to see that," Ace said, backing out into the street. He couldn't entertain Ralph's conversation for long. Lynette had already warned him that she was putting him out at eight o'clock. He didn't care if he arrived at her house with only five minutes to spare. Five minutes with her tonight was better than no time at all.

"You let me know if you see something suspicious going on around here until I get my key back from her," Ace told Ralph. "Hopefully Sheila won't rear her ugly side any more than she has."

Chapter 53

Lynette was furious. "That woman had some nerve. Change the locks—and the alarm code. Then you don't have to worry about getting the key back."

Lynette knew it wasn't the conversation Ace wanted to have after seeing her for the first time in a few days, but her knack for reading his expressions seemed to kick back in already. He'd had more than flirting with her on his mind when he walked in the door. She had stayed on Ace until he opened up and told her about Sheila's audacity.

"And what about the basket?" Ace asked. "I'd feel bad throwing all of that stuff away. Or even giving it away. I mean it's even got a portable GPS in there."

Lynette could care less what gifts Sheila had foolishly spent her money on. That was her problem. Hopefully she still had the receipts.

"The last thing you want to do is agree to meet her, Ace. That's what she *wants*," Lynette said.

Sometimes it seemed that men could be naive over the most obvious things. *Lord, help me. Give us Your wisdom or this relationship is going to be over before it gets started.*

Ace picked through the carton of the vegetable fried rice, even though he said that he'd already eaten. Lynette rushed through the conversation. She wanted to resolve it before the girls came back downstairs and the issue was pushed to another day.

"Drop it off at her job tomorrow. Is there a way you can leave it at a front desk or something without her knowing that you're there?"

"I think I can probably leave it at the downstairs concierge and they can call for her to come get it."

"Sounds good to me." Lynette took her box of rice out of Ace's hands. "Now can we spend some time together without having to talk about drama? People always think women are the only ones with drama."

"Speaking of past relationships and drama. Whatever happened to your little artist boyfriend?" Ace chuckled. "And by the way, I almost started to ask him what his daddy's name was. If his papa was a rolling stone like mine, then I wouldn't have been surprised to find out he was my brother."

"First of all, he never made it to boyfriend status. And second of all, I don't want to talk about Frank at all, even if he is your long-lost brother." Lynette easily scooped her rice out of the box with chopsticks. She knew Ace had always been envious that she had the skills to work chopsticks, while he could barely keep one grain of rice between his sticks on the short journey from the carton to his mouth.

"Now you're showing off," Ace said, evidently thinking about the same thing.

Lynette tossed him a fortune cookie. "Here's something you can handle."

"I don't believe in fortunes. Only blessings and destiny."

Ace gripped Lynette's waist and pulled her toward him. She set the carton of food on the breakfast bar.

"I'm holding one of my blessings and about to walk into my destiny," Ace said.

Lynette wrapped her arms around his fit midsection and rested in his words. She laid her head on his chest and their breathing seemed to fall in sync. After a few cuddling moments, Ace became too comfortable, marked by the way his hands traveled southward down the sides of her hips. Lynette didn't give him time to enjoy the feel of her body, or herself the time to respond to his touch. She knocked his hands away.

"You need to find that Scripture about not waking love before it's time," she said, stepping out of his reach.

"Help me out," Ace held his hands up like he'd been caught stealing sweets from the cookie jar. "Tell me where it is."

"I need to look it up myself," Lynette admitted. "In fact, I had to dig out some of my books and notes about living a godly single life. It was easy for me to walk the walk when I didn't have anybody to test me. Then you came along."

Ace opened the kitchen cabinet above the sink. "I need a glass of water," he said.

Lynette studied Ace like he was a piece of art. Just last night, she'd highlighted some Scriptures during her study time and she knew when he walked in the door tonight that she was going to have to be diligent and purposeful in keeping them. She'd expected him to walk in the door in his pilot's uniform. But God knew best. It may not have been as easy for her to knock his hands away.

"Have you cooled down yet?" Lynette asked after he'd set the empty glass on the kitchen table.

"I'm good," Ace said. "Call the girls down. That's the only way you're going to keep your hands off of me."

"Yeah, right." Lynette walked to the bottom of the steps.

"Carmen. Jada. Come downstairs to spend some time with your dad while he's here. I'm kicking him out in a little while."

Jada was the first to come to the kitchen. She was freshly showered and dressed in a pajama set imprinted in yellow smiley faces. Jada had an affinity for pajama sets, and had amassed a drawerful suitable for every season and holiday.

"I thought you might want some lovey-dovey time or something," Jada said, tearing the paper off of a fortune cookie.

"Nobody in this house needs to be concerned with lovey-dovey time," Lynette said.

"That's right," Ace added.

"You need to tell your other daughter that. She's the one that's boy crazy."

"What do you know?" Lynette pressed her to give more. If she found out that Carmen was still getting in trouble with that boy, she was going to be grounded until the end of the year. If Carmen thought two weeks had been a long time, she'd barely survive an eight-month telephone ban.

"Don't worry," Lynette assured Jada. "You're being an informant, not a tattletale."

"I don't know anything, Mama," Jada said. "A blind man can see she's going through her phase."

"Her phase?" Lynette bopped her daughter on the backside. "Sometimes you act like an old woman."

"Keep it that way," Ace said.

"I'm not worried about boys right now," Jada said, "even though a boy named Cash is running behind me like a little puppy at school."

"Cash? His real name is Cash?" Lynette asked.

"Yes," Jada answered like Lynette had asked a ridiculous question. "He's cute, but he's too immature for my taste."

That's what she is saying now, Lynette thought. But after the school year ended and Cash returned from summer break with two hairs on his chin, a deeper voice, and a half of a bicep, Jada might forget about his immaturity.

"Thank you for giving me his name," Ace said. "With a name like that, that's all I need to keep a check on him."

Carmen rounded the corner. She scooted into the kitchen, her bedroom shoes swooshing over the hardwood floors. "Check on who?"

"Nunya," Jada said.

"Nunya who?"

"Nunya business."

Carmen smacked her lips. "That's so old."

"You still fell for it," Jada said, throwing a fortune cookie at her sister.

It had been some time since the entire Bowers family had convened at the same kitchen table. Lynette could imagine them all years from now. The girls would bring their husbands and children back to the house where they'd grown up, and reminisce about times like these.

Four years had made a noticeable difference in the girls' maturity levels. It seemed like just last week when they were taking their first steps, and like yesterday that she tearfully walked them into their kindergarten classes. Lynette could see the fruit of her labor sprouting in their character and intelligence as their conversations in the kitchen went into politics and current events. Ace noticed it too, and didn't hesitate to say so.

But when the table turned to the latest celebrity gossip and musical sensations, Lynette was clueless. Ace could keep up, and Carmen and Jada were surprised that he knew as much as he did.

"Oh, I know all of the latest dances," Ace was saying. "I can probably teach you some things." He pushed away from the kitchen table and held his hands at his side like he was trying to stay balanced on a surf board. "Let me get my rhythm," he said, as he started humming, then clapping a beat that was obviously familiar to the girls.

Carmen and Jada joined their father in helping him keep the rhythm going, while he performed a dance that looked more like a conniption fit to Lynette. She couldn't stop herself from laughing uncontrollably.

"You don't know about this, Lynn," Ace said above their hoopla.

"And I don't want to know," she said. "I'll stick to doing the centipede." She got up and stood beside Ace and performed her best rendition of the eighties dance. She couldn't believe that back in high school, she was once one of the student choreographers for their step and dance teams. Now, she couldn't pull off a recent dance move to save her life. Carmen was the first to call it quits from their four-person Soul Train line.

"Enough for me. I'm about to work up a sweat," she said, fanning herself off with a junk-mail postcard from the kitchen table.

"It's a shame that you can't keep up with your old man," Ace said, refilling his glass with water. "It's time for me to go anyway."

Lynette didn't want him to leave. They were having so much fun together, and they hadn't had much time alone to talk about more than the Sheila episode. She wanted to tell him to stay, but she thought about Audrey's advice, her weakness for Ace, and the fact that she needed to keep the boundaries they'd established.

Ace said his good-byes to the girls and sent them upstairs with a prayer to cover their night and the next day at school.

"Time flies when you're having fun, doesn't it?" Lynette said as she walked him to the front door.

"Too fast. But I'm off for an entire week."

"I'm not," Lynette said. Owning her own practice had its perks, but it also meant that she couldn't take time off from work without making the proper plans with her staff and business partner.

Ace pointed to the painting over the couch in the living room. It must've been the first time he noticed it and it was definitely the first time Lynette had thought about Frank's work still being displayed prominently in her home.

"You changed up your artwork," he said. "When did you get that one?"

"You don't want to know. But by the time you come back over, it won't be there anymore," Lynette said. Frank's picture was coming off of her wall tonight and going down in the basement until she figured out what to do with it. Maybe she'd take it over to the Landers' house and let Kirk and Audrey work it somewhere into their décor.

Ace must've read between the lines. "Good idea," he smirked. He reached over and wiped a piece of rice off the corner of Lynette's mouth. "Tomorrow morning I have to take care of that business that we talked about."

Lynette sighed. The last thing she wanted was for Ace to run into Sheila. She wished that Ace would go about it another way—like setting the basket on fire. But that was unreasonable, and downright devilish. Lynette had to trust that he'd make the right choices and do the right thing. She'd already prayed, more times than she cared to admit, that Ace wouldn't be lured back to Sheila.

Sheila's latest attempt to try and buy back Ace's love was foolishness as far as Lynette was concerned. It maddened Lynette, but at the same time, she thought it was sad that Sheila thought Ace could be swayed by material things. Sheila's gift basket couldn't compete with the gift that God had given back to Lynette—Ace's love.

Chapter 54

There was plenty of work begging to be handled on Sheila's desk, but no call rang louder in her ears than the one she'd just received from the concierge desk. A package for *her*? Sheila didn't doubt one minute that it was from Ace. She pushed the elevator down button three times as if the first time wasn't good enough.

She could see it now . . . just as she'd imagined it since the last time she'd talked to Ace. She didn't believe that he'd be able to turn down her gift without wanting to thank her in some way. That's why she hadn't called last night like she was tempted to. The longer Ace looked at the time and effort she poured into making his customized basket, the more he'd think about her. She knew what he liked.

Sheila stepped onto the open elevator, grateful that there was no one else on there. Seeing that it was only ten-thirty, most everyone in the building had probably already arrived for their workday and been sucked into the monotony of their jobs, she thought. Overworked and underpaid. Or in the case of the big men in charge at her office, underworked and overpaid. By the time the robots came up for air to grab a lunch, she would've put her relationship back together. That was more than most people could say they'd done in a day.

Sheila fingered her hair and admired her reflection in the mirrored walls of the elevator just in case her "package" was Ace. He'd pulled the same trick their first Valentine's Day together. She'd been expecting to go downstairs and pick up a bouquet of red roses, but got a six-foot-three package of Ace instead.

Ding. The elevators door slid open and Sheila exited like a spotlight was following her to the concierge desk. Then she saw the basket. And the spotlight fluttered out. If it wasn't for Sheila's plan B, her hopes for reconciliation would've done the same.

Sheila painted on a smile, when she really wanted to crumble to the floor. "Sheila Rushmore," she said to Linwood, her least favorite concierge attendant.

"Nice and heavy," Linwood said, as he lifted up the basket. "I hope someone didn't send this to you because they got their orders mixed up. This looks like it's for a man."

"It's a gift for my father," Sheila lied. *He needs to mind his own business.*

"Either your father has expensive taste or his daughter loves him a lot. This must've cost a pretty penny." Linwood rotated the basket so he could peer through the shrink-wrap again.

At least four hundred dollars that she didn't have to spend, she wanted to confess. But at least now she'd be able to return the items and get the money credited back to her cards. The wrapping was still tightly sealed on the basket, and it didn't look like a single item had been jostled around.

"Thank you," Sheila said, and jerked the basket out of Linwood's hands. She was sure he'd attempted to calculate the costs of the items inside, if he even had any idea how much those things cost. His taste screamed thrift store.

"Do you remember what the person looked like who dropped off the basket?" Sheila asked, and listened while Linwood recounted Ace's features like he'd been asked to be an eyewitness for a police lineup. It had been Ace. Definitely.

Sheila went back upstairs and behind closed office doors so that she could rip the basket apart. She placed the items in a box that she'd pushed under her desk so that people wouldn't question her again when they saw her leaving with a massive basket that hadn't found a home with its intended recipient.

If there hadn't been another meeting called at two o'clock, Sheila would've started to make her returns during lunchtime. She didn't want to get caught being late to a meeting again. It would be her luck that a thirty-five-minute run would end up taking two hours because of some inconvenient street renovations that the city of Atlanta thought best to do in the middle of the workweek.

Sheila opened an e-mail with an attached résumé that had been forwarded to her.

J. Morrow had gained a new client and she was responsible for finding experienced candidates to fill positions for their Atlanta and Houston offices. This job had gotten to the point where it was boring her to tears—literally.

After perusing the résumé, Sheila realized that the candidate probably wasn't the most qualified, but she was willing to take a chance and call him in for an interview. Despite how she hated the job, she needed to step up her performance so that she could get a raise following her upcoming performance review. Creditors were starting to leave messages on her home and cell phone voice mails. One even had the nerve to call her office.

"Excuse me, Sheila." Nancy had buzzed into Sheila's interoffice intercom on her phone.

"Yes, Nancy." Nancy was the most pleasant person in the office, and it sometimes seemed like she was the only one who wasn't trying to cut Sheila's head off behind her back.

"You have a visitor up front who's just as sweet as can be," she said.

"Be right up," Sheila said, opening her top office drawer and getting out her purse-sized perfume. It was Ace for sure. This time she knew it. He was coming to apologize for acting so irrational. Sheila spritzed the perfume behind both ears. Not only did Ace need to see what he was missing, but she wanted her scent to wrap around him.

Only it wasn't Ace that Sheila was greeting. It was Cassandra. And she was dressed like she was going to a club instead of to her friend's professional and conservative office. Sheila was tired of painting on her smile today, but she did it yet again until she led Cassandra to her office.

"What are you doing here? And looking like that?" Sheila asked Cassandra after they were behind closed doors.

"I think I look hot," Cassandra said, looking down at her black stilettos.

"For the club, yes. But not for coming up *here*."

Cassandra set her purse on the edge of Sheila's desk. "I was in the area and thought I'd drop by. Forgive me for trying to surprise my best friend and brighten her day."

"Mission *not* accomplished. I've got too much work to do." Slowly but surely, Sheila's definition of best friend was changing. She didn't get the same joy as she used to out of spending time with Cassandra. There was a time when Sheila's life was based so much on Cassandra's desires and opinions. That was starting to change now. It was almost like Cassandra had become an addiction that Sheila was trying to break.

"Let's go for lunch," Cassandra suggested. "I haven't had Benihana's in a while and I want to see that little man flip the egg up into his hat and make a miniature volcano with the rice."

"I brought my lunch," Sheila said, thinking about the peanut butter crackers and microwaveable kid-sized portion of spaghetti in her desk drawer.

"I hope it's something good and filling because you're starting to look skinny."

"Weren't you saying not too long ago that I could stand to lose a few pounds?"

"That was then."

Sheila shook her head. That was typical Cassandra.

"Why are you acting so stank?" Cassandra said. "I think you're taking your breakup with Ace out on me and I'm not the one to stand here and take it today. I know he was a good man to you, but he's gone. G-O-N-E. Let him live his life with his baby's mama." She slung her purse over her shoulder. "Call me when you're back to being the old Sheila."

When Cassandra walked out she bumped into Clive.

"Oh, well hello," she said. "I didn't know such good-looking men worked on this floor."

Sheila got up and closed her door. She was not going to be a part of that. With all of the downtown roadwork, Ace couldn't have gotten that far away from her office building. Not far enough that Sheila couldn't convince him to return.

Sheila tried to call him, but Ace didn't answer. To her surprise, he'd taken his personal message off of his voice mail and let the computerized woman's voice leave instructions. He'd taken away something from her again. It had been a comfort to at least hear his voice whenever she wanted to.

"Ace, please call me. We have something important to talk about. I don't want to leave a message. I want to talk to you directly. I'll await your call." She started to hang up, then added, "It's important. Please."

He'd pushed her to do this. *Please call me so I can tell you about your baby,* she thought. Sheila planned to carry her lie about being pregnant until she was sure Ace was hooked. When the time was right and he was away on a series of international flights, she'd fake an incident that she would say caused her to lose the baby. He would be devastated, but they'd get through it together. Ace was compassionate. He'd never abandon her in that state. Never.

Chapter 55

Ace had been a man of his word. He'd returned Sheila's gift to her office this morning, and to Lynette's relief, they hadn't crossed paths. Lynette leaned back in the front seat of Ace's ride and realized why he'd spent the money on it. Unless it was dealing with his children, Ace held his finances under tight reins. But this was worth it.

It wasn't practical for Lynette to buy a car that was suited for one person and an occasional passenger, but if she ever felt the need to splurge on an automobile, she could see herself in a convertible. Pearl white with tan interior.

Lynette opened her eyes when she realized they'd cruised to a stop. They were sitting at the light in front of the medical office park that housed her practice.

Ace picked up her left hand and entwined his fingers through hers. If he kept looking at her like that, she was going to have to jump out of his car as soon as he pulled in front of her building—she'd do it while the car was still rolling if she needed to.

"All I had to do was take you out to lunch to put a smile on your face like that?"

"It's the joy of the Lord," Lynette said. "And you may have had a teeny tiny bit to do with it, too." Her life hadn't been bad before this turnaround with Ace, but things certainly seemed calmer and more pleasant since it happened. Even her patients were more cooperative and Lynette had finalized some pending tasks with Kelly for the retreat. The same event she'd dreaded had become something she was looking forward to. Lynette couldn't wait to spend time with other women of God. She'd even convinced Audrey to teach a workshop on being partners with your husband in life and business.

Lynette had a feeling that unless she was asked to be a speaker at next year's event, it would be her last time attending the singles retreat. She and Ace would have the opportunity to join the newly revamped Couples in Christ ministry at church instead.

Ace pulled into a visitor's parking space, and like clockwork, Tonia arrived back from lunch at the same time.

What in the world must she think of me? Lynette thought. *This month, Ace. Last month, Frank.* She started to mention the irony to Ace, but decided that he probably wouldn't find the humor in it. When Tonia noticed them, she smiled like she'd happened upon a secret.

"Here comes your girl," Ace said between clenched teeth.

"Don't start," Lynette said and put the window down. "Be nice," she whispered, before Tonia leaned down and stuck her face in the window.

"Dr. Singletary," Ace said. "Long time no see."

"Not so long that you can't call me Tonia," she said. "Such a surprise to see *you*."

"I bet it is," Ace said. "And you'll be seeing more of me."

"Oh, is that so?" Tonia said, looking at Lynette. "Lynette didn't tell me that."

Lynette knew Ace had purposefully set her up. He wanted the world to know what God was doing in their lives. Lynette was the type of person who would stick her pinkie toe in the water. Ace was the type who dove right in.

"I'll see you inside in a minute," Lynette said to Tonia.

"See you next time, Ace." Tonia sang her words.

Lynette watched her walk toward the building. She'd put on her Anne Klein shades with the jet-black lenses. They were perfect, Tonia said, for scoping out men without them noticing, and ignoring those she knew she'd have no interest in.

"You had to put all of our business out there, didn't you?" Lynette asked. Ace was holding her hand again. She could have spent the rest of the day here. Holding hands, yet saying nothing. But there were cavities to be filled.

"Thank you for lunch," Lynette said. "Dating you again is definitely going to make it easier on my purse."

"You won't have to worry about buying lunch or anything else for that matter," Ace said. "I'll take care of everything you need." He pressed her hand against his lips.

"You're pouring it on real thick," she teased. "I wish I had a tape recorder to document everything you're saying right now. You better believe I'm going to hold you to your word."

Ace held up hands. "Um . . . if that's the case, I think I better retract that statement. I was caught up in the moment."

"That's what I thought," Lynette said, unlocking the door.

"Talk to you tonight?"

"Of course. On one condition."

"What?" Ace had always backed her up into a corner by having her make promises before she knew what she was committing to. What was it this time?

"I need some sugar to keep me through the day. I'm feeling a little light-headed."

Lynette leaned her cheek toward him. "Right there," she said, poking her finger on the spot where she had one deep dimple.

Ace pulled her finger away, kissed the tip of it, then kissed her cheek. "I think your lips would be a lot sweeter."

Lynette shook her finger at him. "You're acting like a bad boy. If I give you an inch, you'll take a mile." Lynette opened the door. The kids weren't around, and she had to depend on herself to do the right thing—even when she didn't want to. And Lord knows, she didn't want to.

"Call me, tonight," she said. "And thanks again."

Lynette walked into the building and turned around to watch Ace drive away. Just as she expected, Ace had waited to watch her as well.

Two medical assistants that Lynette recognized from the doctor's office on the floor below her practice walked in the door.

"Now *he* was a cutie," one of them said. "If I had a man like that I'd never let him leave the house without me. I'd hook myself around his neck and let everybody know he was taken."

"He wouldn't be taken for long," her associate said. "Not with you wanting to ride around on his neck all day. That's why you don't have a man now."

They laughed so loud that their voices echoed through the corridor. They joined Lynette in the elevator for the ride upstairs, and when they stepped off at their floor, they were still talking about the reasons why they were single.

Lynette was glad that she couldn't relate. She had a man. Finally. It had taken four years to get one and he'd ended up being the same one she had gotten rid of. God truly had a sense of humor.

◆ ◆ ◆

Tonia was waiting for Lynette as soon as she turned down the private hall with their two offices.

"You didn't tell me you were having a second chance at romance."

"Well, it's new. Different. A little frightening." Lynette pulled on her white lab coat. In the pockets she stuffed a few hand toys that she sometimes used to distract anxious children. "And definitely more than about the romance."

"Are you sure it's not just your hormones talking? Because I know what they're saying."

"Humor me."

Tonia stuck a penlight and a row of stickers in her top pocket. She fluttered her eye lashes and raised her voice an octave. "Maybe we made a mistake. Things could've worked out between us. I wonder how it would be if we were together now—because you know me and the rest of my estrogen sisters could use a little testosterone around."

Lynette laughed at Tonia's exaggerated prissy movements. "You need help," she said. "And even if my estrogen sisters are talking to me, there's a voice that's speaking louder."

"And whose voice would that be?"

"God's voice," she said. "I know all of this seems sudden, and strange. But I'm at the point that I'd rather think I hear God's voice and follow it, than to think I hear it, do nothing, and miss what He was trying to give me. How He's trying to bless me."

Tonia's voice turned to a more serious tone. "I apologize for making light. I hope you know I was just kidding."

"I know that. I've got tougher skin than that."

"And I commend you," Tonia said. "I don't know if I'd have the guts. I don't think I would ever go back to an old flame."

"There's a big difference between someone who was just a boyfriend, and someone you once loved enough to marry," Lynette said. She pulled an elastic band out of her pocket and pulled her hair back into a ponytail. "And it's more about having the faith than the guts."

"That's where we're different. God seems so far off to me. Untouchable. Yet you've managed to build this close relationship with Him that I wouldn't even know how to begin to do. I didn't grow up going to church, but I never thought my parents were huge sinners or anything like that. Sundays in the Singletary household meant sleeping in late or going to football games."

Football games? When Lynette was growing up, missing church for a sports event would never have happened. "Sleeping in wasn't an option for me unless my parents truly thought I was too sick to move, which wasn't often," Lynette said. "For a long time I thought my relationship with God was about how often I went to church or how many ministries I served in. But I came to a better understanding. And when you know better, you do better."

"Most of what I know is from watching you, whether you realize it or not," Tonia said. "And I want to thank you for accepting me the way I am and never being judgmental."

"Who am I to judge?"

"You'd be surprised at the people who try to pull out the gavel on me," Tonia said. "But I'm a lot better than I used to be."

Lynette nodded. "You've grown. *We've* grown. There's a saying my Uncle Sanford always says. 'I may not be the person I wanna be, but I'm definitely not who I used to be.'" Lynette grabbed Tonia's hand. "And only God can truly make that kind of everlasting change in us. From the inside out."

"Let the church say amen," Tonia said, taking Lynette's other hand and facing her friend. She smiled. "You just give me some time. One of these days I'm coming to God for a soul makeover. Pray for me, okay?"

"Always have, always will," Lynette said. She knew Tonia's heart was softening toward God. It was only a matter of time that she'd accept and open her eyes to the seeds of love that had been planted there.

Tonia dropped Lynette's hands. She stepped back, put her hands on her hips, and looked at Lynette from head to toe. "And look at you. You got your man back. I'm so happy for you."

Lynette and Tonia walked out to the main hall with the exam rooms. The assistants and hygienists had already pulled the charts for their afternoon rotation of patients.

"Thanks. And I'm due for a relationship update from you," Lynette said to Tonia.

"Trust me. You'd rather get a root canal than hear what's been going on with me."

"That horrible?" Lynette asked. She took a chart out of the hanging bin on the door of the first exam room.

"Worse. Add that part to your prayer list, too."

"You've officially moved to the first slot," Lynette said, tapping on the exam room door and peeking her head inside.

As soon as she did, the boy sitting on his mother's lap arched his back and launched into a crying fit. Sometimes the sight of Lynette in a white coat could rouse a reaction out of the children who knew what was about to go on. Little Caleb was a regular patient, mostly because his mother was lax in helping him establish a dental routine. Caleb kicked his feet so hard that one of his black tennis shoes flew off and hit the wall, leaving a scuff mark. This little boy had it bad.

On second thought, Lynette said to herself, *I better keep* myself *at the top of that prayer list.*

Chapter 56

Ace spotted Kenny as he lifted the barbell over his head. He was pressing up the fifth count on his third rep, and his friend's arms were starting to shake from the weight of over two hundred pounds.

Kenny growled as he pushed up the weights with Ace's assistance and let them clank down on the bar above his head. Kenny slid clear of the weights and sat up on the bench.

"So it's official?" Kenny asked, wiping his face.

"It's official." Ace had called Kenny to take him up on an offer to work out at Kenny's gym. Because of Kenny's membership, Ace had gotten in on a visitor's pass and they'd been working the circuit in the weight room for at least forty-five minutes now. It wasn't one of the large franchise gyms, so Ace didn't feel rushed to get out of the way for the men he called gym heads—those who looked like they spent more time at the gym than they did at work or home.

Kenny wiped his face with a white towel, then cleaned the weight bench with the sanitizing wipes provided by the gym. "So how you feeling big man? Seems my wife succeeded in praying you two back to the altar."

"We're not there yet, but I don't anticipate it'll be a long time. You know one of those 'suddenly' moves that God is so awesome at performing," Ace said, snapping his fingers. "I think this may be one of those things."

Ace took his place on the bench and lifted his arms to the weights. He took a deep breath that filled his chest, lifted the weights, then let them settle down slowly on his chest. He exhaled each time he pumped the weights in the air. His momentum slowed as he reached the tenth rep, and Kenny offered the same assistance that Ace had done for him.

"One more. You've got it in you big man," Kenny coached. "If you can get Lynette back, you can give me one more rep."

Ace's adrenaline helped him push the weights up two more times.

Kenny looked impressed. "The right woman will make a man do things he thought he couldn't do," he said.

Ace sat up on the bench to catch his breath. "That and some pentup issues, if you know what I mean."

"I know you two are gonna keep it holy. I'll send my wife back in her prayer closet for that one." Kenny laughed.

Ace checked his watch. He didn't like to rest longer than two minutes between his sets.

"It's been a little hard for Sheila to let go, though. She came in my place and left me a gift basket packed with all kinds of stuff. You shoulda seen it."

"Man, she broke into your crib?"

"Let's just say she let herself in. Technically, she had a key."

"And did you get it back?"

"No. I went ahead and got the locks changed. Lynette didn't think I should take chances with that."

"I don't blame her," Kenny said. He propped his left leg up on the weight bench to stretch out his calf. "Just because Sheila would've given you one key back doesn't mean that's the only copy she had floating around. Smart move. In the perfect world, you wouldn't have had to worry about that."

"But this ain't a perfect world," Ace said.

Kenny slapped the back of his calf with his hand, and then went back to his post to help spot Ace. "And except for me, people aren't perfect."

"Except for you, huh?" Ace slid back under the weights and readied himself for his next set. Kenny helped him lift up the bar and Ace pumped through his next set with more ease than he'd done the first. He felt he was lifting the burdens and weights from his chest. *Healing Sheila's hurts wasn't his responsibility. God would fill her empty spaces. Lynette was willing to let them start anew. He was capable of being a good father and husband again.*

Kenny helped Ace finish his last rep, and they wiped down the bench again before moving to the treadmills to cool down. It was nearing closing time at the gym, and only a few patrons remained in the area.

"I can't help but admire you, Ace. You listened to God's voice and you were obedient."

"At the risk of hurting someone else that I cared for," Ace admitted. "I know Sheila is in God's hands, but it does bother me that I had to cut her off cold in order for her to get the message. She keeps reminding me that I wasted two years of her life—over and over again like a broken record. And she's leaving all of these voice messages. I should delete them, but I listen to them, and they play on my guilt."

Kenny pushed the settings on the console of his treadmill, and the belt started at a smooth pace. "I would give it a few days. But if it doesn't stop, you may need to change your number."

"I was thinking the same thing, Pope," Ace said, bending down to tie his loose shoelace.

Kenny slipped an earbud from his MP3 player into his ear. "I'm here for you, man. You've come this far. What are you going to do now? Turn back around?"

"No chance at that."

"Well do like my grandma used to sing at church. Run on and see what the end's gonna be."

Ace picked up speed on his treadmill. He adjusted the setting to emulate a jog up a small incline. "I'm running. I'm definitely running," he said, settling into a steady pace.

Kenny slipped into the musical world of his MP3 player and Ace let the thudding rhythm of his rubber soles on the treadmill belt lull him into a place of prayer. He asked God to not only increase his faith, but that of Lynette and the girls. He prayed that although he felt an urgency to put his family back together again, he wanted their reunion to be based on God's perfect timing. He thanked God for his relationship with Kenny, and a pastor with whom he could seek sound biblical counsel. He honored God for giving Mama Claudette the spiritual discernment to push him to action and for having Pop Walter's silent support. And lastly, he asked God to steer Sheila into another direction so that she wouldn't bring any discord into his life.

A queasy feeling rumbled in Ace's stomach. He'd had a beef burrito before working out, and hoped that was the only reason for the sudden uneasiness.

Chapter 57

It was the third call Ace was receiving from Sheila on his cell phone this morning, and she'd already called him four times on his home line. By the second ring, he'd already decided that he was going to have to change the cell number he'd had for the last seven years. His home phone, too. If it wasn't for the fact that he didn't want to spoil his Sunday plans, he'd do it today. But today was another milestone in his and Lynette's journey. They were attending worship service together as a family at Mount Pisgah, and afterwards, going to her parents' house to eat.

However, it wasn't a normal Sunday lunch with Mama Claudette burning in the kitchen and doing damage to his nutritious eating plan. It was reunion Sunday, which meant there was going to be a spread of more food options than a grown man should have in one day. It meant he was going to have to hit the gym every day before he went back to work to burn off the preplanned calories he was going to consume—the potato salad, smothered chicken, and baby back ribs with Uncle Sanford's secret sauce recipe that was passed down to one person of each generation. And the corn casserole, turnip greens, macaroni and cheese, and strawberry cobbler. Even after missing at least the last five reunions, he knew his favorite foods would be there.

Ace hit the button to silence his cell phone. Again. *No,* he thought. *Sheila is not going to mess up this day.* He'd put the burden of dealing with her in God's hands. And that's where it was going to stay.

Ace turned on the portable personal trimmer that he usually kept packed in his bag, and tapered his hairline and beard. He was running behind. When he'd set his alarm clock, he hadn't built in the extra travel time he needed to get across town. Since Grace Temple was just a stone's throw from his house, he'd become spoiled with being able to roll out of bed, shower, and dress, with barely ten minutes to spare before worship service started.

Speaking of Grace Temple, Ace hadn't made an appointment with Pastor Bailey yet, but he knew the time was coming when he'd have to tell his shepherd of the last four years that he'd be returning to his old church home. It would be a conversation of mixed emotions, he was sure, Ace thought as he used his handheld mirror to get a look at his tape-up line on the nape of his neck. Lynette used to trim him up in the back to make his cut look fresh when he hadn't had time to get to his barber. Those were the simple memories he was looking forward to getting back to.

Ace's cell phone vibrated and he wasn't surprised to see that it was Sheila. Frustration made him answer it. Maybe if he let her get some words off of her chest, she'd back off for the rest of the day. Or forever.

"Yes, Sheila?"

"Ace?" It was obvious that his answering had caught her off guard.

"Why is it necessary for you to call me back to back? There are better things to do on a Sunday morning."

"I really wanted to talk to you," she said, making her voice low and sweet.

"Go ahead. You have one minute. I'm on my way out the door to go to church."

"Oh. Well maybe we can meet when you get out of service."

"No," Ace said forcefully, trying to dash any anticipation she had. "We can't. Whatever you have to say, please say it now, because we're not going to keep having these conversations."

"What conversations? You won't even talk to me."

"And I told you why." Ace wished he hadn't answer the phone.

"It's not fair. You owe me."

She's about to sing that same song. "I gave you what I owed you. And that was to tell you the truth and to treat you in a respectful manner. But you're making that hard."

Sheila's voice sounded exasperated and Ace could tell by the slight quiver in it that she was about to cry.

"Look, Ace. I still think we can work things out if you give me a chance. Give *us* a chance. We had a future to look forward to and I don't think God would shut it down like that. And I have something I really need to talk to you about. You'll see that it's not over between us."

"Sometimes God does things we don't understand," Ace said. Sheila always seemed to find her spiritual side at times that were convenient for her. He continued, "That's why you need to look to Him for comfort because I'll probably never be able to explain things in a way that you're willing to accept."

"But Ace—"

"No, Sheila," Ace said, thwarting her attempt to keep him on the phone as long as possible. "I'm hanging up now. I have to go." Ace disconnected from the call, and after a second thought, turned his cell phone off completely. He turned up his stereo when he recognized the crooning voices of The Mighty Clouds of Joy, and tried to drown out every thought except those that were in agreement with his faith and the new promises for his life that God had shown him.

Sheila's call had set him back even more in time, and Ace had to rush to put on his suit pants and dress shirt. He hung his suit coat on a hanger and draped it with a tie so that it wouldn't get wrinkled on the ride, then threw a change of clothes in a duffel bag so that he could get comfortable after service. Ace settled for an energy drink for breakfast as he hit the new alarm code and walked out the door.

Chapter 58

Sheila flipped past a row of dresses and suits that had hems that she thought were unsuitable for Grace Temple. It was true that it was one of the more progressive ministries in town to be such a small church, but their pews were still full of the kind of elderly mothers who would drape one of those purple and gold cloths over your legs if they deemed it necessary. Besides, in the state that Ace was in now, he wouldn't be moved by any sight of extra flesh showing anyway.

When Ace saw her today, Sheila wanted him to think an angel had walked into the sanctuary and sat beside him. The red St. John's pantsuit would make it look like she was trying to draw all of the attention to herself, and the black dress looked like she was going to a funeral. The only thing headed to the grave today would be Ace's feelings for Lynette.

I don't have much time, Sheila thought, pushing past two low-cut numbers. Thankfully, she'd showered last night, but she'd fallen asleep without wrapping her hair in the silk scarf that she wore nightly. That meant she'd have to add at least another fifteen minutes to her estimated time of departure so that she could be perfectly stylish from head to stiletto-covered toe.

Sheila kept pushing through the clothes in her closet. One day Sheila felt bloated, and the next she would feel like her stomach was a sunken pit. But she finally found a topaz blue wrap dress that she knew she could adjust according to her ever-changing waistline. She moisturized her skin with a perfumed body cream, put on her makeup with special attention to contour her high cheekbones, then spent the rest of the time styling her hair.

When Sheila was ready to walk out the door, she was more confident than ever that there would be a change in her life this Sunday.

Sheila had scanned the pews in front of her at least three times in every section and she still hadn't seen Ace. *What was I thinking? I should've checked the parking lot for his car before I got stuck in here.*

She would've preferred to be closer to the back, but she'd been ushered—nearly pushed—closer up the aisle and to a pew that was about halfway between the back and the pulpit. She'd tried to sit on the end of the row, but those already in the worship service refused to scoot down. She'd been involuntarily pushed to the middle of the pew. Stuck. And the usher who led her there was guarding the door out of the sanctuary like it was Fort Knox.

By the time Sheila arrived, Pastor Bailey had already begun his sermon, and he was deep into the crux of his message now. She couldn't inconspicuously tip out the side door either. Stuck. The woman to her left slid closer to her so that she could put her purse on the pew. More like wedged now.

It was possible that Ace had seen her when she walked in and decided to leave before she could lay eyes on him. It was hard for Sheila to turn around and look behind her without being met by faces that she was sure would wonder what—other than the pastor's sermon—could command her attention. She hadn't heard a single word Pastor Bailey had said other than a few Scriptures he'd recited. She was embarrassed that she'd flipped through the Bible several times with no success at finding Ezekiel or Isaiah. So instead of continuing to leaf through the pages, or looking at the table of contents, she scribbled the Scriptures down in a memo pad that was tucked in her purse.

The woman to Sheila's right suddenly yelled out. "I know that's right, Pastor. You better tell the truth to shame the devil." She repositioned the toddler sitting on her lap and the little girl's feet somehow ended up being propped up on Sheila's lap.

I don't believe this, Sheila thought.

"You're really preaching now, Pastor," the woman said again and waved her funeral home fan toward the pulpit.

Sheila decided that she might as well tune into Pastor Bailey's message since it seemed she wasn't going anywhere until the benediction.

"Why in the *world* would you want somebody else's blessing? You should want what God has for you because anything else that you manipulate to get into your life is only temporary—especially if it's not God's will for your life."

"Amens" rolled across the sanctuary.

"You're looking across the church at somebody else's man because you think he can be the peanut butter to your jelly," Pastor Bailey said, laughing at his own comment. "But you don't know what his wife is dealing with behind closed doors. Trust me, everybody has their issues. And I'd much rather deal with the issues that I'm anointed for."

Pastor Bailey walked to the end of the pulpit. "I don't know why I'm off on this tangent, and I don't know who this is for, but it's for somebody up in here."

"Help 'em out, sir," a man in the front row said, standing up to punctuate his point.

Pastor Bailey picked up the Bible that was lying open on the podium. He shook it in the air. "Stop running after a man, and start running after God. 'Seek ye first the kingdom of God, and his righteousness; and all these things shall be added unto you.' You can't keep living your life the way you're doing. You're going to have to change some things if you ever expect to have the joy of the Lord: leave—the—man—alone."

Sheila tuned out again. A few times when she'd attended church with Ace, Pastor Bailey had preached a sermon that Sheila thought had been just for her. This wasn't one of those times, she thought. First of all, Pastor Bailey was a man of the cloth and it was much easier for him to seek God and be righteous. Second and more importantly, he was a man. He could never feel with a woman's heart.

The woman beside Sheila elbowed Sheila in the side. "He's telling the truth, ain't he?"

Maybe for you, Sheila thought.

For the next thirty minutes until the end of the sermon, Sheila stared at a small piece of lint in the hair of the woman sitting on the pew in front of her. Sheila's heart began to pound loudly against her chest when Pastor Bailey made the call for salvation to the congregation. She always hated this part, and was relieved when he finally dismissed the service.

The women on either side of her were taking their time gathering their belongings and their children. Sheila tried not to let her frustration show on her face, but things were getting worse by the second. Her feet felt like the blood was being squeezed out of them in her shoes.

"Excuse me."

Sheila turned around at a tap on her shoulder. The man's face looked familiar, but she couldn't place his name.

"You're Brother Ace's friend, right?"

"Yes. Sheila," she said, feeling that she could at least be cordial even though she wasn't interested in talking to anyone. Besides, she was still scoping the people who were milling around just in case Ace hadn't left after all.

"I haven't seen him in a while and I was wondering if everything is all right."

"Um, yes. He's doing fine. I think he was here earlier but evidently he had to tip out."

"Oh, okay. I must've missed seeing him. I can usually see most people from my seat in the pulpit."

That's right, Sheila thought. *He was one of the ministers.*

"Well tell him I said hello. And I hope to see you again, too. It's been quite some time, but I can imagine that you have your own church home."

"I'll pass the word to him," Sheila said, ignoring his latter comment. Church home was pretty accurate. Her church was at home. And she could attend several services on one Sunday if she wanted to.

"Minister Lee," the man added. "Tell him Minister Lee said hello."

"I certainly will," Sheila said. She hadn't thought to ask the man his name. But when she talked to Ace, it would be an extra point on her slate if she could prove that she'd actually been at service.

Sheila was finally able to squeeze past the people who were dawdling about on her row. She walked to her car as fast as her aching feet would allow, then rode through the parking lot once to see if Ace's car was there. She hadn't really expected it to be, but she'd gotten out of the bed to come to church so anything was possible. Anything.

Chapter 59

The cars of family and friends were lined up and down both sides of the street and as usual, some of the Moreheads' neighbors had offered the extra space in their driveways for the spillover. Ace had driven over from the church alone since he'd asked Uncle Sanford if he had time for a short one-on-one counseling session with him. Ace thought there was never such a thing as obtaining too much wise counsel. And after speaking with Uncle Sanford about his intentions and his and Lynette's desire to attend marriage counseling he felt even more at peace.

Ace coasted down the street until he found a place to park. It was a benefit to have a compact car in situations like this, and he parallel parked his vehicle between two others. Unless he and Lynette planned to keep his car as their weekend toy, he realized he'd have to get rid of it and upgrade to a car more suited for his family. Whatever his wife wanted. Lynette. His wife. He smiled at the thought of it.

Mama Claudette was the first to acknowledge Ace as he stepped into the backyard. She pushed open the back porch door with her hip, and Ace willingly took the pan of warm macaroni and cheese out of her hands.

"Is my macaroni the only reason why you want to help me?" she asked.

"Now Mama Claudette you know better than that. I'm indebted to you. I owe you a lot more than helping you carry *my* pan of macaroni and cheese. You pushed me past my fear and into a place of faith."

"Not me. That was God. But I know that if I hadn't done it, you would've done it sooner or later. I just wanted it to be *sooner*, rather than later."

"Me too," Ace said, waiting while Mama Claudette adjusted the other pots and aluminum pans covering the tables lined across the backyard. There was barely space to add another pan, but Mama Claudette managed to make room for her family favorite.

"Lynette's inside icing a cake for me," Mama Claudette said. "Don't let my kinfolks get on your nerves. You know some of them are likely to come with a thousand questions, but you can tell them to mind their business. In fact, tell them that *I* said to mind their own business."

Ace laughed. Because even though she said it in jest, he knew she truly meant every word. And it wasn't long from the time Mama Claudette left his side that the questions started.

Lynette's cousin, Dante, slipped up on Ace from nowhere. "Been a long time, bro. Does Lynette know you're here?" he said, attempting to put on a protective front.

It was obvious that Dante hadn't stepped foot in church that morning and had probably slept in and awakened just in time to make sure he would be one of the first to have a Sunday dinner plate. Not only had Ace and Lynette worshiped together, but they'd gone to the altar as a couple when Uncle Sanford called for those wanting prayer for wisdom and direction.

"I didn't see you at church this morning," Ace said, deflecting Dante's probing.

Dante cleared his throat. "I had some business to take care of so I couldn't make it."

"That's too bad," Ace said, picking up a cup of sweet tea from among those set out on the drink table. "But I'm glad to see you here. Welcome back; we've missed you," Ace said, knowing his attempt to turn the tables on Dante had left the boy confused.

Dante hesitated for a moment before he caught the gist. "Oh, I get it. Yeah, bro. Welcome back."

"Uh-huh," Ace said, then shook hands with Dante. "Stay out of trouble."

"Much as I can," Dante said, thumbing the tip of his nose. "If you can get these women to keep their hands off of me, half of my problems would be solved."

"Is that so?" Ace said. Dante had always talked about the number of women he had to constantly fight off, but Ace had never seen any of them at a family function. "I'll leave those multiple women to you. I'm a one-woman man," he said, and noticed Lynette walking out the backdoor. "And here she is now."

"You better be glad she let you back in the game," Dante said, pulling out his tough exterior again. "It's hard to step up and be the star player when you've been a benchwarmer for so long." He walked away with an exaggerated swagger in his step.

If he leans any more to the side he's gonna tip over, Ace thought.

"What's Dante running his mouth about?" Lynette asked.

"Nothing worth mentioning."

"As usual," Lynette said. Her face lit up. "And as usual you look handsome. I didn't tell you that, today."

"Appreciate it," Ace said, remembering his duffel bag with the change of clothes that he'd left in his trunk. "You know I like to look good for you and all, but I'm gonna change out of these clothes. It's bound to get ugly around here."

"You're right," Lynette said. "Nothing's changed. Daddy is going to call for the horseshoes challenge as soon as everybody finishes eating."

Jada and Carmen came outside with a flock of their cousins following behind them. Carmen was carrying a stack of magazines, and it looked like she had an entire electronics store clipped to the waist of her jeans.

"Hey, Daddy," Carmen said. "What took you so long?"

"I had to talk to Uncle Sanford."

Carmen playfully poked her father in his side. "He had to give you the big talk, didn't he Daddy? You should know this time around that it's always the man's fault, so if you want to keep peace in our house, simply apologize and retreat to your corner."

"What?" Ace said. "When she's acting like that she's officially *your* daughter," he told Lynette.

"No. *Your* daughter. And she's been watching too much television. Evidently, I need to deprogram her mind from talk shows." Lynette swatted at her daughter's backside. "Get out of here before your mouth gets you in trouble."

Jada put her hand on her hip. "Really. Get yourself under control, young lady," she said, teasing her older sister.

"I'm going. I'm going," Carmen said, while her entourage of cousins giggled and followed behind her out to a small shed near the perimeter of the yard.

Ace remembered when Pop had bought a new storage house and he'd allowed his granddaughters to keep the old one for an apartment, as he called it. Sunlight through open windows provided the only source of light, but the girls would still recline on the beanbags and futon furniture, content with their battery-operated radio until their grandparents made them come inside.

"Carmen really surprised me today. I still can't believe she belted out the solo part in that song like that," Ace said. "I always knew she had a gift, but it's like it matured out of the blue."

"Tell me about it," Lynette said. "She didn't even tell me about it, that's why I was about to break down crying in the church when she started singing. The one thing that kept me from doing it was that if she would've seen me, she would've refused to sing another song. Ever."

Lynette walked alongside Ace as he went to his car to get his clothes. He purposefully took slow strides so they could enjoy the time together. It was probably the last time that day that he'd be able to steal away with her without being interrupted by folks bringing up old childhood stories and reunions of the past.

Lynette picked up a straw wrapper that had found its way onto the spotless neighborhood street. "Carmen said on the way over here that she'd wanted her solo to be a surprise for us. A gift from her and God for us getting back together."

"She didn't tell me that either," Ace said. He rested his hand comfortably on Lynette's shoulder.

"Well she's a sixteen-year-old now and unfortunately there may be a lot of things she won't tell you. Not voluntarily anyway."

Ace got his clothes from the trunk and started an unhurried trek back to the house. Just as he figured, Lynette was summoned into her family's activities as soon as she walked into sight.

The plate her Aunt Olivia was carrying looked ready to fold in two, but she placed it on the table in front of her third—possibly her fourth—husband. Ace had lost count of the aunt's marriages, but he thought she'd never gotten over her first one, Henry. All of the subsequent husbands looked remarkably familiar to Henry. They were all at least three inches shorter than her and bald.

"Lynette, we've been looking for you," Aunt Olivia said. "Can you please come and tell Nikki that a child can rot their baby teeth before they even come in? She lets that baby of hers crawl around with a bottle full of juice all the time. And sleep with it in the crib, too. It's ridiculous."

"Here we go," Lynette mumbled.

"I'll catch up with you," Ace said to her. "You go ahead and do damage control."

It was a short distance to the bathroom but it still took Ace at least fifteen minutes to make it behind closed doors. He was stopped so many times that he was starting to think that all the food would be gone by the time he changed clothes and was able to make it back outside.

When he unzipped his duffel bag, he remembered that he'd thrown his cell phone inside after he'd turned it off. He decided to power it up. He was expecting a phone call from Grandma Toot today and she absolutely hated to get his voice mail. Instead of leaving a message about what she wanted, she'd use up the recording time complaining about how much she hated to talk to machines.

The message alert beeped as soon as the phone came on. Ace dialed into his voice mail and set the phone on intercom so he could continue to get dressed. The first message was from Grandma Toot ranting about the fact that he'd taken his personal greeting off of his voice mail and she hoped she was leaving a message with the right person. But it was the second message that almost made him fall to his knees.

"Don't hang up on this message, Ace," Sheila said. "You refused to meet me in person so I had no other choice but to leave you a voice message. I even came to church this morning, but you weren't there. I don't think there was any other place you would've wanted to be when you got news about your child, and I'm not talking about Carmen and Jada. I'm talking about our child, Ace." Her voice rose in excitement with her last sentence, but Ace's heart simultaneously sunk to his feet. "I'm pregnant."

Chapter 60

Lynette made herself a plate then went back through the line to make one for Ace. On an occasion like this, he wasn't a discriminatory eater, and she knew he would scoff down everything she put on his plate. There was an empty seat on the bench by her father. Even though she hadn't spent as much time together over the last year as they used to, Lynette was still a daddy's girl at heart.

"Hey Daddy," she said, sitting down beside him. She gave him a kiss on the cheek.

"What up, baby girl?" he said, looking at the extra plate she'd put on the table. "You've got some appetite today."

Lynette slid her own plate closer to her and covered Ace's with a napkin. "If I could eat this much Ace would have some problems on his hands."

"He's already got problems. He's going to have enough to deal with moving back in the house with one grown woman and two wannabe grown women."

"You sound so sure that we're going to be married again."

"I am sure. And you are, too."

"When I'm alone and thinking about it, it makes me nervous, Daddy. I'm scared of failing at marriage again. And it's more than just me I have to think about. It's the girls, too."

"Trust me. Ace is carrying the same kind of weight that you are, if not more. That's why you have to cast your cares on Jesus. All of them."

Her father scraped up his last bit of green beans then went to work on the squash casserole. Lynette always thought it was weird that he ate all of one kind of food on his plate before he moved to another.

"Don't you think God knew you'd come back to this point? There's no such thing as catching Him off guard. Now me? That's another story. But your mama came to me some time ago and said she felt something stirring up in her spirit and that you two would get back together." He snapped his fingers. "I think it was around the time y'all went off on that overnight spa trip for your birthday. And you know how your mama is when she feels like God has shown her something. She fasts and prays until she sees that thing to the end."

"She never told me she had a feeling about me and Ace."

"Because she didn't want you to take off running in the other direction." Her father laughed and turned his plate around to his cornbread stuffing.

Sometimes Lynette felt like her mother had a private line to God.

Ace walked out of the back door and it was apparent to Lynette that his countenance had changed. He'd gone inside strutting like a peacock showing off its feathers, but he'd returned with slumped shoulders. Even when Dante stopped to ham it up with him, Ace's reaction seemed forced. Lynette wondered which one of her family members had said something to him to cause him to retreat into a shell. And what in the world had they said?

"I'll be back, Daddy," Lynette said, covering her plate. She was still hungry enough to go through the buffet line two more times, but there was something—someone—more important right now. She was already starting to become more concerned for Ace than she was for herself.

"Hey," she said, putting her arm around his waist and stopping him from walking. She lowered her voice. "What's going on? You look like something is bothering you."

"Today is not about me. It's about being with your family." Ace clapped his hands together. "I've been waiting all day for some food. Don't hold me back now."

It was a front. Lynette knew it and she wasn't going to let him hold his frustrations inside. It wasn't physically or emotionally healthy. It wasn't how she wanted them to renew their relationship.

"In case you don't know, my sixth sense for you has already kicked back in," Lynette said. "Something is bothering you and I don't see why you feel the need to hold it in. If this is about being with my family, then that's exactly what I'm trying to do. Because you *are* my family."

Lynette took Ace's hand and led him back into the house, pushing past her family and her parents' neighborhood friends that had crammed themselves into the small kitchen. They didn't seem to mind that they had to yell over each other to have a decent conversation with the person sitting or standing beside them. Lynette, on the other hand, still hadn't mastered the fine art of being in more than one conversation at a time.

Lynette and Ace walked into her parents' room and Lynette closed the door.

"Now." She sat down on the edge of their four-poster bed. "What's going on?"

"Lynette," Ace said. He ran his hand across the hair on his face. "I don't think this is the time. We can talk about things later tonight."

"No," she insisted. "I want to talk about it now. Then we can deal with it and move on," she said, her mind already clicking through who she thought would have the audacity to say anything hateful. "Did somebody say something out of line to you?"

Ace pounded a fist into his hand and Lynette gave him the time he needed to get himself together. After a few long moments, he pulled his cell phone out of his back pocket. It was like his body caved in as a sign of surrender as he sat down on the opposite end of the bed from Lynette.

"I'm sorry, Lynette," Ace whispered.

They weren't the words Lynette wanted to hear. She didn't know what story was behind them, but clearly it wasn't a good one.

Ace pushed a series of buttons on his cell phone then handed it to her.

Lynette listened to Sheila speak words with the power to change her life. *I'm talking about our child, Ace. I'm pregnant.*

Lynette felt like she was about to lose the food that she'd already eaten and stain her mother's freshly polished hardwood floor. This couldn't be happening to them.

Chapter 61

Lynette was glad she was sitting down. She felt faint. "There's no way this is possible, right? Tell me it's not possible."

Ace's voice was almost a whisper. "I wish I could say that. But unfortunately I can't."

"What?" Lynette resisted the urge to scream at the top of her lungs. "Are you telling me that you and Sheila were sleeping together?"

Ace paced back and forth across the area rug in front of her parents' chest of drawers. He was stalling. His method of avoiding confrontation. Some things never changed. Lynette repeated her question, but this time she was standing up and ready to meet him in his face once he looked up from his feet.

"Not on a regular basis," he said. "It only happened a few times over the last two years. One of those times was pretty recently. Before me and you got back together."

Lynette could've smacked him for putting them in this situation. For putting himself in this situation. She had no idea what constituted *a few times* by his standards, but like she'd told Carmen not too long ago . . . it only took once.

And she reminded him of it.

Ace's breathing was so heavy that she could hear it. He walked over to her parents' window, even though the blinds were drawn shut. "I know," he said. "It was stupid and careless."

"And wrong. Don't forget that one. Or let's say that nasty little word that nobody wants to use anymore. Fornication."

Lynette guessed Ace realized how ridiculous it was to be standing at a window where he couldn't even see outside. He sat back down on the bed and rested his forehead between his palms. "I don't know what to say. That's why I didn't want to talk about this right now. I hadn't even had time myself to think it through."

Lynette put one hand on her stomach and another on her head. Not only was her stomach swirling, but now she had a headache. The pressure pounded against her temples.

"What's there to think through, Ace? And waiting to talk about it later wouldn't have done anything to change the situation," Lynette said. "You changed the situation from the minute you lay in the bed with Sheila."

She felt the weight of conviction on her shoulders with the last comment. She was letting her emotions speak for her, but it was hard not to.

"I think I better go home," Ace said, standing up.

Lynette almost couldn't stand to look at Ace right now, yet it infuriated her that he would leave her at a time like this. To deal with this mess by herself. And where was he going? To Sheila's?

God, her parents, and Audrey had convinced Lynette to take a second chance at love. And look what it had gotten her. She firmly believed that God knew what was coming. But Audrey and her parents weren't going to believe this.

"I can't believe this is my life right now," Lynette said.

Ace was mumbling something incoherently, and when Lynette stopped to silence her mouth and mind, she realized he was praying. *He'd* better *do some serious praying right now,* she thought.

"I'm going to go ahead and leave," Ace said.

Ace tried to touch her hand but Lynette moved it out of his reach. It would be hard for Lynette to ever let him touch her again. Not when those were the same hands that had caressed Sheila.

"That's fine. Do whatever you feel is best," she said, even though she didn't mean it.

"I'm only leaving because I don't think it's fair for you to have to deal with this right now."

"Whether you leave or not I'm still going to have to deal with it. Or maybe not."

It was a tough truth to swallow, but it was true. It was Lynette's decision whether she was going to deal with it.

"Don't talk like that. Give me time to figure things out."

He didn't get it, Lynette thought. "You can't analyze this away, Ace. This is not a problem you can plug into your accounting software."

Ace tried again to pull her to him, but Lynette wasn't ready. She opened the bedroom door and walked out. Truthfully, he wasn't the only one who was ready to leave.

Soon after Ace left the house Lynette decided to go home. She tried, but she couldn't enjoy her family. She just kept hearing Sheila's voice. *I'm pregnant . . . I'm pregnant . . . I'm pregnant.* She sounded so happy. Too happy.

"You don't have to sneak off to see Ace," her Aunt Olivia announced loud enough for the entire kitchen to hear. "You all are grown, and we know you'll behave yourselves. We don't want to hear any announcements about any little babies until *after* you're married again. Y'all thinking about getting married again, right?"

Lynette ignored her Aunt Olivia's question. Lynette didn't want to hear about any babies either. But it was too late for that.

"I'm not feeling well," Lynette said. "You know how it is when you want to lie in your own bed."

"It's probably all that food you ate," somebody chimed in. "Mixing all this food will do it to you."

Lynette didn't bother to turn around and see who was offering their two cents. She unhooked her purse out of the coat closet and headed outside to round up Carmen and Jada along with the two cousins that were supposed to be spending the night with them. She wished she could renege on her promise, but the girls had been planning for their company since Lynette convinced them it was best to stay in Georgia with their family over spring break instead of going to New York.

Lynette's mother intercepted her. "Let the girls stay," she said. "I'll bring them home."

"Okay, Ma. Thanks."

Claudette sliced off pieces of a caramel cake and passed them out to those awaiting slices of the coveted dessert people usually paid her to make. "Are you sure you don't want to lie down here? You can go in my room and I'll make sure nobody bothers you."

Lynette shook her head. If her mother knew the conversation that happened in her room, she would've never made such a suggestion. Lynette didn't want to return to her parents' room so soon so she could relive the moment. There was no way she'd be able to get a ounce of peace in there.

"No. I'd rather go home," Lynette said, opening the kitchen drawer for a roll of aluminum foil to wrap her plate. The food didn't look as appetizing as it had before she'd left the table to go talk with Ace. In fact, Lynette didn't have an appetite at all anymore.

"Okay, everyone," Lynette said, hugging and kissing her relatives on her way to the door. "Prayerfully I'll see you all tomorrow at Stone Mountain." Unlike most family reunions that concluded their celebration with a Sunday worship service together, the Neils extended their reunion until Monday, which was traditionally a visit to a local Atlanta attraction.

Lynette moved as fast as she could to get out of there, then found the girls to give them her usual outline of parental instructions.

Lynette decided she was going to pray her way through her emotions tonight. She wouldn't let this situation steal what had been an enjoyable weekend. As soon as she closed her car door, she hit her Bluetooth and called Audrey.

"I hope you're not busy," Lynette said, when her friend answered the phone, "because I really need to come over."

"What? You need time away from the family already?"

"I wish it was that easy," Lynette said. She let down her window. It was starting to feel stuffy inside of her SUV. Even though it was a reasonably warm day, the temperatures weren't high enough that she should feel sweaty and suffocated.

I'm pregnant. Sheila had sounded so exuberant. *She'd probably carefully calculated the time when she could spring the news to Ace,* Lynette thought.

"Come on over," Audrey said, as Lynette knew she would. "Do you have any special request before you get here? Kirk put some beef ribs on the grill and I made coleslaw and veggie baked beans."

"I'm not hungry," Lynette said. She realized after all the effort she'd taken to wrap her plate; she'd ended up leaving it behind. She had no doubt that her mother would bring it to her when she dropped the girls off, along with enough food to feed a tribe for a week.

Lynette sighed. "The only thing I need is prayer. And lots of it."

And pray was the first thing Audrey did when she heard the news from Lynette.

338

Lynette folded over in tears, and Audrey cradled her on her shoulder like they were separated years in age instead of only four months. It was the cry she needed to rinse her spirit clean of all the negative thoughts trying to bombard her mind. They told her that she was a fool for thinking that she deserved love again. They taunted her with how hurt her daughters would be, and told her that Ace would build another family and forget about them. But Lynette felt better. And she knew that with God, she could make it without Ace. If she had to.

"What do you mean make it without Ace?" Audrey asked her. "You're not going to let Sheila come in and take back your promise from God. It's not going to happen. I'm not going to let you go down like that."

"I'm supposed to take this with a grain of salt and let me and Ace move on like nothing has happened?" Lynette couldn't believe her ears, especially when those comments came from Audrey.

"You're going to find out the truth. I think the girl is lying. In fact, I know she's lying."

"How can you be sure she's lying?"

"How can *you* be sure she's pregnant?"

Lynette wasn't sure. In her anger, disappointment, and hurt, she hadn't considered that Sheila could be bluffing, especially since Ace had verified that it was a strong possibility that it was true. That's the part that hurt so much. No, they weren't together during the time in question, but now that they were attempting to rebuild their relationship, it felt like he'd cheated on her.

"Have you talked to Ace since he left the house?" Audrey asked, making Lynette a plate.

It was amazing how true friends could discern each other's needs. Lynette hadn't mentioned that her appetite had suddenly returned, but there was a stack of ribs in front of her before the thought could fully form in her mind.

"I can't talk to him tonight. We need our space."

"Now's the time for you to draw together, not push each other away."

Lynette put down her fork. "I must be talking to a clone because this can't be the Audrey I've known all of these years. In a situation like this I thought for sure you would've told me to send him packing."

Audrey laughed, then her face turned serious again. "I'm trying to be the spiritual mind for you right now. You've got to look beyond what you can see. This ain't nothing but a setup, and I'm sure of it."

"But it doesn't change the fact that he slept with Sheila."

"No it doesn't. But he's going to have to deal with God on that. And you know Ace way better than I do. And you know he's already made peace with God about it. That's probably the first thing he did. His only concern now is probably making peace with you."

Lynette nodded so that Audrey would get off of her case for the time being, but things weren't that easy. Audrey was an outsider looking in, so of course she had a different perspective. With no emotions attached. With no dreams and promises riding on it. Sure, Audrey and Kirk had their marital problems before—like most couples do—but Audrey had never been tested in this way before. And if this test was supposed to be part of Lynette's testimony, she wasn't sure she wanted it.

Chapter 62

Don't believe her."

Kenny should've been having a relaxing Sunday evening with his family, but Ace couldn't help but call him. This was not the kind of news that he wanted to take over into the serene atmosphere of his friend's home, but Ace knew he couldn't take it home. Alone. To an empty house where the disturbing thoughts and shock would follow him.

Kenny was shaking his head. "Don't believe her."

"But we—"

"I know what you did, bro. You've told me about a hundred times in the last ten minutes. And I'm telling you not to believe Sheila, but to still do what you need to do to clear your name and your conscience."

"But what if she is? It's a 50 percent chance and you don't get odds like that often. It's a yes or a no."

"It's on her to prove it," Kenny said. He handed Ace a cue stick. "I know it seems like a rough way to handle it, but I don't think Sheila is fighting fair. You're going to have to confront her on a neutral playing field. Don't go to her house and don't let her come to yours. Go to her job."

Ace hadn't even called Sheila back. He knew she was waiting for him to. First, she'd probably start with the tears. He couldn't take tears tonight. He was too mad at himself for making a mistake that could alter not only his life, but the lives of his daughters. And Lynette.

Lynette had made it clear how she felt about things. She didn't have to deal with it. But if this was the end of them, *he* was going to have to deal with it. And he'd have to do it for the rest of his life.

Kenny sunk a striped ball into the corner pocket. "The wise thing to do is to catch her off guard," he said. "If you let her know you're coming, she'll have time to formulate a plan."

"Bro. She called to say she's pregnant. If she's lying, the plan is pretty much formulated."

"Okay, formulate is the wrong word," Kenny said. He propped the cue stick on top of his fingers and leaned down to get a better view at the tricky shot. He stood up like he was second-guessing his approach. "But I'll tell you one thing. A liar always gets caught. Always. It might take a while, but they'll slip up in their story eventually."

"If she's lying, I don't have time to wait until she slips up. By then, Lynette could've already moved on and decided that it's not worth the wait. She's not only dealing with the possibility of a child, she's dealing with the fact that Sheila and I slept together in the first place."

He'd already asked God for forgiveness and knew that he'd received it, but Ace felt like the regret was eating at his stomach's lining. He needed some sort of chewable tablet for indigestion or it was going to be a long night.

"You know what I always say," Kenny said.

The friends recited Kenny's usual words simultaneously. "Pray about it. Ask God for wisdom, and ultimately for His will to be done."

Ace's cell phone vibrated in his pocket. "I hope this is Lynette," he said, wrestling to pull his phone out of his jeans.

It was Grandma Toot. The last thing he wanted to do was pick up the phone at a time like this. Grandma Toot had a sensitized radar and could pick up on anything. But Ace knew that if he let her call go to the voice mail again, he'd get a lashing for it later.

"I'm glad to hear that you're in the land of the living," Grandma Toot said when Ace answered the phone.

"Yes ma'am. I'm living all right."

"Well you sound like the living is not too good right now. 'This is the day the Lord has made; we will rejoice and be glad in it.'"

Ace sat his cue stick on the edge of the pool table and motioned to Kenny that he needed some time to take the call. He'd tried to make his voice sound lively and carefree, but his attempt was no match to Grandma Toot's spiritual discernment.

"Yes ma'am," he said again.

"I'm calling first of all to check on you since you've been so busy that you can't call me."

Ace knew that was coming. He'd been so wrapped up with work, Lynette and the girls, that he hadn't made his weekly call to Grandma Toot in going on three weeks. He hadn't even had the chance to tell her about him and Lynette getting back together. Now he was glad that he hadn't.

"I'm sorry, Grandma Toot. I've been busy. It won't happen again."

"That's right. You should never get too busy for your family," she chastised.

"Yes ma'am," Ace said again. "I'll do better."

Grandma Toot had a series of coughs and sneezes before she

could go on. "Whew," she said, clearing her throat. "I've been battling this old nasty cold for a few days."

Ace was prepared to take a trip out to Griffin if he needed to. He thought it might do him some good to go and tend to his grandmother and take his mind off of his own problems. But in his own selfish way, he wanted to be close to home for when Lynette called him. Lynette might be mad—even disappointed—for a few hours, but she'd come around. Right now, he needed her more than anything.

"Do you need me to come and bring you something?" Ace offered.

"Lord, no. I'll eat me some of this onion I got over here and this cold will be out of my system," she said.

Ace nearly gagged at the memory. Onions were Grandma Toot's cure for everything. Whenever she caught an ailment, she'd try to run it out of her body by either eating an onion like it was an apple, or adding a clove of garlic to her meals. Ace had his share of onions in his days living with her.

"What I really wanted to call and talk to you about was this dream that I had," Grandma Toot said. "It was so real that I needed to call and see if it was true."

"What kind of dream?" Ace asked. His question caught Kenny's attention.

"I had a dream that you were getting married."

"Married?" Ace asked, giving Kenny a glimpse into Grandma Toot's conversation.

"Married. And I thought to myself, surely Ace isn't up and marrying that woman he's been seeing all this time and I haven't even met her before. Since you still ain't brought her out here to see me, I figured she wasn't really somebody you would settle down with in the long run."

Ace had never thought of it that way. All this time, he'd had so many excuses as to why he and Sheila hadn't visited Grandma Toot together. Whenever he went to Griffin for a day's visit, he took the girls with him.

"Ace? Did you hang up?" Grandma Toot interrupted his thoughts.

"No ma'am, I'm here."

"Well you're not getting married, are you?"

"*When* I do, it won't be to Sheila," he said. There was no time like the present to tell Grandma Toot about Lynette. Initially at the beginning of their conversation he was going to keep things to himself until things were ironed out. But now his faith had kicked in. And his faith wouldn't let him keep quiet.

"Grandma Toot. Me and Lynette are going to get married again."

Ace thought he heard her drop something in the background.

"I believe you might need to come out to see me after all," she said, her voice more cheerful than Ace had heard it in a while. "Because somebody is going to have to pick me up off of this kitchen floor." She laughed until she caught a coughing fit. "Whew," she said. "Now that good news might have knocked this cold right on out of me."

Suddenly, Ace's spirits were lifted. He could feel himself getting mentally stronger.

"Maybe that explains the baby I was seeing in the dream, too," Grandma Toot said. "I bet y'all are going to have another little one soon after you get married. I betcha thought you were done with children."

I refuse to get deterred. I can't let this thing take me out. God is in control. Ace started to run confessions through his mind.

Ace finally found the guts to say, "A baby?" The look of shock transferred from Ace's face to Kenny's.

"Yes. But there was a funny thing about the baby, though," Grandma Toot said. "For one thing I couldn't tell if it was a boy or girl because the child was wrapped up so tight in one of those blankets," she said. "I used to wrap your mama up tight like that," she said, running off on a tangent. "If I didn't, she'd only sleep for a few minutes and then she'd be up making enough noise to wake up the city. I believe I wrapped her up like that until she was a good five or six months old."

Ace could care less about that right now. He needed to know about the baby in the dream. "What else was different about the baby?" Ace asked.

"The child kept disappearing. Every time I held my hands out to take it out of your arms it would disappear. Like it wasn't even there."

Ace stood up and pumped his fist in the air.

"Grandma Toot I could kiss you right now," Ace said. "You don't even know how you made my day."

He'd heard the word from Grandma Toot and Sheila couldn't convince him otherwise. Sheila was lying. And he was going to make her come clean.

Chapter 63

Ace had one day to make it good. He was going on flight duty tomorrow morning which meant this Monday was the day to take care of business. He couldn't get on the plane with unsettled issues, and once Grandma Toot had dropped her revelation on him, he realized now that all he had to do was pick up the pieces in his life.

Ace backed out of the drugstore parking lot and hit the highway. Everything today was working in his favor. The department of transportation seemed to have taken a day off from roadwork in downtown Atlanta, because he didn't hit any delays. And although the meteorologist had predicted a 60 percent chance of early morning showers, there wasn't a single cloud streaked across the sky.

When he walked up to the receptionist desk at J. Morrow Corporate Recruiters, the woman manning the front lifted her headset off of her teased hair. Ace couldn't forget a hairdo like that—it was indicative of most styles from the seventies TV shows that he used to watch—and he remembered that he'd seen the woman at the office Christmas party. He looked at her name plate. Nancy.

"How are you doing, Ms. Nancy?" he said.

Nancy looked at him like she was trying her best to place his face. "I know I've seen you before," she said. "I don't want to get myself in trouble, so go ahead and tell me your name."

"Ace Bowers," he said.

"Ace. Ace," she repeated. It seemed her pink cheeks lit up. "Ohhhhhh, Ace. Sheila's man of honor," she said. Nancy looked at the clock on her desk then started clicking through an electronic calendar program on her computer screen. "Was she expecting you? Because her team is in a meeting right now. They should be done in about five minutes, if not less. Someone else is scheduled to use the conference room right after them."

"No problem," Ace said. "I'll wait if that's okay," he said, sitting down. *I'll wait all day if I have to.*

"Please do," Nancy said, lowering her voice. "It'll do Sheila some good to see that you're surprising her like this. She hasn't been herself lately."

Ace picked up a magazine. It wasn't the surprise that Sheila was going to be hoping for. He felt bad for having to do things this way, but he'd been pushed into a corner. Ace hated to be forced into a corner. He would've preferred it if he and Sheila were able to part ways amicably from the start, but Ace was man enough to take part of the blame. From the moment he'd started having feelings for Lynette, he should've backed out of the relationship with Sheila from then. But at the airport, Sheila had basically had her grip around their relationship yanked from her hands. It wasn't fair, but it was right.

Just as Nancy had predicted, the meeting of Sheila's team was over in less than five minutes. Ace couldn't see them, but he could hear them leaving the conference room.

"I'll buzz her," Nancy told Ace. "Sheila. You have a visitor up front." Nancy paused a moment then said, "Will do."

Nancy stood up and motioned for Ace. "You can go on back," she said. "I didn't want to spoil your surprise so I didn't tell her who it was."

"I appreciate that," Ace said. He was doing exactly like Kenny suggested—meeting her on a neutral playing field and letting the element of surprise work in his favor.

But surprise wasn't all that was on Sheila's face when he walked into her office. She looked elated, and the first thing she did was close her office door behind him.

"Baby, you got my message," Sheila said, and tried to push herself into his arms. "I know it wasn't planned, but this is the best thing that could've happened to us."

Ace wouldn't let her snuggle into an embrace with him.

Dejection covered her face. "It's going to be all right," she said, as if she had to give him comfort. "We'll get through it. All of us together." Sheila rubbed her stomach.

Ace wished she'd stop talking. He'd had sympathy for her hurt feelings, but as she kept digging her trench of lies, it was making it hard for him to feel anything but resentment. This wasn't the woman he'd met and been with over the years. It was like Sheila had taken off—or rather put on—a mask that wasn't hers. Her actions made her look like her best friend, Cassandra, and it wasn't the least bit appealing.

Ace didn't bother to sit down. He planned on being in and out with as little drama as possible. Ace reached into his pocket and pulled out the small bag from the drugstore and took out its contents. He handed Sheila a pregnancy test.

"I need you to prove it to me," he said flatly. "It's a shame that I even have to say this, but I think you're lying."

"What do you mean you think I'm lying? Why would I lie about something like this?"

Ace was still holding the test. Sheila wouldn't take it in her

349

grasp. "I don't know," he said. "Why *would* you lie about something like this?"

"I don't have to prove anything to you, Ace," Sheila said. "I'm not a loose woman. I don't go around lying in the bed of a bunch of different men. You know that you were the only person I was with."

"I never called you a loose woman," Ace said. "I think nothing of the sort. In fact, I don't know who you are right now." He changed his mind and took a seat. "And I'm not leaving until you take the test."

Ace put the pregnancy test on top of her in-box.

Chapter 64

Sheila's plan was backfiring and she had no idea how to get out of it. She hadn't expected Ace to walk in the door. She had an interview scheduled in less than ten minutes, and she was sure that the applicant had arrived early in an attempt to impress her even more than he'd already done with his résumé and their phone conversations.

"I have an interview scheduled with an applicant that I'm trying to place in a job," Sheila stammered. Every day she'd had to prove to her superiors that she was worth keeping and not axing during their next round of reductions. "I don't have time for this nonsense." *No time.*

"Neither do I," Ace said.

He didn't budge. Sheila knew that Ace meant what he'd said, and it wasn't an option for her to reschedule because the applicant was driving in from Nashville, Tennessee.

"Either you believe me, or you don't," Sheila said.

How could Ace do this to her? When he'd walked in the door, she was so sure that he was coming to claim his love for her and confess that he hadn't been in his right mind for the past month. Once Ace spent the time with Lynette, she thought he'd surely remember the reasons for their divorce in the first place. That was what she'd been forcing herself to dream. Not this.

Sheila thought she'd gotten off the hook when Ace stood. Either something came upon him and he was accepting her lie as the truth, or he was about to take a drastic measure.

Ace walked close up on her, invading her personal space. On one hand it was what she wanted, but she didn't know how to perceive his actions. Ace wasn't a violent man so she knew that he wouldn't inflict any bodily harm on her. Yet it wasn't a physical touch that hurt her. It was his words . . . and the truth in them.

"Why are you doing this?" Ace said. "This isn't you. You're not this kind of woman. If you were, then we never would've lasted even as long as we did."

Sheila was not going to cry. Crying was a sign of guilt.

"You're too beautiful—inside and out—to act like this. You deserve what God has for you. And if I'm not the one, the best thing you could do for your life is accept it, then expect the next best thing. An even greater thing."

Ace picked up her hands and held them in his. Instead of feeling a romantic connection, she felt like Ace was speaking to her as an older brother. "It may hurt for a while, but it'll get better. Trust me. Sooner or later, I'll be the last thing on your mind."

Right now it didn't feel that way. Thoughts of Ace had consumed Sheila's mind day and night. It didn't even stop when she was sleeping. How would things ever get better?

Sheila's first tear fell. Then a second. Then there were too many to count. Sheila fell into Ace's chest. Her entire body quaked, and the tears begin to back up into her sinuses. She dropped to her knees, and before she could control her actions, found herself clinging to Ace's leg. Ace bent down and peeled her fingers from his thighs.

"Don't do this to yourself, Sheila," Ace said, trying to pull her up to her feet. "Stop for a minute and think about it."

And she did. Sheila imagined how ridiculous she looked, and now she felt the same. She wiped her face and leaned on Ace for support.

"I think God wants to have you to Himself before you ever put yourself completely in a man," Ace said. He'd wrapped his arms around her now, holding her until she was calm enough to hear what he was saying. "I apologize for letting things happen between us that shouldn't have. I should've been more of a man of God, but I know that He forgives both of us and will give us a fresh start. Every day if we need it."

"I don't know how I'll make it," Sheila said. She stepped out of Ace's grasp and looked for her purse. Nancy would probably be buzzing in about her appointment at any minute and Sheila needed to get cleaned up. Pastor Bailey's words echoed in her ears. *"You can't keep living your life the way you're doing. You're going to have to change some things if you ever expect to have the joy of the Lord: leave— the—man—alone."*

Sheila opened up her compact and saw what a mess she really looked. Her mascara was streaked down her cheeks and it looked like she'd been crying for days instead of minutes.

"You still think I'm beautiful?" she asked, looking at Ace and forcing a weak smile.

"I still do," he said. "I'm leaving now," Ace added. He backed toward the door. "But I want you to remember one thing. People may walk in and out of your life, but God never leaves you."

And Ace was gone. She knew that would be the last time she'd see him. He was walking away to a new life now, and as much as she hated to see him leave, she realized she loved him enough to want him to be happy. Sheila ran a makeup remover pad across her face. *Even if it's not with me.*

Chapter 65

Ace pulled up to the gate attendant and paid her the eight dollars necessary to enter the parking areas at Stone Mountain Park. He'd already texted Carmen and asked her where Lynette's family was convening for their closeout picnic for the reunion, and convinced her that the designer shoes she'd been asking for would be hers by the end of the week if she could keep his arrival to herself.

Ace had been in prayer during the entire ride from Sheila's job to Stone Mountain. His burden for carrying Sheila's hurt had been removed and he was confident that he'd done what God had told him to do this morning before he'd left to go to her workplace. Ensure Sheila that she's a woman of worth. Point Sheila back to Him. There was finally closure and Ace was free to move forward. This time with no setbacks—or setups.

Lynette hadn't called him last night, but that didn't deter Ace. He was a man on a mission, he thought, as he wound through the maze of streets until he found the covered picnic shelter where the Neil family—and some visiting Morehead family and friends—had congregated. Lynette was the first person he spotted, and fortunately her back was turned to him. He didn't know why she was flailing her arms about until he walked closer and realized she was engrossed in a game of charades.

"*Gone with the Wind,*" somebody finally yelled out.

"Yes," she said clapping. "Goodness. I thought we were going to be here all night."

"That's not our fault," Aunt Olivia said. "You probably knew Ace was behind you and you couldn't keep your thoughts straight."

Ace shook his head. He could always count on good ol' Aunt Olivia.

"Daddy!" Jada screamed. As always, she was the first of his daughters to his side. "I didn't know you were coming out here."

"Yeah, Daddy," Carmen said, flocking to his other side. "Neither did I." She discreetly pinched him on his elbow as a reminder of their silent agreement.

"Make that three of us," Lynette said.

Ace wished she'd wrap her arms around him, too, but she didn't. He couldn't look at her outward reactions; he had to go with what was in her heart. A woman who was forgiving and virtuous. A woman who'd extend grace to him. The woman who thought they deserved a second chance.

Carmen kissed Ace on the cheek. "Come on, Jada. Let's go ahead and get something to eat so we can go to the Ride the Ducks with Grandma."

"Make sure you let me know before you leave," Lynette yelled after them.

If Ace had anything to do with it, Lynette wasn't going to escape from him. Although he cherished the time they shared as a family, he'd come to the park with specific intentions. To be with her. He knew he couldn't usurp all of her time from the reunion, but they had to have some time alone. It would be days before he saw her again.

Lynette knew he wanted to be alone with her, which is probably why she walked toward a grassy area away from the shelter and the folks that were starting to bombard the grill and picnic tables as if they were eating their last meal. He followed her until she stopped, then Ace jumped in before she could get in a word.

"There's no baby," he said. "I'm sure of it. I went to see Sheila today. It was a lie."

It was a lie that made Ace have to expose his indiscretions. He'd fallen short of the mark. Yesterday he could tell that Lynette was hurt by that more than anything else. He could tell by her reaction to him, that she'd kept her body holy toward God. Four years and she'd known no one since him, just as she'd known no one before him. It made him want her as his wife even more.

"God has forgiven me for sleeping with Sheila. All I'm asking is that you do the same. I know that just because it wasn't planned, doesn't mean it was right."

Ace had always hated to disappoint Lynette. Whenever he did, she'd give him the look that she was giving him now. It affected him more than any verbal harangue.

"What kind of person would I be if I didn't forgive you?" Lynette finally said. "When you left yesterday I was feeling crushed beyond measure, and of course, all I could do last night was pray. God told me He would put the pieces of my life back together."

Lynette was saying nearly the exact same words that Ace had thought this morning.

Ace held out his hand. "Will you come with me?"

"Where are we going?" Lynette asked. She slipped her hand into his.

"To the next level," he said.

Ace had to pull Lynette past her questioning family members, and as usual, Mama Claudette helped him beat off the persistent ones who had nothing else better to do than dig into other people's lives. Like Aunt Olivia.

"Go sit down, Olivia," Ace heard Mama Claudette say. "Go tend to your husband or climb to the top of the mountain."

"If I'm climbing, you're climbing," Aunt Olivia said. "And you know can't neither one of us make it up there. God help us all."

"That's *your* family," Ace said.

"And as crazy as they are, I wouldn't trade them for anything," Lynette said.

Ace and Lynette walked to his car so that he could drive her to the Summit Skyride attraction. Even though she'd married a pilot for whom flying and heights was second nature, Lynette wasn't one for heights. The only reason she could endure airplane flights she said, is because she could sit in an aisle seat and not have to see what was going on thousands of feet below her.

That's why Ace wasn't surprised at her hesitance when she realized where they were going.

"I think you left part of your mind when you went to go see Sheila this morning," she teased. "I'm not going up there."

"Yes, you are," he said.

"No. I'm not."

"Yes. You are. Because this is about trust, and you know I'd never take you anywhere to hurt you."

Lynette looked up in the sky and watched the Swiss cable car slide across the cables, then looked at Ace. "I can't believe I'm going to do this," she said.

Every time Ace came to Stone Mountain Park, it was the first attraction he visited. There was something about being suspended over eight hundred feet above the ground. To Ace it represented a total trust in God. While in the cable car, they wouldn't be able to see the equipment that connected the ride to the car. They would just have to believe that they'd arrive at their destination—at the top of the mountain—at the intended time.

Ace bought two one-way tickets for the Skyride. Although he enjoyed the short three-minute journey where he could see the Atlanta skyline and Appalachian Mountains, Lynette kept her eyes closed until they were on stable ground.

Ace stood behind Lynette, his arms wrapped around her mid-section, as they looked out at the view. The time had finally come. This Monday's intentions were about to be complete.

"So this is the next level?" Lynette said, settling back into his arms. She rested her weight against his chest.

"No," Ace said. He turned Lynette around to face him, then dropped to one knee. "This is."

Reading Group Guide

Dear Readers:

These questions are provided to help facilitate an entertaining and thoughtful exchange about the issues and characters in *The Last Woman Standing*. If you'd like to arrange for Tia McCollors to join your book club discussion (in person or via phone) or visit with your organization, please contact the author at Tia@TiaMcCollors.com. She also welcomes readers to sign her guestbook on her website at **www.TiaMcCollors.com**.

GENERAL QUESTIONS

What was the most memorable scene in the book?

What character(s) could you relate most closely to?

What lessons did you learn from the characters in *The Last Woman Standing*?

What were the characters' flaws? What were their redeeming qualities?

Fiction often imitates life. Did the characters or situations in *The Last Woman Standing* remind you of your life or the life of anyone you know?

Part of the reason for Lynette and Ace's divorce was their passion for their careers more than for each other. Consider your life. Have you prioritized the people and the things that are most important to you?

Do you believe it's possible for a previously divorced couple to begin a new marital relationship with a fresh start?

Did you envision a different ending?

Is there a relationship in your life that was severed that you are feeling a tug in your heart to restore (i.e., marital, friendship, family)?

LYNETTE

Why did Lynette consider dating Frank? What kinds of considerations and issues keep a single mother from dating/pursuing new relationships?

Lynette and Frank's daughter Carmen pushed the envelope when she was caught with a boy twice under questionable circumstances. How do you think her parents handled the situation? Discuss parenting based on biblical principles and life experiences (from the viewpoint of the parent and as the child).

Do you think Lynette's mother overstepped her boundaries by bringing Ace to Lynette's house without her daughter's permission?

What problems (if any) do you foresee the girls having with their parents' reunion?

ACE

Ace tried to ignore his feelings for Lynette and continue with his relationship with Sheila. Was he wrong for carrying on the relationship with Sheila when he realized he was exhibiting feelings of love for his ex-wife?

Was Ace being deceptive by not telling Sheila that he was having dinner at the airport with his daughters and Lynette during his layover?

Sheila doesn't have the same kind of spiritual maturity as Ace (and even Lynette), yet Ace was in a relationship with her for two years. Do you think he considered Sheila's relationship with God (or lack thereof) before he entered into the relationship?

SHEILA

What do you think is in Sheila's future as it pertains to relationships? . . . her friendship with Cassandra? . . . her relationship with God? . . . her job and association with Clive?

Sheila's involvement in church didn't extend beyond attending with Ace and she preferred to watch sermons from pastors on television. Do you consider that sufficient for a person's spiritual growth?

CASSANDRA

Cassandra seemed to have too much influence over Sheila's life. How does she use it to sway Sheila's decisions?

Do you think Cassandra purposely manipulates Sheila? In what ways do people manipulate each other?

How do you feel about the way Cassandra uses/pursues men?

HEART OF DEVOTION

ISBN-13: 978-0-8024-5913-8

Best friends Anisha Blake and Sherri Dawson have been insepa-
rable for the last five years – until Anisha is swept away by Tyson
Randall. When Anisha becomes the object of Tyson's affection,
she believes her prayers for a knight in shining armor are answered. But as their romance grows, Anisha's intimate relationship with God becomes an afterthought instead of her first
thought. With life crumbling around her, Anisha is faced with
choices she was sure she'd never have to make. An inspiring and
emotional journey through adversity and spiritual self-discovery.

by Tia McCollors
Find it now at your favorite local or online bookstore
www.lifteveryvoicebooks.com

ZORA'S CRY

ISBN-13: 978-0-8024-9861-8

Zora Bridgeforth is twenty-nine and grappling with identity issues. While in search of her deceased mother's bridal veil, Zora happens upon a letter that reveals that she was adopted. Zora is devastated and vows to find her biological family. To find an outlet for her feelings, she joins a multi-church women's discipleship group. Unexpectedly Zora finds that the joy of friendship with three women in her group (Monet Sullivan, Paula Manns, and Belinda Stokes) turns out to be God's hand at work. As the ladies drop their facades and learn to find healing through each other's testimonies, a series of events unfolds resulting in an outcome Zora could have never imagined.

by Tia McCollors
Find it now at your favorite local or online bookstore
www.lifteveryvoicebooks.com

THE TRUTH ABOUT LOVE

ISBN-13: 978-0-8024-9862-5

In the anticipated sequel to *Zora's Cry*, revisit the lives of the four women from the P.O.W.E.R. discipleship group. Zora is facing some challenges adjusting to married life after so many years as a single, and the pressure only increases when her new husband, Preston, declares his call to the ministry. Monet is happily dating but still unsure if marriage is for her. Belinda's stepson T.J. has grown dangerously rebellious, testing her faith and her marriage to the limit. And Paula has just given birth to a girl and is stunned when her husband demands a paternity test. The women pull together in prayer as they search for answers and end up confirming the truth about love: that it never fails.

by Tia McCollors
Find it now at your favorite local or online bookstore
www.lifteveryvoicebooks.com

FIFTEEN YEARS

ISBN-13: 978-0-8024-6885-7

Jonah (JT) Tillman, the son of a substance dependent and neglectful mother, spent most of his childhood years living in foster homes throughout Atlanta, Georgia. At the age of fourteen, he was taken from the foster family that he had grown to love, and returned to his negligent birth mother. JT endures the hardships of life. However, fifteen years later, at the peak of success, he finds himself at his lowest. Deciding to reconnect with his foster family, he finds renewed faith and discovers a developing attraction to his foster sister.

by Kendra Norman-Bellamy
Find it now at your favorite local or online bookstore
www.lifteveryvoicebooks.com

LOVING CEE CEE JOHNSON

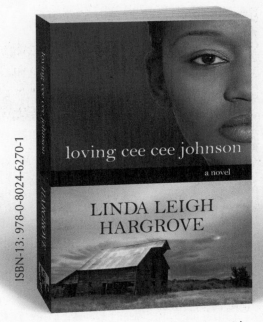

ISBN-13: 978-0-8024-6270-1

The sequel to *The Making of Isaac Hunt* returns with a new character, Cee Cee Johnson, a reporter who lies about her identity. When given an assignment in her hometown, Pettigrew, Cee Cee comes face to face with the truth about herself, her father, and the love she so desperately needs. Join us on this roller coaster ride of emotions filled with suspense, as Cee Cee Johnson discovers what it means to listen, learn, love, and forgive.

by Linda Leigh Hargrove
Find it now at your favorite local or online bookstore
www.lifteveryvoicebooks.com

The Negro National Anthem

Lift every voice and sing
Till earth and heaven ring,
Ring with the harmonies of Liberty;
Let our rejoicing rise
High as the listening skies,
Let it resound loud as the rolling sea.
Sing a song full of the faith that the dark past has taught us,
Sing a song full of the hope that the present has brought us,
Facing the rising sun of our new day begun
Let us march on till victory is won.

LIFT EVERY VOICE

So begins the Black National Anthem, by James Weldon Johnson in 1900. Lift Every Voice is the name of the joint imprint of The Institute for Black Family Development and Moody Publishers.

Our vision is to advance the cause of Christ through publishing African-American Christians who educate, edify, and disciple Christians in the church community through quality books written for African Americans.

Since 1988, the Institute for Black Family Development, a 501(c)(3) nonprofit Christian organization, has been providing training and technical assistance for churches and Christian organizations. The Institute for Black Family Development's goal is to become a premier trainer in leadership development, management, and strategic planning for pastors, ministers, volunteers, executives, and key staff members of churches and Christian organizations. To learn more about The Institute for Black Family Development write us at:

The Institute for Black Family Development
15151 Faust
Detroit, Michigan 48223

We hope you enjoy this book from Moody Publishers. Our goal is to provide high-quality, thought-provoking books and products that connect truth to your real needs and challenges. For more information on other books and products written and produced from a biblical perspective, go to www.moodypublishers.com or write to:

Moody Publishers/LEV
820 N. LaSalle Boulevard
Chicago, IL 60610
www.moodypublishers.com